Fiction
SULLIVAN
Faith

Sullivan, Faith

Good night, Mr.
Wodehouse

OCT 2 2 2015

3/6

D0962595

Good Night, Mr. Wodehouse

Good Night, Mr. Wodehouse

A Novel

Faith Sullivan

milkweed
editions

The characters and events in this book are fictitious. Any similarity to real persons, living or dead, is coincidental and not intended by the author.

© 2015, Text by Faith Sullivan
All rights reserved. Except for brief quotations in critical articles or reviews, no part of this book may be reproduced in any manner without prior written permission from the publisher: Milkweed Editions, 1011 Washington Avenue South, Suite 300, Minneapolis, Minnesota 55415.
(800) 520-6455
www.milkweed.org

Published 2015 by Milkweed Editions
Printed in Canada
Cover design by Mary Austin Speaker
Author photo by Kate Sullivan
15 16 17 18 19   5 4 3 2 1
First Edition

Milkweed Editions, an independent nonprofit publisher, gratefully acknowledges sustaining support from the Lindquist & Vennum Foundation; the McKnight Foundation; the National Endowment for the Arts; the Target Foundation; and other generous contributions from foundations, corporations, and individuals. Also, this activity is made possible by the voters of Minnesota through a Minnesota State Arts Board Operating Support grant, thanks to a legislative appropriation from the arts and cultural heritage fund, and a grant from the Wells Fargo Foundation Minnesota. For a full listing of Milkweed Editions supporters, please visit www.milkweed.org.

Library of Congress Cataloging-in-Publication Data

Sullivan, Faith.
    Good night, Mr. Wodehouse / Faith Sullivan. -- First editon.
        pages ; cm
    ISBN 978-1-57131-111-5 (alk. paper) — ISBN 978-1-57131-917-3 (ebook)
    I. Title.
    PS3569.U3469G66 2015
    813'.54—dc23
                                    2015009151

Milkweed Editions is committed to ecological stewardship. We strive to align our book production practices with this principle, and to reduce the impact of our operations in the environment. We are a member of the Green Press Initiative, a nonprofit coalition of publishers, manufacturers, and authors working to protect the world's endangered forests and conserve natural resources. Good Night Mr. Wodehouse was printed on acid-free 100% postconsumer-waste paper by Friesens Corporation.

For my children

and Grandson Jack, Ace of Hearts,

and

in memory of

Grandson Ixtlali, and Friends Peach, Ty, Hal, and Steve,

the Irreplaceables

♪

She read Dickens in the spirit in which she would have eloped with him.

—Eudora Welty—

Good Night,
Mr. Wodehouse

prologue ♔

IN 1944, AT AGE SIXTY-EIGHT, Nell Stillman wrote her
obituary. (This despite perfectly good health.) Years later,
the new owner of the *Standard Ledger* published the piece
in full:

> In our town, the custom is that an obituary should
> be kind. A kind word at the end is a little reward
> for dying. Never mind that no one spoke well of
> you before death, nor will hence. Death is a serious
> business—"The undiscover'd country from whose
> bourn no traveler returns"—and this one time you
> are owed.
>
> But, frankly, Helen Ryan Stillman was no better
> than she should be. So—contrary to custom—I will
> not reward her for dying.
>
> On October 12, 1876, Helen—Nell, as she was
> called—was born in Woodridge, Wisconsin, to
> shanty Irish immigrants—affectionate and gentle
> Onnie and Donal Ryan, late of Tipperary. Donal
> being an untutored farmer on unimproved land,
> the family struggled with poverty.
>
> After high school, Nell worked her way through

Milwaukee State Normal School, obtaining teacher certification in 1896. In January of 1897, she married Herbert Bartholomew Stillman of Rhinelander, Wisconsin. They moved to Harvester, settling in an apartment above Rabel's Meat Market, where Nell would reside until her death. On December 18, 1898, she gave birth to Hillyard Donal Stillman, a soul without stain. He now dwells in Elysian Fields, where—should it mean swimming the length of the River Styx—Nell plans to join him.

In 1909, Nell discovered P. G. Wodehouse, who became her treasured companion and savior. She recommends his books to all who know distress. And, of course, to all who don't.

But, further, she simply commends reading— Dickens, Austen, Steinbeck, or whom you will. In books are found solace, companionship, entertainment, and enlightenment. The stuff of our salvation.

Mrs. Stillman taught third grade for thirty-seven years in the Harvester Public School.

Preceded in death by both husband and son, Nell Stillman knew the kindness of dear friends and, eventually, the love of a good man.

For days, folks in Harvester spoke of little but Nell's obituary. Bonita Hansen had never heard of the Elysian Fields. Nor of the River Styx.

Of course, even today—mass communication notwithstanding—there are many things of which people in Harvester have never heard.

Irma Blessing felt that the obituary was eccentric: "A sign of mental instability. I blame it on the Bomb."

But to Harvey Munson it was "More like egomania. *Imagine* thinking you were smarter than Mr. Estes at the *Standard Ledger*, writing your own obituary."

"'Eventually, the love of a good man'? What's *that* supposed to mean?" milkman Casey Birnbaum wondered.

Out in Elysian Fields, Nell agreed; composing her own obituary *was* perhaps eccentric and egotistical.

But as for the 'Elysian Fields'?—look it up.

chapter one

Wiping egg from his plate with a scrap of toast, Bert cast Nell a dubious smile. "I'm not sure a good Catholic woman oughta enjoy the bedroom." He reached to pinch her breast. "Like you did last night."

Nell winced and pulled away. In bed he often treated her like a whore, but if she responded like one, he'd press, "Who taught you *that*," though she'd never been with a man before their marriage.

Pushing back from the table, Bert rose to fetch his cap from a hook by the door. Turning, he grabbed Nell's waist, squeezing it in a sinewy arm even as she stiffened.

"Now, girl," he said, affecting a brogue, "no wild carryin'-on because y' miss me. A man's got t' put food on the table and clothes on his lad." He saluted the eighteen-month-old peeking out from behind his mother, clutching her skirt in his two plump hands.

Bert was a physical man, one who had to work off his impulses, and he looked forward to the lifting and hauling and driving of horses that made up his days at Kolchak's Dray and Livery. Kolchak was a fair and canny boss, and he had plans for Bert. Horseless vehicles, that was where the future was, Kolchak had told him, and Bert knew that the man was right.

Back in the Wisconsin logging camps, Bert had yearned for a job like this, something with a future—a town life, a pretty wife if he was lucky. Well, he'd been lucky. But, by God, she'd been lucky, too. And she'd better be careful they didn't get another kid.

"I'll try to behave," Nell told her husband, pulling back and laughing rather too lightly.

"And next time I'd appreciate meat with my eggs and potatoes. A working man needs meat." Bert released her and swung away, out the screen door and down the outside stairs, admonishing, "Meat, Helen old girl!"

She frowned. He *would* insist upon calling her "Helen," though no one else did.

"'Nell' sounds like a barkeep's daughter," he'd assured her often enough.

And "Meat, Helen old girl!"—where was she supposed to find the money for that?

Nell lifted the baby into her arms, watching her husband cross Second Avenue, whistling, headed for work. The heat of the day was already cruel. From beneath Bert's heavy boots, a close-woven cloud of dust rose up, enshrouding him.

Summer heat pays no mind to death. The temperature was ninety the morning following Bert's death.

Dressed, Nell sat in the wicker rocker, nursing the baby. It was important to feign calm, not to upset the child. Even so, she must make her way through a tangle of questions. The first being, where could she turn?

Panic swept through her with a chill, and she shuddered despite herself. Beneath her arms her dress was wet with cold sweat.

At the screen door, a hard, familiar knock.

"Come in." Nell plucked a piece of flannel from her lap, placing it over her breast and the baby's head.

Trailed by her husband, Bernard, Bert's Aunt Martha let herself in, wheezing, "Poor Herbert. Only thirty-five years old. *Just* thirty-five." Dabbing at her wet hairline with a handkerchief and laying a tapestry reticule on the table by the daybed, she turned. "The heat . . . and the dust. I'm not well. The drive to town has done me in."

Nell noticed Martha's gaze falling upon the wicker rocker, which the older couple had given Bert and Nell as a wedding gift. Martha's eyes narrowed acquisitively. Then her finer nature appeared to prevail and she sank down onto a straight chair, the dry wood crepitating beneath her.

"What will you do now?"

Nell could only shake her head.

Tucking the handkerchief inside the cuff of her dress, Martha considered her husband, perched with hat in hand at the edge of the daybed—as if all of life were, for him, quite tentative, including this visit. "Bernard, where's the ground-cherry jam and the preserved chicken? Left them in the buggy, did you?"

Shoulders sloped in perpetual resignation, Bernard rose, shambling down to the street to fetch the jam and chicken.

"Thought you'd be able to use them," Martha told Nell. "I don't imagine you and Herbert had much put aside for . . . something like this."

For something like death? No. Bert's salary at Kolchak's had barely covered their modest expenses. There was nothing put by. Though Nell had a teaching certificate, the Harvester school board did not hire married women, especially not of childbearing age.

Another cold panic washed through her.

No money. No work. She couldn't return to Wisconsin. Her father was dead, her mother living with Nell's sister, Nora—who already had enough on her plate thanks to her shandy husband, Paddy; two young sons; and an acreage of no consequence.

"I'm not clear about something," Martha pressed, adjusting her glasses. "Why was Herbert lifting a heavy trunk by himself on a blistering day?" Her tone implied that a fine Italian hand, possibly Nell's, must be somewhere involved.

"No one else was at the livery. Ted Shuetty had gone home for lunch, and the trunk needed delivering. Eudora Barnstable had already sent a boy to see about the delay."

Martha suspired audibly, pursed her lips, and threw her head back. "*That* one," she said, referring to Mrs. Barnstable. "Imagine forcing a lone man to load a heavy trunk on a ninety-degree day."

"She didn't know he was alone."

"Doesn't matter. That's her way." Martha whipped the handkerchief from her cuff, mopping her throat.

Nell was sorry she'd mentioned Eudora Barnstable.

"May I get you a glass of cold tea? There's a pitcher in the icebox. Or I can fetch water from the pump out back." Hoping Martha would refuse, Nell didn't rise.

"Here's the jam and canned chicken," Bernard said, appearing in the doorway.

"For crying out loud," Martha told him, "shut the screen before you let in every fly in town."

No refusal coming from Martha, Nell rose, the baby still in her arms. "I was about to pour cold tea for Martha," Nell told Bernard. "You'll have a glass, won't you? And cookies. Only store-bought I'm afraid. Too hot to fire up the cookstove."

Moments later, one handed, Nell set the tray on the table beside the daybed, handed Martha and Bernard tea, and passed around napkins and a plate of ginger cookies. Martha snapped open the coarse linen napkin as if it might conceal a viper, then tucked the fabric into her ample bosom.

"Now, back to Herbert . . ." she began.

"Dr. Gray said he died instantly. He showed every sign of a burst artery."

Martha blew crumbs from her shelf. "Doctors don't know everything."

"Hillyard needs changing," Nell told her. When she'd returned with the freshly diapered child, she asked, "Would you like to hold him? He's a very good baby." Nell patted the satiny skin of Hilly's plump thigh and looked from Martha to Bernard.

"We have to be going," Martha said, rising and tugging at her overburdened corset. "When do you need us for the funeral?" She might have been inquiring the schedule of the westbound train.

"At ten. The women's sodality is serving lunch in the church basement afterwards. I hope you can stay."

"Depends on my dropsy. I haven't been well."

"Of course." Nell moved with her in-laws toward the door. "We don't want you overdoing." She kissed the top of the baby's head and smiled at Martha, now on the outside landing.

"We'd like to be more help," Martha said, one hand grasping the rail, the other clasping the tapestry reticule to her breast, "but you understand, we're still paying for our new buggy."

The baby blew little bubbles and waved as the aunt and uncle descended the wooden stairs.

chapter two ◈

AND NOW? Nell shifted the baby and stared at the altar; at the linens, beautiful, immaculate; at the gold cup and paten. In this little church in this small village, a *gold* cup and paten. Who had paid for those?

She was in debt for the coffin, the undertaker.

Did Kolchak owe Bert wages? She tried to recall. *For God's sake, Nell, stop it.* Nothing was owing. Her chest constricted. *My God . . . My God . . . My God . . .* The baby whimpered. She was holding him too tightly.

The next day dawned fiery. Not a day of kindly portent. Lethargic with the heat and despair, Nell lay in bed, absently running a hand along her left arm, testing the tender spot above the elbow where a bruise had not yet healed. Another on her right hip was deeper, more painful.

Bert. Her mind was an awful confusion this morning. So much to consider. Yet it would wander back, where it never should: Bert's fist . . . last winter. Afterward, snow and blood. Then, the outhouse.

She flung the damp sheet away with a suppressed cry, hurling herself from the bed. Trembling, she leaned heavily against the bureau.

What now, Bert? I've got sixty-five cents in a jar in the kitchen.

Dressed, she roamed the four sparsely furnished rooms.

What furnishings they had, apart from the wicker rocker, Bert had haggled off a foreclosed couple moving back east. Would she soon be carrying this small collection down to the street to sell?

A finger absently dragged across the top of a bureau and the back of a chair came away soiled. Though Nell cleaned daily with a damp cloth, in the warm months dust collected on every surface, drifting up from passing wagons and buggies on the unpaved street below.

She had fed and bathed the baby and set him on the floor with wooden blocks and a battered pie tin when she heard steps on the outside stairs. Crossing to the open door, she was perplexed to see the Lundeens, Laurence and Juliet.

Nell knew the two only by sight; they were Methodist, not Catholic. Laurence owned a dry-goods store, a bank, and a brand-new lumberyard. He sat on the school board and his son, George, had graduated from Harvard this past spring. Did Herbert owe them money?

"May we come in?" Juliet Lundeen asked as Nell opened the screen door. "We won't stay but a minute, but we wanted to pay a call."

"Please. The apartment is very warm, but there's cool tea."

Ignoring the offer, Mr. Lundeen removed his Panama hat and followed his wife into the stifling living room. He had the rosy, healthy complexion common to Scandinavian faces, and his eyes were the unclouded blue of bachelor's buttons.

"We'll only be a minute," Mrs. Lundeen repeated.

"Please have a seat, at least. It's kind of you to call."

Diminutive Juliet Lundeen, with her prematurely graying auburn hair and small, eloquent hands, sat on a straight chair, the soles of her black calfskin boots barely brushing the floor. Though her frame was delicate, Nell suspected that the woman was not in the least fragile. Bent a little forward, as if by urgency, Juliet said, "We were saddened to hear of Herbert's death. And shocked. My goodness, he was so young. And the two of you with a darling baby."

As though he understood, Hilly proffered Mrs. Lundeen a wooden block. She bent and kissed his hand. Laurence, now settled into the rocker, cleared his throat. "We want to be useful, Mrs. Stillman," he said, his tone both avuncular and businesslike. "May I call you Nell?"

Nell was amazed that these people knew her name. And Bert's. And that here they were, wanting "to be useful."

"Laurence is president of the school board," Mrs. Lundeen pointed out. "And we've been told that you have a teaching certificate. That was farsighted of you. Many women would not be prepared to provide for a child."

My God, it's true! thought Nell. I'm no longer a married woman!

Looking up from the pale Panama held in his hands, Laurence Lundeen again cleared his throat. "We're losing our third-grade teacher this fall."

"And the board was wondering if you might consider the post," Juliet Lundeen pursued. "They'd rather not go afield if someone local is available. Someone qualified, of course."

Nell reached for the arm of the daybed, lowering herself onto it. "To substitute, you mean? Until you find someone?"

"No, no. We're offering you a year's contract," Laurence Lundeen said.

Nell's eyes filled.

"Of course you'll need time to think about it," Mrs. Lundeen added.

Nell willed back her tears. "I don't need time. I need work." She withdrew a handkerchief from the pocket of her apron and dabbed at her nose. "I'm overcome," she said.

"Don't be," Lundeen told her, rising. "We need a teacher, and you are one."

His hand went to an inside pocket. "You may need a bit of cash to tide you over until September," he said, handing her an envelope. "With an infant, there's always something, isn't there?" He smiled and donned the Panama. "Good day, then."

Weak from the Lundeens' improbable kindness, Nell clasped the envelope to her middle and slumped against the doorjamb. As the Lundeens rounded the corner of the street, she wandered back toward the kitchen. Had she owned whiskey, she'd have enjoyed a tot; as it was, she poured cool tea and sat down at the kitchen table, staring at the unopened envelope.

In the living room, Hilly crawled to the wooden chair and pulled himself to his feet. Toddling into the kitchen, he grabbed his mother's apron and looked up at her in the demanding way that infants do. Still moving in a daze,

Nell took him on her lap. At length she ran a fingernail under the envelope flap and extracted five twenty-dollar bills and a slip of fine vellum on which Juliet Lundeen had written, *Nell—A small recognition of your loss. Use as needed. J. L.*

One hundred dollars. As much as Bert had made in three months at the Dray and Livery. Then she wept loudly, and the child bawled to see her tears.

chapter three 🙌

"Aunt Martha!" Nell called the next day, as Bernard helped his wife down from their new buggy. "Glad I caught you."

What fresh incommodity was this, Martha appeared to wonder, fanning herself with a handkerchief. "I'm in an awful hurry," she said.

"I won't keep you. I know the heat is bothering you." Nell shifted Hilly on her hip. "I'm going to be teaching this fall, and I'll need someone to look after Hillyard. I hoped you might know of a girl."

"Teaching? Where?"

"The school board has offered me a contract for third grade." Nell brushed Hilly's hair off his damp brow. "It's a godsend. I didn't know which way to turn."

"But you've only just begun your mourning. What will people think if you rush out to work?"

"I can't care. Do you know of a girl?"

"Well . . ." Martha began, "Herbert's cousin Roland has a daughter—Elvira. Left school after eighth grade to help at home. But her younger sister's twelve now and old enough to take hold, so Elvira will be looking for a place. I'll talk to the mother."

"You're so kind," Nell said, holding Hilly close. "So kind."

When the baby was down for the night, Nell stood in the semidark at the west-facing window of his bedroom. Below, voices rang out, mostly farm families starting late for home, wagons creaking, horses nickering, the dusk of nine o'clock lighting their way to country roads. One by one, they emptied Main Street.

On this, her third night of widowhood, Nell listened to men going in and out through the propped-open door of Reagan's Saloon and Billiards, a strident piano accompanying them. And from a two-block distance came the hushed tinkling of the piano at the Harvester Arms Hotel, these reaching her like memories of country dances.

She had let down her hair and braided it into a single plait. Now she thrust it over her shoulder. Inside her cotton nightdress, perspiration trickled down the flume of her spine, and she reached back to wick it with the gown.

Soundlessly she fetched two kitchen chairs and placed them against the low bedside to prevent Hilly from rolling out. Despite the heat, he slept as if drugged. She wished that she could take him in her arms, absorbing his untroubled serenity like a sleeping powder.

Back at the open window, she fell to her knees weeping, but weeping for what? At length, a wisp of night breeze, what her mother called a "fairy kiss," lifted the damp strands of hair clinging to Nell's nape and temples. She breathed deeply and rose, staring down at Hilly's blurred form against the sheet.

Life's purpose grew as clear, then, as a drop of pure water. *This child must grow up gentle—and happy, of course. And I must see to it.*

"I'm Elvira." The girl at the door spoke softly, shifting an ancient carpetbag from one hand to the other.

Nell had expected a girl with thick ankles and thicker wits. But the young woman on the landing was tiny and well formed, with intelligent dark eyes set in a perfect oval of pale skin.

"Come in, come in." Nell held the door. "You'll share Hilly's room," she said, leading the way. Nell had purchased a twin bed and bureau from the newly opened Bender's Second Hand. A new kerosene lamp stood on the bureau.

Since the baby was asleep, Nell whispered, "This will be your bed and this"—she pointed—"is your bureau. Mrs. Rabel gave me lavender from her garden to scent the drawers. I hope you like lavender."

The girl nodded a blank face.

"The Rabels are good to us. To *me*. I still forget that Herbert's gone." Odd the way she'd begun thinking of him as "Herbert," not "Bert," as if in death she'd put him at a little distance. As if he were both strange to her now and, at the same time, finally coming clear. "Well, I'll let you put your things away. Would you like a glass of cool tea when you're ready?"

Turning back, Nell said, "There's a commode in the bathroom. I'm afraid emptying the pot will be your job."

Again the girl nodded.

Shy or anxious, Nell thought, setting out ginger cookies on a plate and pouring tea into two glasses.

"The baby's handsome," Elvira said, pulling out a kitchen chair from the table.

Nell smiled. *Handsome.* "Thank you. He looks like Herbert." Did he? She was no longer quite sure. She sat down. "Think you'll like town life?"

"Oh, yes!" the girl said. "So many things going on." She hugged herself. "Exciting."

"I forgot to ask. Are you Catholic?"

"Yes. I've brought my missal and rosary."

"It wouldn't have mattered, but this way we can go together." Nell held the cool glass to her temple. If the heat continued, the classroom would be hot, the children restless.

"Do they have parish dances here, Cousin Nell?" the girl asked.

"No, but there are dances at the hotel every Saturday night. Herbert and I used to go before we had Hilly. But—please—just call me Nell."

The girl took a bite of cookie and chewed. Then, "Do you have to have a beau to go to the dances?"

"Heavens, no. All the girls go. Town girls and country girls."

"Are the town girls stuck up?"

"I don't think so. You'll have to see for yourself."

"You wouldn't mind if I went to a dance?"

"Goodness, no. Maybe you'll find a beau. How old are you?"

"Sixteen. Ma says I oughta be married."

"What do you say?"

"I want to find out about town life first." She paused. "Maybe find a town beau." She peered up from beneath black lashes to see if Nell was shocked.

"Why's that?"

"Had enough of the farm." She smoothed the oilcloth covering the table.

Nell noticed that the girl's hands were rough and sore. Small burns marked the wrists. Canning; probably milking and cooking for hired men. No fieldwork, though: Elvira's face was fashionably pale. At the Saturday dances, she'd give the other girls a run for their money.

When the girl picked Hilly up from his nap the next afternoon, she told Nell, "He's the best baby. Not like the ones in my family. Such fussers. Colicky, most of 'em. That'll tire you out." She rolled her eyes and held Hilly close, kissing his warm cheek. "This one's like a doll." She changed his dirty diaper, sponged his bottom, and powdered him with baking soda.

They'd taken to each other, Elvira and Hilly. Both were children, really, Nell thought. For all Elvira's talk of a "town beau," the girl was artless and vulnerable. And Nell soon saw that Elvira liked pretending that Hilly was her own. She playacted the little mother, dreaming of a town husband, Nell supposed.

A few days later, Elvira took Hilly for the first of many walks to the Milwaukee depot, three blocks away. Having lived on a farm, far from a railway, Elvira now gravitated to the depot. She timed the walks to coincide with the arrival of the 2:30 p.m. passenger train. After the first excursion, she reported that she and Hilly had seen a commercial traveler alighting with his satchel and sample case. "Least, that's what Mr. Loftus"—the depot agent—"called him. Commercial traveler."

One afternoon, while Elvira and Hilly were out, Nell sat at the kitchen table drumming her fingers. A week until she must prove herself. She had a teaching certificate, yes, but almost no practical experience. Just a few days substituting in a country school.

What if town children were cannier than country children? What if they set out to bring her down? Such things happened. Hadn't she heard of a young woman in Minneapolis who'd hanged herself when the school board wouldn't renew her contract? She'd been unable to control her pupils, they'd said. And no other school wanted a teacher whose contract hadn't been renewed.

What if, after all their kindness, Nell failed the Lundeens?

chapter four

THE DAY BEFORE IT OPENED, Nell walked down Main Street to the Harvester school, an impressive three stories and built of dark-red stone. Unusual for so small a town. In a lofty belfry hung the bell she had heard on many mornings, calling children in. Clearly Harvester placed great value on education and expected only the best from its teachers. Nell's step faltered and she held a clammy palm to her middle.

Earlier, she had carried home textbooks, poring over them, mapping out lessons and quizzes. Now, alone in her classroom, she printed her name on the blackboard. Moving on, she wrote, "'A day of the learned is longer than the life of the ignorant.' Seneca. Do we know what this means?"

Mercifully, the first day of school was a half day. Desks were assigned. Attendance was taken. Texts were distributed. Monitors were chosen: one to keep order should Mrs. Stillman be called away from the classroom; one to check the cloakroom at the end of each day; one to assist at recess; one to clap erasers and clean the blackboard.

"I will reassign these jobs at the end of the first six

weeks," she told them, "and I may find that I need more monitors as we go along."

Everyone wanted to be a monitor. Everyone wanted to be important.

Before dismissing the children at noon, Nell told them, "Tomorrow, we'll talk about what Mr. Seneca meant in his quote." The following day, Cletus Osterhus was so excited and desperate to explain the Seneca quote that, after he'd raised his hand and been called upon, he found that he must first run to the outhouse.

Returning, breathless, he gasped, "I asked Grandpa Hapgood. He was in the Civil War, and he knows a lot. That wasn't cheating, was it, asking him?"

"No. That was research. Going in search of information."

"He said life's more interesting and full of good stuff to . . . to fill the day if you know a lot of things. And life isn't so interesting and not so full of good stuff if you don't."

Though these first days of teaching passed without event, Nell felt no relief. She would be on trial for a long time. With a child to provide for, she could not afford a misstep.

On the sixth of September, days after school had opened, President McKinley was shot, succumbing on the fourteenth of the month. News of his death arrived with the westbound train. On Friday, school was canceled.

"What'll happen now?" Elvira asked at breakfast, her eyes huge with alarm.

"Theodore Roosevelt will be president," Nell said, ladling out oatmeal.

"You think he knows how to be president?" Elvira pressed, ignoring the pitcher of milk Nell set in front of her.

"I believe he's intelligent and well-educated. No one can know if he'll be a good president."

"My gran remembers when President Lincoln was shot. Those were terrible times, she says. Everybody thought the country was gonna come to an end. The country won't come to an end now, will it?"

"No, no. I have a good feeling about Mr. Roosevelt." Did she? "Anyway, President Garfield was assassinated, too, and the country kept on going." She spooned a little brown sugar onto Elvira's oatmeal. "Now, eat and stop worrying. I'll look after you."

Late in September, Elvira told Nell, "Hilly and I saw Father Gerrold outside the post office. He reminded us that the St. Boniface bazaar is next month. Will we go?"

"It wouldn't be proper for me, so soon after Herbert's passing," Nell said, "but you must go and take a pie. I'll give you a bit of change to put in your pocket for the wheel of fortune."

Clapping her hands, Elvira cried, "You're so good to me," and ran to embrace Nell. "Nobody's ever been so good to me."

The night of the bazaar, Nell brushed Elvira's hair, tying it back with red ribbon. "You'll need a heavy sweater," she told the girl. "Take mine." Before Elvira stepped into the dark, carrying an apple pie, Nell dabbed vanilla behind the girl's ears. "You'll be the prettiest girl there."

"Best-smelling, too."

It was ten before Elvira returned, cheeks flushed. "Our pie was the best-looking one," she rhapsodized. "And guess who bought it—Mr. Lundeen!"

The girl flung herself onto the screeching daybed. "We got to talking and he said they could use an extra hand at the dry-goods store on Saturdays, at least till after Christmas. And Mrs. Lundeen said yes, they were short-handed and they'd probably need me till after inventory, whatever inventory is." She sat up. "Would you mind?"

"Saturday afternoon and Sunday are your time. If you want to work at the store, that's fine. You can make your-self a little cash."

"That's what I was thinking. Wouldn't Ma be surprised to get a store-bought present for Christmas?" Elvira hugged her little body.

"Now, tell me who all was at the bazaar," Nell said. "Any likely beaux?"

"There was one kinda sweet on me. But he's from the country, so that's that."

chapter five ✐

"I CAN'T BELIEVE IT!" Elvira said. "They let me write up a sale and ring it on the cash register. And I helped Mrs. Rabel find the thread she needed. I felt so grown-up, Cousin Nell."

"There's a little coffee left from supper," Nell said. "I'll heat it while you get into your nightdress."

"Oh, don't bother. It's only nine-thirty. I thought I'd look in at the dance. I wish you'd come with me."

Pulling on the old alpaca coat that hung to the floor and had once been a man's, Elvira kissed Nell's cheek. "I know, I know. It wouldn't be proper for you to come." And then she was gone.

Smiling, Nell drew the rocker close to the lamp and opened the copy of *Sense and Sensibility* she'd come across in Bender's Second Hand while searching through used housewares for another iron skillet.

So much about Elinor in this book reminded Nell of herself. Her calm, her self-sufficiency. And wasn't it a good thing to have an aspect of one's nature illuminated by a character? A book could be a mirror helping one to understand oneself, accept oneself—maybe even one's more refractory parts. We were ourselves probably the sphere we least understood.

On a typical afternoon, when the three-o'clock dismissal bell rang in the school tower, Elvira bundled Hilly up, walking him up Main Street and into the school. In the third-grade room, Nell corrected papers by a kerosene lamp and entered the marks in her grade book.

Impressed by the school, Elvira invariably exclaimed to Hilly, "Isn't this the biggest building you ever saw?" While they waited for Nell to finish, Elvira carried the little boy to the windows, pointing to the rim of the western horizon where a spectacular sunset yielded to the icy blackness of a winter night. In the darkening village, lamps flared to life inside houses where wives tossed more wood into cookstoves.

Catching sight of the sudden flame of a freshly lit lamp, Hilly threw his head back, laughed, and pointed. "Light," Elvira told him. He tried to repeat the word, but "light" was difficult, and every time came out as "wite." Still, Elvira told him that he was a good boy.

Sometimes they helped Nell by picking up items fallen to the floor, or checking the cloakroom for lunch buckets and mittens. If the appointed monitor had failed to stay behind to wash the chalkboard, Elvira and Hilly carried the galvanized pail to the pump in the yard and fetched water to scrub it. "Isn't this fun?" Elvira asked, and the lad clapped his hands.

On the way home, the three occasionally stopped in the pharmacy for aspirin or mentholatum. Inhaling odors edgy and foreign, Elvira lingered over exotic treasures, identifying each for Hilly. "Dr. Aspenwall's Cure for Gout, whatever that is. We'll ask your mama. And here's Neat's-Foot Oil. Ma puts that on her feet in the winter." In the grocery store, shopping for potatoes, Elvira cooed, "Green beans in a *can*, Hilly, imagine that."

Elvira soon became a familiar face in Harvester. She was a friendly little thing, eager to know everything she could be taught, whether it was the meaning of "gout" or the price of a railway ticket to Chicago. "Not that I plan to go there," she told the depot agent, "But you never know . . . do you?"

The Lundeens were taken with her. "That girl knows how to work," Mr. Lundeen told Nell when she ran into him in the meat market. "We'll have work for her through January, maybe later. Juliet thinks Elvira's the cat's whiskers."

By now, young George Lundeen had returned from his Grand Tour, a graduation gift from his parents. At the dry-goods store, he was training to take over management from his father, who was increasingly tied up at the new Square Deal Lumberyard across the street from the depot.

Sitting at the battered oak table one night, spreading apple butter on a slice of bread, Elvira told Nell, "Mr. George really hoped to go into the bank, but his pa wants to start him out in the store."

"My goodness, how do you know that?"

"You hear things."

"Have you met him?"

"Last Saturday. He's very nice. No airs, even though he's been to Paris and Rome and almost everywhere."

"I don't think I've ever seen him," Nell said, cutting cheese into small pieces for Hilly. "He must have graduated from high school about the time Herbert and I came here."

"He's very good looking."

"I heard somewhere—maybe at sodality—that he's engaged to a girl from the East."

"Boston," Elvira said.

"You do have your ear to the ground."

"In a dry-goods store you hear a lot. Especially about the owners."

"I suppose." Nell held a cup of milk to Hilly's mouth. "Think of it. Europe. It takes my breath away."

"Mine too. I've never even been to St. Bridget!"—the county seat.

Sitting on the living-room floor by the three-foot-square hot-air register, Hilly played with a spoon and pie tin while Nell and Elvira washed and dried the dishes.

"My Christmas vacation begins at the end of this week," Nell told the girl. "If you're planning to go home for a visit, better have someone fetch you."

"I don't think they can spare me from the store," Elvira said. "It's so busy now, Mr. George says they can use me every day till Christmas." She added, "That is, if you don't mind looking after Hilly." She wrung out the dishcloth and wiped down the oilcloth.

"Are you disappointed not to go home?"

"I've bought little presents for everyone. Mrs. Lundeen helped me pick out nice things I could afford, and then she gave me a discount because I'm an employee. Isn't that something?" Setting the teakettle over a burner, Elvira continued, "Everybody at home's going to be knocked off their feet. They never get anything new-bought except, you know, like a plow. When they see those presents, they'll never miss me."

The little group celebrated Hilly's third birthday on a December Sunday when the store was closed and Elvira could be present. After early Mass, Nell baked a cake and, once they'd all eaten potatoes and sausage, Elvira ran out to gather a bowl of fresh snow.

"Hilly, it snowed just for you," she told him as she stirred a little maple syrup into the bowl and spooned some of the mix over a slice of cake that Nell had torn into pieces. "Taste that, you little dumpling."

He dug in with both hands, stuffing cake into his mouth. "Nithe," he mumbled.

Once Hilly was asleep, Elvira sat near Nell and said, "When I told Mrs. Lundeen we were having Hilly's birthday tonight, she sent this home for him." She handed Nell a book, gorgeously bound.

"*Beautiful Stories About Children* by Charles Dickens," Nell read. "How will I ever repay the Lundeens?"

"They don't seem like people who expect it."

One day, Nell thought, maybe there'll be *something* I can do.

chapter six

CHRISTMAS CAME AND WENT, and Elvira was still needed at the store on Saturdays. Early in February she told Nell that she was depositing a little money in the bank each week. "In the Bank of Harvester. Mr. Lundeen's bank," she added, as if there were another in town.

"When you marry, you'll have money of your own. That's always a good thing," Nell said. Indeed.

"Maybe I won't marry. Then I'll really be glad I saved it."

The subject reminded Nell. "There's a Valentine Dance at the hotel," Nell said, laying aside the weekly *Standard Ledger*. Lately, Elvira had been giving the dances the go-by.

"It'll mostly be married people and girls with beaux," Elvira said.

"Nonsense. There's bound to be unattached girls at a Valentine Dance. And boys. What if this is the dance where you lose your heart?"

Wearing the rose party dress that Nell had made her at Christmas, Elvira did attend the dance. Nell waited up, now reading *Pride and Prejudice*, a loan from Juliet Lundeen. Jane Austen, despite being from a different place and time, well understood human frailties in their many costumes.

Elvira should be reading novels and biographies. Life could toss your sanity about like a glass ball; books were a cushion. How on earth did nonreaders cope when they had nowhere to turn? How lonely such a nonreading world must be.

But Elvira had demurred when Nell suggested sharing the books from Mrs. Lundeen. They were "too deep," she'd said. Nell sighed now and rose to check on Hilly, tucking the quilts around his bootied feet. This room and her own were always cold in winter.

Bertha Rabel had long ago given Nell lace curtains for the living-room window and those in the bedrooms. Though kindly meant, they did not keep out the cold.

After setting the teakettle on the stove and heaving a chunk of firewood onto the embers, Nell struggled into her coat and slipped down to the street, stepping gingerly onto the snow and ice.

At each corner of Main Street, a gas lamp was lit, but the stores, robbed of the light and vitality of the business day, stood bleak and black. In a village like Harvester, the collection of stores and offices strung loosely along Main Street—with odd little intervals here and there, like gaps between teeth—were the clearinghouses of news and gossip.

Telephones were still a rarity. There were perhaps half a dozen in the town. Laurence Lundeen, with plans for the future of Harvester, had set up a telephone company, called Five Counties Telephone Communication. This involved installing a little switchboard in the office of the dry-goods store, where Anna Braun, the bookkeeper, could connect Edward Barnstable in his real-estate office with Dr. Gray in *his* office, one floor above.

Similar switchboards were being installed in St. Bridget and Red Berry and not a few other towns in the area. Laurence was quoted in the *Standard Ledger* as saying that one day soon every household would possess a telephone. The idea gave Nell pause. Wasn't it a little frightening, everything so instant? First the telegraph, now the telephone.

She rubbed her bare hands and peered down Main Street toward the Harvester Arms Hotel. On the broad front porch, several young men huddled together, smoking or sharing a flask. Inside, all the lamps on the first floor were burning, and Nell thought she caught the strains of "After the Ball." Herbert had been partial to that tune; its sadness fed something in him. She trembled, turning away from the sound.

"You waited up," Elvira said when she came home around half past eleven. An air of warmth clung about her despite the cold night.

"I was reading and fell asleep. My, it's chilly in here." Nell's shawl had slipped and she gathered it around her shoulders, shivering. "The fire's gone out." Rabel's, downstairs, let their fire die at night, so no heat rose through the register until morning, when the shop reopened.

Elvira slipped out of her coat, hanging it on a hook by the door. "Should I start the cookstove?"

"No. We'll be going to bed. I don't like to waste the wood."

"I'll get into my nightdress, then."

"How was the dance?" Nell asked, rising.

"Dull as dishwater for an hour, but then Mr. George stopped in," Elvira said, returning with her nightdress in hand. "He knows so many dance steps—steps nobody around here's even heard of." She wandered into the kitchen to see if the stove still held any heat. "And he showed us how to do them. Things got lively then! I wish you'd been there."

Back in the living room, Elvira went on, "There's still a tiny bit of heat in the stove if you want to undress out there before it's all gone."

"I think I will. I should have heated bricks for the beds before the fire died. Wear your heavy woolen socks," Nell cautioned, leaving to fetch her gown.

When she returned, Elvira was riffling the first pages of *Pride and Prejudice*. "'It is a truth universally acknowledged,'" she read, stumbling only a little, "'that a single man in possession of a good fortune, must be in want of a wife.' What does that mean?"

"What do you think it means?"

Elvira wrinkled her brow. "That girls think rich men want . . . or should want . . . to get married?"

"I expect that's about it."

"I wonder if that's what Mr. George's fiancée thought."

"Why do you wonder?"

"Well, she's marrying a rich man, isn't she?"

Nell considered. "But she's probably marrying him for love."

Elvira laid the book back on the table. "Some men probably get more than their fair share of love."

"I don't follow you."

"Think about it. A man like Mr. George, for instance. He's got money and looks and nice ways. Lots of girls must have set their caps for him. It doesn't seem fair."

"To other men?" Nell asked.

"To other girls."

Had Nell set her cap for a husband? She didn't think so. But she'd been fresh from college, teaching certificate in hand, with no prospects. Hanging around Nora and Paddy O'Neill's farm, where she was an extra mouth, had been unthinkable.

Then, she'd met Herbert at a village dance. He'd been a roustabout with a lumber outfit up north but was on his way to Harvester, having already taken the job at Kolchak's. "I've been looking for a town job. Not much advancement in lumbering."

"Got the letter here," he went on, patting his shirt pocket, "from my schoolmate Ted Shuetty. Says the boss will hold the job till I get there. Ted's given him a pretty good spiel about how hard I work. Besides, I got relations near Harvester." He spun Nell through a waltz. "Just stopping over a couple of days with cousins here in Woodridge."

Two days later he asked her to marry him, and she said yes. Was love any part of it? She doubted.

But when they danced, the firm pressure of his hand on the small of her back had caused her to feel out of control. He'd had extraordinary hands. Nell turned on her side now, in her dark bed, with none but her own clumsy hand for excitement.

chapter seven ✑

"Isn't this exciting!" Nell said, settling into the rocker.

Late in May of 1902, Nell and Elvira received invitations to the June wedding of Cora Mary Pendleton and George Laurence Lundeen in the Methodist Episcopal Church of Harvester and to the reception following, at the home of Mr. and Mrs. Laurence Lundeen of 248 Catalpa Street.

An interview in the *Standard Ledger* quoted Miss Pendleton: "I want to acquaint myself with George's world as quickly as possible, so I've chosen to be married in Harvester rather than Boston. George grew up here, and I know that I shall love it."

The article further stated that a considerable number of family and friends would be journeying by train from the East. "The charming Miss Pendleton laughed, saying, 'Daddy has pretty much booked up the Harvester Arms.'" It was noted that Miss Pendleton had graduated from the Greybriar School for Young Ladies in the Berkshires.

"This calls for new dresses," Nell told Elvira, laying her invitation on the end table beside a stack of third-grade geography tests. "I haven't had a new summer dress since

I was married. Have you seen a fabric at Lundeen's that you like?"

"Haven't looked," Elvira said without glancing up from the floor, where she and Hilly were building a house of blocks.

"I think it's a good sign that Miss Pendleton wants to marry here, among George's people," Nell said. "It shows that she really loves him and wants to fit in."

"What's a 'school for young ladies'?"

"A finishing school, I suppose. Where families send their girls to learn to be ladies," Nell said, taking up the geography. "They learn French and German or Italian so they'll feel at home in Europe. And I suppose they learn how to entertain and dress and carry on a conversation."

"I used to speak a little German," Elvira said. "We had a hired man taught me some."

"It must be grand to speak foreign languages . . . like being able to play the piano or sing an operatic aria. I wonder if Miss Pendleton plays the piano."

Rising from the floor, Elvira said, "I'll start supper." At the kitchen doorway she turned. "An operatic area?"

In Lundeen's the following Saturday, Nell decided on ivory linen and lace to sew a boudoir pillow for a wedding gift, then chose a soft lilac yardage for her new summer dress.

"And a yard or so of lilac ribbon to trim your hat?" prompted Elvira, who was waiting on her.

"Perfect. But how about you? Have you found a fabric you like? The peach lawn is very pretty. I was tempted myself."

"I don't think I'll go to the wedding," Elvira murmured.

"Not go?" Nell was taken aback. But Marcella Kolchak was approaching with a packet of needles in hand, and Nell said no more.

Elvira had taken a sandwich to work with her, so Nell didn't see her again until the store closed. The May evening was warm and Main Street was noisy with the Saturday-night crowd. Nell sat by Hilly's open window, watching the throng below as it fetched and flowed, sweeping along smoothly here, eddying there, folks laughing and calling to each other as if Saturday night in town were the grandest regalement to be found.

The women in their Saturday best hesitated over a yard of lace in Lundeen's, parted with a bit of egg money for a bag of horehound drops in Petersen's, loitered in little clots along the walk, then gossiped in wagons and buggies. Nell longed to be down there, strolling among them, catching their fun, warming herself at their fever.

She needed to laugh. Some best part of herself—her wild humanity—was held in a closed fist, had been since ... well, for a long time.

George Lundeen's wedding would be her "coming out." Nearly a year would have passed since Herbert's death. After the wedding she would begin accepting invitations, should any come her way. She'd once known how to play whist. And though she had lived in Harvester for only three years and wasn't universally acquainted, she hoped to cultivate a little social life, maybe with the other teachers.

Observing Elvira leaving Lundeen's, slouching along Main Street looking like the frayed end of a rope, Nell went to the kitchen to fetch cold tea for them both. The day had been hot and dusty, hotter in the dry-goods store than anywhere, she didn't doubt. Fortunately, the iceman had delivered a fresh block that day.

"You're wilting." She handed Elvira the tea as the girl let the screen door close behind her.

Elvira set the glass on the living-room table, sank into the rocker, and began unlacing her shoes, sighing and groaning as they came loose. When her feet were free and she had rubbed and stretched them, she took up the glass and drank.

"I'll fix us bread and butter," Nell said. "Brown sugar on it?"

"Mmmhmm." Elvira rose. "I'll shuck outta my dress."

In that muslin nightdress she looks about fourteen, Nell thought, as Elvira slumped onto a kitchen chair. "When's your birthday?"

"Same day as Mr. George's wedding. June 16," Elvira told her.

"Is that why you don't want to go to the wedding?" Nell laid a plate of bread on the table.

"No."

"Don't you think the Lundeens will be hurt if you stay away?" Elvira shrugged and bit into a slice of bread.

"Is anything wrong at work?"

Elvira shook her head, then wiped her mouth. "I like the Lundeens. They're good people." She was near tears.

"Well, then?"

"I'm not a lady. I hadda leave school when I was twelve. I don't know anything."

Nell raised her brows. "You know how to keep house and care for a baby and work in a dry-goods store. You can read and write. You have curiosity. You have a good heart. Without that, any lady's counterfeit."

"You're just trying to make me feel better, and that's because *you're* a lady. . . ."

Nell threw back her head and laughed. "What do you think a lady is?"

"Somebody who talks nice and knows what to wear and how to write a thank-you and how to act when she meets somebody. I don't know any of that, and it's too late now." Elvira laid her head on her arms. "I'm a yokel."

"You're not. Elvira, you're already a lady. The things you're talking about are just . . . the trimmings."

"Well, that's what I want—the trimmings! And I'll never have 'em."

Nell didn't want Elvira believing that "trimmings" made the lady—and she certainly didn't want to play Pygmalion to Elvira's Galatea. It would be false and patronizing. But the girl looked brokenhearted.

"If I teach you some trimmings, will you come with me to the wedding?"

Elvira nodded. "I'll come. If you teach me what to say when I meet Mr. George's bride."

chapter eight

EACH TIME SHE GLANCED at the sewing machine in her bedroom—a wedding gift from her family—Nell warmed with gratitude. The family had gone without in order to buy it. But patting Nell's hand, her mother had said, "Think of the money it'll save you. And yer poor fingers, too."

When not in use, the pale oak body made an attractive table, and Nell had always been pleased by the iron treadle with its intricate open-work design. Though she was not particularly adept, rocking the treadle back and forth with her feet was a satisfying exercise. And, as Mam had suggested, it had saved her fingers this week as she'd fashioned Elvira's dress.

Now, though it meant starting up the cookstove to heat the iron, Nell spread towels on the kitchen table and pressed the birthday gown of peach lawn that she'd raced to finish before the wedding.

"Oooo, it's pretty," Elvira fluted, running her hands over the satin waistband. "Can I try it on? *May* I try it on?"

"Of course. Only be careful not to wrinkle it."

Nell was pleased to see how the color set off the girl's dark eyes and hair, and how the fitted bodice showed off her supple figure and small waist. "There was enough satin left to tie your hair back."

Elvira stood before the mirror in Nell's bedroom, turning around, studying herself over her shoulder. "I look like a town girl!" she cried.

George and Cora had scheduled their wedding for a Sunday so that no one from the store need miss it.

Since it was a Lundeen wedding, a few of the less scrupulous Catholics were on hand in the Methodist Episcopal Church, a matter that would surely find its way into Father Gerrold's next sermon. Missing the occasion would have offended Nell's conscience more than attending.

The weight of Bertha Rabel's German Catholicism would not allow her to attend, though she did not begrudge Nell and Elvira, and so had offered to look after Hilly. "You'll tell me all about it when you come home."

The wedding was all that Harvester might have hoped. Though the church was plain, with only dark beams and paneling to relieve the simplicity, lilacs and peonies had burgeoned with timely consideration, and masses of them filled every possible space.

As the organ in the choir loft pumped out Handel, and the six bridesmaids in simple pink gowns hesitation-stepped their way toward the altar, the congregation stood "to gasp at the delicate beauty of Cora Pendleton in a seed-pearl-embroidered gown of silk organza over lightweight silk satin," as the *Standard Ledger* would report.

In the first pew, Cora's mother stood at her daughter's approach. Mrs. Pendleton, blonde and youthful, smoothed her pale-blue gown, touched a handkerchief to her nose, and smiled a watery salutation. Mr. Pendleton, square shouldered and proud, led his daughter to the altar.

Following the ceremony, Mendelssohn accompanied the couple back up the aisle, the bride merry and laughing, dancing toward the open doors. Nell thought it a pity that all brides didn't laugh and dance as they left the church.

Elvira pulled a tiny handkerchief from the waistband of her gown. Nell eyed her askance, noting tears gathered in the girl's eyes.

Reception guests made their way to the picket-fenced backyard of the Lundeen home where crab apple trees, planted when the house was built, were coming into their maturity and dropping late-blossoming confetti onto the assembly. Beneath a grape arbor, a string quartet imported from Minneapolis played Offenbach, Mendelssohn, Gilbert and Sullivan, and Strauss.

Following Nell through the receiving line, Elvira cast the bride a nervous smile and in clarion voice improvised, "I'm Elvira Stillman, and I work for the Lundeens at the dry-goods store. I think you're the most beautiful person I've ever seen. Best wishes."

A moment's pause followed. Then Cora Pendleton Lundeen grasped the girl's shoulders and lay her cheek against Elvira's. "Thank you."

Smiling, Nell took the moony child's hand and led her toward a long table dressed in pink linen where a banquet was spread, and girls in white frocks brushed away flies with palm fans. On a separate table, a tall wedding cake sat amidst a snowy scattering of white-satin rosettes.

After filling their plates from an array of fancy sandwiches, caviar and its accompaniments, several salads,
and delicate cookies with pale icings, Nell and Elvira
moved along to the drinks—fruit punch and champagne,
ladled and poured by two young men who had declined to
sign the temperance card at the Epworth League.

Recovering from her rosy oblivion, Elvira cast Nell an
inquiring look.

"*One* glass of champagne," Nell conceded, nodding to
the servers.

Toward the back of the deep yard, the women found a
table among the many that were dressed—like the buffet—in
pink linen and furbished with squat vases of roses, satin
streamers, and tiny boxes of groom's cake.

Minutes later, fortyish Anna Braun, who operated the
little telephone switchboard at the dry-goods store, came
scurrying along, heedful not to spill champagne on her
best gown. She settled herself at the table, placing an open
palm on her breast as if something inside threatened to
explode.

"Don't this beat all?" she said, spreading a napkin across
her lap and glancing around with visible delight. "Everything so beautiful. They don't do it any better in Boston,
I'm sure. Not that I've had the pleasure, but what could be
more elegant than this?" She bit into a salmon-salad sandwich, wiped crumbs from her lips, and swallowed. "And
young George. Where could a bride find a nicer, hand-
somer groom?"

Elvira set down her glass abruptly.

"May we join you ladies?" The assistant manager at Lundeen's, Howard Schroeder, and his wife, Elsie, pulled out chairs.

"*Fruit* punch?" Anna teased Howard, looking at his glass, her heroic laughter audible at wonderful distances. Elsie Schroeder peered around, anxious lest their table appear raucous.

"Elsie here signed the pledge," Howard said. "I keep tellin' her I never signed the darn thing, but still I gotta be a long way from home b'fore I can get next to spirits."

Anna laughed. "That's the advantage to being Catholic," she told him, lifting her glass. Elsie pursed her lips but said nothing.

"These chairs—" Howard confided, "rented from an outfit in Chicago. Brought in on the train. How 'bout that? None of yer borrowed church chairs that collapse under a fella."

"Excuse me, please," Elvira interrupted. "Anyone need something from the buffet?" She left the table.

"That's a good girl," Howard said of Elvira when she was out of earshot. "She's the pet down at the store." To Nell he whispered, "She's been practicing her manners on us. Wants to be like a lady, she says."

"I told her a lady is someone with a good heart. She thinks there's more to it," Nell told him.

"Too many girls these days are trying to be a *somebody*," Elsie said. "Putting themselves forward, my mother called it." Elsie's was a voice one might hear exclaiming, "I don't think I've ever been *completely* well."

Taking umbrage, Anna said, "Elvira wants to make something of herself. If that's putting herself forward, I'm for it."

Straightening, Elsie observed, "Getting married and keeping house was good enough for *some* of us."

"Not everybody's cut from the same cloth," the unmarried Anna said, rising. "May I refill someone's drink?"

As Anna wandered away, Nell asked, "Does anyone know where George and Cora will honeymoon?"

Howard lifted his chair away from the table and crossed his legs. "France and Italy, his dad told me. They'll come home in the fall. By that time, the new house'll be ready."

"The Lundeens are building George a new house?"

"Building *themselves* one."

"Where?"

"On Second Avenue, across from the school. George loves this old house, grew up in it," he said, gesturing toward it. "So Juliet—Mrs. Lundeen—said, 'take it.'"

"Wasn't that kind."

"Well, he's an only child. They dote on him."

And so the conversation continued. After ten minutes, Nell missed Elvira. Ah, there she was, at the drinks table—but seemingly caught in a trance. Was it the wedding couple she was staring at? Moments later, though, she was holding a glass of punch and returning arm in arm with Anna.

While guests basked in the warm afternoon, Juliet Lundeen made her way from table to table, thanking everyone for coming. "We'll soon be getting to the toasts," she warned, "so be sure your glasses are full." Laying a hand on

Elvira's shoulder, she said, "My, but you look pretty. Is the gown new?"

"Yes, ma'am. For my birthday."

"Don't tell me today's your birthday?"

"Yes, ma'am. I'm seventeen."

Juliet bent and kissed the girl's cheek. "I wish you the same as George and Cora—a lifetime of happiness. Now, before you leave, take a satin rosette from the cake table. There's one for each woman." At this, she moved on, telling them that the two servers in charge of drinks would be coming around to refill glasses.

From beneath her lashes, Elvira surveyed the others, hoping they had noted Juliet including her among the women. And when the servers came around, Elvira requested champagne. "For the toasts," she told Nell—a statement, not a question.

Nell worried about the second glass, and she knew that Elsie Schroeder's eye was bent in their direction. "Just this once," Nell said. "We don't want people talking."

Toasts were drunk—Laurence Lundeen's, "It is fortunate when your only child is the one you'd hoped for, and his bride is the daughter you'd have chosen. To George and Cora!"

From a table of family intimates, a gentleman of high color and assurance was the last to rise. Lifting his glass, he said, "As a Dutch uncle, I'm allowed to offer advice: After 'I love you,' the four happiest phrases in the language of marriage are: 'I'm sorry,' 'What do *you* think?', 'It's *just* what I wanted,' and 'Let's have a glass of beer.'" Laughter. "Cora and George."

Nell looked inquiry at Anna, who leaned toward her. "John Flynn. Lawyer." Cupping her mouth with her hand and nodding significantly, she added, *"Widower."*

Later, the bridal couple, wearing street clothes, were seen off in a festooned buggy destined for the depot and the Chicago-bound train. Nell and Elvira rose now to thank the Lundeens and say their good-byes. As she and Anna followed the girl, Nell noted that Elvira was not altogether steady on her feet.

At the gate, drawing on her newly acquired "trimmings," Elvira managed to blurt at the Lundeens, "Thank you for a grand time. Everything was . . . grand," before dashing headlong down the drive, pulling the handkerchief from her waistband for the second time that afternoon.

"She's a little overcome by it all," Nell explained, and hurried to follow.

It wasn't until Elvira reached the park across the street and slowed that Nell caught up. "What on earth . . ." she began, clutching the stitch in her side.

Elvira sank onto a bench, weeping and bending over the side to vomit. Nell dug in her bag for a handkerchief. Emptied and weak, Elvira laid her head on the back of the bench, eyes closed.

"What's going on, Elvira?"

The girl shook her head slowly, not opening her eyes. "Nothing," she whispered. "I am so sad. That is all that is going on."

chapter nine 🎵

DURING THE REMAINDER OF THAT SUMMER, Elvira begged for trimmings and more trimmings. "Teach me how to set a table! Proper!" Or how to carry on polite conversation— and what *was* polite conversation?

Before marrying Donal Ryan and moving west, Nell's mother had been in service in Boston. She knew how things were done; Nell might have grown up in homesteading poverty, but she had "better ways," as Mam would say, so now Nell could only imagine Elvira's sense of inadequacy.

To Nell's satisfaction, however, Elvira wanted at last to read—*good* books. "Nothing too hard to start out," she cautioned, so Nell brought home fifth- and sixth-grade readers. But Elvira's country-school education had been solid, as far as it went, so it wasn't long before she graduated to adult books on loan from Juliet Lundeen.

For all Nell's delight in Elvira's progress, she was disquieted. Behind Elvira's new needs lay a troubling *something*. And the normally chatty and candid child was silent regarding that something.

Autumn exploded in a flash of gold. School reopened, the young Lundeens returned from Europe, and George's parents moved into a substantial new house across from the school and half a block off Main Street.

In mid-September, the *Standard Ledger* noted:

"Young Mrs. George Lundeen hosted a tea on the fourteenth of this month. Present to enjoy ribbon sandwiches and tea cakes were Mrs. Laurence Lundeen, Mrs. Edward Barnstable Jr.," and so forth.

"The weather continuing mild, tea was poured in the garden beneath the grape arbor, asters and sedum lending a riotous setting for the conviviality."

Elvira, who followed news of Cora Lundeen with feverish devotion, had begun a "George and Cora" scrapbook. Clipping social items from the *Standard Ledger*, and picking up orts of hearsay from the store—"They have a telephone now. In the kitchen. And a hot-water heater. Imagine. Everything so up to date"—slavishly she entered these into the growing scrapbook. The white rose from the wedding reception was pressed in amongst the other Lundeen miscellanea.

Nell wondered at Elvira's hero-worship of George; still, she smiled at Elvira's devotion. It did no harm to have models. And young Cora was a proper model: visiting shut-ins with her mother-in-law, serving as hostess at Ladies Aid gatherings, and spearheading a Christmas toy drive for children living south of the railroad tracks.

In a village, however, the gears of social converse are oiled by gossip, so, in spite of good works, Cora was bound to be a topic of back-fence talk. So lovely, so well dressed, so well educated, so social: "Yes, of course she's good natured, but wouldn't we *all* be, if we had her money?"

Nevertheless, one Saturday night after work, Elvira stomped up the outside stairs, slammed the apartment door, and stood in the living room shaking her fist. "I can't believe some people!"

Pulling a nightshirt over Hilly's head, Nell asked, "What's wrong?"

"Aunt Martha!"

"What's she done now?"

"She came into the store to return a corset she'd ordered from St. Paul. She's had it two months and I'm sure she's worn it, but today she said it was too big and we'd have to take it back. What could possibly be too *big* for Aunt Martha?"

Suppressing a smile, Nell rocked Hilly and waited.

"I went up to the office and asked Mr. George—really the finest gentleman you'll ever meet—what I should do. He said to give her the money, it wasn't worth fighting about. I told him I didn't mind fighting with her, but he said no, he didn't want to put me in that position."

"You wouldn't want to create a scene in the store," Nell said.

"I wouldn't mind creating a scene with *her*. But I gave her the money. Then what does she say? How do I like working for a high-hat who's too good to marry a local girl?"

"*That* was uncalled for."

"Well, I gave her a piece of my mind. I said Mr. George was a prince and Cora Lundeen was a perfect angel and anybody who said otherwise was a jealous troublemaker."

Nell laughed despite herself.

"That got her goat," Elvira continued. "'Jealous of a snip

who's too good to buy clothes in her husband's store?' she said. I was so embarrassed. It was a blessing no one was close by, but they could've been. Poor Mrs. George, if it got back to her . . ."

Nell carried the sleeping Hilly into his bedroom. When she returned, she said, "It's admirable to stand up for friends, but there's always going to be gossip in a whistle-stop like Harvester. Don't take it seriously."

Elvira flopped onto the daybed. "What *should* I have said?"

Nell considered. "When you're in a public place, you have to be discreet, or you may generate more gossip. Let's see. You might have given Aunt Martha a sharp look and said, 'I think highly of the Lundeens, and what they do is none of my business.'"

"Why didn't I think of that?"

"Because you're still a girl. But you're a quick study. You're becoming a lady."

Elvira clapped her hands. "You really think so?"

Nell loved the warm semidark of Lundeen's, the sense of possibilities. Standing there, she drank in the crisp perfume of fabric bolts and new-minted overalls, the serious and promising smell of work boots, the dreamy waft of women's soft leather shoes.

In yard goods, she searched through the fabric remnants for a dark, heavy piece to sew short pants for Hilly. The boy stood at her side, watching customers come and go, listening to the palaver as they jawed with each other and with Elvira, behind the counter.

"And Hilly will need a pair of kneesocks," Nell told Elvira.

After some minutes, Hilly wandered from Nell's side—at first only a few steps; then a bit further; finally, crossing what seemed a great expanse of store, turning again and again to be certain that his mother hadn't left without him. Did mothers ever do that? He didn't think she would, but maybe she would forget that he was there.

Most of these tables, piled with merchandise, were taller than he was. If she didn't see him, maybe she'd think that she hadn't brought him. What if she went home and they closed the store and he was still in it? And he hadn't had his supper?

And shouldn't there be someone working on *this* side of the store? Hadn't there been a man when Elvira had brought him here once, a man who'd bent to shake Hilly's hand and call him "little man"? Now, beyond the reach of women's voices, it was too quiet.

There, ahead of him, mounted against tall shelving, was a pair of men's long underwear. He himself had never worn anything like them. They were huge and pale and headless. And weren't they moving, just a little? Yes, yes, the arm—he was pretty sure—had moved a tiny bit, reaching out.

Eyes wide, heart pounding, he backed away, bumping into table after table but backing still, until at last he was near the front door and someone was coming through it and he could see his mother, over by Elvira. He finally breathed and ran to Nell, grabbing her skirt, and she said, "What on earth . . . ?" And he was safe.

Elvira was on a ladder, fetching down boxes of gloves for a customer who seemed determined to try on most of the stock. The woman finally shook her head and turned away just as Cora Lundeen hurried up.

"Elvira, you're the very one I want."

The girl blushed and clasped her hands at her waist—cap in hand, so to speak.

Cora hurried on. "Mother and Father Lundeen think you're a corker. And George, well, you should hear him carry on." She smiled, drew a breath, and continued, "I'm planning a Christmas party at our house for everyone from the store, the bank, and the lumberyard. Mother Lundeen will help, of course, but I need your thoughts—what people here like to eat and drink, what kind of music they like, all that sort of thing."

Reaching across the counter, she placed a hand on Elvira's arm. "Please say you'll help?" She tipped her head to the side imploringly. "Could you come to my house tomorrow after church? George will be duck hunting. You and I can have a cozy lunch and make our plans."

She turned to Nell. "You wouldn't mind, would you, Mrs. Stillman, if Elvira had lunch with me?" Both Cora and Elvira looked at Nell.

"Of course not." Who could refuse such a creature?

"I'm awful to take advantage of Elvira, but I love to plan parties. Isn't it fun to see people enjoying themselves?"

"You have a good heart," Nell told her.

"Maybe I'm just indulging myself. There's nothing I love better than dancing. I don't know what I'd do if I couldn't dance." She laughed, casting a brief glance heavenward, petitioning for an endless waltz. Then she smoothed the fingers of a glove, adjusted her little fur hat, and started for the door, calling over her shoulder, "My house at noon, Elvira?"

Adoration lit Elvira's features, lending the pale oval a seraphic glow. Nell waited a long moment before saying, "I need some twill. Maybe the dark gray. And the knee-socks. Gray. We mustn't forget."

Elvira was a fortunate young woman, to be acquiring a friend like Cora Lundeen. Nell only hoped she wouldn't break her heart in the process.

chapter ten ☙

Harvester had only ten installed telephones, yet the social news of early 1903 traveled as if over a thousand wires. George and Cora had canceled their planned trip to London in June. Cora was expecting! Over back fences, the lying-in was predicted for mid-May.

Cora wanted to deliver in Boston, near her mother, and, since Dr. Gray advised no travel during Cora's late months, the young Lundeens journeyed east shortly after Valentine's Day.

On the first of May, Laurence and Juliet Lundeen boarded the train to Chicago, from there traveling to Boston. Elvira was beside herself with expectation.

"May's a good month to be born—I mean, with the weather warm and everything green. If it's a girl, maybe they'll name her May. If it's a boy, they should name him George Jr. George is a . . . heroic name. Well, remember, St. George slew the dragon, and George Washington was the father of this country."

Wednesday, May 14, after the dismissal bell rang, Elvira took Hilly's hand and walked up Main Street toward the school. The temperature had climbed to eighty, unusual for the date. From the west, the sharp, not-unpleasant odor of manure drifted in from plowed fields, commingling with the lilac scent of town.

Elvira thought that the red-stone school, gazing down over Main Street, looked upon her and Hilly with the tender glance of an affectionate grandmother. She was inclined to make relatives of buildings; they stood in for the pitiful lot God had given her.

For instance, Lundeen's Dry Goods, a substantial two-story brown-brick building, was the courtly yet entirely approachable uncle who took the train to St. Paul every year to serve in the state senate—and after the session closed, brought you a tiny replica of the majestic new capitol building.

The Harvester Arms Hotel was a sophisticated, distant cousin who drank champagne and thought nothing of traveling to Chicago. She let you try on her rococo hats—grand with ostrich feathers and velvet roses—and taught you songs from the latest operettas.

Thrusting open the heavy schoolhouse door, Elvira helped Hilly climb the stairs to the main floor where he ran to the third-grade room, calling, "Mama, Mama!" His voice and steps echoing in the near-empty building.

Nell was moving from window to window, closing the upper sashes with a long pole. The western sun beat in upon the oak floor and desks, releasing an exhalation of varnish and wax.

"Look who's here," she called, standing the pole in the corner and spreading her arms to her son. "Did you have a good day?"

"We went to the . . ." He turned to Elvira.

"Post office," she told him.

"Post ossif."

"And what did you do there?"

Hilly shook his head.

"We mailed a letter to Cora," Elvira said, "telling her we are thinking of her and hoping that she is well."

Hilly nodded. "She's getting a baby in Boss . . ."

"Boston."

"But we don't know if it's a boy," he told Nell.

Later, on the way home, Elvira asked, "Can we stop at the store? Maybe word came on the telephone." She grabbed up Hilly and ran with him.

At the rear of Lundeen's, past the yard goods, an open stairway led to the office and switchboard in a loft that overlooked the sales floor. Elvira set Hilly down and ran up the stairs, calling to Anna Braun, "Any word?"

Nell and Hilly waited below. Moments later, Elvira appeared, snuffling and wiping her eyes. When Hilly saw Elvira's face, he began to whimper.

"What's happened? Is it the baby?" Nell seized hold of the banister.

Starting down, Elvira shook her head. "It's a boy and his name is Laurence, after his grandpa. But Cora had a hard time."

"She's not . . ."

"No! But she can't move her legs. The doctor said not to worry, it's probably temporary . . . but still, you do worry, don't you?"

Hilly grabbed Elvira's skirt and bawled.

At the head of the stairs, Anna Braun sagged against the newel post. "Imagine. Our pretty little dancer."

chapter eleven 🌀

WHEN GEORGE AND CORA brought baby Laurence home in August, Cora was still in a wheelchair, though her Boston doctors remained hopeful.

Cora hired both the recently widowed Mrs. Krautkammer to keep house and fourteen-year-old Lizzie Jessup to help with the baby. Elvira burned with envy. Lizzie might be a willing girl, but she was also a dough-faced, pigeon-toed, ignorant one, who hadn't finished sixth grade and didn't know the difference between a bread plate and a pastry fork. What kind of influence was that for baby Laurence? Elvira felt passed over—unreasonably, as she would never abandon Hilly or give up her part-time work at the store. Still, wasn't life unfair?

One day in late October, the bloodless Lizzie wheeled Cora up to the fabric counter, where Elvira stood wrapping a length of lace around a scrap of cardboard. "I've come to throw myself on your mercy again," Cora said, handing the baby to Lizzie. Elvira watched the girl trail off, breathing through her mouth. "I'm planning this year's Christmas party."

Cora laid a gloved hand on the wooden counter and cast her eye around the store. Nothing could be further from her city background than this village dry-goods store, yet she was at ease here and grateful for its prosiness. Its very odor—offcastings of fabric sizing, plus woolen mittens, beaver felt, and dogskin coats—lent an odd sense of refuge.

In the East, refuge had never occupied her thoughts. But here, where the sky and land stretched forever, civilization felt precarious. People still spoke with sharp pain of the blizzard of 1888, which had killed so many. And they shuddered to recall the Hinkley fire, in which more than four hundred had perished.

In this dry-goods store, with a staunch country girl named Elvira wrapping lace around a bit of cardboard, Cora felt cosseted and sheltered, oddly at home.

That Sunday afternoon, in the Lundeen parlor, Cora told Elvira, "The lady's chair by the fire is comfortable."

Sitting in the chair, lavished with friendship, Elvira found herself borne across the boundary between Earth and Heaven, ushered into a world lovelier, more secure, more comfortable, even better smelling than any she'd dreamed of. What *was* that scent which seemed to be nothing laid on, but a part of the house itself?

The oil paintings; the deep, soft Turkey carpets; the upholstered furniture and shimmering draperies; the mahogany mantel and marble fireplace—surely these spoke of ease and gaiety.

Cora wheeled herself across the room, frowning and setting her mouth as the carpets resisted her. Elvira rose to help, but Cora motioned her off. "This is good exercise," she explained, screwing up a thin smile.

From the sofa she gathered up a dress of navy-blue faille, one of several dresses heaped there. Tiny fabric-covered buttons marched up the sides of the sleeves. "You could wear this, don't you think? You might have to shorten it a bit." She held it up.

Elvira crossed the room and took the dress in her hands, caressing it. "It's beautiful. But why can't you wear it?"

Cora turned the dress to show Elvira the sleeves and the back. "Look at all these covered buttons. Can you imagine how uncomfortable they are when I lean back against this chair?" She grimaced. "Torture."

"But you'll be walking again soon," Elvira said. "And then you'll regret giving this away."

"Certainly I'll be walking again—and dancing! Oh, how I miss the waltz. George loves to waltz. But think of the fun I'll have buying new things." With a kind of scorn for herself, she turned the wheelchair away from the sofa. "Now, let's plan the party."

When Lizzie looked in later, the two women had finished making their party plans. "The baby's down for his nap," Lizzie said. That girl's strained through a sieve, Elvira thought. No spirit. What Cora needs is someone to buck her up.

Cora asked the hired girl, "A pot of tea? And slice us some of the gingerbread, please. Get yourself a piece while you're at it."

Turning back to Elvira, Cora said, "It's none of my business, but I have to ask." She clasped her hands beneath her chin in a girlish gesture, as if meaning to coax a secret. "A girl as pretty as you must have a swain."

Elvira looked confused. "A swain?"

"A suitor?"

"I . . . no, no."

"I didn't mean to embarrass you. But you're lovely and fun. Someone should be setting his cap for you."

Cora sounded like Nell. "I guess I'm just not interested in that kind of thing."

"Well, someday."

Easy with one another, they sipped tea and finished two slices of gingerbread each before Elvira said good-bye, taking the dress with her.

"George could deliver the clothes," Cora told her.

"Oh, no," Elvira said, "I can't wait to show them to Nell."

Walking home through the early November gloom, with a bleared sun low behind banked clouds, Elvira relived the afternoon's plummy pleasures: the strong, pliant baby, soft and warm against her; the genuine appreciation she felt from Cora; the beautiful clothes she held in her arms, given without condescension or patronage. She clasped them to her face, savoring the scent of friendship. *A swain?*

With a puzzled scowl, she shook her head and plunged on.

chapter twelve

FINGERS TREMBLING, Elvira slipped into a watered-silk moire the color of red grapes. "What do you think of the color?" she asked Nell.

"It's beautiful. It changes when you move. Sometimes it has a green cast." Nell began buttoning the back. "Poor Cora."

"I know. I feel guilty wearing this to a party at her house."

"She'll be happy to see you in it."

"But it feels . . . like I'm walking on her grave."

"You're in a strange mood."

Moving to the parlor, Elvira paraded up and down. Hilly, in his Dr. Dentons, watched from the kitchen door.

"I can't get used to it," Elvira said. "It's one thing to stand still in a dress like this. But dancing in it!"

Without warning, Hilly cried, "Wanna go!" and flung himself sobbing at Elvira, grabbing handfuls of her skirt. "Wanna go dance!"

"It's a grown-up party," Elvira told him, trying to loosen his grip.

"No! Wanna go!" he screamed, beating her thighs with his fists.

Then Nell was on him, snatching him roughly, twisting

him toward her. "Don't ever hit! Do you hear me? *Never! Never!*"

"Mama," he bawled, clutching her knees. "Mama!" When had his mother ever raised her voice to him? What was happening? He had only wanted to dance with Elvira.

A few minutes later, shaken by the scene with Hilly—what had gotten into Nell?—Elvira studied herself in the mirror above the bureau. Even by dim lamplight she saw that her cheeks were flushed. She felt feverish and weak.

She had an unsettling sense that she'd attended this very party a long time ago. For weeks she'd heard echoes of it in her head, voices and music, like the scratchy sounds from the graphophone tube at the Harvester Arms. And when she heard them, she grew melancholy.

In George and Cora's dining room, Elsie Schroeder, wife of Howard the store manager—Elsie who had taken the pledge—poured herself a cup of fruit punch. Across the broad table, Elvira ladled out a cup of the brandy-laced version.

"Imbibing, are we?" Elsie lifted an eyebrow and smiled.

"As Anna always says, 'That's the advantage in being Catholic.'" Elvira moved toward the door and stood watching dancers in the parlor, where the furniture had been pushed against the walls and the carpets taken up.

Elsie followed. "That's a mighty fancy dress."

"Mrs. Lundeen gave it to me."

"Mrs. George Lundeen?"

"Yes."

Elsie pondered this. "Well, I suppose it was too nice for the missions box at church."

At this, Cora appeared around the corner of the parlor door and wheeled across the hall. "There you are," she called to Elvira. "Would you be a dear friend and pour me a cup of brandy punch?"

"I was just complimenting Elvira on her dress," Elsie said. "She's fortunate to have a fairy godmother."

"Oh, no, Elsie. The fairy godmother is fortunate to have Elvira." Cora took the cup and drank deeply. "Now, Elvira, I want you to save several waltzes for George. He's too kind to say it, but I know he misses dancing."

"I'm not very good."

"Doesn't matter. He's a strong lead. Just let yourself go."

Over the course of the evening, Elvira lost count of her dance partners. The manager of the lumberyard asked for two or three schottisches. A teller at the bank stole the polkas, while Howard Schroeder was partial to the two-step. In the dining room, finishing off a roast-beef sandwich, Anna told Elvira, "Elsie's given up dancing now. Howard says she's immodestly virtuous." Anna wiped mustard from the corner of her mouth and looked up as George Lundeen approached.

"Elvira? I think you owe me a waltz or two." The quartet had struck up "The Sidewalks of New York," and George led Elvira into the parlor.

"The color of your gown becomes you," George told Elvira, whirling. "The men in the back parlor are saying you're the prettiest young woman in Harvester."

"Cora's the prettiest woman in Harvester! And she gave me the dress." Then, afraid she'd spoken sharply, she added, "Because of the covered buttons in the back."

"They're a problem," he agreed. "Cora's had to make a lot of adjustments. She's a good scout about it all."

"She says she'll be dancing again, maybe this time next year."

George said nothing.

"Don't you believe?"

Again, he said nothing.

"Anything's possible," Elvira finally told him.

"True."

But Elvira sensed his doubt. Maybe the doctors had told him something they hadn't told his wife.

Tempering, though, George said, "Who knows what a year might bring?"

"Life changes so fast," Elvira said. "Look at me. I'm a totally different Elvira from the one who came to town. I don't believe I'd know that girl anymore."

He smiled. "You've grown up since you came to the store."

"Well, I've been there two years now."

"Only two years? So much has happened, I feel like I'm forty."

After "Annie Laurie" and the "Blue Danube," George returned Elvira to the dining room and poured her a cup of punch. "I'll be back later for another waltz."

Elvira watched him wander from the room, turning toward the back parlor, where men disappeared to smoke. The strains of "Annie Laurie" and the rumbling-tumbling words floating past were the same sounds she'd been hearing in her head for weeks. She felt a little faint.

Later, Elvira sat visiting with Cora. It was nearly one in the morning, and several guests had already said good night.

"I should leave, too. Nell will be waiting up to hear the gossip," Elvira told her friend.

"George will drive you," Cora said.

"No need."

"At this hour? Don't be silly. What kind of friend would I be?"

"You and Nell are the best friends anyone ever had," Elvira said, grasping Cora's hand. "And you *will* dance by next Christmas. I say so."

Cora looked away. "We'll see."

A few minutes later, George arranged a fur robe over Elvira's lap and around her legs, then climbed into the buggy and snapped the whip over the black mare.

The girl leaned back against the seat. "Thank you for the party. It was . . . splendid."

"You were the belle of the ball. To quote father, 'The girl's a treasure.' How many times did he dance you around?"

Elvira laughed. "Three or four."

"Mother says you've got him wrapped around your little finger."

"She didn't."

"She did."

"I'm straw masquerading as hay."

George laughed, a sound rare and affecting.

Halting the buggy in front of Rabel's, George saw Elvira

up the outside stairs. In the parlor the lamp was burning and Nell sat dozing in the rocker, but started up when the two opened the door. "I fell asleep!" She set aside *The Adventures of Huckleberry Finn* as George said good-bye.

When the two women were alone, Nell headed for the kitchen and lit the lamp over the table. "I'll toss another bit of wood in the fire so we can each warm our brick for bed. Put on your nightgown and bring me your brick."

Elvira did and, returning, said, "It's 1:30. We'll have to go to barmaid's Mass."

Nell adjusted the flue and left open the door on the stove. Elvira huddled beside her in front of the little blaze.

"So, the party—how was it?" Nell asked. When Elvira didn't answer, Nell saw that the girl was wiping her eyes. "You didn't have a good time."

Elvira averted her face. "I had a wonderful time," she countered.

"Then what on earth is wrong?"

"Nothing." Shaking her head in seeming perplexity, Elvira said, "I do not know."

Nell wasn't sure she believed that. They were both silent, then Nell asked, "Should I make hot chocolate?"

"Not for me, thank you."

Minutes later, Elvira said good night.

Though Nell was tired, she wasn't yet sleepy. She made a cup of hot chocolate, carrying it with the Mark Twain to the bedroom. Even before the party, Elvira had been overwrought, restless, and preoccupied. Now, there were tears. Was she frightened? Angry? Sad? Well, yes, she'd said she was sad. But about what?

chapter thirteen ☙

In early June of 1904, George and Cora sailed to England, taking one-year-old Laurence with them—as well as Lizzie Jessup. Once again Elvira stewed. "That lump! And in England! She's got the grace of a plowhorse, and she picks her nose. I've seen her do it. What if that poor little boy becomes a bumpkin like her when he grows up?"

But when George and Cora had settled into a small house in Surrey, postcards began arriving for Elvira. And finally, a fat letter. Here, then, was recompense for having to stay at home.

Dear Elvira,

I wish you could see our cottage and this village that looks torn from a children's picture book. Such flowers! Such vistas of lush rolling green in every direction. What would I give to run across those fields!

Blessed George takes me for a drive every afternoon, and we've been invited twice for croquet and whist at "friends of friends." Since croquet isn't possible, I'm polishing my whist and becoming a cardsharp. The ladies are shocked, I believe.

Next week we're taking the train to London so I can

visit doctors and dressmakers. I have more faith in the dressmakers than the doctors. While we're in the city, I will shop for a little London remembrance for you. You would lose your senses there, with so much to do and see. Theater and music and museums. Far more than Boston even. And so much history. Sadness, too—I mean, sadness in the history.

My great failing these days, Elvira, is that I get blue. I don't think it's my nature. I used to be a flibbertigibbet, always looking for fun. This awful seriousness has come on since the wheelchair. I try not to let George see; being blue is so unattractive. And George is the kindest, most loving husband—he deserves everything good and golden.

Forgive me, Elvira, for unpacking my blue laundry this way. I had not intended to. When I've posted this, I'll be sorry and embarrassed, I'm sure, but I need your kind ear, and I trust you. Lizzie Jessup is a good girl and loves the baby, but I wish you were here, with your jolly enthusiasm.

Despite what I've written, I implore you not to worry. I have plenty of sunshine, notwithstanding the English climate. And if I learn to be a good person—a loving, generous, blithesome person—I can be a good wife and mother and friend. Isn't that so?

Until later, Elvira.

With affection,
Cora Lundeen

P.S. George asks to be remembered.

Because Nell could keep secrets, Elvira felt no disloyalty in sharing the letter with her.

"Poor little girl," Nell said when she'd read it.

"That business about having more faith in the dressmakers than the doctors—that worries me. How can I buck her up?" Elvira asked.

Nell pulled a darning needle through the heel of a stocking. "Tell her about the runaway horse on Main Street." She knotted the thread and set the needle aside. "And try to reassure her without being obvious. If she's embarrassed at letting down her hair, she won't want to be reminded."

For three days, Elvira spent her spare moments writing and rewriting the letter to Cora. Leaf after leaf of cheap lined paper went into the kitchen stove. At length she handed Nell the latest draft and, with a few teacherly corrections, Nell pronounced it fine.

Dear Cora,

Thank you for your letter. I was so happy to receive it. In the post office I let out a squeal as if somebody had stuck me with a hatpin. Everybody turned around to see if I'd been stabbed. I had to explain that it was my first letter from a foreign country.

Even now, just holding the letter in my hands and thinking of the miles and miles it has come, across a whole ocean, makes me want to jump up and down. The stamp is beautiful, and the London postmark sends a shiver right down my back.

Also, the paper, which is the nicest I've seen—crisp like a dry leaf—was touched and written on by you, so in a way it's as if you took my hand to talk to me. See how much pleasure you have given me?

Things are going along smoothly at the store. Four more businesses have ordered telephones and two or three houses also. Anna says if the switchboard gets any busier, she'll have to grow another arm. But she is tickled. That switchboard makes her feel important. The other day she said, "Someday the whole world is going to be connected by telephone, and here I am, in at the start."

I wonder. Do you think the whole world should be connected? I can't make up my mind. I mean, we do have a transatlantic cable, and I suppose that's handy, but personally I believe people already know too much about each other's business.

A good example of this is Aunt Martha Stillman. I hope that woman never gets a telephone, because she will be a menace. She was in town shopping last Saturday and she came into the store. I hate to see her coming as she always has a nasty something or other to say about someone.

I was ringing up a box of handkerchiefs and she started telling me about Lucy Shellam, who is the country teacher in Aunt Martha's township. According to Aunt Martha, Lucy Shellam was seen with a man at a dance in St. Bridget. Not only that, but alcohol was served!

A. M. said she was going to bring the matter to the school board and have Lucy "dispatched."

"Was Miss Shellam drinking alcohol?" I asked.

"I wouldn't know," A. M. said.

"*If she wasn't drinking alcohol, I can't see how she was doing anything wrong.*"

"*It isn't what she did. It's what she might have done and what people will think she did.*"

Are you able to follow that, Cora? I had a hard time.

"*Your argument won't hold up in a court of law,*" *I told her,* "*and Lucy's gentleman will have you in court, you can bet on it. Probably for defamation or something.*" *I'm not sure what that is exactly, but it sounded scary.*

Aunt Martha gave me an evil look, but I could see that she was going to think twice about "dispatching" Lucy Shellam.

I am not Aunt Martha's favorite relation, but she's the kind of person whose favorite relation you don't want to be. (Cora, I couldn't have gotten myself out of that last sentence without Nell's help, just in case you're thinking I've been to college since you left.)

I have babbled so much, you'll have eyestrain if you get to the end of this. To save your poor eyes, I will close, but first I have to tell you that everybody here misses you. You are all the things you said you wanted to be— good, loving, generous, and blithesome, which Nell tells me means cheerful.

> *With affection,*
> *Elvira Stillman*

P.S. Please remember me to George.

chapter fourteen ❧

CORA WAS STILL IN HER WHEELCHAIR when the young Lundeens returned in late August. Her girlish lightness had fled. Without being self-pitying, she was older, more sober.

"She's still an invalid. How *could* she be the same?" Nell pointed out when Aunt Martha spoke of Cora's "comedown."

"She's furnished the Methodist sunday school with expensive toys and books and I don't know what all." Martha commenced to fan herself. "Meanwhile, *we* have to count our pennies to buy a new carpet for the parlor."

Nell's patience was thin. "She and Juliet Lundeen have also contributed a beautiful bookcase for the lobby of the new Water and Power Company."

"What on earth for?"

"So folks can leave books and magazines for others to borrow. *I* call that bighearted. I've already been over there taking advantage."

Martha set the fan aside and rose with much wheezing and importance. "If you have to buy people's affection, what's it worth?"

"Has Cora Lundeen offended you?"

"I don't approve of people flaunting their money. If I were rich, I wouldn't throw mine around."

Nell waited until Martha was down the stairs before she started laughing.

Hilly wouldn't start school for another year, so Elvira had begun taking him for walks to "build up his stamina." It was her opinion that school required a good deal of stamina—and that Hilly, because he lived in an apartment, needed his improved.

Besides, the walks fit in with her plan to "buck Cora up."

One mild late-September day, as she and Hilly marched around the schoolhouse block and then around the park, Elvira said to the boy, "And while we're at it, we'll stop at Cora's to see if she'd like to take the air." "Take the air" was a phrase Elvira had picked up from one of the English novels she'd grown devoted to.

"I'd love to go," Cora told her. "We're going to the park, Lizzie. Get my shawl and Laurence's sweater. Also the little package on the buffet."

George had ordered a ramp built onto the porte cochere so that Cora could come and go. Now, while Cora held Laurence on her lap, Lizzie guided the wheelchair down the ramp.

In the park, Cora released Laurence and he tottered away, following Hilly, who was headed toward swings hanging from a pair of maples. On the swing, Hilly held the baby in his lap with one hand and clasped the rope with the other, pushing off gently with his foot. When finally the boys tired of this, Hilly called to Elvira, "Can Laurence come on the teeter-totter?"

"He's not big enough," Elvira told him.

"I'll go with him," Lizzie said. She showed Laurence how to cling to the grip, then she applied her weight to his end of the teeter-totter, forcing it up and down.

"She's very willing," Cora said to Elvira's silence. She smiled and handed the "little package" to Elvira.

"It's too pretty to unwrap," Elvira said, but pulled on the satin ribbons. "Oh, my," she gasped, lifting the lid and then the contents, a cameo brooch. "Oh, my. I've never had anything so beautiful. You shouldn't have. But I love it!" Tearful, she embraced Cora. "Thank you, thank you. You are so good to me."

"It is you who are good to me," Cora said. Then, indicating the face on the brooch, "The silhouette is Queen Victoria. Thank heaven, it's the *young* Victoria."

Pinning the cameo to her breast, Elvira said, "It'll soon be time to plan the Christmas party."

Cora shifted in the chair and gazed toward the back of the schoolhouse. "I've been thinking, though . . . maybe it's time to have it at Mother Lundeen's."

Recalling Cora's earlier hope that she'd be dancing this Christmas, Elvira changed the subject. "Do you have plans for the fall?"

"I'm scouting furnishings for the kindergarten."

"Kindergarten?"

"For young children. *Next* fall. The school board's adding one. It's a shame Hilly will miss out this year."

"What do they do in kindergarten?"

"It's a new idea from Germany," Cora said, leaning toward Elvira. "They learn their ABCs and simple numbers and they color pictures with crayons and cut shapes out of paper. And there'll be a sandbox. And the teacher will read the children stories."

Elvira was pleased that her question had lit a spark of animation.

"They'll play games, of course," Cora went on. "I want to find beautiful books for them and colorful pictures for the walls. Four more years and Laurence will march off to kindergarten."

Then Cora grew quiet, perhaps imagining *Lizzie* marching Laurence to his first day of school.

When Nell arrived home the following day, Elvira told her, "I have shopping to do." In Lundeen's, the young woman gathered up a pair of children's scissors, a thick pad of cheap paper, and a wooden box of crayons.

George Lundeen himself rang up the sale. "What's this all about?"

"It's about Hilly and kindergarten. I don't want him to miss out on all that." Elvira smiled. "I sound like a mother hen."

Wrapping the items in brown paper and tying them with string, George said, "Hilly's a lucky boy." Like Cora, George was moving into that pale landscape where the sun shines dimly through a scrim of vanished possibilities. Elvira wished she could lay a comforting hand on his.

Outside, Elvira stood pensive for a moment, then plunged on toward the Water and Power Company to scour the shelves for children's books. Like the post office, this building was golden brick, and the broad interior lobby boasted a terrazzo floor. Elvira thought it hinted at a promising future for Harvester. Entering, she squared her shoulders and hoped that she looked a tiny bit *soigné*, a word newly acquired from Cora.

Shuffling through the bookshelves, Elvira found a little primer, nearly lost among the larger books. Seeing its quaintly illustrated alphabet, she tucked it into her satchel.

"What's kindy garden?" Hilly asked, later, when Elvira showed him her purchases.

She repeated what Cora had told her. "Doesn't that sound like fun?"

He nodded. "I kin do those things?"

"Most of them. We can't have a sandbox, but we can learn the ABCs and numbers and do coloring and play games."

"You're a lucky boy," Nell told him, echoing George Lundeen. "What do you say to Elvira for being so good to you?"

"I love you, Elvira."

Elvira lifted him, hugging him. "Someday I want a little boy just like you." Setting him down, she added, "But I don't know how to manage that without a husband."

"You could go to Boston and get a baby," said Hilly. "Mrs. Lundeen got one there."

An autumn Saturday morning, flaxen and mild. Nell sat at the kitchen table, drawing up lesson plans. Hilly had descended the stairs, promising not to wander off. "I'll play by the pump," he told his mother.

On one side of the vacant lot behind Rabel's, a three-hole outhouse squatted; on the other sat one of the village pumps where, winter and summer, Nell and Elvira drew water.

The vacant lot was now drifted with leaves. Hilly ran through them, bending to toss them into the air, gathering them into piles and throwing himself down on them.

Someone moved into the space between the boy and the sun. Shielding his eyes, Hilly looked up. "Gussy," he said, struggling to sit up.

"Not 'Gussy,' *dummkopf.* 'Gus.'"

"What's *'dummkopf'*?"

"You. A dummy. Somebody who doesn't know nothin'."

"Elvira's gonna teach me. Like kindy garden."

"I'm in first grade, *dummkopf.* I know lots mor'n you." Young Gus Rabel kicked leaves into Hilly's face. "*Dummkopf.*"

Hilly flung his arms in front of his face. "Please don't, Gussy."

"I told you, my name is Gus. Now you're gonna get it, *dummkopf.*"

The bigger boy fell upon Hilly, knocking him backward and rubbing leaves into the boy's face.

"Please, Gussy . . . Gus. Please don't." Hilly struggled to roll away, but Gus's knees dug into his ribs, pinning him. "Hurts."

"Ooooo, poor little *dummkopf.* Little baby *dummkopf.*" Gus's face was so close, Hilly could smell the pickled pig's feet on his breath. "Does it *hurt*, baby?"

"Yes." Hilly had begun to whimper, as Gus bounced his weight on top of the smaller boy's ribs.

"Here! What you think you doing?" Butcher Gus Rabel, wearing a broad white apron over his work clothes, grabbed his son roughly by the arm and yanked him to his feet. "What kinda *dummkopf* are you?" He smacked the boy hard on his backside. "I am ashamed. You should learn from this little fellow how to be a *man! A gentleman.*" He shoved young Gus out of the way.

"I am sorry," he said, helping Hilly to his feet. "You come. I give you oyster crackers. You like oyster crackers? We get you a little bag of oyster crackers."

Hilly took the butcher's hand and followed him through the back door of the meat market. Never before had he been in the big room where Gus butchered meat. How important he felt, being let into the mysterious place behind the meat counter.

It was dim and smelled of a number of things: blood and sawdust and pickling spices and smoke. It was a homey, familiar smell since these odors rose up through the big hot-air register into the Stillman living room.

When Gus had filled a little bag with oyster crackers, handing it to Hilly, he said, "You always be a good boy, won't you? Everybody love a good boy."

chapter fifteen 🙰

ELVIRA HANDED CORA A CUP of holiday punch and drew a chair close. "Every year you're more elegant," she said, admiring the simplicity of Cora's pale-gray gown. Near them, dancers swept across Laurence and Juliet's parlor floor to the insistent pulse of "Under the Bamboo Tree."

"Thank you." Cora set the cup aside and took one of Elvira's hands. "And every year you're kinder."

"Baloney, sez I."

"I'm going to ask a favor again," Cora said.

Elvira laughed. "'Dance with George?'"

"He needs to dance," Cora said, her gaze so unwavering Elvira had to look away. "He's growing old." Eyeing her husband from across the room, immersed in store talk with Howard Schroeder, Cora continued, "It's because of me—don't say a word. Not a word.

"If I could . . . dance, everything would be different. If I could do so many things." Her voice grew sardonic. "I'm becoming a *matron*, Elvira."

Never had Cora spoken so plainly, never had she and Elvira been so close. For Elvira this closeness was both flattering and disturbing, involving as it did responsibilities only half understood.

There was no question that she loved Cora, and Cora's need made Elvira love her all the more. And George? Well, of course, no dearer man lived. She had recognised that fact the night, long ago—it *was* long ago, wasn't it?—when he'd taught the little crowd at the Harvester Arms the new dance steps. No airs about him; only goodwill and generosity and an unconscious charm, charm that got under your skin because it was without guile.

"You're fond of him, I know you're fond of him," Cora went on. "And he's still young. He needs the warmth of a young woman, Elvira, so please make him feel young. Make him feel warm." She squeezed Elvira's hand until the young woman winced. "For me."

Elvira glanced around the room of dancers, a room that ought to feel familiar. But in this strange moment, the room and the world in which it existed were suddenly unknown, utterly new. A thrill—or was it a terror—ran through her.

"Elvira! Just the person I've been looking for," George's mother broke in. "Let's find a quiet corner. I have a proposition." She led the way to a sunroom at the back of the house, away from the music.

Dazed, disoriented, Elvira followed. *Another* proposition?

They took seats on a settee before a small hearth. "Now then, Elvira, Mr. Lundeen and I have been discussing you. And we're agreed that you're too bright for the store."

Elvira tried to focus. "I . . . love the store."

"But you don't want to spend your whole life there."

How difficult it was, finding her way back into known territory. "No?" Cora's words did not want to give way to Juliet's. "For me," Cora had said.

Juliet went on, "Now, what I suggest is only a proposal. And you're free to tell me to mind my own business. But Laurence and I think you should go to college. Maybe the Normal School in Mankato. From what we've seen, you're a born teacher."

The older woman settled back and stared into the fire. "We're very fond of you. You know that. When we were younger, we hoped to have a daughter. And, well, we do have a wonderful daughter in Cora—but we think of you that way, too."

Elvira was silent, still dazed by the earlier conversation.

"Have I upset you?"

Catching hold of Juliet's question, at last, Elvira shook her head, slowly, from side to side. "You couldn't upset me. You and Mr. Lundeen have been so good to me, ever since the night at the church bazaar when he bought my apple pie."

"Well, then, hear me out. We want to pay your expenses to college."

"I don't think . . ."

"Laurence says you're not interested in marriage. That's as may be. But a young woman without a husband needs a career."

"I don't know what to say."

"Don't say anything. You could start in the fall, if that was convenient." Juliet rose and shook out her skirts. "I have to get back to my guests. You think about it."

Elvira felt as if she were in a game of blindman's buff and, blindfolded, had been spun round and round. She sat, dizzy and unstirring, her brain groping.

If she'd understood correctly, the Lundeens were offering her college. *Teacher's college.* Such a thought had never crossed her mind. She was a country girl who'd been happy to find a place in town. And what of Cora and George? Stupefied, drugged with confusion, she massaged her brow.

"Cora says you've promised me some waltzes." George Lundeen appeared in the doorway, light from the chandelier in the next room silhouetting him, projecting a figure of mystery. He held out a hand and Elvira rose, a pulse beating hard in her throat, her bones melting. She did not think she could stand upright if he did not hold her—and she him.

chapter sixteen

"COLLEGE!" NELL CRIED. "My stars, Elvira, what did you tell her?"

"Nothing. She said I should think about it."

"But of course you'll go. Such an opportunity." Nell poured tea and they sat at the kitchen table. "Did George bring you home?"

"Yes." Grains of sugar scattered across the oilcloth.

"Is anything wrong?"

"No."

"You seem . . . shaky."

"The brandy punch, probably."

Nell studied Elvira. "You do want to go, don't you? To college?"

"Yes. No. I don't know. I want to learn. I want to be somebody. But I don't want to leave the store."

"Really?"

"What's so strange about that?"

"Well, the store is only a small world, that's all. College is a big world. Are you frightened of college?"

"I don't think so."

"Mankato's bigger than Harvester. You'd meet so many new people."

"I just don't know, Nell. Please." The teacup clattered in the saucer as she rose.

The querulousness in Elvira's voice was unfamiliar. "I'm sorry," Nell said. "I won't keep at you."

Lifting her skirts in her fists, Elvira fled to the bedroom.

Here again was the girl warm and intelligent enough to win love and respect yet secretive and untrusting enough to close a door behind her, shutting Nell out.

For months, Nell purposely refrained from mentioning college again. Juliet Lundeen, respecting Elvira's indecision, said only that there was no hurry, the Normal School wasn't going anywhere.

And Juliet remained patient, if puzzled, by Elvira's silence during the coming year. But, after all, the girl was young and there was plenty of time.

However, in the fall of 1904, while Hilly started first grade, Elvira began working full-time at the store. This, Juliet had not anticipated, and she did wonder if Elvira intended to turn her back on college altogether. And, if so, why? Nor could she ever have anticipated what the year would bring Elvira.

Once or twice over the year 1904, Nell broached the subject of college, but each time, Elvira drew an icy curtain around herself and walked away, saying that she was still thinking about it.

Apart from these occasions, Elvira was much her own self, and from her increased salary, she was paying Nell a small room and board consideration. So, really, from September of 1904 to March of 1905, life above Rabel's Meat Market was genial.

Nell was occupied with teaching and with overseeing Hilly's first-grade projects and lessons. Additionally, she had acquired a small social life. One night a week, three or four elementary teachers, among them Hilly's teacher, Diana Hapgood, joined her in the apartment for an evening of darning and mending followed by tea and cake. Diana referred to them as the "Darn It, We're Good Club."

As she herself was busy, Nell was pleased when Elvira once again began attending the Saturday dances at the Harvester Arms. And she paid no particular attention when, occasionally, the girl returned late from work. Elvira was, for heaven's sake, grown-up now, old enough to be a wife and mother, certainly old enough to have an independent social life.

But then, sometime in May—Nell wasn't sure just when—Elvira fell into a strange mood, jumpy and lethargic by turns, quick to flare. Had the girl fallen in love with a boy from the dances?

Around 2:00 a.m. one night, Nell woke to sounds from across the hall. Rising, she padded into Hilly and Elvira's room. Arms flailing, Elvira was tossing on the bed, sobbing.

"Wake up!" Nell shook the girl.

Instantly, Elvira was awake and sitting, her eyes large with panic. "What did I say?"

"You were sobbing," Nell told her. "What's wrong?"

"Nothing, nothing." Elvira whipped the light blanket around herself and lay down, face to the wall. "Just a nightmare."

Two days later, Hilly asked, "What's wrong with Elvira? She got mad when I asked if we could go to the park with Mrs. Lundeen and Laurence." He sat at a desk in Nell's third-grade room while she corrected spelling tests. "And now they've got a push-go-round at the park. Laurence would love that."

"Well, maybe Elvira doesn't have time right now."

"And she's never home."

"She's a grown-up, Hilly, and she's not responsible for you now that you're in school."

"Doesn't she like me any more?"

"She loves you. But she's got other things to think about."

"What things?"

"She's got to decide about college. Or maybe she's thinking about getting married."

"Married? But what about *us?"*

"I don't think Elvira ever intended to live with us all her life. Someday *you'll* get married and have your own house and probably a baby like little Laurence."

"Don't worry, Mama. I'll never leave you."

"Elvira, we need to talk," Nell said one Sunday when they'd returned from Mass. "Hilly, would you go outside, please?"

Elvira looked balky. Seated on the daybed facing her, Nell clasped her hands tightly together, nervous, but beyond caring if the girl resented a call to account.

"I feel responsible for you while you're living with me," she said. "In the past two or three weeks you've lost weight. You're edgy and secretive. Something's wrong. You're a different girl from the one who came to live here."

"That's right. I'm a grown woman now. And I don't want to talk about it."

"Well, we have to. Or I'll have to go to your parents."

"No!"

"Then tell me what's wrong. Is it a young man? Did someone bother you at work? Do I need to talk to the Lundeens?"

"For God's sake, no!" Eyes skittering, panicked, the girl looked about to break down.

Then, Elvira went calm. The terror disappeared and her body relaxed. She smiled. She's found a lie, Nell realized.

"Oh, all right," Elvira said, "I didn't want to talk about it but you won't be satisfied until I do."

Nell wanted to cry. Elvira was feeling her way through the story.

"If you must know, I'm thinking about taking a little trip. I never had a vacation." Nell waited. "I deserve a vacation."

"Of course you deserve it, but why would you lose weight over that?"

"Well, it's scary, isn't it? I've always wanted to see Chicago, and that's a big adventure."

This is her story and she'll stick to it, Nell thought.

At work, Elvira gave notice that she would be away for a week beginning June 17. She was going to Chicago.

Something wasn't right, Nell knew. In desperation she

called on Cora after school one day. "Elvira is miserable—moody and quarrelsome—and she won't explain. Has she said anything to you?"

"I haven't seen Elvira since the Christmas party." Cora studied her pale, desiccated hands, locked together on her lap.

"She says she's taking a vacation. Going to Chicago for a week."

Cora looked up. "I didn't know."

"It's come up all of a sudden." Nell rose. "I'm sorry to bother you. I had hoped Elvira might have said something." Nell left, unsettled and dissatisfied. Was Cora lying? And why would I think *that*?

chapter seventeen ⬎

AFTER SEEING NELL OUT, Cora wheeled herself from room to room, pausing several times to beat her fists on the arms of the chair.

"Lizzie, I'm going to the park. Can you help me?" Once Cora had been positioned in the sunshine, she told the girl, "Take Laurence down to the hotel and buy yourselves tea and doughnuts. Don't hurry."

For an hour Cora sat, by turns agitated and mournful. God forgive me, she prayed. I meant no harm.

Walking home from Cora's, Nell met Anna Braun leaving Lundeen's, a store money bag in hand. "Running an errand to the bank," Anna said.

"I'll walk with you as far as the post office," Nell told her. "You've heard that Elvira's going to Chicago."

"Yes."

"You and she see each other outside the store, don't you? Is anything troubling her?"

Anna shot her a speculative glance. "I don't see much of her outside the store. Lately, she keeps to herself."

"Lately?"

"Since Christmas, I'd say."

"You don't go to the dances at the Harvester Arms?"

Anna shook her head. "I haven't been to a dance in two years."

"I must be mistaken. I thought the two of you went together."

"Must have been someone else."

A week later, Cora Lundeen removed five hundred dollars from an evening bag in the bottom drawer of her dressing table, slipped the money into an envelope without an accompanying note, and mailed it.

Despite Elvira's protestations that it was silly, and her reminders that she would be back in a week, Nell insisted on seeing her off to Chicago. Hilly too. They sat in the depot waiting room, warm Saturday-afternoon sunlight pouring through grimy windows. A horsefly, buzzing a frantic message to the world outside, hurled himself repeatedly against the glass of an upper sash, driving himself mad.

The sooty smell of trains permeated the dusty wood floor, the railroad-tan walls. In the center of the room, a gritty potbellied stove sat cold, extraneous out of season.

Nell struggled for conversation. "You still don't know where you'll stay?"

"No. Someone at the Chicago depot will know a place."

"It worries me that you don't know where you'll be. If there's an emergency, find a telephone. Mr. Rabel has one in the store now, you know. He'll holler up to me."

Elvira nodded, holding her straw hat with the peach ribbons, twisting the brim round and round. She was wearing the same peach dress she'd worn to Cora's wedding. It was a little out of date now, but she favored it, and it was cool for the train. Pinned to the bodice was the cameo Cora had given her.

Elvira crossed to the window. With her hat she tried to shoo the fly out the open lower sash, but he was crazed beyond recognizing escape. "Poor thing," Elvira said, and returned to the bench. "They get addled and you can't help them."

A strange farewell it was, Nell thought, Elvira now and then pretending excitement, flashing quick false smiles. But she was opaque with concealment.

She'd never traveled before, not even to St. Bridget. She should be pacing and quivering, if only with the welcome fear that accompanies adventure. Instead, she looked as if the undertaking were already carved on stone tablets. Nell felt as though she were seeing someone off to war.

"I'd say 'write,' but you'll be home in a week."

"Yes."

"You're sure you have enough money?"

"More than enough."

"Will you bring me something from Chicago?" Hilly asked.

Elvira hugged him. "You'll have something from Chicago. I promise."

In the distance they heard the train wailing. Elvira tensed, then seemed to shrink.

Without thinking, Nell said, "You don't have to go, you know. You could turn in your ticket. The weather's lovely.

We could pack a picnic and walk out to Sioux Woman Lake. Maybe Cora would like to come. And little Laurence. Cora could take us in the buggy."

Elvira clapped on her straw hat, grabbed the two valises, and spun toward the door, Nell and Hilly following. She stood at the edge of the platform, peering down the tracks, the muscles in her jaw working.

Nell stood next to the semaphore, watching. *She despairs that the train will come and fears that it won't.*

Though the train was still a mile or more away, the depot agent came out and walked down the platform to fetch a mustard-yellow freight wagon with "Milwaukee" printed on the side in green letters.

Hilly stood by Nell, trusty and straight as a soldier but with tears beginning to gather. "Send us a postcard from Chicago," he said. "I never got a postcard before."

Elvira nodded but didn't glance at him. She, too, was soldiering.

Moments later—or so it seemed—the engine was panting and groaning and letting off steam as it ground forward into the station. The conductor threw down the iron step, and Elvira hurried toward it, handing him her bags.

Now she turned, as turn she must, and her mask crumpled. Nell rushed to her. "You don't have to go. You don't have to go."

Hilly tugged at Elvira's arm and she hauled him into her embrace, tears wetting his shirt. And then she was gone, up the stairs and into the coach, and the conductor was tossing the iron step into the train as a crate was unloaded from the baggage car onto the freight wagon.

When the depot agent pulled the freight wagon away from the train, the great engine snorted and began to huff. The conductor jumped onto the first step of the passenger car and waved to the engineer. The huge wheels, with inexorable heaves, moved forward.

chapter eighteen ☙

THEY CLIMBED THE WOODEN STEPS back to the apartment, neither Nell nor Hilly speaking. An envelope stood propped on the living room table.

"Elvira," Nell said, perplexed.

Dear Nell and Hilly,

I'm not coming back. I've disgraced you. I can't say more than that. Don't ask around. Nobody knows about this but me.

Someday when I'm settled, I'll write and maybe tell you what I did. Don't worry—I didn't steal anything. I have plenty of money to get me by until I'm able to work again.

I love you more than any kin of mine. All my life I will keep the dress you made me for George and Cora's wedding.

If you were with me now, you'd see that I'm throwing you kisses.

Love,
Elvira

Nell fell back into a kitchen chair.

"What is it, Mama? What does she say?"

"In a minute. Mama needs to sit a minute." The poor little girl, Nell thought. I promised her I'd look after her. God forgive me.

"Mama, why are you crying?"

"Fetch me a handkerchief from my top drawer, son."

When Hilly returned, Nell wiped her eyes. "I'll read Elvira's note to you. I want you to hear that she loves you. I want you to remember that."

She read, and afterward the boy burst into tears. "Why won't she come back? And what does 'disgraced us' mean?" He pounded the table and buried his head in his arms.

"Don't be angry, Hilly. She didn't want to go. She thinks she did something bad—I don't know what—and she can't face us."

"Face us?"

"Think of how you feel when you've been naughty. You don't want people to look at you. You're embarrassed and ashamed." He sat aloof.

"She should've told us what it was. Did she shoot somebody?"

"Heavens, no. I don't know any more than you do, but I do know that she didn't shoot anybody." Nell reached to hold him, but he would not be held. When his father had died, Hilly had been only eighteen months old and hadn't understood. Now he was six and a half, and understood enough to feel betrayed.

At bedtime, as Nell tucked him in, Hilly told her, "I think I felt like this when Papa died. I think I remember, Mama. I was a baby, but I think I remember."

However, at breakfast the next morning, after Mass,

he said, "I don't care if she never comes back." He'd been spurned.

"Well, I care. I love her and want her here with us."

"If she confessed to Father Gerrold and went to Communion, God would forgive her, right?"

"That's right."

"Then why did she leave?"

"Who knows. She had a powerful reason."

When the breakfast dishes were washed and put away, Nell said, "I thought I'd walk out to the cemetery later. Would you like to come?" She needed to move, to work the anxiety out of her limbs.

"Yes," he replied from the living room.

He was lying on the daybed reading from *Beautiful Stories About Children.* Such a serious boy; Nell worried sometimes. She carried her missal, rosary, and gloves to the bedroom, recalling how Hilly's first-grade teacher had confided, "When he started reading, it was as though he'd always read."

Nell knew that he was reading far better than many of her third graders. Well, it wasn't surprising. Elvira had taught him his ABCs, even how to read a few simple words.

Elvira. Where are you? You who've never been any place bigger than Harvester.

After lunch, Nell and Hilly started for the cemetery, Nell carrying a sky-blue parasol Elvira had said Cora had given her, one she'd left hanging on a peg by the door.

"Would you like to bring your hoop?" Nell asked Hilly.

He shook his head. "I'm bringing a book."

"Me too." She held up Twain's *Life on the Mississippi*. She'd thought at first to bring *Tess of the D'Urbervilles*, but knew Thomas Hardy was too dark for her mood. Some found a novel of despair to be purgative for their own grief. Not Nell. If she'd had something downright jolly on hand, she would have grabbed that.

But for the racket of a thousand singing birds, they tramped along in silence. The cemetery wasn't distant—maybe ten blocks from the apartment. The last bit followed a country road where the chirring of cicadas nearly drowned the birdsong.

"You'll never forget Elvira, will you?" Nell asked as they turned into the Catholic cemetery. "She taught you your ABCs."

"And she read to me every day. She liked to read out loud, she said. And I liked it when we used to go to the park with Mrs. Lundeen and Laurence."

"Maybe on the way home we can stop at the Lundeens', and if Laurence isn't down for his nap, you can say hello." Nell led the way to the second row of graves where Herbert was buried beneath a small granite marker.

Herbert. He'd been a mercurial man. No—more than mercurial. How many times had he told her that he regretted having married her? He'd proposed while riding one of his high, whirling moods. But when those moods gave out beneath him, he'd fall, as from a cliff, taking her down with him. "Without a wife and kid, I could've gone places."

"Is it all right to sit on Papa's grave?" Hilly asked.

"Of course. He'd be disappointed if you didn't stop and

say hello." Nell leaned against a nearby headstone and helped a ladybug down from her skirt and onto the grass. "What would you like to tell him?"

"I wish he was here. Really here, like you and me." He pulled a seedhead from a plantain. "Now that Elvira's gone, we hardly have any family." Hilly told his father about Elvira's leaving and about the Dickens stories, then he and Nell strolled further along and sat to read, their backs against an old cottonwood.

Beyond the cemetery fence, the land stretched west to the Badlands. The countryside was an undulating sea of wheat and corn, rye, oats and timothy—a sea of loneliness. Nell looked out at the farms and marveled at those who had first homesteaded them or even pushed on to a more distant outpost, a harder existence. She had never had the itch, as some called it. Oh, she would have loved to travel—to at least see Europe—but that was different. One came home again.

She was a home girl, warmed by the glow of lamplight, a stove boiling water for tea. To sit in the rocker and read Jane Austen or Hardy, to play checkers with Hilly—these entertainments spoke of her unsophistication, and she did not mind. To be unsophisticated was no crime if you weren't narrow, and she hoped that her reading kept her from that. Through novels you glimpsed the grim night that could eventually overtake the intolerant.

Over near the fence, she saw a white cob swan marching across the grass with stately intention, extending its graceful neck and lifting its head as though in greeting. Nell touched Hilly's arm.

"A daddy swan," she breathed. "He's wandered over from the lake."

"I never saw one at the lake, except far off, did you?"

Nell shook her head. "He looks as if he's come to visit." The swan did indeed. He approached, not stopping to peck in the gravel path but stepping with purpose and unusual delicacy for so large a bird, until he reached a spot not four feet distant from them.

For long minutes he stood eyeing them with a sad, bright glance, as if there were things he would have liked to say. At length he cocked his head and turned, wandering away among the graves. Nell let out her breath.

No buggies stood before George and Cora's house nor in the drive, so Nell and Hilly rang the bell. Lizzie answered.

"They're in the back," she said, leading the way out to the yard. Cora sat in her wheelchair and George on a wooden bench beneath the grape arbor, each of them with a book in hand. George wore one of the vanilla-white ice-cream suits he favored in summer. From his watch fob dangled a gold charm in the shape of an ocean liner.

"Visitors," Lizzie announced.

Cora laid her book aside and called, "Come join us." She looked drawn, new lavender shadows in her temples and the hollows of her cheeks.

Nell and Hilly settled on the bench opposite George. "I hope we're not intruding," Nell said. "We've just walked out to the cemetery. The lilacs and peonies are beautiful. So mature. Someone must have planted them as soon as the cemetery was marked off."

"Eudora Barnstable, when she was a young bride," George said. "Also the evergreens along the north fence."

"I won't keep you from your reading," Nell told them. Folding the parasol, she leaned it against the bench.

"What a beautiful parasol," Cora noted.

"Thank you." Nell recalled Elvira saying that it had once been Cora's. Perhaps Cora had forgotten.

Nell tried to sound light but felt heavy and reluctant. "I thought I should ask if Elvira had said anything to you about not coming back. From Chicago."

The Lundeens stared. "Not coming back?" Nell saw that she'd knocked the pins from under them.

"She told us she was taking a vacation," George said, trying to grasp the situation.

"That's what she had told *us*," Nell explained. "But she's been worried lately, or unhappy."

Cora's shoulders flinched.

An awkward silence. Nell glanced toward the fruit trees at the back of the lot, trying to recall in every detail the parting at the depot. "When we saw her off, I saw that she was distressed, but I thought she must be frightened of the big city.

"But when we came home, we found that she'd left us a note." How much should Nell tell them? "She seemed to think she'd done something . . . wrong. I can't imagine what it could be. She was a good girl."

George gave his head a convulsive twist, as though his collar chafed. "Maybe she wrote to us at the store," he said, tossing down his book. "I'll check the box at the post office." He sprang up. "I'll do that now."

He's taking this hard, Nell thought.

Eyes squeezed shut, Cora rested an elbow on the arm of the wheelchair, and with thumb and forefinger pinched the bridge of her nose.

Noting her distress, Nell said, "Cora—don't. This was none of your doing."

chapter nineteen

DAYS LATER NELL AND HILLY both received cards from Elvira, postmarked "Chicago, Illinois."

On the front of Hilly's was a scene of bathers on Lake Michigan, and on the back:

Dear Hilly,
This lake is as big as an ocean, and this city is so big, I've gotten lost three times already. I'm leaving before I get lost again. A little package will be coming for you.

I love you,
Elvira.

The picture on Nell's was of the Palmer House Hotel. The cramped handwriting read:

Dear Nell,
I didn't stay here, but I went in and looked around and had a cup of tea. It's surely grand. I wish you could see it. I'm leaving today. I'll write from wherever I end up.

Love,
Elvira.

The following afternoon a harmonica arrived for Hilly. And almost daily, for a while, some item seemed to turn up in the apartment to keep Elvira's presence fresh. Hilly found a hairpin under the rag rug beside her bed and kept it on the bureau like a museum piece. Nell had the previous Christmas given Elvira a box of monogrammed handkerchiefs; one of these was found mixed in with Nell's. Then, of course, there was the blue parasol.

But the George and Cora scrapbook was gone.

After the harmonica arrived, a week passed with no word. "Would you like me to sell Elvira's bed?" Nell asked Hilly. She stood in the doorway of his room. "You'd have more space."

"Let's keep it, in case she comes back. I'll sleep in it till she comes."

After three weeks, Nell felt it was time to talk to Juliet Lundeen, to apologize for Elvira. The couple had offered to send her to college, and Elvira had pulled up stakes without thanking them.

"Come in," Juliet stood aside.

Dreading this visit, Nell followed Juliet into the front parlor. Beyond the windows, the afternoon was blinding and hot. But in here, soft northern light, filtered through lace curtains, bathed the room in cool shadow. Though she knew better, Nell sometimes found it hard to believe that people living in such surroundings, with sumptuous chairs and sofas, soft carpets and tea trolleys—like Henry James characters—knew the same worries and sadnesses as the less fortunate.

"You'll have a glass of lemonade," Juliet said, skirts

whispering as she left the room and returned, pushing a tea cart.

"You shouldn't trouble for me," Nell said.

"Nonsense." The older woman passed Nell a cool glass and a plate with two slices of pound cake. "You can set those on the malacca table," she said, drawing up a chair and pouring herself a glass. "Now, then, you have the air of someone on a mission."

"I'm here to apologize for Elvira."

"No need. She already did that herself. Sent me a note from Chicago at the same time she wrote George to say she wasn't coming back." She shook her head and bent toward Nell. "I'm worried about that little girl. What's happened?"

"I don't know. All I can think is there's a man in this."

"My thought, too."

Less tense now, Nell sliced off a bite of the pound cake. "Beyond that, I have no idea—who it could be or what happened."

"In her note she said she was sorry to let me down. She felt she was a disappointment to me, and to you."

"She's never disappointed me," Nell said. "I couldn't have asked for a better girl to look after Hilly. We love her dearly. She worked hard and she was sweet-tempered—at least till the last few weeks."

Thoughtful, Juliet nodded. She wanted to ask something, Nell saw, but either scruples or delicacy prevented her.

"I can't help wondering if she's . . . *expecting*," Nell said.

"Oh, God, yes," Juliet sighed, her mouth working. She rose, crossing to a window where she looked out toward the school. "That occurred to me, too, and I've hated myself for it." She turned back to Nell. "But Elvira was a pretty girl, and lively. Men were attracted to her."

"Still, we don't know where she is, so what can we do?"

"An awful thought. If you hear where she's gone, let me know. Please. She's so alone."

The following morning, a Saturday of tropical heat, Nell woke to pounding. She'd hooked the screen door and left the inside one open all night, hoping to capture a breath of air. Now, at 7:00 a.m., someone was banging on the door-frame. *Elvira?*

"I'm coming," Nell called, grabbing her robe.

Hilly wandered into the hall, curious.

On the landing, Aunt Martha waited, huffing with impatience. "I came as soon as the milking was done," she said. "You, apparently, are not an early riser."

"I was up late reading." Nell unhooked the screen, and Martha hove in, heading for the rocker.

"Well, the fat is in the fire now," she said, settling down, weapons in place.

"What's wrong?" Nell pulled her robe tighter.

"Elvira! That's what's wrong." Martha struck the flat of her hand on her thigh. "What kind of guardian *are* you?"

"Guardian? Elvira's a grown woman."

"Well, she was living under your roof."

"And?"

"And she's run off pregnant."

"Pregnant? What're you talking about?"

"Are you telling me she's run off for no reason?" Martha's mouth twisted with scorn.

"I don't know why she left. I saw her off to Chicago. She said she was taking a vacation."

"Well, I tell you, you're in big trouble."

"Trouble?"

"I heard it from Minnie Monk, and she as school secretary ought to know. They've called a special meeting of the school board."

"But why?"

"Because a girl's in a family way, with no husband, and she was living under your roof while it was going on."

"Who says she's pregnant?" Nell felt not fully awake.

"Zeke Dormeier just came in from Denver a day ago. He knows what Elvira looks like, and he saw her in the Denver depot. Elvira. In a maternity getup." Tears sprang to Martha's eyes. "We're disgraced."

"We?"

"She's relation. Everyone knows that. Poor Herbert must be spinning in his grave."

Not likely. "I still don't see why the school board is meeting."

Extracting a handkerchief from her reticule and blowing her nose, Martha rose. At the door she paused long enough to warn, "You'll find out."

chapter twenty

"THE FOOLS WANT TO CANCEL your contract," Juliet Lundeen said. "They've actually scheduled an emergency school-board meeting for Monday night. Laurence is talking to John Flynn now."

"The lawyer?" Nell remembered him from George and Cora's wedding. She gasped, gulping air. Since Aunt Martha's visit, she had had difficulty breathing.

"Laurence wants your legal rights protected."

Nell's insides twisted.

"A tempest in a teapot," Juliet continued, closing her eyes as if the whole business didn't bear thinking about. "People in villages need drama. You can't talk about the weather forever."

A tempest in a teapot? If Nell lost her teaching position, her small bank account would dry up in a week.

Juliet took Nell's hand. "We're not going to borrow trouble. I promise you this will come to nothing."

No, thought Nell. It will come to *something*. "I don't mind for myself, but I don't want Hilly hurt."

"He won't be," Juliet assured her, but not even a Lundeen could promise that.

◆ ◆ ◆

As Nell and Hilly were returning from Mass on Sunday, George and Cora stopped them on the street. From the buggy, Cora called to Hilly, "We've been hoping you could spend today with little Laurence. He's been missing you." Cora knew that a woman doesn't want to moan and pace and wring her hands in front of her child, and so Hilly was welcomed into the buggy.

Indeed, moan and pace and wring her hands was exactly what Nell did all that day. Beyond tea and toast—and the toast only half eaten—she could not remain seated long enough for a meal, even had she an appetite. Gnawing her cuticles and yanking her hair, she sat, rose, then sat again, only to leap up and pace.

Late in the afternoon, she tried reading Balzac. In Milwaukee, studying for teacher certification, she'd heard a professor remark that reading, especially something deeply affecting, was a sure way to escape the moment. In the present case, this proved untrue. If she had something humorous . . . but, really, could *anything* fetch her away from this day while a knife tip of panic was driving her back and forth, back and forth?

Monday night found Nell waiting, like a naughty pupil, on a bench outside Superintendent Brewster's office. Both Juliet and Cora Lundeen waited with her, George and his father having carried Cora and the wheelchair up the stairway. Hilly was in Lizzie's care for the evening.

Sitting in the hall, the three women and George caught only scraps of debate as the all-male board argued her case. "This is madness," Juliet declared at ten o'clock. She turned to Nell. "Whatever happens, you're coming to our house for a whiskey when it's over."

At that, the door opened to disclose a company of silent, grim-faced men. Last to emerge were Laurence Lundeen and John Flynn, wearing thin, remote smiles.

"We're heading to our house for whiskey," Juliet said. "John, you'll join us." The shadowy halls of the school felt foreign to Nell as the group headed down the stairs, John Flynn carrying the wheelchair, George carrying Cora.

No one spoke as the little party made its way under moonlight to the senior Lundeens', where lamps were burning. Once inside, they settled in the larger parlor, and Juliet fetched whiskey and glasses.

"Nell, you'll need this," she said, handing the woman a bourbon. "Cora, what's your poison?"

Preoccupied, Cora ran her hands back and forth along the arms of the wheelchair. "Sorry . . . I'll have the same."

Laurence stood at the mantel and took a breath. Nell focused on him; they hadn't discussed the outcome yet. "I can't reveal who voted yea or nay, but here's what happened: Nell, you'll keep your position. John scared 'em, told 'em he'd sue if you were sacked."

Nell felt gratitude to both men but no elation. Another shoe was to drop.

"But," Laurence continued, "our side carried by *one* vote—always bad in a little burg. Very divisive. The others are talking about setting up a church school. We'll see how far they get with that."

"I'm not worth this," Nell said. "I'll resign."

John Flynn rose from a wing chair. "No, you won't. I understand your feelings, Mrs. Stillman, and I don't want to make a martyr out of you. But we can't encourage this nonsense. A town has to decide early the kind of place it wants to be."

Laurence broke in, "Don't desert us, Nell. Superintendent Brewster isn't any happier about this mess than we are."

Nell set her glass on the malacca table. "May I have a day or two to think it over?"

"Naturally."

"I owe all of you a good deal."

"You owe us nothing!" Cora suddenly exploded, startling everyone. "You're the victim here. We damned well ought to be kind." She glanced around. "Pardon my vulgarity."

Uncertain, Juliet laughed, and then the men.

On Monday morning, first-grade teacher Rhoda Cheney dropped a pencil as she stood beside her classroom door. By bending to retrieve it, she was able to avoid greeting Nell, who was crossing to her own room.

Except for Diana Hapgood, the second-grade teacher, the rest of the elementary faculty also maintained its distance, unable now to afford association with a colleague touched by scandal. No more darning and mending club. Nell sympathized. Small-town teachers were a pitifully vulnerable lot.

When she entered the classroom, Nell found the students scattered in knots and buzzing, full of the gossip they'd heard at home. They took their seats, looking both contrite and curious, glances passing back and forth among them. Would teacher say anything about the school-board meeting?

Nell had spent hours considering this question, and her voice was full of trepidation as she told them, "I'm sure most of you have heard that the school board voted last night whether to keep me as your teacher." Hands trembling, she sat down at her desk and opened the attendance book. "The majority voted that I should stay. I'm happy about that, and I hope you are, too. But your opinion is your own. You don't have to share it with anyone, unless you choose."

From there, the school day went forward pretty much as usual. When the other children had filed out at three, Delilah Dempsey hung back, slowly gathering her books and papers. At last, she started for the door, but hesitated at Nell's desk.

"Mrs. Stillman?" She stared at her shoes.

"Yes?"

"Well, I just wanted to say . . . well, I wanted to say that almost all the kids are glad you're still our teacher. Including me."

Later, as Nell stood in Rabel's Meat Market, eyeing the ring bologna, Gus came out from behind the counter, wiping his big hands on his apron. With a hand cupped beside his mouth, he said, "I'm not supposed to tell, but I voted for you, Missus, and I'm not taking little Gus out of the school neither."

But when Nell entered Petersen's Groceries, Arvina Petersen swung about and headed to the back room, leaving the clerk to tot up Nell's order.

Over the following days, three letters appeared in the

Standard Ledger complaining of a 'heathen element' in the school, and two ministers preached sermons decrying godlessness in public education.

Nell walked on eggshells.

"There may be children at school who don't want to play with you—not because of *you*, but because their parents are upset with me," Nell told Hilly. "Maybe I could get a job in another town." She was not sanguine about that prospect.

But the boy wept, "We know people here. We won't know people some other place. And what if Elvira comes back and she can't find us?"

Nell thought it might be the final straw, though, when she received a stiff-looking letter one day. When she saw the embossed return address, she fled the post office: another sanction, and this from a woman of influence, Eudora Barnstable. Nell had never met Eudora, but Juliet had once referred to her friend as "the mother superior of the village."

Nell put off opening the envelope until she had set the kettle on the stove and changed into her housedress. A cup of tea and a ginger cookie from Petersen's at hand, she slid a paring knife under the flap and extracted two sheets of creamy paper, written upon with a plain but firm hand.

Dear Mrs. Stillman,

I am appalled by the recent action of the local school board in bringing you to account for an unverified indiscretion by a young woman with whom you shared your home.

But what can one expect? Put two or three men in a

room together, give each of them a title, and you have the makings of a silliness akin to that unnecessary horror called the Spanish-American War. We can only be thankful no lives were lost in this local folly.

I have always believed that women should occupy school boards, since children are more generally their responsibility. Until we gain our rightful enfranchisement, alas, that belief remains a dream—but a dream to strive for.

Sincerely,
Eudora W. Barnstable

When Nell next spoke with Juliet Lundeen, she recounted the letter. "It was so kind. Were you behind it?"

Juliet laughed. "No. Eudora is a force unto herself. Nothing I could say would sway her if she weren't already convinced."

Nell wrote Eudora a note of thanks, and kept the Barnstable letter on the kitchen table for those moments when she was most in need of assurance—moments which were not infrequent. Some people, both men and women, had made a point of turning away from her—even at St. Boniface, which in some way was hardest.

Two weeks after the school-board meeting, Nell made a confession, not because she felt guilt concerning whatever sin Elvira might have committed, but because she hoped for a sympathetic ear from the priest.

Spring's chill was gone and the Saturday-afternoon sidewalk was pleasantly warm beneath Nell's leather soles. Within St. Boniface, only a handful of parishioners waited beside the confessional. Genuflecting, Nell slipped into the backmost pew to wait.

When her turn came, and when she had confessed her transgressions, among them anger at the school board and at those who shunned her, she waited for Father Gerrold to comment or at least to assign penance. Instead, he was silent.

"Father?"

"Yes?"

"My penance?"

"Isn't there something more you'd like to tell me?"

"Something more?"

The silence between them was a widening moat. Finally it came to her: he was waiting for her to confess a sin of omission. She had omitted vigilant oversight of Elvira, and because of that, the girl had been led into sin.

"There's nothing more," she said.

With a heavy sigh, the priest said, "Five Our Fathers and ten Hail Marys. And use the coming days for an examination of your conscience." So briefly was he able to dismiss her.

Nell escaped, not pausing at the holy-water font nor saying the Our Fathers and Hail Marys but fleeing home to read again the note from Eudora and to praise Hilly who, as she had asked, waited alone, reading a little book of Kipling poems that Elvira had found at the Water and Power Company.

Village memory is prodigious. Though summer intervened, when school reopened in September of 1905, Nell's prediction to Hilly was borne out. As the Christmas holiday drew near, Diana Hapgood's second graders began decorating colored-paper tree ornaments, gifts for their parents and for one another. From his twelve classmates, Hilly received just five presents. At home, his mother was always quiet, a silence that shut him out. She'd been that way for a long time. To fill the void, he "played" the harmonica.

Then one blustery day in mid-December, Diana Hapgood stopped by the apartment with her grandfather. "Hilly says he has a harmonica," she told Nell. "If he wants, Grandpa will teach him to play."

And so lessons with Grandpa began. Every Saturday morning through the remaining winter and coming spring of 1906, the old man came to instruct Hilly and to play duets. Hilly applied himself with severe discipline, and late in May, Grandpa Hapgood told Nell, "I've taught the lad as much as I know. It's been a pleasure. He's a deep little fellow, not like some scamps I could name—that butcher's kid for one."

Hilly and Mr. Hapgood were friends now, two old men together. Hapgood taught the boy to fish with a cane pole on Sioux Woman Lake. If Hilly caught anything worth carrying home, Grandpa cleaned it and sent it along to Nell.

That following June, after months of keeping her head down, Nell encountered Juliet Lundeen in the lobby of the Water and Power Company.

"Can you come for whist Saturday night? There'll just be the four of us—Laurence and I and you and John Flynn. You have no objection to cards with John?"

"Heavens, no. How could I?"

The florid widower was solid and shrewd, according to Cora Lundeen, who a day later wheeled across Seidman's Pharmacy to waylay Nell, paying for aspirin at the counter.

"You'll like John," Cora said sotto voce as Elsie Schroeder, the perpetual pietist, passed them on her way out the door. "He's good company. An easy man. But keen as a new knife."

"I'm predisposed to like someone who saved my life," Nell assured her.

Cora's face clouded. "A horrid affair. I am sorry for what you've been through."

"It wasn't your fault."

Cora murmured something under her breath, then said, "Since you'll be playing cards Saturday evening, send Hilly to us. He can spend the night. He's teaching Laurence how to play checkers."

As they parted, Cora grasped Nell's hand. "Please have fun."

But, at 3:30 a.m. Saturday morning, in her sleep, Nell strained to scream, squeezing out only a wordless whimper.

In her dream the night was solid black, bereft even of gaslight, as she felt her way home from school along Main Street. Something brushed her arm, and she pressed her back against the window of Blankenship's Hardware. In the clotted darkness, eyes flashed. Pinpoints at first, but growing bolder. Across the street. At the corner. In front of Reagan's Saloon and Billiards. She spun around. But there they were, inside Blankenship's, peering out at her.

Nell's whimper woke her and she sat up in bed, cold and shaking. With hands that seemed not her own, she thrust aside the quilt, felt for matches on the bedside table, and lit the lamp.

chapter twenty-one 🙴

"Young Laurence is learning to play checkers, I understand." The boy's namesake poured Nell a glass of wine.

"Cora said."

"Well, it beats all. I don't know which of the boys is smarter: Laurence, for learning at age three, or Hilly, for teaching him."

"Hilly has the patience of Job," Juliet observed.

Footsteps sounded on the front steps. "Here's John." Juliet left the others standing by the hearth and went to the door. "Come in. We're having a glass of wine."

"D'ya have beer?" the lawyer asked, entering. "I've got a powerful thirst, and I'd soon go through a bottle of wine."

Laurence guffawed. "There's beer in the root cellar. I'll fetch it. Come in and say hello to Nell."

"Mrs. Stillman, a pleasure. Sorry to come busting in begging for beer, but I've been out on the lake all afternoon, trying to catch a few miserable bullheads. Skunked, I was. Too hot. Should have gone early morning."

"My Hilly went early with Grandpa Hapgood. We had fish for supper."

"Shown up by a boy."

"A six-year-old boy," Juliet added.

The party moved out to the screened gazebo in the backyard. The women carried lamps though the sky was still light enough to see the cards. As they passed outside, Juliet had thrust a platter of cheese and homemade crackers at John. "It's humid, so they may have gone soft."

"They wouldn't dare."

A table, chairs, and scorepad were already in place, and now the players cut the deck for partners, Nell and Laurence pairing for the first game. As they took their designated seats, Nell leaned against the back of the chair and closed her eyes. She had grown bodily stiff from tiptoeing through the past year.

"Anything wrong?" Laurence asked.

"Absolutely nothing. I was only thinking how fortunate I am to be sitting in this lovely spot on a beautiful evening and in such fine company."

"It's a good and rare thing to realize when we're happy," John said. He and Juliet won the first game, and all cut for partners again. This time John and Laurence played together, and the women won.

"I haven't played whist since I was a girl," Nell said. "I'm surprised I remember how. Da liked whist. Sundays, after dinner, he, Mam, my sister, Nora, and I played all afternoon."

Later, while Laurence poured more wine and beer, Flynn said, "Saw George and Arnie Kolchak out fishing today. My God, but your boy is gray. Seems like overnight he turned."

"More like over a year," Laurence said.

"What is he, twenty-nine?"

"Twenty-eight."

John shook his head. "Funny how some folks go gray early. Well, it's distinguished looking, I'll say that. Gives him gravitas."

Night was gathering. To anyone observing, Nell thought, we must appear a floating island of well-being. She savored being seen in this way—not as a disgraced teacher, but as someone well regarded, if that was the word. She sorted the cards John had dealt.

"Have you used the bookcase in the Water and Power Company yet, Mrs. Stillman?" Flynn asked.

"Every week. And please call me Nell—especially if we're going to discuss books." He eyed her closely and nodded.

"I'm reading *The American*," she continued. "And you?"

"*The Mill on the Floss*. But I'm only ten or fifteen pages into it so, for God's sake, don't quiz me," John paused. "Excuse my profanity. I'm too used to men."

"Since I doubt God will take offense, why should I?"

Night was full-on now, and, save for the light of stars and an apricot moon, the darkness bordering the Lundeens' yard was as black as an undertaker's new suit.

An apricot moon . . . Nell drifted in reverie.

She had been twelve. The late summer day had been warm, and she had completed her morning chores.

"Girl," Mam said, "we need sorghum. Y'll have t' walk t' town."

As Nell tramped into the raggedy Wisconsin village, the eastbound train stood at the station, snorting like a wounded bull. Nell lingered on the platform, captive to the stories she suspected the train was transporting—stories exotic, romantic, maybe even wicked and thrilling.

The day being warm, the windows in the passenger car were raised. From one of these, an arm extended, reaching down toward her, palm upturned and holding—she saw as she drew near—a fruit, orange, but smaller than she knew an orange to be.

"Apricot," the man said.

Nell had never seen an apricot. Dazed, she could only thank him with a hand uplifted in farewell. In the other hand lay the apricot, golden and pink-tinged and warm, the surface, like her own flesh, at once firm yet yielding.

Hadn't she known that trains carried riches? Here were riches lying in her hand—a story complete in itself, an apricot unblemished and wafting the perfume of sunlight unending.

Mam should have a bite of it, Nell thought, but when she raised the fruit to her mouth, extracting the sweet juice, she forgot everything but the succulent meat of it.

When only the rough pit remained, she sucked it clean and dropped it into her pocket, a tangible memory of surpassing delight. . . .

Now, under this apricot moon: surpassing delight once more. A dog barked across town, and a rooster woke to crow out of time. Nearer, from between the buildings of Main Street, the faint sounds of the piano at Reagan's filtered toward them. "In the Good Old Summer Time," jaunty and sad. Nearer yet, luna moths flung themselves against the gazebo screens, petitioning.

Later, Juliet announced, "I have baked beans and cold chicken." She stood.

"I'll carry a lamp for you," Nell told her, taking one from the table, and also, from beneath it, the extra card that explained where the deck had been manufactured, and where to send away for another, concluding, "Wishing you luck in cards and love."

In the kitchen, pulling a platter from the icebox, Juliet observed, "John is a nice fellow, isn't he?"

"Yes. 'Easy' is the way Cora described him." Nell slipped the card into the bodice of her dress.

Later, as the party broke up, John Flynn said, "I'll walk you home. Saturday night, you never know what you might run into downtown."

Now, with the echoing sound of their steps on the wooden sidewalk, the two strolled along Main Street. The businesses were all dark except for Reagan's and, further on, the Harvester Arms. The few gas streetlamps burned dimly, their light casting no shadows.

At the foot of Nell's stairs, John stopped and said, "Been a long while since I had such a good time on Saturday night. You're a crackerjack whist player. Would you be willing to try it again next Saturday at my place—if I can pull a foursome together?"

Nell laughed. "Yes, certainly."

They shook hands, and Nell climbed the stairs, waving from the landing. *Crackerjack.*

chapter twenty-two 𝒫

IN THIS WAY John and Nell fell into a routine of Saturday-night foursomes. With Flynn, Nell felt moored to something strong and large minded. She was liberated to be witty occasionally and to have opinions. He was chivalrous and affectionate without being amorous. On their second evening of whist, he noted that he was fifteen years her senior, and she took that to mean that he had no romantic expectations. A relief, really, since she didn't plan to marry again.

But best of all, Hilly liked John. His new friend gave him several volumes of Horatio Alger and took him for buggy rides in the country, visiting farms that Flynn owned. A town boy, Hilly returned from these outings with tales to tell:

"I was *this* close to Mr. Jessup's bull."

"You be careful when you're around bulls," Nell cautioned.

"There was a fence between us but still, the bull did look pretty mad. And he pawed the ground and put his head down like this."

Or: "Mrs. Schoonover showed me how to gather eggs. Sometimes the hens don't like you to take 'em, but I was brave, John said."

And, "Did you know the milk we buy, some of it comes from one of John's farms? They let me try to milk a cow, but nothing came out." The relationship extended beyond field trips, however. John bought Hilly a chessboard and taught him to play. Then Hilly taught Grandpa Hapgood, ensuring himself a back-up partner.

To John, Nell could only say, "You're a good man."

"He's a good lad," John replied. "Very serious. I call him 'the Professor.'"

In the second week of May 1907, the third-grade boys were restless, the girls dreamy. No one wanted to correct geography papers. In the hall, beside the door, Nell ushered in the last of the stragglers from recess. Behind her, in the classroom, Berma Bentine stifled a whimper. Nell turned.

Young Gus Rabel stood by his desk, back to the door. Berma sat across the aisle, massaging her right arm. In the back of the room, little Anders Holm was saying, "I'm telling Mrs. Stillman."

"You do, and I'll twist her arm till it breaks."

"What's going on here?" Nell asked Berma.

Gus swung around and sat down, all nonchalance.

Berma shook her head. "Nothin'."

"Gus." Motioning the boy into the hall and closing the door behind them, Nell held Gus's cold gaze with her own.

"Nothin'. You heard her. She said I didn't do nothin'."

"You and I both know better. What did you do?"

"She kicked me."

"Berma has never kicked anyone."

"Well, she called me names."

"Do you think the principal will buy that? Would your mother?"

"Don't tell 'em," the boy cried. "Please, don't tell 'em."

"I want to know why you do these things. Last week you told Phyllis you were going to set fire to her cat."

"I dunno." He'd begun to snivel, and he wiped his eyes on his sleeve though no tears had gathered. "I dunno. I can't help it. Somethin' gets inta me. Maybe the devil?" From beneath his brows, his eyes calculated whether this was selling.

"That won't do, Gus."

"But somethin' *does* get inta me. Maybe not the devil, but *somethin'*." A further thought occurred to him. "And I'm too big. I'm the biggest in the class. Maybe if I wasn't so big, I'd be better."

"Big can cut both ways. *Heroes* protect smaller children; *bullies* pick on them. Which would you rather be?"

"I dunno. A hero, I guess."

"Next time there's mischief or I just *hear* of mischief, you're off to the principal's office. Do you understand? Do you? Now, go in there and apologize to Berma for whatever you did." She turned him around and opened the door. Three weeks until school let out. Nell would warn the fourth-grade teacher. Something was wrong there.

When Hilly passed into Nell's third-grade class in September, he faced a fresh set of problems. Because Nell was his teacher, if she gave him an A, deserved as it might be, boys called him teacher's pet. Nor did he enjoy the roughhousing the bigger boys got up to after school. They all planned to be the next Jim Corbett or Jack Johnson.

To avoid confrontations, Hilly remained in the class-room after school, doing homework. This did nothing to enhance his reputation. John Flynn showed Hilly some wrestling moves and how to keep one's dukes up, but Hilly had an exaggerated notion of the harm he might inflict and was loath to fight. That was fine with Nell.

Throughout third grade, Hilly spared his mother knowl-edge of the bullying and teasing: shoves on the stairs, elbowing in the cloakroom, taunts on the dusty patch of playground—"Hey, guys, it's Milly! Little Milly Stillman."

Hilly wouldn't fight, but he dreamed of glory that would cow these bullies. Recently the Volunteer Fire Department had organized a kitten-ball team and staked out a playing field beneath Bacall's Hill, at the edge of the village. Benny Knobler was currently the pitcher. Though a fine tinsmith, Benny was only a fair pitcher; nonetheless, he was becom-ing a celebrity among the town's kitten-ball enthusiasts. If Hilly learned the art of pitching—and maybe with John's help this summer he could make a start—in a few years he would be a whizbang pitcher and local hero.

But that summer of 1907, on a Sunday afternoon seem-ingly too cloudless for disappointment, Nell and friends were gathered in Laurence and Juliet's backyard for a pic-nic, some of them in the gazebo, others at a table under a black maple.

At the table, John was laughing at the question George Lundeen had asked. "My God, do you have to ask? Democrat, of course. I'm a wild Irishman."

"That is a damned fact," George said. "But the legislature?"

"Blame my boy, Paul. He's a noise up there in St. Paul

politics, and the Democrats are looking to pick up an out-state seat. Old Soren Jansen's retiring, thank God, and the Party thinks I might pick up this district."

From her wheelchair at the end of the table, Cora said, "John, we don't want to lose you here."

"I'll be here, running my practice, looking after the farms, except during the session. It's only a few months a year." He turned to Nell. "What d'ya think, darlin'? Do I have your vote?"

She laughed. "You would, if women could vote. But I'm like Cora. I'm afraid we'll lose you."

Nearby, Hilly tossed a rubber ball back and forth with little Laurence. Hearing John's plans, he realized pitching kitten ball wasn't going to be the answer to his problems after all.

chapter twenty-three ♪

FOR MUCH OF THE NEXT YEAR, as Cora and Nell had feared, they did lose John. He was gone frequently, laying the groundwork for his legislative run.

Nell missed his verve and optimism. Without him, life was paler and somehow less defined. She missed asking his opinion, hearing his assurances. He was a bulwark. Without his company, she was back to feeling a stigmatized schoolteacher.

Often he slipped into her mind late in the afternoon, when the dismissal bell had emptied the classrooms and the building had settled into its evening rest; when only the tread of the janitor measuring the length of the hall again and again with his wide dust mop, or the tick of the clock high on the wall behind her desk, broke the solid silence.

As she graded papers, she'd look up, tapping the pencil against her chin and wondering what John would think of this student's answer or of that one's. How he'd laugh to hear Mamie Madden's response to the question, What do you want to be when you grow up? "I want to be a wife," she'd written, "and have three childrun and some of the modurn conivances."

When asked what an example of modern *convenience* might be, the girl had replied, "A store-bought broom, for one thing!"

On such an afternoon, early in October, Nell set aside both her grade book and thoughts of John Flynn, then rose and checked the floor for trash. Slipping into a sweater and pulling together a pile of spelling papers, she locked the door behind her and left. Strange, she thought. Hilly hadn't shown up after school to walk her home. Well, he was in fourth grade now, possibly growing too sophisticated for such activities.

When she passed Seidman's Pharmacy, it was nearly five, according to the clock in the store window. If she hurried, she could stop for mail. Leaving the post office with a grubby-looking envelope added to the stack of school papers, she crossed Main Street and climbed the stairs to the apartment. The inside door stood open. "Hilly?" she called, closing the screen behind her.

A muffled "What?" from the direction of his bedroom.

Setting aside the envelope and schoolwork, she knocked on his bedroom door. As a rule, the door was open unless he was dressing.

"May I come in?"

Hilly was lying on the bed with a kitchen towel bunched in front of his nose and mouth.

Alarmed, Nell sat down beside him, pulling his hand away from his face. "Oh, dear," she said, "you've been in a fight." His nose and upper lip were swollen and bleeding. "Come out to the kitchen and I'll clean you up."

Afterward, sitting at the table, she said, "I don't think

the nose is broken, and the lip is only cut on the inside, so that'll be okay. You won't have a scar. Who did this?"

"Ozzie Arndt."

Fifth-grade son of Adolph Arndt, school-board member. "How did it start?"

But Hilly simply shrugged and didn't answer. She wanted to question him further, but someone was at the door.

"John! Am I glad to see you."

"I hope you're not sitting down to supper. I'm on my way from work and thought I'd drop this off for Hilly." He indicated a rolled-up sheet of paper.

"We haven't seen you since the picnic! Have a seat," Nell told him, holding open the door, then called, "Hilly, John is here." Turning to the lawyer, she explained, "He's been in a fight. He'll be embarrassed."

"Nothing to be embarrassed about, Professor," Flynn said when the boy appeared in the doorway, reluctant and trying not to show his face.

"Black eye?" John asked.

Hilly shook his head.

"His nose and lip are swollen," Nell offered.

"That all? Come on out. I've got something for you." John removed the string from around the parcel and unfurled the sheet, revealing a map. "Remember you telling me you wanted to see the world? I recall you mentioned India because of *The Jungle Book*. If you tack this on the wall of your room, think of the plans you can make." He handed the map to Hilly.

Hilly cast him a macabre lopsided smile. "Thank you," he slurred.

"So, tell me, did you fight back?" John asked.

Staring down at the map in his hands, Hilly shook his head.

"Why was that? Did the fella take you from behind?"

"No, sir. He came right up and said he was going to lick me."

John nodded. "But you didn't put up your dukes and give him what for?"

"No, sir. I was afraid I might put his eye out."

John reflected. "If you don't want to fight—whoever it is—that's your business, Professor. But at least put your dukes up next time, so you don't get your nose broken, OK? Your mother'd take after me with a carpet beater if you got your nose broken."

chapter twenty-four 🙑

THE STRANGE, GRUBBY ENVELOPE had fallen behind the kitchen table and been forgotten in the ado surrounding Hilly's nosebleed and cut lip. A week passed before Nell moved the table to sweep. On the envelope, "Mrs. Stilman" and "Harvester, Minnesota" were printed in a childlike hand. Setting the broom aside, Nell lifted the corner of the flap and eased it open, extracting a single sheet of lined paper.

"Jezzabel."

For a few seconds Nell was merely amused, but gradually the intent dawned. As if the page harbored a fatal disease, she recoiled. The paper floated to the oilcloth. Both heartbeat and breath faltered as she gripped the edge of the table, lowering her body onto a kitchen chair.

Who?

Later, when Hilly was down for the night, she sat in the rocker, raking her mind for answers. At first she thought the note might concern Elvira. But surely not—Elvira had been gone for several years now.

John? Had it anything to do with John? Did the writer imagine that Nell was his mistress? Anger blotched her face and throat, and she pressed fists hard to her breast. John mustn't know about this.

Over the next year, John Michael Flynn threw himself heart and body into the political arena, and in the fall of 1908 the district rewarded his labor with a seat in the state House of Representatives in St. Paul.

The following Saturday, George and Cora threw a victory party, and the town came out—even the Republicans. A harvest table sagged beneath washtubs of Reagan's beer, bratwursts and buns, sauerkraut, coleslaw, potato salad, baked beans, and an array of cakes.

In the parlor, a crowd clustered around the piano singing "In My Merry Oldsmobile" and "Wait 'Til the Sun Shines, Nellie." In the backyard, faces candescent in firelight gathered around an emptied oil barrel stacked with burning logs. As the logs shifted, they spat sparks that flew toward a nonpartisan moon shining cold and clear over a snowless November.

Nell drank in lungfuls of tangy wood scent. Beside her, a nearly ten-year-old Hilly squirmed and danced with exhilaration. "Isn't it exciting? Aren't you happy?"

Nell smiled. "I'm happy for John." She hadn't actually prayed that John would lose the election, but she wouldn't have shed a tear had that happened. That was her little secret.

John moved among the guests indoors and out, thanking them for their support, lingering to inquire about families, crops, businesses. No political palaver: He would never have a great stock of that. In the backyard, he worked his way toward Nell and Hilly. "What d'ya think, darlin'?"

"Congratulations are in order." Though she felt shame for begrudging his victory, she would not say that she was happy. And she would never mention the "Jezzabel" note. Evil was fluid and could seep into places, like John's career, where darkness was unearned. One must throw a wall around it.

Once established in St. Paul the following January, John was pressed into service. A popular speaker, inevitably he was drawn into the social life of politics. A new man of taste and intelligence was not a glut on the market. In addition, John's son, Paul, and his family lived within walking distance of the capitol building. John would of course spend much free time with them.

In John's absence, Nell read. And read. Eliot and Balzac and Trollope and yet more Austen, starting over when she'd read the last's novels. Where would she be without the Lundeens' library?

And then Nell discovered Chekhov. First the short stories on loan from Juliet, then the plays after writing John and asking if he could secure them. Though she'd read some Chekhov before, it was in this new reading that she suddenly saw what he was saying. So it is, often, that in the passage of time a story takes on new meaning. These were people she knew, Harvester people! Set down in the provinces of Russia they might be, but she daily nodded to many of them on Main Street or sat beside them at St. Boniface, people with awful longings, a sense that life was happening elsewhere, that this little world was suffocating them. Nell had seen all that in pair after pair of eyes; she had witnessed it in young fellows stumbling out of Reagan's on Saturday night, shoulders bent.

Not all of Chekhov's characters were so disaffected, however, nor were all the folks in Harvester. The chumminess of a village suited many; others simply ceased to consider their own estrangement. Still, the intimacy she felt with these Russians was nearly unsettling. She found herself speaking aloud to them, to Vanya or Sonya or an old servant. "There, there. Can you find consolations *here*, in this place?"

That was another thing about fiction; it could expand your humanity. Not that Nell flattered herself in that regard, but she recognized the possibility and hoped that reading might eventually help her. Who knew? If she read enough fiction, she might even soften toward Aunt Martha. *Might.*

When John returned from the legislative session in late spring, he began motoring the back roads of his district, reconnecting with constituents, and this in a gasoline-operated Sears High-Wheel Buggy that frightened horses, terrified geese in farmyards, and raised storms of dust everywhere. In his law office, he caught up with the backlog and invited folks to stop in with their concerns.

Occasionally that summer, he managed to attend a card game. One evening at Juliet and Laurence's, he fell into a doze while sitting dummy. Snoring softly, he jerked to attention when Juliet prodded him, "You're driving yourself too hard."

"It's the nature of the beast, this political hobbyhorse I'm on," he replied.

Nell shook her head.

Now and then John dropped in to see her on his way home from the office, sometimes as late as nine or ten at night, always apologizing for neglecting her and Hilly.

One night he said, "If I asked how you're spending your time now that I'm not hanging around, I'd sound presumptuous as hell. I expect you have more offers than you have evenings. But . . . how *are* you spending it?"

"Being courted by Monsieurs Balzac and Flaubert and Misters Trollope and Twain, to name but four. I'm also on excellent terms with Miss Austen and Miss Eliot. We manage to fill the hours profitably."

"Well, don't spend too many evenings with Monsieur Balzac. He's a dour chap, I think."

Nell laughed. "My latest courtier is a fellow named Chekhov. You were instrumental there. Mr. Chekhov and I understand each other profoundly."

As he was leaving, John kissed Nell—not a simple buss this time, but something more. "I hope you won't grow too fond of this gent Chekhov. Not sure I could compete with a *doctor*."

He needn't have worried about Chekhov. That autumn Nell found another intimate altogether—a soulmate.

On an October afternoon when the air was extravagant with the scent of bonfires and apples, Hilly joined Nell to walk home from school, stopping at the Water and Power Company on their way. Nell spied a book on a high shelf titled *Love Among the Chickens*, by someone named P. G. Wodehouse—a book left there by Cora, as it turned out.

As though bewitched, Nell sighed, "Ah, yes," and pulled the book down. Well, one doesn't often come across a title like that, she thought.

While Hilly leafed through an illustrated Wild West magazine from a lower shelf, Nell opened the volume and read. The scene selected at random took place on a golf course. The narrator recounted, "I drove off from the first tee. It was a splendid drive. I should not say so if there were anyone else to say it for me. Modesty would forbid. But, as there is no one, I must repeat the statement."

Later, dawdling along Main Street and casting an eye into store windows at goods she couldn't afford, an irrational giddiness shook Nell, and her hand fluttered to her throat. *Love Among the Chickens.*

Mr. Wodehouse, it turned out, was an entirely new experience. He was delicious, lighter than air. Generous to a fault. He made her laugh as no man ever had. Surely, he wrote only for her. His rhythms, the way his wit kissed a phrase and sent it dancing—these warmed her like summer. She laughed aloud and fell in love again and again.

Since she had a great hunger to feel weightless and amused, to dismiss out of mind grubby envelopes and school boards and men who breezed off to state legislatures, Mr. Wodehouse came to live with her. No. She went to live with *him*. He was a friend who took her hand, saying, "I'll show you an innocent place, and I'll be there when you need me." A gentle man.

Other than that extra card from Juliet's deck—"Wishing

you luck in cards and love"—never had Nell stolen anything. But she did not return *Love Among the Chickens*
to the Water and Power Company, and later, she would
filch *The Swoop!* And, should any *other* volumes by Mr.
Wodehouse fall into her hands . . . well, they would meet
the same fate.

chapter twenty-five 🙢

DURING THE TWO YEARS of John's term in the legislature, Nell watched Hilly growing into a young man. That he was plagued now and again by tormenters at school she was only peripherally aware, since he went to great lengths to protect her. To borrow a saying, Hilly played those cards close to his vest.

But one December Saturday, late in 1911 and just before Hilly's thirteenth birthday, Nell came across a note in a trousers pocket as she was gathering up laundry. "Little Milly Stillman. Any time you wanna show me you're not made outta yellow crap, let me know so's I can beat the rabbit shit outta you." Nell sighed and tossed the note into the stove, thinking, if he can make it through these next several years, he'll be fine. Then she sighed again, hating the wishing-away of his life in this manner.

She had hoped that after John's legislative stint, he would be back in their lives as he had been once, a strong masculine presence for Hilly. But in St. Paul, the Democrats had persuaded him to sign on for another run.

The April morning was unseasonably warm. Through the open windows of the classroom came the sounds of birds racketing in the trees, horses clop-clopping in the street, and the occasional snort of an automobile.

"Pass your spelling quiz to the person behind you," Nell told her students. "Back row, bring yours to the front."

As the class exchanged the quizzes and prepared to correct them, someone knocked at the door, and Nell crossed to answer. Stepping into the hall, she half-closed the door.

Minnie Monk, the secretary, stood outside fidgeting with a balled-up handkerchief. "That big ship went down," she blurted.

"What 'big ship'? The *Titanic?*"

"That's it. Yes. It sank. Lots of people drowned. Mr. Brewster wants people to know in case anybody had kin on it."

A bolt of fear stunned Nell, followed by dizzying relief. George and Cora weren't leaving for Europe until June, when young Laurence would be out of school. And of course this ship had been sailing in the opposite direction, *toward* America.

Still, for the rest of the day and long after, the *Titanic* occupied a substratum of Nell's consciousness. An entire ship. So many people. So quickly—virtually in the snapping of one's fingers—they were gone. The cosmic capriciousness of it shook her. She felt as if she were only half-breathing—as if everyone was only half-breathing—waiting for a giant to stamp his foot.

At lunch break, further details had come in on the Teletype at the depot. Walking home, she could not shake the vision of passengers unable to get into lifeboats, struggling in icy water, losing strength and finally hope. And the Titanic had been the finest ship ever built.

Sitting on the bed, changing out of her shirtwaist, her heart was leaden, too heavy to hold up. She lay back on the quilt. So many poor in steerage. So many souls, each unique. She closed her eyes and groaned, mostly in anger.

And then a strange thing happened. A part of her mind began drifting, and for minutes she had two minds, one agonizing over babies slipping from their mothers' arms into the cold north Atlantic, the other floating, not quite against her will, into a daydream:

Nell was walking to the depot with a letter for Mam, in Wisconsin. If the letter went east on today's train, Mam would have it tomorrow. Handing the letter to Mr. Loftus, Nell turned to leave.

There, on a bench in the waiting room, a traveler sat, his bags at his feet. He nodded and she returned the greeting. But before she could reach the door, he rose—and she could see that he had a question.

"Ma'am," he said, "may I trouble you?"

She hesitated.

"I'm between trains on my way to Denver to deliver a talk at a university. I have several hours' wait, and I was hoping to find a restaurant where I could enjoy a meal and while away a bit of time."

His accent was British, his voice pleasant, his manner winning.

"I'm sorry—I should have said—my name is Pelham Grenville Wodehouse." He extended a hand and she shook it.

"Nell Stillman."

Nell was so shaken that she did not acknowledge recognizing his name. She groped for words. "There's . . . there's not a lot of choice," she told him. "But I should say your best bet is the Harvester Arms Hotel. I've never eaten there, so I can't vouch for the food, but I'm told it will do in a pinch."

"Well, this seems to qualify as a pinch."

"If you follow me, I'll walk you there. It's on my way."

Well, it was nearly on her way. They left Wodehouse's bags with Mr. Loftus and set out.

For her kindness, Wodehouse invited her to join him for the meal, and so it was that Nell "whiled away a bit of time" with her literary hero, discussing all manner of things but mostly books, including Love Among the Chickens. *Though her collection was limited, she confessed to being a devoted fan.*

"Is that so?" He seemed surprised and inordinately pleased.

Then, as often happened in the middle of a stimulating conversation, the quotidian intervened. Nell heard the outside door, and the two halves of her mind slowly merged. Hilly was home. The bedside clock read five past five, and there was supper to put on the table.

chapter twenty-six

"HILLYARD, MAY I SPEAK WITH YOU?" Abel Timms, who taught history and coached the school's scant physical-fitness program, called to Hilly in the hallway.

"Yes, sir?"

"I'm getting together a running club. Some schools in the county are holding competitions next spring. I figure it's not too early to get started."

Hilly nodded.

"It wouldn't take much of your time."

An outright "No" felt impolite.

"You've got the build," Timms continued, "and I need a man in the two-mile category. Think it over."

A man. What he meant, Hilly knew, was an "available body." Still, he was flattered. He'd never been asked to join anything. "I'll think about it, sir."

Timms nodded. "Let me know what you decide."

That night at supper, Hilly told Nell. "Mr. Timms wants me to join the running club. He thinks I could be a distance runner."

"That's grand," Nell said, passing Hilly the bowl of gravy. "How far does a distance runner run?"

"He mentioned two miles."

"Will you say yes?"

"Now that I'm working after school, I don't have much time."

"True," she said. "But it would do you good to be out exercising with the other boys." She slid the plate of sausage patties toward him. "It's up to you."

In the end, the decision was made *for* him. While he paid for a roll of kite string in Blankenship's Hardware the next day, he overheard two women discussing a mutual acquaintance. He reddened as he realized it was Nell.

"I hear she's set her cap for John Flynn."

"Oh, yes."

"Well, you know, Elsie saw her drinking champagne at the Lundeen wedding reception. And her a teacher, mind you."

"And there was that girl who got in a family way."

"Maybe I'm old fashioned, but in my day a schoolmarm didn't try to be more than she was. Which in this case is shanty Irish."

Hilly paid for the string and left, cheeks flaming. *Witches. Clucking hens.* How dare they discuss a fellow's mother in public! His anger only ripened through the day. If he were older, he'd join the army and be heroic and earn medals— then everybody would know that his mother was a good person. And he'd send home his pay so she could buy a real sofa like the one he'd seen in the Sears, Roebuck catalog. But he wasn't old enough to join the army. Yet.

Then he recalled Mr. Timms. What if he became a champion runner? People wouldn't dare disrespect his mother then. If the boys on the team called him mama's boy, well, maybe that was all to the good. He'd show them what a mama's boy could do!

After school the next day, Hilly found Timms and told him, "I guess it'd be okay, you know, to run."

"Good for you, son," Mr. Timms said, grasping Hilly's shoulder. "Start running in your spare time, build up your lungs and legs for spring."

Son.

With school out, Hilly began working full-time at Kolchak's Dray and Livery, where his father had worked. It pleased him to do some of the same jobs Herbert had done—cleaning out the horse stalls, making sure the animals had fresh feed and water, and currying them when they came in at the end of the day.

Sometimes Hilly climbed on a dray wagon with Arnie Kolchak or Ted Shuetty. Riding along to the depot to pick up freight, or to the furniture store to deliver a sofa or icebox, the men often let Hilly take the reins. He always hoped that one of the school bullies would see him driving the horses. He felt bigger than himself then.

Hilly enjoyed the heavy lifting as well. "Look at them muscles you're getting," Ted Shuetty told him. "Another year or two, you'll be boxing at the county fair." And the next time somebody pushed Hilly around, maybe he'd push back.

But he still saw his mother's livid face. *Don't ever hit! Do you hear?*

To find time for running, Hilly rose at 5:30, heading into

the country before breakfast. Most mornings he jogged past the school, through the park, down the cemetery road, and a mile beyond.

At first, running felt pointless and arduous, so he began imagining that he was running to someone's aid: his mother had fallen, turning her ankle; John's car was stuck in a ditch; a big dog had taken off after Diana Hapgood.

He had ongoing dreams of heroism. Oh, not just a running hero, winning trophies—but also a hero who did good in the world. Maybe someone like . . . well, he wasn't quite sure yet, but a person who saved lives in some way.

One thing he noticed about running was that after fifteen or twenty minutes, a knot in his gut he hadn't known was there began to unclench. He didn't know what that was about, but it felt good. He seemed lighter by about five pounds. And faster, as if he had wings on his feet. Like Mercury!

And when he flew like Mercury, sometimes he flew to India—he saw himself floating down the Ganges on a big raft with a makeshift shelter so he could escape the sun in the heat of the day. Along the shore women chattered and washed clothes against the rocks, and mellow temple bells sounded, and smoke writhed from funeral pyres.

Then, on another morning, his winged feet took him to Delphi, in Greece, where he raced in the Delphic Games in a magnificent stadium halfway up a mountain. There he was crowned with laurel, and his mother was proud, and they both drank from the Castalian Spring, which gave men (and surely women, too) the gift of eloquence.

Every morning he flew somewhere. Usually far away. But, closer to home, the cemetery road was his favorite flight. Often he stopped to visit his father's grave. But never again did he see that huge white swan—though he kept hoping.

Nearer town, on the cemetery road, lived Grandpa Hapgood and Diana. Unmarried, she was an object of conjecture in the village. So pretty and neat about her person, people said. Pleasant when met on the street. Why had she remained unwed? Early orphaned, she seemed content to keep house for the old man and to mentor new teachers. There must be a story there, people figured. It wasn't natural.

"Miss Hapgood," Hilly called one day, seeing her at the porch railing, shaking dust from a rag rug.

"Hilly. Can you stop?"

"For a minute." He still enjoyed an occasional game of chess with Grandpa, but he had less free time since he'd taken up running.

Inside, Grandpa Hapgood rose from the breakfast table, a cup of coffee sitting by his egg-smeared plate. "Have some breakfast, Hilly?"

"No, thank you, sir. Mama's waiting with mine before I go to work."

"Still at the dray?"

"Yes, sir. Sorry I haven't been around. How are you keeping?"

"Pretty fair. Diana looks after me. Coffee at least?"

"Could you come for supper?" Diana asked, pouring

coffee from an enamel pot and setting a cup in front of Hilly. "George Lundeen came by with a string of fish, and we have new peas." Hilly nodded.

"Larry is what his dad calls him now," Grandpa Hapgood said that evening, referring to young Laurence, now in the sixth grade.

"Fine-lookin' boy. Dark. Takes after his dad, though George's gone gray. Darned young to go gray. Must be hard on him, the wife being crippled. He don't complain, though." The old man paused, sucking on his corncob pipe. He shook his head. "Nice woman, the wife. She and her mother-in-law'll build us a library one of these days, I don't doubt."

Diana Hapgood stood in the kitchen doorway, wiping her hands on a towel. "More coffee, Grandpa? Hilly, would you like another piece of cake?"

At the cleared dining table, Hilly looked up from the chessboard where he had lined up his men. "No, thank you, ma'am."

"Mr. Timms has got you running," the teacher noted.

"Yes, ma'am. He says that next year our club will get together with clubs from St. Bridget and Red Berry and we'll run races. He says I'm built for long-distance running. Probably the two-mile."

During their second game, Grandpa asked Hilly, "Whatever happened to that pretty little thing that lived with you and your mother? The one that worked at the dry-goods store?"

"She left, sir." Hilly swallowed. "She got on a train for

Chicago, and she never came back. I was five or six then."
He wanted to be manly, but still couldn't talk about Elvira.

"Well, there's a mystery for you," the old man breathed.
"What's your theory?"

"Theory?"

"Let's say some fellow who was passing through town
came into the store one day and she waited on him. And
say he was an important government . . . emissary—that's
what they call those fellows on secret missions, isn't it,
Diana? And say they fell in love, what they call 'love at first
sight.' Well, you can see all the ways that might turn out.
You think about it."

"And she couldn't tell us about him because he was on
secret business," Hilly added. "And . . . maybe still is."

"Was she sad when she left?"

"Very."

"Because she couldn't tell you where she was really
going." Grandpa moved a chess piece. "Anyway, that's one
possibility."

Rolling her eyes and laying aside her knitting, Diana
said, "I'm going to make popcorn." Pausing at the kitchen
door, she eyed her grandfather. Still full of surprises.

chapter twenty-seven 🙢

THE WEEK BEFORE CHRISTMAS 1912, Hilly and Ted Shuetty hauled an upholstered armchair up the stairs to the Stillman apartment.

Nell peered out the door. "What on earth?"

"An early Christmas present," Hilly told her. "I've been saving up. Mr. Bettin at the furniture store says I can pay the rest on time." They set the chair down in the living room. "D'ya like it, Mama?"

"Like it? It's beautiful." She ran a hand over the tufted back. "The green is perfect. It goes with everything. Hillyard, you really shouldn't have. But I'm thrilled."

Hilly grinned. "See how it feels."

Nell sank down into the chair, resting her hands on the cushioned arms. "Like sitting on a cloud."

"Now you have a nice place to sit when John Flynn calls," he told her. "When he sees you in that chair, he'll probably ask you to marry him."

"What an idea!" she said, embarrassed that Ted Shuetty was hearing this.

Hilly shrugged and waved, heading back to Kolchak's.

Nell relaxed into the new chair, caressing the soft fabric. Hilly's careless remark made it impossible to keep John at a distance. She wouldn't marry again and John knew it, but she sometimes dreamt of him and moaned as she woke, excited and spent. With rue she considered the horrid saying that you couldn't have your cake and eat it too.

Glancing toward the bookcase where her meager but blessed collection of Mr. Wodehouse resided, she rose and crossed the room. The latest addition, *Psmith in the City*, had been a holiday remembrance from Cora Lundeen, amused by Nell's fondness for feckless young men from English public schools.

Slipping *Psmith* from the shelf, Nell returned to the new chair and let the little volume fall open: "Dignified reticence is not a leading characteristic of the bridge-player's manner at The Senior Conservative Club. . . . Mr. Bickersdyke's partner did not bear his calamity with manly resignation. He gave tongue on the instant. 'What on earth's' and 'Why on earth's' flowed from his mouth like molten lava. Mr. Bickersdyke sat and fermented in silence. Psmith clicked his tongue sympathetically throughout."

Oh, the darling. Oh, the bliss.

Choosing a French design from one of Cora's magazines, Nell spent several days assembling a dress for the Lundeens' New Year's party.

"You look like an actress," Hilly told her when she emerged from the bedroom. "I saw one on a poster for the St. Bridget Opera House. She was wearing a dress like yours."

"I'm sure," Nell said, her tone sardonic.

"Now go sit on your new throne." Hilly led her by the

arm. "The color of your top is excellent against the green chair. What do you call that?"

"I call it maroon."

"I'll let John in. He's got to see you in that chair."

Nell laughed. "Hillyard, I never knew you to be such an 'arranger.' The man is nearly old enough to be my father."

"Does that make a big difference?"

"What if he became my husband, and then died next year? You'd feel terrible."

"If he died, I'd feel terrible anyway."

She eyed him with concern. "Well, don't get your hopes up."

When they heard steps outside, Hilly flung open the door and, ushering John in, helped him out of his coat.

"You have a new butler," John observed, laying a couple of small packages on the lamp table.

"Yes," Nell said, "and the butler insists I sit here so that you can see how well my dress goes with our chair."

"And indeed it does," John said, sitting in the rocker opposite as Hilly had indicated. "The chair's new. Very nice."

"My Christmas present from Hilly. The nicest piece of furniture I've ever owned."

"The Professor has good taste."

"Doesn't she look like an actress?" Hilly asked. "She made that dress herself. Isn't it excellent?"

"Oh, for heaven's sake, Hilly, you're embarrassing me. Get going if you're going." To John: "He's looking after young Larry tonight."

"Open this first, Professor." John rose, handing one of the packages to Hilly, who tore into it at once. "*Riders of the Purple Sage* and *Smoke Bellew*. Excellent! Thank you, John. This is excellent!"

When Hilly had left, Nell said, "'Excellent' seems to be the pet word of the moment."

"My pet word at that age was 'profound.' Everything was profound, from the laying of the Atlantic cable to the latest penny dreadful." He handed Nell the second package. "Here. I understand you're infatuated with a Mr. Wodehouse."

"You dear man." Unwrapping the package, Nell held up three books—*Mike, A Gentleman of Leisure*, and *The Prince and Betty*. "How on earth did you find them?" she asked, clasping the books to her breast.

"A fellow in St. Paul could probably get me a Gutenberg Bible if I wanted."

"They're perfect. Thank you." She rose and started for the kitchen. "I'm afraid all I have for you is a tin of cookies I baked—the soft ginger ones you said your mother made."

He followed her and slipped his arms around her waist. "Nothing could please me more."

Later, in the car, Nell inquired about John's Christmas.

"Christmas was just as Christmas oughta be. Everyone was well, and the three grandchildren are the right ages for St. Nicholas—Grace is three now, Harry five, and Caroline eight. Caroline recited 'A Visit from St. Nicholas' on Christmas Eve, and we all went skating Christmas Day before sitting down to Mathilda's roast goose and trimmings."

"Mathilda?"

"Paul's wife."

Hearing John talk of his family made Nell feel remote from him. He owned so much past in which she played no role.

"Are you all right?" he asked.

"Yes. I'm fine."

"We don't have to go inside," he said as they drew up in front of the Lundeens'. "I can go to the door and explain that you're under the weather."

"And miss showing off my new dress?"

Juliet had invited two tables of whist. With John and Cora as their opponents, George and Nell partnered the first game. George told Nell, "Hilly's going to teach Larry to play whist."

"Well, Hilly taught him to play chess when nobody thought he could," said Laurence, who was sitting at the second table. "Whist will be a breeze."

"Your dress is good enough to eat," Cora told Nell.

"Copied from one of your magazines." Nell concluded dealing and laid down a spade in the center of the table. "After I'd made it, I was afraid it might be too . . . fashionable for a schoolteacher." George laughed.

Smiling, Nell told him, "There's always the risk of 'getting above ourselves.'" She hoped that the Elvira scandal was well behind her, but in the ashes of disgrace, some would always find a spark.

"What you're above is the hoi polloi who concern themselves with your clothes."

George was always thoughtful, pleasant, and the soul

of breeding, but, like a September frost, middle age had overtaken him early.

Nell noted Cora's glance straying to her husband. How much did she blame herself for George's decline?

Now Juliet was turning from the second table to ask John, "Will you be in town for the Businessmen's Variety Show? February 28 and 29?"

"I'll be back for the performance. Couldn't miss Charlie here and Laurence doing the 'Tap-Dancing Honeymooners' number."

"Laurence is already rehearsing," Juliet told him, and rolled her eyes.

"Will you run for the legislature again?" Cora asked, leading a small trump.

Holding her breath and bracing her spine against the back of the chair, Nell prepared for a blow. If he ran, this would be his third term.

"I'm damned if I know. I'm weighing a couple of options. I'll let you know as soon as *I* know."

"It's your turn to play, partner," George prodded. "Nell?"

"Oh, sorry. I was woolgathering. What are trumps again?"

The others laughed.

John pulled the car to the curb outside the meat market and turned off the engine. The machine snorted to silence. The late night was quiet after the earlier barrage of gunshots announcing the New Year.

"If we sit here, you'll take pneumonia," John said. "May I come up for a few minutes?"

When Nell hesitated, he took her hand. "I doubt anyone will notice on New Year's Eve, Nell. I won't stay long." She nodded.

Once inside the icy apartment, Nell lit lamps and John started a fire in the cookstove. They sat down at the kitchen table.

"Cora asked if I would run for the legislature again," he said. Nell nodded. "I've actually been approached to run for Congress next year."

Nell was silent.

"D'ya think it's a terrible idea, darlin'?"

"It's probably a wonderful idea," she said. "But remember what Cora said when you ran for the legislature? 'I'm afraid we'll lose you.'"

"But you didn't lose me, did you? And you won't now. You'll see."

Washington wasn't up the road a piece, like St. Paul, but it was *his* career. If she tried to stop him, one day he'd resent it.

"You'd be a wonderful congressman. Just don't expect me to smile as I wave good-bye."

"I'd be disappointed if you did."

After John had left, Nell heated a brick on the stove, wrapping it in a towel and slipping it between the bed-sheets. Returning to the kitchen for a last cup of tea, she paused in the living room to fondle the books he had given her.

Opening *A Gentleman of Leisure* at random, she read: "'Personally,' said Jimmy, with a glance at McEachern, 'I have rather a sympathy for burglars. After all, they are one of the hardest-working classes in existence. They toil while everybody else is asleep. Besides, a burglar is only a practical socialist. People talk a lot about the redistribution of wealth. The burglar goes out and does it.'"

Turning the wick down and blowing out the flame, Nell sighed and headed to the bedroom, teacup in one hand, brick in the other, book tucked under her arm. *It's up to you now, dear Mr. Wodehouse. You must see me through the winter nights when he's in Washington, and the summer afternoons when he's on the hustings.*

A book was not flesh and blood; John was. But a book was nearly everything else: companion, instructor, travel guide, entertainer, philosopher, sometimes healer. The list was endless.

And Mr. Wodehouse, well, he was a conjuror, summoning a world that had never been but was more real than any that had, a world that provided all that the so-called real world withheld—most especially, friends who didn't leave.

Well, John Flynn, she thought, folding back the covers and slipping the brick into the cold bed, if you lose my affection to P. G. Wodehouse, it's your own damned fault.

chapter twenty-eight ☙

SOUTH OF BACALL'S HILL, on the east side of Harvester, stretched a flat, open area, once a community pasture. A portion of it was now marked off for kitten ball.

In the spring of 1913, Coach Timms dragooned a couple of high-school athletes to mow a crude running track on another section. Later, lanes would be drawn for formal meets, but for now Timms's runners loped around the track in casual clots.

Ten boys made up the team, the youngest an eighth grader. To accommodate everyone's schedule, Timms arranged practice for Sunday mornings—before church, of course, to head off the objections of Baptist mothers.

The first practice for the scheduled May 19 meet was held in early April. Most of the snow had melted, but a frigid westerly breeze sliced through the boys' clothing as they awaited instruction from Timms. *At least in church, we'd be out of the wind.*

Young Gus Rabel was quiet till Timms was out of earshot, then sneered, "Watch out, fellas. Get too close to Stillman, you'll catch something."

Sensing a joke, Nils Petersen, a good-looking senior boy, stamped his cold feet and asked, "Like what?"

"Mommy-itis," Gus told him, adding, "Stand over there, Stillman. Nobody wants to catch what you've got."

Hilly moved a couple of steps away. *Here it comes.* The eighth grader, a head shorter than Hilly, darted from the pack and charged. Hilly simply stood aside, but could see that this boy would be the bullies' mascot, while *he* would become their goat.

"Afraid of a little kid, Stillman?" Gus called.

He wasn't; neither was he going to hit one.

"All right, you bums, let's see what you've got," Timms called. He began to send the runners off in groups of twos and threes, sprinters first. When the sprinters had all finished, Timms gave them a few pointers and dispatched them to church.

"Stillman, Arndt, and Petersen, get over here." Hilly and the two others jogged to the track, peeled off their jackets, and waited for Timms to blow his whistle. Hilly felt ready. While snow had still lain piled along the cemetery road, he had begun training again, a mile and a half out of town, then back.

"How far?" Petersen asked the coach.

"Till I blow the whistle," Timms told him.

In March, John had sent Hilly a proper pair of running shoes. Hilly kept them in his bureau, saving them for meets. Jogging in heavy winter high-tops the rest of the time was awkward, but Hilly knew it was building his legs. Later, when he ran in light footwear, he'd feel buoyant.

Hilly owed John a lot. For one thing, John took him seriously. While John was in Washington, he wrote once a week—letters you might write a college man, Hilly thought. Monday's letter read:

> Dear Hilly,
>
> Your mother tells me you practice your running every day, getting up before school to get to it. I admire folks who pay due regard to the activities they undertake.
>
> Every man needs a pastime or two that he respects and that recompenses him. By recompense I mean gives some deep reward to mind or soul, not the reward of money or loving cups or ribbons—though they may accompany the other.
>
> If you ever have the time or inclination, I'd be interested to hear about the recompenses of running. I was never any kind of runner, tending more toward Greco-Roman wrestling myself, but I can imagine the satisfaction in something as solitary and challenging as the long-distance run.
>
> In looking over what I have asked, I see that I may have requested the impossible. To describe what is ineffable is a tall order.
>
> I enclose a pat on the back along with my love.
>
> John

Hilly looked up "ineffable" and was glad to add it to his vocabulary. The word surely applied to a great deal of life, at least his.

But besides the pleasure of being taken seriously— and that was huge at fifteen—when you were with John, a sureness took hold of you. Sort of like when you were running. You felt you could make something of yourself, something your mother would be proud of. If Nell married John, would they live in Washington? That'd be the answer to his prayers. No more "Mama's boy."

With John Flynn dreams at his back, Hilly flew forward around the rough track, losing himself in motion.

Not until the coach stepped in front of him did Hilly realize that it was time to stop. The other runners were laughing at him for his mooniness. Hilly's face burned.

Timms blew his whistle again. "Too bad the rest of you lead-foots aren't as crazy as Stillman." He turned and walked away.

But Hilly knew the sneers would continue. Lily-liver and yellow streak. The only way to prove them false was to fight.

But his mother . . .

Monday, May 5, Hilly returned from his morning run winded, his cheeks red with exertion and the chill of early May. "Your first meet—the one in Red Berry—it's Friday, isn't it?" Nell asked as he sat down to oatmeal. "Are you excited?"

"I guess."

"Frightened?"

"Yes," he said. But he had something else he needed to say and couldn't put it off. "Mama?"

"Yes?" She sprinkled brown sugar over his cereal.

"About Friday?"

"You'd rather I didn't come to the meet?"

She'd read his mind. "Would you be disappointed?"

"I'd make you nervous if I was there."

He nodded.

She added milk. "Anybody could understand that."

"Really?" She was hurt, he knew. But if she heard someone calling him names . . . it was better this way.

The day of the Red Berry meet dawned dark and bone chilling. May in Minnesota was contrary, sometimes hot enough to fry eggs on a tin roof, sometimes as cold as Jesse James's heart.

Again and again during algebra—then history, and English—Hilly peered out at the sky. Was it growing lighter? Darker? If it rained, would the meet be canceled? *Excellent.*

Around 1:30, the sun pierced the clouds and a light westerly breeze began sweeping ragged gray shreds eastward. At two o'clock, the club members assembled in front of the school, where three automobiles waited to carry them the seven miles to Red Berry. Both George Lundeen and his father had volunteered to drive, as had Arnie Kolchak, who'd taken an interest in Hilly's running.

Hilly, along with three other team members, was assigned to George Lundeen's 1911 Overland, Hilly climbing up in front. George was telling the other boys, "I'd like to see the school organize more teams—a football team, say, and a baseball team. And wouldn't it be grand if we had a real gymnasium so you could play basketball?"

Hilly was too nervous to reply. The three boys in the backseat didn't have much to say either. George Lundeen was pretty impressive: could be the boys were intimidated. *Excellent.*

When they reached the grassy field at the edge of Red Berry, they saw that a running track had been laid out, much like the one in Harvester. George pulled the Overland onto the verge, and the boys in the back tumbled out, heading toward their teammates who'd driven up behind them.

"Good-looking shoes," George said.

"Mr. Flynn."

"He's a good friend."

"Yes, sir, he's excellent."

The boys in the dashes ran first. Harvester took a first, a second, and two thirds. St. Bridget, the biggest town represented, had more runners, more firsts and seconds. Harvester didn't have a relay team, so that competition was held only between the others.

During the dashes and relays, Hilly paced up and down near the automobiles, away from the running track and his teammates. When a cheer went up from the small crowd, he halted long enough to determine who had won, then resumed pacing.

Tonight, fathers would order a beer in Reagan's or at a meeting of the Volunteer Fire Brigade, and they'd snap their suspenders and brag of their son's winning the hundred-yard dash or the four-forty. Hilly imagined having someone brag about him.

"Stillman, step on it," Timms was calling. "Get over here and line up."

Moments later, someone shot a starting pistol, and six boys bounded away from the line. Running, Hilly was blind to the others—blind to who was ahead and who behind; blind to the scruffy track, not mown short enough; blind to the seedy, tar-paper hem of Red Berry, a couple hundred yards distant; blind to this domestic sky.

He was winged Mercury now, soaring untethered in a sky anchored close to the sun. Below him were spread millions of acres of sand as blazing as that sun in their radiance and heat. And, there, off to his right, the Sphinx reposed— inscrutable, regal, silent—while a lone ibis, forsaking the Nile, drifted pale as a ghost around the statue's shoulders.

Past the Sphinx, one pyramid—and then another, and another. He'd like to join that distant caravan, carrying dates and carpets toward Cairo and Alexandria. But now he must change course.

There, beyond a bank of low, thready clouds, the obelisk of the Washington Monument floated into view, while nearby, the Potomac was swimming along, lazy and dark, toward Chesapeake Bay. In irresolute sunlight, the White House shone bravely and over in that direction lay the Capitol building, where John labored.

Hilly, his mother, and his new stepfather, John Flynn, were living in Washington—had been for a couple of years. Returning to Harvester for a visit following some great, unspecified triumph of John's, half the town met them at the depot. A band played "For He's a Jolly Good Fellow."

Young Gus Rabel was there, as were Ozzie Arndt and Nils Petersen, all slapping Hilly on the back and saying, "Remember when we were in the running club? Didn't we have a helluva time in those days?"

Women exclaimed over Nell's dress and hat, men pumped John's hand and gathered up the suitcases. A little parade formed, marching toward Main Street and then north toward the school and John's house. Someone—members of a committee assembled by Cora and Juliet?—had decorated John's front stoop and porch with bunting and flags. It was all so jolly, Hilly's heart was bursting.

John was his hero, the kind of man Hilly hoped to be. A natural leader, he'd heard someone say. Well, *he*, Hilly, was no natural leader; nobody ever followed him, except to give him a shove. But maybe there was such a thing as an unnatural leader, someone who learned to lead. If so, Hilly might still stand a chance. Then he'd make his mother proud. He knew she was proud of him now, but that was motherpride. Motherpride just *was*. He needed to know he'd *earned* it. If he did well today, would that be a start?

Now, in real time, in this Red Berry moment, Hilly's heart pumped like a great straining oil drill. Perspiration poured from his skin and into his eyes, blurring his vision. Ahead of him was the finish line—though he could not have been certain of this but for the shapes of several people standing beyond it, waiting. One of them was cheering and walking slowly toward the line as Hilly approached. John Flynn—as if Hilly's dream had conjured him!

Gasping, finally it came to Hilly that he had won his race. And John was there, snapping his suspenders and saying to Abel Timms and everyone else in hearing, "The boy's a natural. Championship stuff. Championship stuff."

chapter twenty-nine

THE FIRST NOTE HAD ARRIVED IN 1905, ten years earlier; they had continued, two or three a year, until the latest, several months ago—*"Hores git punished."* Who had written it? Was the poor spelling meant to mislead her? And did it matter? Someone hated her. At times the hatred struck her such a blow, she stood turned to stone.

Might it be Adolph Arndt? Nell wondered, as the man turned away from her in the post office. Ten years ago, serving on the school board, he'd voted against her—she was certain. And he made a point of turning away whenever he encountered her. Had he hated her then, and did he still?

Queer that she should be wondering this as she called for her mail, for in the batch was yet another envelope addressed, *"Mrs. Stilman, Harvester, Minnesota."* Glancing around, she was tempted to toss the envelope into the wire wastebasket beside the post-office door. But no. She slid it into her bag.

Later, she sat benumbed at the kitchen table, not removing her coat. At length, she picked up a table knife and slit the envelope open: one sheet of lined paper. *"John Flyn aint gonna mary a hore with a yellow kid. Get that in yer head."*

The writer could be anyone she encountered on the street, anyone standing behind her in Seidman's Pharmacy or in Lundeen's. Huddled at the table, she recalled that day soon after the school-board meeting when Arvina Petersen had walked away from her in Petersen's Groceries. The little bell above the door had jangled as Nell entered; Arvina had glanced up, an expression of surprise and distaste eclipsing that look of cheerful anticipation routinely cultivated by tradespeople.

The woman had lain her pad of yellow sales slips beside the register and turned as squarely as a wind-up toy soldier, marching down the row of bins containing crackers and sugar and flour and salt. Her heels hit the wooden floor with such aggressive purpose that heads turned. At the rear of the store, she snapped aside the door curtain hung on clacking wooden rings. Those heads that had turned to observe Arvina now spun back to discover the source of her wrath, and to wonder.

The young clerk—Harry, Nell thought he was called—appeared from some nether region as she raced to gather the few items she required, dropping them into the basket on her arm and hurrying to the cash register.

"That be all, Mrs. Stillman?"

She nodded dumbly.

He wrote up the sales slip and tucked the store copy into the metal clip which held her account. Apparently unaware of Nell's disgrace, he chatted the weather, the condition of the road to Red Berry, and the splendor of the new grain elevator by the depot.

Crumpling her copy of the sales slip into her bag, she

rushed out, then stopped short on the top step, trying to recall the direction home.

Now, rising to remove her coat, Nell recalled Arvina Petersen in those days. The woman had worn her hair in braids, twisted into a high crown. Her cheeks, though unrouged, were nonetheless rosy. But as Mam would have observed, Arvina's eyes were small and set too close, lending her a judgmental aspect—as if she'd been born with a gavel in her hand. In that way, at least, Arvina had changed very little. But was she the tormentor?

Nell surveyed the cramped kitchen and small dining space with its shabby furnishings. There were still a few places that provided sanctuary—this little apartment; the Lundeen homes; and her third-grade room. She supposed that the offspring of the poison pen might sit before her in class, but the first rule of that room was: everyone must be safe here.

Fear closed down expansiveness, and surely it was the desire, the need to expand that led an eight-year-old to reach out for a new thought, a new methodology. Also, fear bred hate, and they mustn't learn hate in her class.

Nell always encouraged her students to share their fears, but she had no desire to divulge her own. She didn't want to soil those she most trusted: People like John and the Lundeens, and even Gus and Bertha Rabel, lived in kind and privileged worlds. It would be dreadful to sully those worlds.

In the meat market, nevertheless, Gus Rabel often regarded her with concern. "Missus," he'd say, "what are you needing? A ring of bologna, or a chicken?" But beneath the words, his empathy spoke clearly: "If there are problems, maybe I could help." Nell was certain that Gus remembered her life with Herbert, that it had been loud and sometimes frightening. Still, she wouldn't repay his kindness by making him privy to this nastiness.

Maybe if she felt more intimately connected to God and religion, she could turn in that direction. But she'd been born a skeptic—not quite a believer—and you didn't turn for help to something you weren't certain was itself standing upon firm ground.

Then, too . . . did Father Gerrold know something? Following Mass, as he stood in the vestibule greeting parishioners, grasping a hand, inquiring about an ill family member, he sometimes cast Nell a speculative look. After all these years, it couldn't concern Elvira. What, then?

And why was the connection between fear and guilt so strong that when she passed the Virgin and St. Joseph while receiving Communion, she felt censure? She'd committed no great sin. But something about being hated made you feel guilty.

She felt manipulated by the writer. With each note, the scope of her activities shrank. She no longer felt free to walk through town on a whim, but must wait until an errand demanded attention. For Hilly's sake, Nell continued their walks to the park and cemetery, but the outings were less frequent.

This shrinking was most obvious in the weeks immediately following the arrival of a note. After a month or two passed, she relaxed involuntarily; a person could only hold breath or fear for just so long. In these blessed weeks of calm she allowed herself to imagine that the hatred had burnt itself out.

On her most anxious days, Wodehouse became a *place*, and she retreated there. Like the apartment and her class-room, Wodehouse protected her, leading her far from Harvester, into London's Chelsea. There, artists with-out much money or even talent nevertheless mingled absurdly, critiquing each other's work in both grave and fawning tones and finding unlikely romance.

Such was the opening story in *The Man Upstairs*. In the next, Wodehouse spirited Nell off to a village in Hampshire. . . . The stories were compellingly funny and she became lost in them. And that was all she asked—to lose herself in the abundant goodwill of Wodehouse.

What a pity she couldn't spend all her hours with her nose in his books.

LIZZIE JESSUP ANSWERED when Nell turned the doorbell clapper. The woman looked even more discomposed than usual.

"Mrs. Stillman."

"Is Cora at home, Lizzie?"

"She's in the back parlor." The young woman held the screen door open and stood aside, mumbling something about war and ships. "Glad I'm not going."

"I'm so pleased you stopped by," Cora called, wheeling herself into the hall. "Lizzie, bring us tea and whatever's sweet." Turning to Nell: "What I'd really like is a tall whiskey, but I suppose that would be too shocking at three in the afternoon."

"I've come to return *O Pioneers!*" Nell explained.

"Have a seat and put your feet up," Cora told her, indicating a wicker chaise. Cora's color was unnaturally high, her movements tremulous.

Nell set aside the book and her bag. Cora needed to be calmed and soothed. "Do you ever wonder how many lives you've changed with the books at the Water and Power Company? Think what you set in motion for me when you donated *Love Among the Chickens!*"

The younger woman cocked her head.

"Mr. Wodehouse is my savior." Nell tugged off her gloves. "If I'm down in the dumps, I run away to his books. Everybody needs a place like that where they're happy and . . . safe." Nell gazed out at the arbor, where the vines were coming into leaf. "You gave me a priceless gift." She tried to keep the tone light but inviting, if Cora needed to talk.

"I'm pleased to hear it. I'm not sure I have anything comparable. Little Larry, maybe. But you have to be careful not to burden a child with responsibility for your happiness."

"I understand. Hilly's far too willing to assume responsibility for my happiness. That can be a weight for both of us." Nell smiled.

Since Cora wasn't going to share her preoccupation, Nell set off on another path. "I don't like the sound of this war, my friend. Have you considered waiting a year to travel, till things settle down?"

"Not you, too! Absolutely not. You sound like George. He wants to cancel." She smoothed her dress across her thin thighs. "But this is my last chance. And I'm going to be selfish about it, damn it, and maybe even reckless. I'm thirty-five, Nell. The doctor says I may already be too old for the treatment. I have to try."

"Of course you do."

"Bless you." Cora looked tearful.

Nell rose, laying a hand on Cora's shoulder, thin as a blade. "I should be going."

"Don't you dare. You sit right down." Cora turned her chair. "I'll be back," she said, wheeling away.

Minutes later, she returned, two ice-filled glasses held between her thighs, a bottle of whiskey beside her.

"Here," she said, handing the bottle to Nell, "you pour." She held up three fingers.

Nell looked reluctant.

"I'll give you licorice to chew before you leave."

Nell poured the whiskey and sat down again, lifting her glass to Cora. "As the ice melts, the whiskey dilutes," Cora assured her.

"Juliet said she wanted to give you and George a bon-voyage party, but you were against it."

Cora held the glass to her cheek. "If there's a hullabaloo, people get their hopes up. I don't want that. Especially not for Larry or George's parents." Rolling the glass back and forth across her cheek, she changed the subject, studying Nell: "You and John make a good pair."

Now it was Nell's turn to demur.

"And he's so good with Hilly," Cora plunged on. "Every boy needs a man in his life, don't you think?"

"We're very grateful to John. He's a wonderful friend."

"I'm surprised he hasn't asked you to marry him—or maybe he has?"

Nell squirmed and sipped her liquid courage. "No. He hasn't." The probing question was not typical of Cora.

"I wonder why."

"There's quite a difference in our ages."

"Would that matter to you?"

"Oh, Cora, I don't think I should be discussing John this way."

"Don't be absurd. That's what women friends are for. Would Hilly mind if you got married?"

"Not if it were John."

"Well, then?"

Nell laughed.

"Damn him for not asking you," Cora swore. "I'd like to leave knowing that certain things are settled. How old are you? Thirty-five?"

"Thirty-eight in October."

"You could still have another child."

"No." *Not really.* Beads of perspiration broke out along Nell's hairline and between her shoulder blades.

"I'd give anything to have another one," Cora confessed.

Nell was curious.

"As I am now," Cora said, "they tell me it would be too risky. Even so, I wouldn't mind. Especially for Larry's sake. Think how he must blame himself, for the way I am."

"Oh, but that's . . ."

"Irrational. Of course. But we all have irrational guilts, don't we? I certainly do—and some that aren't so irrational."

"Not you, Cora."

"Yes, me. I'm a very nice woman. But money can make people meddlesome. We think we have rights we don't have. We think we can order things the way we want them. But there's only so much anybody can order. People are messy."

"I don't know what you mean."

"Neither do I. I'm just in a mood." Cora finished the whiskey and set the glass aside. "Do you ever hear from Elvira?"

No, Nell hadn't heard from Elvira. And while whole days passed when she didn't think of her, no week did.

Every time Aunt Martha stopped in, the old woman still trotted out Elvira's "disgrace" as an unsolved mystery, casting herself as detective. "Girls like that get themselves murdered. It's peculiar how she hasn't written, though I daresay her folks wouldn't be happy to hear from her."

"Maybe that's why she hasn't."

After the most recent visit, Nell asked herself if the letters could have come from *Aunt Martha*? But she dismissed the thought; surely not.

Meanwhile, John Flynn's first year in Congress was dense with work. To keep his law firm going, he hired a young law-school graduate, Apollo Shane. "Funny name," people said, but they were inclined to accept him, despite that he read Greek and Latin.

Those weeks when John was back in his district, he spent long hours in the old office, meeting with townspeople. Otherwise, he was out on the road.

He'd sold his Sears High-Wheel and bought a Cadillac touring car. "More practical," he said, though he frequently found himself mired up to the axles and needing the hire of a good draft horse to pull him out. "It's amazing the constituents I meet when I'm stuck," John laughed.

It was obvious how much he loved his work. When

Nell saw him—and that was not often—he was full of stories of Congress and the district. Over a game of whist at Juliet and Laurence's, he told them, "I was out at Anders Bloom's the other day. He's got a three-legged chicken. Damnedest thing you ever saw. Had to build a separate pen and roost for it, or the other hens'd peck it to death. I said to him, 'Anders, why don't you just kill it and fry it up, then you wouldn't have to go to all this trouble?'

"Well, you know Anders, he's not a loquacious man. Fifteen, twenty words in a day. But he looked at me as if I belonged in the state hospital. 'What kinda fool d'ya take me for?' he said. 'Kill that chicken? Why, that bird's my fame.'" Everyone laughed.

"Had a photographer out taking pictures," John continued. "And didn't they have the damnedest time getting the bird to stand still. Paid the photographer good money—not Anders's usual habit. But when the chicken finally goes, he said, he'll have the proof of his fame. I said maybe he oughta get it stuffed. He said he'd think on that."

"Don't most people want a scrap of fame?" Juliet wondered. "Think of Eudora Barnstable's plantings at the cemetery. It's *her* cemetery."

"I think you're right," Nell said. "Even if you're only famous for your gingerbread recipe or your solos in the church choir."

"Ah, vanity," Juliet sighed. "Mine's probably the bookshelves at the Water and Power Company. And someday, mark my words, a real public library. Oh, won't I be conceited then?" She folded her cards against her breast, caught in the rapture of plans.

Laurence reached for a piece of fudge from a dish beside his wife. "Then there's folks who get themselves real fame," he said, looking at John.

His friend hooted. "Being a first-term congressman is pretty small potatoes."

"What are you hearing about the war?" Laurence asked.

"Wilson's still trying to keep us out, but don't bet on it. What's got me worried is this U-boat zone the Germans have thrown around Britain. Thank God they don't have enough of the damned things to set up a full blockade." He paused. With Cora and George on the verge of their ocean voyage, this was a delicate subject. "But you know all this." He turned to Nell. "I believe it's your lead, darlin'."

"They sail May first," Laurence said. "I'll be glad when they get to Liverpool. I always feel better when folks are on dry land."

chapter thirty-one ๑

HILLY APPROACHED LUNDEEN'S DRY GOODS as a tearful Howard Schroeder was hanging a Closed sign on the door.

"How can you be closed on Saturday?" Hilly asked.

A sob. "Mr. and Mrs. George's ship went down."

"What?"

"The *Lusitania*. Sank."

Hilly reeled. "But . . . but, how could it?"

"Torpedoed. German submarine."

Dazed, Hilly made his way home. George and Cora. How was he going to tell his mother?

He'd better buck up. He was the man of the family. Wiping his face, he mounted the stairs.

When John heard the news, he caught the first train from Washington. Following the memorial service in Harvester, Laurence, Juliet, and Larry traveled east for another in Boston. Overnight, Laurence had become stooped and trembling, Juliet completely gray—yet she made the arrangements and cared for him.

"Let me come with you," Nell said. "I could help with the luggage and see to Laurence."

"You're too kind, dear Nell. But I think I need to do

this on my own. Still, if Hilly could give Larry some of his time when we get back, we'd be grateful. Whatever he can spare. I know how busy . . ."

Juliet's eyes filled and she let go of Nell's hand to dab at them.

Some days later, John was sitting in Nell's living room. The two had been talking in the disjointed way people do in days of crisis, sorting through a welter of thoughts, beginning sentences that went nowhere. How could one speak sensibly of something so senseless?

Now, as shadows piled up in the corners, the silence felt companionable. Nell glanced at the clock. "I'll fix supper," she said, rising from her chair.

"Don't bother for me."

"You have to eat and so does Hilly. He'll be home in a few minutes, and he'll be upset if he's missed you. Hang up your hat and light the lamp."

That evening, after a meal eaten in near silence, Hilly said, "I don't want to run Friday."

"St. Bridget. I'd forgotten." Nell began clearing away. "But you've been running all week."

"That's different. Out in the country, I can cry," Hilly said without embarrassment.

"So, why not run Friday?"

"Friday feels like, I don't know—like showing off. Disrespectful."

Nell turned from the sink. "Mr. Timms will understand."

John rose and grabbed a dishtowel from the hook by the sink. "I don't know as it'll make any difference in the way you feel, Professor, but I planned to ask Larry if he'd like to ride along to St. Bridget and watch you run. I thought it might be a distraction for him."

So it was that on Friday Hilly found himself at the track, standing on the far side to watch the sprinters and relay runners. Spectators from St. Bridget ringed the oval, and he lost himself among them, waiting for the longer distances when he would have to wander back to his team.

John and Larry were subsumed in the band of Harvester men gathered near the team. They wouldn't mind his ignoring them.

Nervous and determined, Hilly paced behind the onlookers. Today he was running for George and Cora. He recalled how excited George had been when he'd chauffeured the boys to last year's meet. "It's a grand thing to compete. At recess, when I was a kid, a handful of boys raced each other, all ages together. I still remember that feeling—a damned fine madness, when you're rushing across the pasture with the wind whipping your face, and the blood humming in your ears."

Hilly imagined the Irish beach where people had stood watching as the few lifeboats had landed and bodies washed ashore. John had brought newspapers from Washington describing the anguish of the surviving passengers and of the Irish who had helped them onto land.

But now Abel Timms was waving his arms, hailing Hilly to the starting line. Hilly trotted across the infield and took his place with six other boys, including young Gus Rabel. Hilly hated beating Gus, now a senior, in the fellow's last race, but the Lundeens came first.

And now, as the gun sounded, and the Irish beach extended before him, Hilly ran. To reach them. To reach them. To haul them ashore. He was fast. They were there ahead, calling him, George exhausted, swimming with Cora clinging to his side. No one could make it ten miles to shore in the cold Atlantic, not hauling another body—but George was there, not a gasp nor an ounce of strength left. The grass beneath Hilly's shoes was sand; the air not bright and dry but filled with a misty chill; gulls, not blackbirds, wheeled overhead.

And then the tape was breaking across his chest—and Hilly hadn't reached them. He staggered past Abel Timms; past John holding his hand out; past Larry, calling to him. He staggered down the field sobbing, his spirit breaking against a distant shoal.

When they found him weeping, he told them, "I couldn't run fast enough."

Timms approached with Hilly's first-place ribbon. "Good work, son," he said, then turned and walked away. You didn't probe a boy's heartbreak.

Waiters in black silk vests and bow ties moved from kitchen to dining room, from one linen-covered table to another, smiling, nodding, taking and filling orders, replenishing water in glasses where ice snapped like the breaking of tiny crystal bells.

John had taken Hilly and Larry to the St. Bridget Hotel after the meet. Now Hilly sat straight as a post, hands knotted in his lap, studying the comings and goings, the flourished menus, the waiters' bows to departing customers. He pondered the maître d', who lingered with special clientele. To Hilly this was all as alien and as fascinating as a glimpse into one of the great pyramids at Giza.

The maître d' had recognized John when they entered and treated him with a deferent bonhomie that implied a long and happy familiarity between the Representative and this dining room. The boys, by association, were welcomed as minor celebrities. Following the maître d' to their table, John nodded and waved to several other diners, but made it plain that he was engaged by the two lads.

Hilly found it impossible to be unimpressed. On wine-red walls hung gilt-framed oil paintings, mostly portraits, by an artist of provincial note who worked from photographs. That one over there was the soprano Nellie Melba, Hilly was pretty sure; and there was Zebulon Pike, the great explorer; and further along, there was Henry Wadsworth Longfellow—their glances approving, seeming to say, "We're all good fellows and gentle ladies here."

Though electric lighting was finding its way into St. Bridget homes and businesses, the hotel dining room was still flushed overall with a golden gaslight that flattered women and threw an aura of authority and substance around men.

"Well, boys, what'll it be?" John asked.

"Boeuf Bourguignon, sir," Larry said, closing his menu and laying it to one side.

"And you, Professor?"

"Um . . . I'm not sure." Hilly found it difficult to detach

his attention from the surroundings long enough to think about food. The Harvester Arms was pleasant, he knew. But this was, well, a different world entirely.

"D'ya like beef stew?" Larry asked.

"You bet," Hilly replied.

"Well, that's what Boeuf Bourguignon is: beef stew cooked with red wine."

"Excellent." Hilly closed his menu, and they ordered.

"That was a fine run today," John said, not for the first time. "You'll be welcomed to the running club at any college."

"I still have another year of high school, sir. And . . . I don't know about college."

"It's never too soon to start planning. And of course you'll go to college, a bright lad like you. It'd be a damned waste if you didn't."

Hilly was silent. He didn't want to mention the cost; John might think he was looking for help. The boy rolled the edges of the napkin lying across his lap and glanced away, as if studying a portrait of Colonel Josiah Snelling.

"I wonder why Gus Rabel joined the running club," Larry said. "He's kind of . . . bulky."

"Not the model of a runner," John agreed.

"Still, he came in third today," Hilly pointed out.

"That's because one of the St. Bridget boys turned his ankle at the start." Larry was silent for a moment, then, "He's a terrible bully."

"That so?" John asked. "I'm surprised. His dad's a fine fellow."

"Young Gus is always picking on smaller boys. He'd be all over me if he weren't afraid of Granddad."

John laughed. "Doesn't want to get on the wrong side of the bank?" The food arrived and he forked into his trout amandine.

Interesting, thought Hilly. Apparently Hilly hadn't been young Gus's only victim. Well, all that would end now that Gus was graduating.

As the small group was leaving the dining room, the maître d' bowed and again embraced them with his ardent professional cordiality. "Always a special pleasure, Representative," he said, his warm glance taking in the boys as well.

Hilly couldn't help feeling a little important.

During the drive back to Harvester, talk was sparse—the gravel road being rough and words being shouted. But bellowing cattle along the way, impatient for the barn and milking, would have heard three male voices raised none-theless. "On the Road to Mandalay" and "Swanee River" and "I'll Take You Home Again, Kathleen" rang across pastures and farmyards beneath the pale early moon.

If it weren't for George and Cora—and that was a mon-ster If—Hilly thought that life couldn't get better than this day. He'd won his race, eaten Boeuf Bourguignon in the St. Bridget Hotel, and ridden in John's car, the spiffiest in Harvester.

Flynn pulled the Cadillac to the curb in front of Rabel's Meat Market. "Congratulations again, Professor," he shouted above the engine clatter as Hilly climbed out of the car.

"Thank you, sir. And thank you for dinner. The beef stew was excellent. Really excellent."

Hilly stood watching the car pull away, remembering

the tender beef in red wine, the carrots and potatoes, and the pecan tart with whipped cream. When John turned the Cadillac toward the Lundeens', Hilly swung around and headed for the stairs at the side of the building . . .

. . . and then someone was knocking him down, dragging him, kicking him. Then that same someone fell atop him, pounding, grunting. "Think you're somebody." Half-heard, the attacker was whistling through his nose, leaning close, hissing into Hilly's face, "You're nobody. The little man who wasn't there." The voice laughed low. "Little Milly Stillman."

Nell leapt from her chair when she saw Hilly. "What's happened?" The boy leaned against the jamb, squinting into the room, eyes already swelling shut, lips split and bleeding.

After she'd led him into his room and sat him on his bed, she fetched a cloth, a pan of tepid water, and a jar of ointment. Gently dabbing his face and neck with the cloth, she asked, "Who did this?"

"I didn't see him. He came from behind, and it was dark."

Nell helped Hilly out of his shirt and undershirt, then left him while he removed his trousers. Returning, she handed him a chunk of ice wrapped in a clean rag, then placed three aspirin in his cupped hand and held out a glass of water.

"Now, lie down, and I'll pull the sheet up."

Once she'd picked up the bloodstained shirts lying beside the bed, she stood for long seconds not moving, remembering. Water in a galvanized pail swirled in a pink eddy of blood as a dress and petticoat swam dizzyingly.

"You know I hate violence. But this—person—who beat you could have killed you. How could I live if anything happened to you? I'm going to the constable."

"No, Mama."

"At least let me tell John."

"No, Mama."

She bent and brushed Hilly's cheek with her lips. "Then next time, put up your dukes."

chapter thirty-two ☙

WHEN THEY HAD RETURNED FROM BOSTON, Juliet and Laurence were stunned to find a letter in Cora's hand, written on hotel stationery and postmarked New York. It had been a long time on its way.

Dear Mama, Papa, and Larry,

I've been to a New York doctor who practices techniques similar to those of the Zurich fellow we'll be seeing and I'm feeling more hopeful than I have in years. I honestly believe I'm feeling something!—it's only a "buzzing" sensation in my right thigh, but . . .

On the other hand, don't count your chickens, as Nell's Mr. Wodehouse would say. No need to break out the champagne yet.

Anyway, I'm more eager than ever to meet the man in Switzerland. Apologies that this note is so brief, but we are repacking for the ship. We both send kisses to the three of you and our greetings to the "whist gang."

Love,
Cora

Bumping into Nell in the post office, Juliet described the note. "It was so hopeful, it broke my heart. I debated whether to show it to Larry. In the end, I decided not to for now." She removed her glasses and folded them, shaking her head. "He's being brave, but he doesn't sleep well. Terrible dreams. I suppose that's to be expected, but you worry anyway. Hilly's been good, bless him, making time for Larry."

That fall of 1915, Juliet and Laurence had moved back into the old house on Catalpa. "For Larry," Juliet said to Nell one day. "His memories of George and Cora are in this house."

"And the lovely home you built for you and Laurence?" Nell asked.

"There's a new manager at the Water and Power Company, Eli Weatherford," Juliet said as they stood on the post-office steps. "Wife and two children—another baby on the way. They'll rent the place indefinitely." She nodded to Grandpa Hapgood, coming from a game of billiards at Reagan's. "Maybe someday, when we've gotten past all this, we'll turn the house into a town library."

"How's Laurence?"

"Still frail, but finally getting over his chest cold. Wants to get back to working full-time. Suddenly everybody's ordering a telephone."

"If there's anything I can do . . ."

"You can tell Hilly how proud we are. I don't think he lost a race this past spring, did he?" He hadn't.

In September, Hilly began his senior year, relieved that young Gus Rabel was gone from the high school. Gus was working for his father in the meat market, mostly in the back, learning butchery and brining. Old Gus had added a Reliance Motor truck to the business so his son could make pickups from farms and deliveries to town customers. He was big enough and strong enough to handle sizeable carcasses.

Young Gus's path rarely crossed Hilly's; Hilly was busy working part-time at Kolchak's and running. At school he excelled. Mrs. Cooper, the English teacher, told Nell, "The boy has a gift for writing. I don't know what a man would do with that after college. . . ." She played with a lace frill at the neck of her dress. "Maybe newspaper work? He does love writing stories about exotic places—Constantinople and Rio de Janeiro and Nanking and I don't know where all."

Though foreign lands fascinated Hilly, they were not much on the mind of the average villager. When the Archduke got assassinated in Europe back in '14, that was unfortunate, and of course the sinking of the *Lusitania* was a damned shame—but most folks were pretty sure the president would keep the country out of any serious mess. The average villager was more interested in local gossip, the condition of the streets, and whether his supply of coal and firewood would last the winter.

In the spring of 1916, Hilly increased his training. This would be his last year running for Harvester, and he wanted to make a good show. When Timms called the team together in April, Hilly was ready—and by the time John visited in early May, the season was off to a good start. One evening John told Hilly, "I see by the *Standard Ledger* that you won your first two meets."

"Yessir. I've been lucky."

Hilly took a bite of potato; Nell had cooked dinner for them at John's house, where she enjoyed working in a larger kitchen.

"I'm afraid I won't make it to any of the meets this year. I hate missing them, Professor, but things are heating up in Washington."

"Europe?"

"We're gearing up. For what, I'm not sure, but Wilson thinks we oughta be ready, so we're arming." Seeing Nell's discomfort, John changed the subject. "I'll try to get back for graduation."

Following the meal, Hilly went home to study, and Nell and John retired to the screened front porch to watch the sunset. Late twilight was blurring the world's outlines as the two sat in the swing.

"I was hoping to talk to the Professor about college," John said.

"He's determined to pay for it himself."

"Maybe I can reason with him."

"If you paid, there'd be gossip."

"I'd work it out."

John took Nell's hand, and they sat observing lamps being lit against descending night. To be alone in the dark, together, murmuring the inconsequent observations that mark intimacy and trust, was a rare treat, and the pleasure was unspeakably sharp and sweet.

In the Battle of Jutland, at the end of May, Germany inflicted serious damage on the British fleet. Congress was alarmed, and John remained in Washington for meetings with the War Department. He sent Hilly a long wire upon the boy's graduation and promised a gift. Hilly thought the telegram alone was a gift; few in Harvester could boast of one. He tacked it to his bedroom wall, beside John's map of the world.

At the actual graduation ceremony, Hilly was amazed to be singled out for a silver medal, Mr. Timms telling those gathered that Hillyard Stillman had distinguished himself by his character, his scholarship—nearly an A average—and his athletic performance. Hilly was further stunned when the *Standard Ledger*, covering graduation, mentioned his award right along with the honors given the valedictorian and salutatorian. Nell insisted they frame the newspaper piece and hang it on the living room wall along with the silver medal. And so they did.

In another surprise, Hilly received a letter from Eudora Barnstable. The only time the boy had ever laid eyes on Eudora had been when he and Ted Shuetty delivered a tall mahogany bookcase to her house. Hauling the furniture up the porch steps and into the front hall, he'd glanced into the parlor, noting more bookcases on either side of the fireplace, bookcases burdened by what looked like a thousand volumes. Hilly had felt sorry not to know this woman better, but she was not routinely seen on the street or in the stores. Little wonder, when she owned a library such as this.

When Hilly and Ted had hoisted the monstrous bookcase up the stairs and into a room which in novels would be called a study, Eudora plied them with glasses of lemonade. Later, at the front door, she thanked them and pressed twenty-five cents into each man's hand, unwilling to hear their protests. She was not one to be gainsaid.

At any rate, here was a letter from the woman, a week after graduation.

Dear Hillyard,

I address you informally since, as you may recall, we met when you helped to deliver a bookcase to my home. At the time I was struck by your good manners and apparent intelligence. Your mother has made a good job of you.

I was present at the graduation ceremony and not surprised to witness your recognition by Mr. Timms and the administration. As one who reads newspapers, the local one among them, I was aware of your success as an athlete and, again, was not surprised that it was in long-distance running. I cannot help pondering if that isn't the physical choice of a thinker. . . .

Have you had time to read about the ancient Greeks and their athlete/philosopher ideal? It might be something to look into and contemplate as you venture forward to college and beyond.

I'm hoping that you will accept the small gift enclosed, tendered in the spirit of admiration.

Sincerely,
Eudora Wellington Barnstable

Enclosed was a five-dollar bill. Hilly sat down at once to thank Mrs. Barnstable and John, who had himself sent a check for one hundred dollars—a sum the boy could not even contemplate, this to be applied to Hilly's college savings. John had written, "Congratulations, Professor. I couldn't be prouder if I were your father. We will talk further about college and the financing of it. With love, John."

Following graduation, Hilly went to work for Kolchak's full-time, driving Arnie's new General Motors truck. But he still rose early each day to run. He had to; an engine inside him thrummed. At night, waiting for sleep, he heard its urgency, and he almost heard its purpose.

All that year of 1916, warnings rolled across the Atlantic. Then, on April 6, 1917—Good Friday—John Flynn voted in the House of Representatives for a resolution declaring a state of war between the United States and Germany. As in the Senate, it passed by a huge majority.

In Harvester, public sentiment was not so clear-cut. John's constituency contained a sizable bloc of German-Americans. They read German-language newspapers; attended German Lutheran churches, where services were conducted in German; and often felt a loyalty to the Kaiser.

Yet the headlines in the Minneapolis Morning *Tribune* were unimaginable, some battles claiming as many as fifty thousand men. A large part of a generation of men was vanishing.

When John finally returned from Washington in July, Nell stood at the door masking her shock. He'd lost weight. An unhealthy gray had crept beneath his skin, and his thick, once salt-and-pepper mane was a dull steel. With a weary smile, he said, "And I wanted to be in politics."

Nell led him to the green chair, taking his Panama hat

and suit jacket. "I'll get you a glass of iced tea. Loosen your collar and put your head back."

When she returned, John was asleep. She placed a pillow from the daybed behind his head, then unlaced his shoes and removed them.

At supper, Nell set a platter of sauerkraut, ring bologna, carrots, and potatoes before John and Hilly. "Good men in our delegation voted against the declaration, and for good reasons," John said. "I hope I did the right thing."

"But it would have passed even if you'd voted against it," Hilly pointed out. "And I read in the paper that guys are already going across, volunteering to fight with the English."

"Who wants mustard? Ketchup?" Nell tried to change the subject—but she knew the subject would continue to be war, now and for a long time.

Following Mass the next Sunday, the three sat staring at Sioux Woman Lake, John's cabin behind them, the remains of Nell's picnic lunch collected on the table before them. In the slight breeze, evergreens shifted uneasily.

On the water, the paths of indolent canoes and several small sailboats crisscrossed. The lake had already begun to give off the rotting odor of algae, hot sand, and fish carcasses, washed up in the shallows where birds and raccoons picked them over.

Seated with his back to Nell, Hilly said, "I'm going to sign up, Mama."

"You're all I have."

John frowned. "It's early days, Professor."

"Please talk to him, John." Nell washed their few dishes at the kitchen pump. "Go out there now and talk to him."

Hilly sat at the end of the dock. Behind him, John stood shielding his eyes from the water's flashing light.

"Could you hold off a bit? Give your mother a chance to live with this?"

Hilly was silent. John waited, knowing the boy was collecting his words.

"Ever since the *Lusitania*, I dream that I'm there. On the Irish coast, watching for them. I run as fast as I can, down the shore. I see that they're swimming toward a point further along the beach. When I get close enough, I'm going to dive in and help George. But then, they're gone. I've lost them."

"It was ten miles to shore, son."

"I know. And they didn't even make it off the ship. But that's not my dream."

John nodded and touched Hilly's shoulder. The power and the impotence of old men were terrible things.

After a silent drive from the lake, John dropped off Nell and Hilly and continued home. Just inside the door, Nell whirled on Hilly, screaming, "This can't be!" For a split second, she looked as if she had startled herself. Then she fell on her knees at Hilly's feet, sobbing, "Oh God, please, don't go!"

Hilly stared down at Nell, who was suddenly hysterical, her face distorted. This was not the mother he knew. He reached to pull her to her feet, but as she rose, she twisted away, screaming, "I'll die!" Her hands snatched at her hair. "I promised to look after you, don't you understand?"

Her body was so rigid, he was afraid she might somehow break. He started toward her. "Mama . . ."

Then she went limp, almost as if she *had* broken, and he caught her before she fell. "Mama, Mama."

She was weeping and choking and telling him, "It was a hot night. You were so beautiful and peaceful. A baby. In your bed. And I swore I would look after you."

He led her to her chair and knelt beside it. "And you *did*, Mama. You always did look after me. But, Mama, I'm grown up now. You did your job. Remember what Mrs. Barnstable said? 'Your mother has made a good job of you'?"

He smiled at her, proffering a handkerchief. She ran a hand down his cheek, trying to see the grown man in him. "I'm sorry, son. I'm ashamed of what just happened. Can you forgive me?" She swallowed the remaining tears and blew her nose.

"There isn't anything to forgive." He rose. "I'll make us tea now."

chapter thirty-three ☙

WEDNESDAY NIGHT, after supper, Hilly walked out to Grandpa Hapgood's for a last game of chess with the old man.

When Diana answered the knock, Hilly noted that a streak of gray flowed back from her temple. When had age crept up on Diana, and how had he not noticed? You had to pay attention every day, or it all moved on without you. A sudden sense of passing time filled his mouth, and his throat ached swallowing this huge new intelligence. When he came home from war, everything would have changed. That shook him.

"Be here when I get back," he told them at the end of the visit.

"Come home," was all Diana could manage.

"Keep your head down," Grandpa said.

On Thursday, Hilly, Nell, and John spent the evening at Juliet and Laurence's. At the house on Catalpa Street, thirteen-year-old Larry answered the bell, showing them to the screened back porch where Juliet was pouring cold beer. She handed a glass to Hilly, making no ceremony of his first beer. It would only call attention to his vulnerable youth, and his awful leave-taking. Already she was unsure that she could survive the evening without tears.

It was Larry who actually asked Hilly, "Your first beer?" and lifted his own half glass to his friend. The others followed suit, though Juliet turned away. She had read too much about this war; she had to shut down her mind to Hilly's departure. It was impossible not to see the babe she'd played with the day after his father's death.

The next day John and Nell drove Hilly to Minneapolis. The boy wanted to join the Ambulance Corps, and the recruiters were only too happy to accommodate. Nell scarce believed that a boy could be taken so swiftly from his mother and with so little ceremony. But one moment they were weeping and embracing, Hilly promising to write every day; the next, he was gone, hurried along with other young men for physical examinations, as if the war had waited in suspension for just this handful of volunteers.

"He's ours now," a recruiter told Nell and John. "You folks can head home."

And Nell insisted they do head home. She would not stay overnight in Minneapolis. "I need to be in my own bed."

Despite miserly illumination from the Cadillac's headlamps, they reached Harvester at a quarter to eleven, Nell asleep beside John.

As he saw her up the stairs, Nell began to weep. "Don't go."

"Just to move the car. You don't need gossip."

When he returned to the apartment, a bottle of scotch under his arm, she was in a cotton nightgown, her hair down, looking lost—like the Serbian refugee woman pictured in a Washington newspaper. He felt unreasonable guilt, as if he were somehow responsible—and, having voted for war, perhaps he was.

"I took the car home," he said, hooking the screen door.

For an hour they sat, she in the green chair, he in the rocker. "I can't speak the things I worry about," she told him. "They might come true."

He nodded. What could he say?

"I feel so alone," she said. "You don't realize how much space someone takes up until they're gone and there's too much emptiness. This place never echoed before. Now it does." She was mystified.

"My mind feels untethered," she went on. "All these years it was focused on Hilly. Now it's flying loose like a kite that the wind grabs. I chase after thoughts like you'd chase a kite string, but I can't catch hold of a single one." Shaking her head, baffled, she raised the glass John had poured and absently sipped.

He let her ramble, exhausting herself.

"How will I put my mind back together?" she asked. Her look implored.

"I don't want to go back to Washington, Nell, but I have to."

"Not right away."

"Soon. I'll come home as often as I can."

"He's such a good boy."

"You're worn out," he said. "Come to bed."

"I won't sleep."

They sat on the bed, backs against the headboard, a

pale wash of light from the streetlamps below picking out Nell's bureau and sewing machine, and the drinks in their hands.

From the street came the sounds of Saturday-night men at Reagan's and of the piano, cranky after so many tunes of loss and bravado: "When the *Lusitania* Went Down" and, now, "Over There."

"When Hilly was small, right after Elvira left, we walked out to the cemetery one Sunday, to visit Herbert's grave. I wanted Hilly to have a sense that Herbert might be looking out for him.

"At any rate, we sat and read in the quiet. Hilly was reading something from Dickens, I think. Then a beautiful cob swan, as white as an angel, came toward us. He studied us so intently, it was uncanny.

"I don't know why I'm telling you this. I suppose I hoped in that moment that there was a connection between Herbert and the swan—and someone looking after Hilly."

Below them, on Main Street, Reagan stood at the door shooing the Catholics out at midnight so they could attend Communion in the morning. "Now, mind, you don't drink any water if you're takin' Communion."

At length Nell handed her empty glass to John, who set it on the bedside table next to his. She reached for his hand and kissed the first knuckle of each finger. When she had done, he laid her down and buried his face in the curve of her neck. She felt his tears gathering there as he caressed her breast beneath the thin fabric of her gown.

When Reagan's finally closed, and the strident piano

and the men's raised voices and "click-clock" of billiard balls fell silent, they could hear the night breathe, as prairie nights do—the heave and sigh of warm earth, of things growing and waiting to be cut down.

chapter thirty-four 🎵

NELL HEARD NOTHING FROM HILLY FOR A WEEK, and the rooms echoed with her footsteps. Sometimes she sang to fill the air, but with her mood that didn't last. Instead, she opened the windows to let in whatever sounds were in the street. Then two short letters arrived, filling a bit of the emptiness:

Dear Mama,

I miss you, and I miss John too.

I had a physical examination in Minneapolis and was found to be in excellent health. Well, we knew that. I told the Minneapolis doctors that my mother fed me well and that I've been a runner for four years. I figure I must be as right as rain.

By the time you receive this, I'll be far across the country. And before too many months, I'll be sailing across the Atlantic Ocean. Makes me dizzy. Who knows what all I'll see in this war.

But someday I want to see Egypt and China and Greece and any other place I can get to. You'll come with me.

I am enjoying the train. I like the way it sways and I like the sounds it makes. Of course, I'd heard the sounds before, but they're different when you're on the inside. It's like they're part of you.

I will write every day that I am able, and when I have an address, I will send it so you can write back. Please greet John and the Lundeens, including Larry of course. Maybe you will pass my address along to them, and to the Hapgoods.

When I was at the Hapgoods, I could see that Grandpa was feeling bad about my leaving. So I tried to let him beat me at chess—but he tried to let me beat HIM. We both caught on, and had a good laugh.

> *I will always be*
> *Your loving son,*
> *Hilly.*

Later, from Pennsylvania, he wrote:

Dear Mama,

Not much to say about camp except that it's big. There are thousands of us here. Like a city. I miss my quilt. We live in barracks, not nearly so cozy as home. And every one of the barracks looks exactly like every other one. A guy could get lost.

We get up before the birds and go to bed before them, too. The food isn't bad, and they give you enough to feed a thresher. I'm wearing a uniform now. I'll get my picture taken to send you. They cut your hair short here, so don't be surprised when you see the picture.

I did have another physical, and a Pennsylvania doctor said I was a credit to my mother. True.

I am looking forward to learning about ambulances, but first I have to learn to march and to shoot a gun, regular soldier things. I wish they could send me to France right away.

Well, Mama, they will turn out the lights pretty soon so I will say good-bye for now.

> *I will always be*
> *Your loving son,*
> *Hilly*

Every morning, until school reopened in September, Nell hurried across Main Street to the post office. While Hilly was in Pennsylvania, a brief note was waiting most days—and sometimes there was even a letter of several pages. Hilly wrote of the Pennsylvania countryside. More hills than at home: "Pretty. Still, I miss the prairie and all the little lakes, like oases." Nell noted with maternal pleasure how accurate his spelling remained.

As summer in Harvester faded into a warm and listless autumn, Hilly wrote:

Dear Mama,

I have a good friend here. His name is Sylvester Benjamin and he's from Dubuque, Iowa. He's heading into the Ambulance Corps, too, and we're hoping to team up when we get to France.

You'd like Sylvester. He's going to be a doctor when the war is over—his dad's a doctor back in Dubuque.

The fellows here tease him about his name. They call him 'Silly' and me 'Hilly.' But Sylvester doesn't mind. He's a great big fellow and everybody respects him.

He says when the war is over, he'll come up to Harvester to visit, and we should come down to Dubuque. It sounds like a nice place, right on the Mississippi River.

Until John drove us to Minneapolis, I'd never seen the Mississippi. And we live only two hundred miles west! Though that is a fair distance. Since you and Papa came from Wisconsin, I guess you saw it on the trip to Harvester. On the train to Pennsylvania, I saw the river at night, with the moon shining on it, and it made me cry. I've got to stop crying at things.

> *I will always be*
> *Your loving son,*
> *Hilly*

The several German families in the parish notwithstanding, Father Gerrold extolled Hilly at Mass, citing him as the first boy from the county to enlist. "He could have waited for the draft to call him, but he heard the cries of the heartsick, the weary, and the wounded, and he answered *their* call. God is proud of the Hillyard Stillmans of this nation, and of the families who send them forth to bandage the ravaged world."

The *Standard Ledger* ran Hilly's graduation picture with an article about his enlistment. Abel Timms was quoted: "Hilly Stillman is a credit to his town and to his high school. I am proud to have been his running coach. He is an outstanding athlete and an outstanding young man—not so big or tough as some, but with more character."

For all her pride in Hilly, Nell was uneasy in the role of the Hero's Mother, especially when she found in the morning mail an invitation from Eudora Barnstable:

On Saturday the Fifteenth of September, at 2:30 p.m., Mrs. Edward Barnstable requests your presence at a tea to be held in your honor at 734 Catalpa Street.

Despite being an entire carpetbag of contradictions, Mabel Eudora Barnstable (she preferred "Eudora" to "Mabel," which she claimed was "common") reigned as the doyenne or matriarch of the village—feared, respected, and not infrequently ridiculed. She prided herself on being twenty years behind the fashions.

Adjusting her pince-nez, she informed anyone who stood still long enough, "Fashion is for fools. Quality is always in style."

And it was economical. The town knew of the financial losses Ed Barnstable was suffering, real estate being a fickle mistress and Edward having no head for it. It was also rumored that he'd taken to the bottle.

But Nell wasn't going to blame Mrs. Barnstable for that. And she must keep in mind that it was Eudora Barnstable who'd written a kind note after the school board to-do. And Eudora Barnstable who'd sent Hilly a lovely note at graduation.

"What's this tea about?" Nell asked Juliet Lundeen.

"You'd have to know Eudora. Her father was English. Her maiden name was Wellington, as in the Duke of Wellington.

Eudora allows people to make assumptions about that and doesn't correct them when they do. So any friend of England is a friend of Eudora's, and Hilly is her particular knight errant. Hence, you must be feted."

"Feted? Oh, dear."

The Thursday before the tea, Nell received another "Mrs. Stilman" message: "Huns gonna shoot him. Dead." Two or three drops of what looked like blood were smeared across the paper. She had saved every note, but now she burned the packet, and knew hatred.

But, this once, her loneliness and apprehension for Hilly tempered fear of the poison pen. Instead of stiletto-sharp anxiety and hatred, she felt only a continuous, abstracted nausea.

In bed that night, she read through Hilly's letters again, then—as nearly every night—she reached for Wodehouse, in this case, *Uneasy Money*. Poor Lord Dawlish, in love with Elizabeth, pursued by Claire, and in possession of Polly's dead monkey, Eustace:

"Lord Dawlish stood in the doorway of the outhouse, holding the body of Eustace gingerly by the tail. It was a solemn moment. There was no room for doubt as to the completeness of the extinction of Lady Wetherby's pet."

Nell gave herself up to the story, slipping unresisting into the antic perils of a young, moneyed lord of the realm, caught in a web of complexity only Wodehouse could design. A Wodehouse plot was a wonder, the solution to each knotty problem leading inevitably to another, knottier problem. And wasn't that always the way?

Anyone who lived in a small town knew that real

life could be complicated. Maybe not as complex as a Wodehouse plot, but . . . She remembered that farmer—had his name been Wilder?—who had been fooling around with his neighbor's hired girl. When his wife found out, she tried to hang herself in the barn. A hired hand cut her down—but in the process the wife fell and broke her hip.

The neighbor, all unaware, sent over his hired girl to nurse the wife. The women became such pals, the girl gave the unfaithful husband his walking papers.

Well, there you were.

chapter thirty-five

MOUNTING WIDE WOODEN STEPS to Eudora Barnstable's porch, wrapped around three sides of the tall white clapboard, Nell hung back. These chattering women would want her to share Hilly. She wanted to withhold him, accumulate him, hoard him. Hadn't she that right?

"There you are." Eudora Barnstable held the door, her pince-nez swinging from a black ribbon pinned high on her breast with a brooch of seed pearls. "I was beginning to worry."

"My goodness," Juliet breathed, "are we that late?" She glanced down at her watch. "It's just 2:30."

"Well, now that you're here, come in." Eudora's manner was brusque, her voice powerful. "Mrs. Stillman, find a seat. We want to hear all about your son."

Nell and Juliet stepped into a broad front hall where umbrellas and parasols jammed a brass container near the door, and a wide assortment of wraps and headgear eclipsed a coat- and hat-stand nearby. Further along the hall, past the pocket doors leading to the front parlor, an accumulation of correspondence, piles of books and periodicals, and two tall lamps burdened a mahogany console table above which hung a haphazard grouping of quite good watercolors in gilt frames. An oriental carpet, soft and frayed, led down the hall to whatever lay beyond. This room bespoke a busy, headlong life.

Following Eudora, Nell and Juliet veered right, into a front parlor only a little less cluttered, with a manyness of armchairs, tables, and lamps. And books—everywhere, books. How lovely, Nell reflected, to own both so many spots for reading and so many books to read.

Guided to a chair by Marcella Kolchak, Nell sat and peeled off her gloves. The other women had not removed their hats, so Nell left hers, though the room was warm and the air thick.

Within minutes the last of the nine guests had arrived, and Eudora directed them to the dining room, saying, "I'll be mother." Seating herself at the head of the table, she commenced pouring tea. Recalling that her own mother used that expression, Nell felt an unbending toward Mrs. Barnstable.

Beside the table, dressed in navy-blue cotton with white collar and cuffs, stood Lizzie Jessup slicing the Lord Baltimore cake. With Larry nearly grown, she'd gone to work for the Barnstables.

Still, Nell glanced at Juliet. When someone close to us dies, we are proprietary of whatever constituted their lives. Curatorship, again. Wasn't Lizzie still part of the George and Cora museum? Not quite part of the Barnstable collection? Lizzie made her way around the parlor gathering plates and refilling teacups.

"Now, Mrs. Stillman, we all want to hear whatever you can tell us of your valiant son," Eudora said, standing before the mantel and glancing around the room, calling them to order. "What can you reveal about his decision to enlist?"

"Not much, I'm afraid," Nell said. "He told me on the fifteenth of July. A Sunday. Naturally I tried to talk him out of it."

"You did?" Eudora was surprised.

"Heavens, yes. Who would send their son to war?"

"But such a just and critical cause..." Eudora murmured.

"Hilly is all I have."

"Well, at least you have the satisfaction of knowing he's protecting something *worth* protecting. Civilization," Eudora went on, placing the pince-nez on her nose as if better to note the group's response. "I've been reading that if the Kaiser wins, all of Europe will be in Germany's control. Our Navy alone isn't big enough to take on the Hun. We'll find him on our shores. Look at the trouble the Germans tried to stir up in Mexico! I shudder."

A few of the women looked nonplussed and stared into their teacups, unsure what the Mexican "trouble" had been.

"What was Hillyard's ... *aim* in enlisting? What did he hope to do?" Eudora pressed.

"He wanted to save lives," Nell said, aware that "save lives" was terribly noble sounding. But then, Hilly was noble, wasn't he? Sensing that Eudora wanted more, Nell added, "In high school he was a runner, you know."

"Won every race he ran," Marcella Kolchak put in.

Nell smiled at Marcella. "After the *Lusitania* was torpedoed, and George and Cora were lost, I think he became preoccupied by what was happening and how he could be useful. He's not an aggressive boy, so he considered his running and how that might fit in."

Nell paused. She was saying more than she had intended, giving away bits of Hilly—bits she had meant to store up against winter, one might say.

"Put it this way—I lost him. He was determined." She shook her head in pain and disbelief.

"And you're very proud of him," Eudora prompted.

"Of course I'm proud," Nell said. "But imagine. Each of you has a child or probably will have. Imagine losing that child to a war that shouldn't have taken place. Pride can't bring him back."

The room was silent.

"Well, I still say to be proud." Eudora was standing her ground. "There are plenty of sons out there who ought to come forward like Hillyard."

Could she be thinking of young Gus Rabel, Nell wondered.

Eudora wrung her hands together. "I fear they don't know the gravity of the situation."

A flutter of consternation ran through the party. "Do you really think the Germans could win?" Mrs. Doctor Gray asked.

Eudora leaned heavily against the mantel. She seemed to be feeling the unusual September heat, compounded now by her own high fervor. Slipping a handkerchief from her cuff, she blotted her temples and cheeks.

"I know everyone laughs at my pride in being English— well, of English descent. Juliet calls it gilt and varnish. And you probably think it's why I'm so keen on fighting this war." Her shoulders heaved as she dragged forth a deep breath. "We all have our follies, but I am truly frightened. I'm not horridly anti-German. There are no dearer people in this village than Bertha and Gus," she said, nodding at Mrs. Rabel. "But this war is different from other wars. This is a *world* war. Think of that."

Nell was concerned for Mrs. Barnstable. The woman's color was too high, and her voice too strained.

Lizzie Jessup slipped into the room, setting a tray of small glasses on a table.

"Lizzie has brought us sherry," Eudora said, handing the glasses around. "I hope you'll all join in raising your glasses to Nell and Hillyard."

"We're all insane in our own way," Juliet observed as she and Nell drove home through streets littered with fallen leaves, the perfume of bonfires hanging in the air. "Eudora's insanity is a little more apparent than most, but I salute her for that. She wears her heart on her sleeve."

"Yes."

"You were uncomfortable being the center of attention. She didn't notice, I'm sure. She's not cruel. But she's intense. Headlong." Juliet turned the Ford onto Main Street.

"In her defense, she accomplishes a great deal," Juliet continued. "You've seen how she's organized the women, rolling bandages, assembling toiletry kits, even writing letters to orphan soldiers. She doesn't spare herself."

chapter thirty-six ☙

EARLY 1918 SAW HILLY IN FRANCE. For Nell, it was excruciating to wait through the school day before stopping at the post office. His letters, notes really, felt like a shared lifeline—a buoy he threw to her and that she threw back to him, their mutual assurance that each would survive.

Of course, the realistic side of her brain, the side that screamed into a pillow at night, understood that he could die before her next safety line reached him. It was a mystical game that they played, but that game was more real than the chalk dust on the blackboard, more urgent than the strange lightning that split the low sky one day, in the midst of a roaring snowstorm.

"Mrs. Stillman, what is that lightning? I've never seen lightning in a snowstorm, have you? Could it hit us?" Imogene Weatherford, her thin back rigid with apprehension, pulled as far away from the nearest window as her desk allowed.

As though fired from a cannon, a crack of thunder shook the windows. Isobelle Schoonover screamed and laid her head on her desk, wrapping her arms over her ears.

A few seconds later, after the next explosion of thunder,

Win Norton asked, "D'ya think that's how the guns sound in France?" The treble in his voice betrayed him.

"I imagine so," Nell told him, turning to the others. "All of you, come to this side of the room, where it isn't so noisy. Let's sing 'Take Me Out to the Ball Game.' Imogene, you start us off."

And so the child sang, head high, notes clear, thin, and determined.

Not forty yards away, a bomb exploded, showering earth and metal on the ambulance. Hilly recoiled but kept his hands on the wheel, navigating the fog of debris, minus a windscreen. The glass cuts were nothing a bit of bandaging wouldn't put right.

There was so little he could share with his mother—not even that he and Silly had been assigned to a British Expeditionary Force field hospital. There were Army restrictions, and there were also things you couldn't tell someone you loved. It would all have to wait until the war was over.

If it weren't for Silly, Hilly didn't think he could handle any of this. He'd lost ten pounds, probably just from vomiting, never mind the running, lifting, and carrying. Sylvester Benjamin kept him sane. After a month they had acquired a reputation for being fearless, but in fact they were scared all the time, cold all the time, and hungry most of the time.

In some ways, Silly was an odd duck. Nineteen years old, as Christian-minded a fellow as you'd meet—yet an atheist.

"Not that I'd want the whole world to know," he told

Hilly one day. "Most folks are hard on nonbelievers. Shun us like we got the plague."

Hilly was stunned. He considered himself a pretty good Catholic—confession and Communion once a week, Mass sometimes twice, if he could manage it. Silly knew this, yet he felt safe in his revelation.

"Have you always been a . . . nonbeliever?" Hilly asked. It was a quiet moment, and they'd climbed down from the ambulance to sit beside the snow- and mud-clogged cow path they'd been traveling.

Tearing apart a hunk of dry bread and handing the larger piece to Hilly, Silly told him, "I had a little sister. 'Teenie,' we called her; her real name was Altina. Anyway, she was so pretty and good, you wouldn't believe it. You know how some damned clucks say 'too good for this world'? Like there is another one you can count on? Well, that was our Teenie."

He picked a crumb from his bloodied jacket and popped it in his mouth. "She had the most delicate little face. Like somebody in training to be a queen, you know? And pretty manners. Mama taught her all the right ways to act."

In the distance, sporadic gunfire. "But she was so funny. When she'd get mad, she'd stick her head in a pillow and swear a blue streak. I mean, like a drunken gandy dancer. She repeated every bad word she'd ever heard Dad's patients let out when he had to stitch 'em up.

"Teenie was four years younger than me, so I was twelve and she was eight when she came down with malaria. Can you believe that? Malaria in Iowa?"

He peered off, as if to that distant Iowa.

"As soon as Dad knew what ailed her, I started praying. At church any time of the day. Beside the bed night and morning. Even if I was just sitting in the swing on the porch. I prayed till I practically didn't know any other language but praying.

"And then she left us." Silly had fallen silent and swiped his sleeve across his eyes.

"You don't have to explain," Hilly said. "You can be an atheist—or any kind of heathen religion—and you'll still be my best friend."

The ground was frozen, and the cold was penetrating the layers of clothing they wore. Silly stood.

"I never told this to anybody," he said. "It feels good to say it out loud. After Teenie's funeral, I told God he could go to hell. 'Course, by that time, I'd pretty well decided he was a fairy tale. And, I'll tell you the truth, nothing's ever changed my mind." He yanked out a grimy handkerchief and blew his nose, then held out a hand to pull Hilly up.

"So you don't think prayers get answered?"

They began walking back to the ambulance. "I figure things fall out the way they're gonna fall out. If they fall out for the good, folks think their prayers got answered. If things fall out for the bad, they say, 'God's will be done.' Guys say there ain't atheists in the trenches. I'm proof otherwise."

Silly climbed in behind the wheel. "I'll never try to convert anyone to my way. People have to believe what they have to believe. You go on being a Catholic. It's all the same to me. Whatever you are, you're all right."

Hilly cranked the engine, tossed the crank into the ambulance, and slid in.

He thought long about the things Silly had said. Instead of being upset, he felt honored that he'd been trusted. It was a big thing, being trusted. He would never let his friend down.

Hilly had never imagined France so desolate. Further back from the lines, it wasn't. But here, near the front, any remaining trees had been ripped apart, splinters of them standing out against the sky, looking like shattered soldiers. Besides these, there was nothing to see but an occasional farmhouse, often shelled to kindling.

Volunteer drivers from America and Britain joined the ranks of the regulars, but many of them left after one too many grisly scenes. The ambulance driver's job was to fetch fallen men from aid stations in the trenches, where wounds were patched and limbs amputated—the sooner the amputation, the less likely gangrene—and to remove them to hospitals.

When the enemy line advanced, the aid stations themselves were under fire. Hilly and Silly's first ambulance was destroyed by an enemy shell, probably an accidental hit. Mistakes were the daily business of war. Mistakes in requisitioning, mistakes in the trenches and in no-man's-land, mistakes in aid stations and field hospitals. How did anybody ever win a war? Hilly suspected that they just wore each other down to dust and ran out of shells.

Hilly and Silly hadn't been in that first ambulance when it was struck, but they'd had a hell of a time getting the man they'd come for back to the field hospital, carrying him all the way on a litter. He died in surgery. Hilly blamed himself, but Silly kept telling him that he was just the litter-bearer of bad news, not the cause.

Another of their ambulances was horse drawn. That was tricky. Even horses accustomed to battle will shy and bolt under particularly bad conditions.

But the worst of all worsts was coming across parts of men. Though their orders were to see to the living, you couldn't leave parts for animals to find—or at least Hilly and Sylvester couldn't. The first time they'd gathered parts, they'd been so close to the lines that dirt from the shelling was flying in their faces. The enemy had taken a forward trench, sending the Allies, under machine-gun and rifle fire, scurrying like rats into a fallback trench.

As Hilly and his partner scuttled toward the trench, a soldier erupted from another, screaming, "Aw, Jesus. Aw, Jesus." One moment he was running, and the next he was flying apart like a piece of cheap machinery. A flywheel here, a rod there—and blood everywhere.

Silly ran back to the ambulance for the rubber bag, and the two gathered up what they could find, including a blood-smeared letter, which might help someone identify the poor devil.

That night, by the illumination of an acetylene lamp in a field hospital, Hilly wrote,

Dear Mama,
We've had a busy day, though it's pretty much the same every day. Coming and going. We're fast. Silly and I make more runs than anybody, if I do say so myself.
The weather's raw, so thank Mrs. Barnstable for the

gloves and scarves and socks, please. Bad frostbite can take a man out of commission. Oh, and please thank the Women's Committee for the blanket.

I had a nice letter from John a while back. The fellows razzed me because it came from Washington, with the seal of the House of Representatives on it. "How come you're over here?" they asked. "You could be sitting behind a desk, cabbagehead." They like me, though. Also had a letter from Mrs. Lundeen and another from Diana Hapgood. Sorry to hear that Grandpa is down with the grippe.

I miss you, Mama. Take care of yourself. I'll be home soon.

> *I will always be*
> *Your loving son,*
> *Hilly*

Nell kept Hilly's letters beside the bed in a box from Lundeen's with an English garden on the lid. Each night, she took them out and read them through. Along with Mr. Wodehouse, they helped her fall asleep.

This evening, returning the letter box to the table, she blew her nose and plucked up Mr. Wodehouse's *The Man With Two Left Feet*, turning the pages to a favorite short story titled "The Mixer."

"I don't know what I am," the dog observed. "I have a bull-dog kind of face, but the rest of me is terrier. I have a long tail which sticks straight up in the air. My hair is wiry. My eyes are brown. I am jet black, with a white chest. I once overheard Fred saying that I was a Gorgonzola cheese-hound, and I have generally found Fred reliable in his statements."

She wished she had let Hilly have a dog.

God love you, my darling Mr. Wodehouse. But when she whispered, "Good night, Mr. Wodehouse," put him aside, and turned out the lamp, she found herself in the dreaded no-man's-land between awake and asleep. There big guns pounded—these guns, she knew, were only her blood throbbing through an artery and, as the weeks passed, strange to say, their drumming brought Hilly closer.

Nell couldn't blame people for staying away from Grandpa Hapgood's wake. Everyone was frightened of influenza. Grandpa's was already the fifth death in town, and Dr. Gray expected more.

Diana Hapgood stood near the casket, the man at her side much younger than Grandpa but bearing an uncanny resemblance to him. "This is my great-uncle Chester," Diana told Nell. "Grandpa's youngest brother." Chester, at Diana's invitation, was leaving Waterloo, Iowa, to move in with his great-niece. "The house is too big without Grandpa," Diana said.

"I've put off writing to Hilly about your grandfather," Nell said.

"Let me," Diana replied. "I was the one who told him that Grandpa was down in bed."

"I hope your grandfather knew that Hilly took the harmonica to France."

Diana nodded and took Nell's hand. "Hilly wrote how he played for the men. He said the late-night hours were the hardest for the badly wounded, but sometimes the music helped—especially if a man was close to the end. He said there was often a hymn or a sweetheart song a boy wanted to hear."

Hilly didn't tell Nell about his foot. His and Silly's ambulance had broken down a few miles from the field hospital. The two men tried without success to restart it, so when darkness closed in, they climbed into the back, swaddling in rough, government-issue blankets and the blanket from the Women's Committee. Inside his boots, Hilly's feet were wet from the snow he and Silly had stood in trying to seduce the engine. He'd worn extra socks, but they didn't help. Two toes on his right foot were frozen.

By the time another ambulance could fetch the men, the toes needed to be amputated. Hilly was temporarily out of commission, and when he returned to his ambulance he hobbled with pain and the loss of the toes.

Again, the other drivers called him cabbagehead, insisting that the pain and the crippling should send him back to a rear hospital, if not home altogether. But the Brits were tough on their own wounded, sending the patched-up back into action as soon as possible, even if they'd been to England for hospitalization. Hilly wanted no dispensation for being a Yank—and, besides, he wouldn't abandon Silly.

Over the weeks that followed, the two men had glazed over. He and Silly hurtled back and forth over impossible roads and cattle paths, never thinking a sentient thought, operating on a kind of wind-up response. Hilly had no time for his feet. The swelling and cracking open—the bleeding, burning, throbbing, and constant peeling—were conditions he mostly noted from a distant corner of his mind. When, rarely, he did pay them closer attention, he realized that his feet ached up to his hip bones, and sometimes they ached all the way to his armpits.

Run as he once had? Forget it.

chapter thirty-seven

IN FEBRUARY, Nell received a letter. The handwriting was both familiar and not.

Dear Nell,

Heaven forgive me, fourteen years have passed since I left Harvester. I expect you gave up wondering about me long ago. I'm sorry I haven't written. At first I didn't want to cause you more worry. And later—well, I just don't know why.

You probably guessed that I was in a family way. I won't say more about that. The first years in California were hard. I put my hand to any work to support my baby, Mary Cora. I was working in a hotel in San Francisco when the earthquake struck.

I was so frightened! I thought I had lost my baby. A woman in our boardinghouse was taking care of her. When I went looking for them, they were gone—and so was the boardinghouse.

Eventually I found them in a tent in the Presidio. The money I had was lost, of course. I headed south then, carrying Mary Cora and begging as we went. I found out there isn't anything you won't do when it's your baby.

I don't know how we ended up outside of Oxnard, hundreds of miles from San Francisco. But I was there, sitting beside the road holding Mary Cora, when the smartest little buggy pulled up with a young woman driver.

I guess she could see that we were half dead, because she took us home—I mean to her mother and father's house. She was visiting from Los Angeles, where she was in college.

I loved the house from the start and I knew I wanted to live there. It was perfect in every way, as pretty as a picture. And I took to the mother right off too. Her name was Mrs. Edwin Kerchel but she asked me to call her Belva. Isn't that a beautiful name?

Life is so strange. Belva was in a wheelchair, like our dear Cora. The daughter, Camille, told me that her mother had been hurt in a buggy accident. Camille was home from college because the lady who'd been looking after Belva and keeping house had dropped dead of a heart attack right at the kitchen sink scraping carrots.

After the baby and I had a bath and I put on some old clothes of Camille's, I told them how we'd left San Francisco after the earthquake. God forgive me, I also told them a big lie: I said my husband had been killed in the quake and that I was desperate to find work. I don't know if they believed me.

When Dr. Kerchel came home for lunch, Belva and Camille and I had already discussed my staying on and I had put a meal on the table for everyone. I could see how relieved the doctor was. We were solving his problems.

Belva was forty then, and she had money of her

own. Aren't those the prettiest words you ever heard?—
"money of her own." It had come from grandparents in
New England.

I've been with the Kerchels for twelve years now. Mary
Cora is thirteen, and the family has all but adopted her.
She is a pretty child, nearly taller than me already, with
dark hair and eyes. She is also the sweetest girl who
ever lived. She has her father's disposition—but I said
I wouldn't write about all that. I'll just say that Mary
Cora's father was a good man and that I loved him.

So, dear Nell, I've brought you up to date. In case
you are wondering, Camille still lives in Los Angeles and
is now married to a successful land speculator. Mary
Cora and I are well and happy. Happier than I deserve
to be but I won't look that gift horse in the mouth.

Though you may want to put "Paid" to your memo-
ries of me, I pray that you will write and tell me about
yourself and my darling Hilly. Is he going to college? I
have told Mary Cora that we have kin in Minnesota,
but she thinks that I met her father in San Francisco.
There is no lie I wouldn't tell to spare her shame. Will
God forgive me all of this, Nell? I need to hear your
thoughts.

I will save further details of our lives for later—if I
hear back from you.

> *Love to you and Hilly,*
> *Elvira*

P. S. I am enclosing a photograph of Mary Cora and
me, taken by Belva. We are standing beside a fishpond

in the backyard. Mary Cora is wearing the peach lawn dress you made me for George and Cora's wedding! Remember, I told you I'd keep it forever.

Here, in the midst of constant concern over Hilly and the periodic arrival of the poison-pen notes, here was joy. Elvira was not only alive, she was well, the mother of a fine thirteen-year-old child, and, to top it off, splendidly situated with a kind family.

The earthquake and the ensuing poverty and dislocation must have been harrowing beyond Nell's comprehension. So much destruction, so many deaths. But that was all behind mother and child, part of history. Elvira and Mary Cora had been a part of history—The Great San Francisco Earthquake.

Nell must answer Elvira's letter at once, assuring her that she and Hilly were still very much a part of the young woman's family. Wouldn't it be grand if Elvira and Mary Cora returned for a visit? Like Hilly's safe return, that was something to contemplate with great relish.

Dear Elvira,

It is a joy to hear from you! The lost is restored. I have thought of you every week and wondered how it was going with you.

Thank you for the photo. What a lovely girl Mary Cora is. And you look as young as when you left us. I can see that the Kerchels take as good care of you as you do of them.

God forgave you long ago. He sees into your heart.

He is a loving and tender God, despite what we are some-times told from the pulpit.

You asked about Hilly and college. I wish I could report that he was at the University. But he volunteered for the Army Ambulance Corps and is seeing terrible fighting in France. Remember him in your prayers.

I am well and continue to teach third grade. I see the Lundeens regularly. I am sad to tell you that George and Cora went down with the Lusitania. *It took Laurence a long time to recover, but in recent months he is looking stronger and more like his old self.*

Young Larry is a great blessing to his grandparents. Juliet insisted that they move back to the old house since that was Larry's home and where he wanted to be. Despite the differences in their ages, Larry and Hilly are great friends.

Dear Grandpa Hapgood was recently taken by influ-enza. He taught Hilly to play the harmonica that you sent him. And Hilly has taken the instrument along to France, so your gift has seen a good deal of the world and brought entertainment and perhaps a bit of com-fort to young men you and I will never meet. I know you'll take pleasure from hearing that.

I am still above Rabel's Meat Market. Thanks to old Gus, I have electricity now and soon will have running water! But I do not have a telephone—I am old fash-ioned. Maybe someday.

The Rabel boy has come into the business with Gus. I'm afraid he bullies his father. The boy wanted to raise my rent, but his father put his foot down. Apollo Shane, our lawyer here, drew up a paper saying that my rent would remain the same as long as I choose to live in the apartment. You can imagine that did not go down well with the son.

Well, darling Elvira-restored-to-me, I want to see this onto the westbound train today, so will close in haste, sending my own trainload of love to you and Mary Cora.

Nell

chapter thirty-eight

WITH CHARACTERISTIC DIFFIDENCE, Aunt Martha's husband, Bernard, passed away in his sleep. The funeral was simple and sparsely attended, but the coffin was grossly splendid. In the vestibule, Anna Braun commented, "Poor old devil finally got some respect."

During the reception in the church basement, Aunt Martha held court. A few cronies in ancient black dresses who'd come primarily for the ham, escalloped potatoes, and peas, paid their respects, tut-tutting and pursing their lips sympathetically to earn their lunch.

To Nell, Aunt Martha confided that she was selling the farm. "Top prices now. Ed Barnstable says it won't be on the market a week."

And Uncle Bernard in his grave a whole half hour.

"Where will you live?" Nell asked.

"In town of course. Someplace north of the park."

Nell unclenched her jaw, drained her coffee, and said good-bye.

That afternoon, a letter from Hilly was waiting at the post office. Setting the kettle to heat for tea, Nell changed into a muslin housedress, poured the near-bubbling water into the pot (Mam: "Don't let it bile on and on, darlin'.

Somethin' blessed biles away."), sat down in the green chair, and with care slid open the letter.

Closing her eyes and holding the unread pages in her lap, she waited for the tea to steep. She liked to create a bit of ceremony around Hilly's letters, give them the time and due they deserved. Rising after some moments to pour the tea through the proper strainer and into the delicate Haviland cup she'd found at Bender's Second Hand, she returned to her chair and to the letter.

> *Dear Mama,*
>
> *You'll be happy to hear that my foot is better. I'm generally better all around. We're finally hearing good news. Fellows are saying the war will soon be over. I'm not saying that the Germans will surrender tomorrow but only that things are changing.*
>
> *Silly and I are back from a few days' leave. We found space on a train to Amiens. Mama, we had real baths with hot water, real beds with clean sheets, and real meals with red wine!*
>
> *We drank a whole bottle one night. And so did a fellow named Rudy, from St. Bridget (Can you believe it?). Rudy and I are going to get together in Minnesota once this is over.*
>
> *Don't worry—I haven't become a boozer. It's just that when you get away from the front, you try to erase it from your mind.*
>
> > *I will always be*
> > *Your loving son,*
> > *Hilly*

P. S. Silly and I are going to be decorated by the French and English governments. It's crazy! But maybe it's some kind of mistake, so don't get excited yet. . . .

Nell prayed that the end of the war was indeed near. In Washington, John was optimistic, but she would not let herself hope until Hilly was home in one piece. What had he meant when he said that his foot was better?

What had been wrong with his foot?

And what was this about decorations? His news was piecemeal.

Over the next days, by means unknown to Nell, word of the decorations spread.

"About these honors Hilly's getting from the French and English. What can you tell me?" Ev Dunn, the owner of the *Standard Ledger*, asked one morning.

"Nothing. He wrote that he'd been told about them, but he thinks they might be a mistake."

"Well, they're not a mistake, that much I know. I called John Flynn first thing, and he said he'd just received word from the Secretary of War. But all we know is that Hilly and another driver are being decorated."

"I wish I could be more helpful, Ev."

"Oh, God, I should mention: The Women's Committee is getting up an event in the new high-school gymnasium, something to honor our boys, but especially your son. And, by association, you."

"I wish they wouldn't," Nell sighed.

"Hah! Go talk to Eudora!"

A heaviness, a weariness, plagued Nell over the next

few days. It went against her grain to be made much of. To stand out was to invite comeuppance, or worse. The universe operated a leveling device, a harrow, to bring down anything that rose half a head above the commonplace.

But Eudora Barnstable would not be denied. The doors of the new gymnasium were flung open on the evening of Saturday, August 31, and strains of "Keep the Home-Fires Burning" and "Roses of Picardy" rang down Main Street.

Eudora's red, white, and blue evening inaugurated the new gymnasium while celebrating the absent Hilly. And, as Ev Dunn had predicted, it honored Nell. On the stage at the far end of the echoing room, a dozen bunting-draped chairs were lined up. Nell occupied the most central and grandest of these, elevated on her own individual dais.

Overheated and groping in their bags for hankies, the mothers of other Harvester soldiers sat on either side of her. In the remaining three chairs, Eudora, Mayor Anton Lindstrom, and Representative John Flynn chatted together as townspeople found seats among rows of folding chairs.

Nell shifted on her throne. Perspiration gathered between her breasts, crawled down the backs of her legs, and puddled inside her shoes.

Most of what was said during the hour-and-twenty-minute program floated in one portal of Nell's consciousness and out another. The stifling air in the big room—and the nagging certainty that no good could come of such spectacle—conjoined to visit Nell with a dull headache.

She did hear John tell the audience, "In early January of this year, our Hilly was reassigned to a British ambulance unit. I have a letter from a Major Willis of that British contingent. He writes:

> To Family, Friends, and Fellow Countrymen of
> Private Hillyard Stillman:
>
> It is my pleasure to advise you that Private Stillman will receive commendation by the governments of both France and Great Britain in recognition of extraordinary courage, initiative, and diligence in the rescue of fallen men.
>
> Private Stillman has saved more lives and under more brutal and perilous circumstances than perhaps any ambulance driver serving on this front. Members of his own outfit report his dogged valor and stubborn refusal to leave a man behind, no matter that man's condition.
>
> A policy exists admonishing ambulance personnel to choose the more likely survivors from among the wounded. Again and again, Private Stillman found a means of taking everyone possible, even resorting to tying men on the bonnet and the roof of his vehicle. And while the Army's orders are meant to be obeyed, in a case such as this, disobedience could not but be recognized for what it is: extraordinary heroism.
>
> Major Hiram Willis,
> in the Service of His Majesty
> King George V

At the evening's culmination, John presented each mother with a star-shaped brooch; the band played the national anthem; and the audience, pleased to have come and grateful to leave, processed out into a breathless summer evening.

"That was a splendid letter from Major Willis," Eudora said later, as they settled onto Juliet's screened back porch with cold beer from Reagan's.

"I was over to St. Bridget today and saw a big story on the front page of Wednesday's *Examiner*," Ed Barnstable told them.

"What are Hilly's plans when he's home?" Dr. Gray asked.

"I hope he'll rest for a long time," Nell said, aware it wasn't the answer Charlie Gray was looking for.

"Of course," Juliet murmured.

"We must expect a different man," John told them quietly. He rose from his chair, crossing to the screen door to light a cigar. "I had a long talk with Ben Hapgood last February." He sucked flame into the Havana with insistent pulls. "He was with the First Minnesota during the Civil War. Those men saw horrors.

"When Ben got back, he didn't want to talk to anyone for a long time. He wasn't comfortable with people who hadn't been there. Not even family. He was caught between two places so different, they'd never understand each other." The cigar glowed in the growing pitchiness of the porch, the thick, fruity scent curling around the room. "Hilly's going to need time to put it behind him the best he can," John went on. "He's been to hell. We'll have to be patient."

Beyond John, heat lightning zigzagged low across the

horizon. Nell laid her head against the wicker chaise and listened as the others talked of the war and of high farm prices. Pools of illumination from the kerosene lamps created a little world within a world, its corners shadowed. Nell preferred these kerosene lamps to the electric ones they all had now. Electrification of the town had taken several years, but it had come too fast for her, and now it was moving out to the nearer farms.

Something in her clung to the old ways, unlike Hilly, who wanted to reach out to the new and the unknown. Look how he'd taken to the automobile, never frightened for a moment. Beyond this screened porch, safe and close, lay the vastness of a world he'd set his heart on exploring.

Guilt stirred her. She knew she would try to dissuade him. Did every mother feel this need to have her grown child close? Motherhood was the most insecure of all undertakings. If you stopped to think, even for a moment, every choice you made was the wrong choice.

"Well, all I can say," Eudora began, "is that I'm terribly thankful that Pershing and our men are over there. With the Hun on their doorstep, what would the dear English have done?"

"Or the dear French, for that matter?" Laurence teased.

"I suppose," said Eudora. "But I always think there's something not quite *solid* about them."

John returned to a chair near Nell and took her hand. "Sad to say, Eudora, many French boys *weren't* solid enough to turn away bullets."

"Thank you for bringing me to account, John. My Anglophilia carries me away. But I am glad our boys are putting an end to this war. And I thank you again, Nell, for the loan of a splendid son."

Nell stirred in bed, throwing off the sheet. At the open window, sinuous curtains yielded to a whisper of air, caressing themselves, fold against fold, lace flowers bending, pliant. When he was small, Hilly stood at the open window and mashed his face into the curtains as if kissing or inhaling them.

On the bedside table, a piece of delicate crochet work, resembling rime on a winter window, covered the surface. She'd purchased that in June, at a St. Boniface bazaar raising money for the Red Cross. Standing in the church basement, doily in her hands, she'd imagined some small portion of her pennies leaping the miles, like seven-league boots, to the Front. John and Hilly's photographs stood on the doily. The day after his death, she'd removed Herbert's to Hilly's room.

Climbing back into bed and pulling up the sheet, she turned on her side and ran a hand across the pillow where John's head had recently rested.

chapter thirty-nine 🙿

Dear Mama,

All through this summer we've pushed the Boche back. "We" means the Commonwealth fellows—but I do feel like one of them. Anyway, I'm sure I'll be home soon. Silly thinks we might be home for Christmas, at least on leave. Please send my best to Diana, and to John and the Lundeens.

Love to everyone—even Aunt Martha.

> *I will always be*
> *Your loving son,*
> *Hilly*

But then weeks passed without a word. Nell entreated John in Washington to discover what he could. By turns she was giddy with the certainty that Hilly was alive—then mad with the sure knowledge that he was dead.

When the bomb exploded beneath them, Silly was driving. Hilly was riding in the empty rear of the ambulance. The smell of burning trees and sometimes of burning farm buildings—if Hilly closed his eyes—could almost be the scent of autumn leaves burning in the backyards of Harvester.

And then, there was no sound, no smell. Just Hilly running barefoot on a cold Irish beach, while a ship in the gray distance disappeared. He was running and crying and calling out, "I'll save you!"

In early October, a note addressed to The Family of Hillyard Stillman arrived from Major Willis, who had earlier informed them of Hilly's honors.

> I apologize for the tardiness of these tidings. Events of late have moved with such speed that I am a good deal behind in my duties.
>
> In early September, while making ambulance runs near the town of Brie, the vehicle operated by the team of Privates Stillman and Benjamin struck an unexploded bomb. In the subsequent explosion, Private Stillman, though wounded, was thrown free. Private Benjamin was not.
>
> I share this latter knowledge with you only because the two lads had operated together from the first and I feel certain that you would want to know.
>
> Private Stillman was removed to an English field hospital and, later, to an American hospital at the rear. I have been unable to determine his whereabouts or condition beyond this point, though I feel sure that your own government will soon share this information with you.
>
> I wish to thank you for the services of Hillyard Stillman

in the cause of the Commonwealth. He has served the Allies with great distinction.

> *Major Hiram Willis,*
> *in the Service of His Majesty*
> *King George V*

Hilly was alive.

On October 12, stopping to collect mail, Nell ran into Eudora on the post-office steps. "Mrs. Stillman!" Shifting the bag beneath her arm, she snatched Nell's hand in a fierce grip. "Word came on the wire down at the depot. The Germans want to talk peace!" She gasped for air. "Hillyard will be home soon! We'll give him a grand welcome, won't we?"

And yet the fighting continued over the coming weeks. Fierce fighting, according to the newspaper. But at least Hilly was out of it.

Late that same month, Nell received a hastily scratched note from a Dr. Blaise at an army hospital in New York. Hilly was being treated for physical injuries and "what is commonly referred to as shell shock." While visits might provoke an "excitation" that could impede Private Stillman's progress, "we have every hope of Private Stillman achieving full recovery."

Shell shock: Nell had heard reports of other boys coming home with this condition. What did it mean? And when would she be able to see him?

She wrote to the hospital at once, but received no answer.

Less than a month later, the war was over. The following Saturday, November 19, a parade marched from
the schoolhouse down Main Street. High overhead, rac-
ing clouds veiled the sun, while on the street, the honed
edge of November gusts whipped shifting islands of dead
leaves.

From a chair beside the bedroom window, Nell watched.
Men and women waving handkerchief-sized flags lined
up on the sidewalk to cheer the combined town and high-
school bands, newly outfitted in their first-ever uniforms,
purchased in anticipation of the war's end.

Across the street, Aunt Martha, cane looped over one
arm, leaned against the handrail of the post-office steps
and fanned herself, despite the chill of the day. Now and
then she glanced up at Nell.

Behind the passing colors shambled two hoary Civil
War veterans, bent and uncertain, then a handful of men
who'd served in the Spanish-American conflict, portly now
and comfortable. Like office seekers, they waved and smiled
to the crowd.

Finally, a dozen already-returned survivors of the war
"to end all wars" made slow procession down the street.
Two of them struggled with crutches, one walked with a
cane and carried an arm in a cast. The sleeve of another
hung empty and pinned. They waved not at all, nor did
they call out to friends.

Nell hesitated before answering Aunt Martha's stento-
rian knock. She entered in full sail. "Didn't see you marching with the third grade."

"I'll make coffee," Nell volunteered.

"Not for me. I'll only be a minute. There's refreshments at the school. That's where folks will be. Honoring the boys." She pulled a lace-trimmed handkerchief from her bosom, mopping her face. "What do you hear of Hillyard?"

"Only the letter from the doctor."

"Can't your good friend the congressman pry out some information?"

"It was on his account that we heard from the doctor at all."

"Well, *I* am proud of our Hillyard," Martha said, thrusting out her chin. "Look at how the French and English decorated him. When he comes home, he has to have a fuss made over him. Your responsibility."

"We mustn't plan something he wouldn't want," Nell said.

"Nonsense. He'd be tickled pink to have folks turn out."

"Martha Stillman is a gossip and a mischief maker," Nell told John over a game of gin rummy that night.

"Well, you can at least stop her gossiping about us, if that's a problem."

"Yes?"

John set his cards aside. "This isn't how I planned it," he said. "I was going to take you to St. Paul for dinner."

"A long way to go for dinner."

"Well, I hardly ever ask a woman to marry me."

"Marry you. Because of gossip?"

"Not for a minute. Because I love you and want to take care of you."

"You've always said you were too old for me."

"I'm still too old for you, but I'll overlook it if you will."

Lifting his hand, she licked the saltiness in its palm and kissed his lifeline.

"Is that a yes?"

"That's an I-have-to-think-about-it."

In bed that night, John was patient. Nell lay on her side, studying John's profile. He was a fine-looking man despite a nose broken in college wrestling. The nose gave him a rakish, dangerous look, appropriate for the man he was: someone to be reckoned with.

But *marriage.* Nell's breath ruffled like something alive and alarmed in her throat.

chapter forty

OVERNIGHT, the temperature had dropped to three degrees above zero, and at 10:00 a.m. it hadn't budged, despite a blinding sun. The January day was the sort one mistakenly ventures into because it appears vivid and welcoming, the light on the snow as flashing and gay as a jewelry-store window.

On a depot platform cleared of snow, the town band had assembled, its members laughing, chafing hands and stamping feet to keep blood circulating.

The Army notice had been brief: Private Stillman, accompanied by a medic, would arrive by train on Saturday, January 18. Nell had begged Eudora Barnstable not to organize a grand welcome.

But Eudora insisted, "I'm sure the medic is simply de rigueur, Nell dear. You'll see. Hillyard may be on crutches and need a little assistance." Tears stood in Eudora's eyes and her nose reddened. "I couldn't bear for our greatest local hero not to be feted."

Now, Mayor Lindstrom stood near the band, cradling in his arms a three-foot-long Key to Harvester while some two hundred townspeople flocked around, with others huddled in the little parking lot at the end of the depot.

At his request, Nell stood to the left of the mayor. And to *her* left, John, Laurence, Juliet, and Larry lined up. On the mayor's right, the tall, tutelary figure of Eudora gazed about at her subjects. Beside her, husband Edward, beset and gray at forty-two, dug gloved hands into the pockets of his overcoat.

To his father's right, young Ed, eleven now—a late and solitary birth in the Barnstable household—tapped his feet and waved a small flag in time to "It's a Long Way to Tipperary."

From the eastern distance, the sound of a train whistle called them all to attention, its cry barely succeeding against a west wind that tossed sound, smoke, and steam back the way they'd come. Nell shuddered and drew herself up.

John squeezed her gloved hand. "It's going to be all right."

"Well, this is it," the mayor said.

Then, before Nell was ready, the train whistle was blowing again, this time at the crossing only a mile from town. Though Nell had dressed in layers of warm clothing and drawn her coat collar around her ears, she could not stop shaking. John slipped behind her, shielding her from the wind.

Suddenly, the train chuffed and squealed to a halt before them, exhaling a solemn cloud of steam. A conductor, with the dignity of a pallbearer, descended the steps of the passenger car, placing the portable step with care.

Nell didn't see Hilly at any of the windows. Then, at the top of the iron steps, a soldier appeared, his body half turned to assist another—surely Hilly—to make his way to the platform. Hobbling, faltering, but without crutches, Hilly was at last framed in the entrance, peering out as if this place were unknown to him and possibly dangerous. At sight of the hometown boy, the band director waved his arms, and the musicians struck up a galloping "For He's a Jolly Good Fellow." The escort soldier flashed a glance of disapproval.

With the escort's hand to guide him, Hilly lurched down the several steps. On the ground, he stared for long moments at the crowd, swiveling his head first in one direction, then the other. Forgetting his apprehension and slipping free of the medic's grasp, he rushed forward. Grinning and drooling a little, he stood behind the music director, waving his arms in imitation. *Excitation.*

The escort followed, trying without success to catch hold of Hilly. But as he neared, his charge broke away and began jigging back and forth across the empty portion of the platform. Behind the two, with a shrill lament, the train began to pull away.

As suddenly as he had begun jigging, Hilly faltered. Momentary comprehension lit his face, like the brief burning through of dawn on a sullen day. He looked down in amazement at the front of his trousers where a urine stain was spreading. His face puckered and tears welled in his eyes. His body trembled. He turned his head to hide his shame. Gradually, with the escort standing behind him laying a hand on his shoulder and speaking softly into his ear, Hilly sank to his knees.

The fringes of the crowd in the parking lot started to crumble and disperse, heads ducked, as if by looking down they could seem not to have been there, not to have seen. The metal clasps of rubber galoshes flopped metallically as men moved toward cars and buggies. A few young people nudged each other, tittering.

Gone now were the flag wavers, gone the band, the mayor, and the Key to Harvester. Nell knelt beside Hilly, speaking in a low voice. At length he stood, looking into her face. *Tell me who I am.*

chapter forty-one

"You're my son. I'm your mother. I'll look after you. I'll keep you safe," Nell crooned in the backseat of John's car. In the front, the young soldier who'd accompanied Hilly sat beside John.

Pictures passed through her mind, as they would a thousand times in the coming days and nights: a baby handing Juliet a wooden block; a boy in the park, swinging with little Larry on his lap; a flushed adolescent returning from a run in the country; and a young man shedding quiet tears after Cora and George's deaths.

John left the soldier at the Harvester Arms Hotel. In front of Rabel's, Nell told John, "Hilly and I need to be alone."

In the apartment, Nell led Hilly to his room. She had laid out his old flannel pajamas on his bed that morning. Now he held the worn softness to his face.

Bathing him later, she noted the raw emptiness where two toes had once been, toes lost to frostbite, and she ran hesitant fingertips along the shiny red welt on his side where shrapnel had been removed at a field hospital.

When he was toweled dry, she showed him the commode and explained its purpose, hoping he had some recollection of it. But she could take nothing for granted.

She helped him into the pajamas, and he crawled into his bed, showing neither curiosity about nor familiarity with the room which had for so many years been his. He was an unquestioning animal who submitted to being led. And he was a boy who had wet himself on the depot platform.

Nell pulled the rocker close to his bed and watched him sleep, rising only to make tea and toast early in the afternoon.

Hilly was home. He was where he belonged, and Nell was grateful. Off and on through the day and evening, she wept for the wounds to his body and mind. And when several times he moaned or cried out, she held his hand, touched his cheek, sang to him. Tending him thus, she did not try to imagine what their lives would be like as the weeks passed. She made no plans. It was enough to see this day out.

The hunger to watch him sleep, to touch him, to draw the blankets over his shoulders when they had slipped— that hunger was so powerful, it did not permit her to leave his room until long past midnight.

When she did climb shivering into her own bed, she lay for an hour massaging her temples and reviewing the improbably long day. Then, without thinking, she reached for Wodehouse.

What would she do without Mr. Wodehouse to lift her almost bodily into his world—into a clean, sunny place where no wars drew sons from their beds and all young flesh was sound and golden? Where else could she find the guarantee of half an hour's escape? When you hadn't the courage to face the future head on, you could still approach it obliquely, on a circuitous route through the printed page. Was there anyone on earth who'd understand how grinding fear could be locked away for a moment of laughter?

Opening *Something Fresh*, Nell read, "The sunshine of a fair Spring morning fell graciously upon London town. Out in Piccadilly its heartening warmth seemed to infuse into traffic and pedestrians alike a novel jauntiness, so that bus drivers jested and even the lips of chauffeurs uncurled into not unkindly smiles. Policemen whistled at their posts—clerks on their way to work . . . It was one of those happy mornings."

Sunday morning, Nell opened Hilly's closet and bureau drawers to show him where his high-school clothes were still kept. He glanced at them, puzzled.

She chose trousers, an undershirt, an outer shirt, and warm socks, laying them across his rocker. Mewling, Hilly looked from the clothes to Nell and back, sensing that something was expected. His frustration was tormenting, and so she began unbuttoning his pajamas, explaining each step as she did.

Hilly paid little attention, instead pointing to an old stain on the ceiling where melting snow had seeped in from the roof. The jigsaw-puzzle shape seemed to fascinate him.

"Yes," Nell said, "that's where the roof leaked."

He shook his head, agitated. "Nah. Nah." The rest of what he said Nell was unable to translate.

"There's breakfast on the table," she told him, leading him to the kitchen, where a fire burned in the cookstove.

She had prepared oatmeal. Toast, cut into triangles and spread with strawberry jam from Diana Hapgood, lay on the plate beside the cereal. Again, the mewling and the perplexed gaze.

Nell picked up the spoon, placing it in his hand. Guiding it, she stirred butter, brown sugar, and milk into the oatmeal, and raised the spoon to his mouth. After a few such trips from bowl to mouth, Hilly grasped what was expected, but like a small child's aim, his was not always true. Nell fetched a dishtowel and tied it around his neck.

She wondered what they had taught him in the hospital. Had it been easier to feed and dress him than to teach him?

When he had eaten half the oatmeal, Hilly rose with jerking hesitation and returned to the bedroom, his gait awkward, protecting the wounded foot. Climbing into bed, he curled up like a caterpillar unkindly touched.

"No one will hurt you here," Nell told him from the doorway, her hands in the apron pockets fisting with grief and anger.

Breakfast dishes were put away and pails of water hauled up from the pump behind Rabel's when the knock came: the young soldier who'd accompanied Hilly.

Settled in the rocker, he handed Nell a small but heavy package and a little box tied with twine.

"I didn't think yesterday was the time to give you these, ma'am—your son's belongings. The gun is a German sidearm he must have picked up in the field. The bullets are removed. They're in the box. There's some other things in there with the gun. Not much, but the folks at the hospital thought you'd want everything."

Nell nodded. Indeed. She was silent for a long minute.

The soldier waited, either accustomed to this reaction or dispirited by it. Maybe each of these meetings ate at him, diminishing something solid and sure.

"Thank you," Nell said, rising and laying the package on the table beside her chair, "for all you did for Hillyard. I know you tried to protect him yesterday." Surely there was something she could do or say to tender small payment for his kindness and awful duty? "What about a cup of tea? There's store-bought cookies."

"Nice of you to offer, ma'am, but I've got to catch the eastbound pretty quick." He rose.

At the bottom of the outside stairs, he fitted his cap back on and gave Nell a solemn salute before heading toward the depot. How could it be, Nell wondered, that someone so important to one's life was there and gone, in less than five minutes? *I didn't even ask his name.*

She climbed onto a chair and thrust the gun and the box of ammunition to the back of the top shelf in the kitchen cupboard.

His harmonica; several handkerchiefs, washed and ironed; a Catholic missal and rosary; and a tiny address book were the remaining contents of the package. She sat down in the rocker to leaf through the address book, finding Sylvester Benjamin of Dubuque, Iowa—Silly. She would send condolences to his parents, and perhaps inquire if they had a spare photo of their son. It might comfort Hilly.

Six callers stopped in the afternoon: first, Laurence, Juliet, and a manly young Larry, all offering help—"Please let me stay with Hilly afternoons," Juliet insisted, "while you're at school, just till he's settled in"; then Eudora, face swollen and red, apologizing for the elaborate homecoming—"I will never forgive myself for putting you and Hillyard through that." And, finally, some time later, Aunt Martha. Inside the door, she glanced around. "Hillyard?"

"Lying down."

Nodding, the old woman settled herself into the green chair. "The girl's doing my shopping." The "girl" was Agatha, a maiden lady probably Nell's age, who met Martha's standards: she was without family, could handle a horse and buggy, and was accustomed to abuse.

"We need to talk, don't you think?" Martha opened.

"About?"

"Hillyard."

"What about him?"

"Where will you send him?"

"Why would I send him anywhere?"

"You can't possibly care for him."

"But I'm *going* to care for him." Nell had failed to offer Martha tea, and now knew she wouldn't.

"Don't be foolish."

"I've never been less foolish."

Martha shifted in her chair, glanced toward the kitchen as if something might yet be forthcoming from that quarter, then turned an imperative gaze on Nell. "You saw what happened at the depot. He's not in control of himself. He'll be a public spectacle."

Nell rose. At the door, she said, "Out."

Martha pushed herself to her feet. Obviously there was to be no tea. "I'll come again when you're sensible."

At length, John arrived, bearing doughnuts from a bakery in St. Bridget. "Hilly lying down?"

"Since breakfast. The only time he's spoken was when he noticed the water stain on the bedroom ceiling. And then I couldn't understand what he said, except that he didn't think it was a stain." She set cups and saucers on the table. "He'll have to learn to talk again."

John was silent, licking sugar from his fingers, then wiping them for long minutes on his handkerchief. Finally he rose and dipped his hands in the washbasin. "It's going to take a while. But in Washington we can get the best help for him."

Nell handed him a towel, then sat. "He needs to remember this old life. And this apartment. Maybe after that."

"And if he's never better?"

Nell was silent.

"I shouldn't have said that."

"No."

Later, when she had seen Hilly to bed for the night and was herself preparing to end the day with a cup of hot chocolate, Nell sat at the kitchen table, staring into the near distance, at the day that must follow this one, and the one after that. The chocolate cooled and grew a wrinkled skin.

Leadenness held her on the chair.

Long minutes passed, and as they did, from the side of

her vision, stage right as it were, a verdure crept slowly forward, gold coins of sunlight dancing on green carpet, surrounding her with warmth. . . .

As she waited, wondering, a wooden lounge chair, a kind of deck chair, coaxed her, and she moved toward it, ran a hand along the cross-slat at the back, and slipped down onto the cushioned seat, between the broad, flat arms, smooth as satin beneath her fingers.

Now voices, light and untroubled, soothing in their buoyant lack of care, approached from between a pair of willows. Several figures in summer whites materialized, fresh from tennis perhaps. Catching sight of Nell, one called out, "How good to see you! Let us get you a lemonade—or you might rather a cold tea?"

Nell rose from the deck chair. Wodehouse clasped her hand. "So glad you could get away."

chapter forty-two ☙

THAT FIRST WEEK, Larry, now a high-school senior, ventured into Hilly's bedroom with a deck of cards. "Rummy?"

Hilly shook his head and turned toward the wall. Failing the card game, Larry grabbed Hilly's harmonica from the bureau and blew into it.

"Unhh, unhh, unhh," Hilly screamed, clapping his hands over his ears and churning from side to side in the bed. Juliet and Nell came running.

Shaken, Larry backed from the room. "It made him remember something, don't you think?"

"That's the problem," his grandmother said. "We don't know what will jog his memory. Something opens a door, maybe only a tiny way, but it's too much."

On his next visit, Larry brought one of his childhood books, the *Just So Stories*. Sitting in the living room, he began reading in a carrying voice:

I've never sailed the Amazon,
    I've never reached Brazil;

His voice was calm and cadenced, hypnotic as he continued:

But the Don and Magdalena,
They can go there when they will!
Yes, weekly from Southampton,
Great steamers, white and gold,
Go rolling down to Rio
(Roll down—roll down to Rio!)
And I'd like to roll to Rio
Some day before I'm old!

I've never seen a Jaguar,
Nor yet an armadill—
O dilloing in his armour,
And I s'pose I never will,

Unless I go to Rio
These wonders to behold—
Roll down—roll down to Rio—
Roll really down to Rio!
Oh, I'd love to roll to Rio
Some day before I'm old!

Within minutes, Hilly emerged, tentative and wary. Had the words struck a buried childhood memory? His robe was clutched tight around him, armor against an assault. At the living-room doorway, his glance caromed from corner to corner. Larry read without pause.

At length Hilly circled the room. Reaching the daybed, he lowered himself and lay with legs pulled up, arms still clinging to himself.

Larry and Juliet began to read aloud to Hilly daily. Some

days he ventured forth to listen, many days he did not. One could neither explain nor anticipate. On those days when Hilly emerged and listened with tolerance, Juliet felt girlish exhilaration, as if a reluctant beau had shown her attention.

One day, she told Nell, she had giggled with joy at his presence, then glanced quickly to see if that had frightened him. Making a mental note—it's all right to giggle—she had turned the page and continued.

From a large and stiff envelope, Nell extracted a photograph and accompanying letter.

Dear Mrs. Stillman,

We were saddened to hear of Hilly's problems and gladdened to know the delight and comfort your son had in our boy's friendship. Thank you for copying out lines from Hilly's letters. I believe they will bring some solace to Sylvester's mother.

Mrs. Benjamin is still recovering from our boy's death. We lost an eight-year-old daughter to malaria when Sylvester was twelve, so this loss has felled my wife.

We would both be interested to hear of Hilly's progress. From what we learned of him from "Silly," he is an extraordinary lad.

Yours truly,
Sylvester Benjamin Sr.

Silly's photo showed him as Hilly had described: a big, brawny boy with a winning smile. When Nell handed it to Hilly, he kissed it and fell on his bed weeping and laughing.

In the fall, when Nell returned to her classroom, Hilly had been home about seven months.

"Eudora or I will check on Hilly in the afternoons," Juliet said. "He does love being read to. Settles him, don't you think?"

Good women.

Eudora had been reading aloud from *Little Lord Fauntleroy*. Listening, Hilly hung his head, physically upset that a boy—just because he was a lord—could be taken from his home in America and sent to live in England. Eudora further bewildered him by trying to explain titles and ascendancy.

In November, she began teaching Hilly to read. He was less enthusiastic about reading than being read to, but Eudora thought that he should have the rudiments. Besides, she was in her element, carting in books from her son's early school years, plus a thick album she herself had put together, each page containing a picture and beneath the picture a word printed in India ink. Hilly could not yet sound out words intelligibly but he was learning to associate printed words with shapes and colors and sounds.

His sleep, however, continued to explode in nightmares. When she heard him cry out, Nell rushed to his room and held him. On a night early in January 1920, he screamed, "Silly, Silly!" over and over.

"You have no idea the stories I'm hearing," Aunt Martha

said a week later. "They can't all be lies. Hillyard's going to get you into trouble, my girl."

"I won't put him in St. Peter."

Aunt Martha hadn't moved from her spot just inside the apartment door. "I've tried to be helpful, but my patience is at an end. That boy will disgrace the Stillman name."

"When did you ever try to be helpful, Martha? When Herbert died and you brought ground-cherry jam?"

"I'll hire a lawyer."

"That's your privilege." Nell wasn't concerned. The woman was too tight with her purse for that.

Weary, John said, "Dear woman, I don't understand you. You're afraid of the stories she'll spread, yet you won't consider going to Washington. You and Hilly." Home for Easter week, he stood beside her at the stove, an arm around her waist.

Water was on the boil, and Nell moved John aside to pour it into the waiting pot, nodding toward Hilly, standing in the doorway. "Not in front of Hilly," she said, and the subject was dropped. But John was silent during their tea, not quite reachable.

Dinner out of the way, John built up the dwindling fire in the cookstove with fresh wood from the stack behind the building. Nell studied him as he worked, his sleeves rolled to his elbows. He was the man nearly every unmarried woman prayed for—loving, gentle, intelligent. She set aside the chemise she was mending. Folding the garment, she hesitated, choosing her words: "I'm a conventional woman with a damaged son."

Punching the needle into a pincushion and without

looking up, she went on, "Whatever you may think, there's nothing remarkable about me. If I were a remarkable woman, I would marry you right now, move to Washington, and, by some manner or means, turn the move into a good thing for Hilly.

"But, not only am I ordinary, I'm a mouse who creeps along the baseboard, my nose twitching for the scent of a cat.

"At the moment, our hidey-hole is the safest place for us, Aunt Martha notwithstanding. From the stain on the bedroom ceiling to the patched screen door, it's our known world, and I think I can navigate Hilly through it with as little shock and humiliation as possible. He's confident that this place won't blow up in his face. And right now, that's everything."

"And I, dear Nell," he replied, his voice solemn, "am a man who needs a lover and companion who is there each night when he turns out the light, and each morning when he ventures forth to slay dragons. I have a great need to be helpful—and I need a helpmate." No hint of a smile blunted the message.

He stayed, however, and their lovemaking, if anything, was particularly tender and ardent. Later, he fell into a doze. Nell watched him, whispering, so as not to wake him, "You are my great love."

"I heard that," he murmured, sliding on top of her. She loved the weight of him on her body. *Oh, God, let this last.*

But two months passed before she heard from John again.

chapter forty-three ↷

LYING BENEATH THE OTHER MAIL in May of 1921 was the latest note. *No more runnin, I gess.* How many years had this dark patch lain across her life? Fifteen? The meanness or madness behind it had always felt like something that would burn itself out.

When school let out for the summer, John returned from Washington, cordial but reserved. During his absence, Nell had imagined both his loss (unthinkable) and marriage (equally unthinkable). There simply was no answer, and that meant she would lose him. He would not allow matters to drift.

With June's arrival, Hilly's teaching "faculty" suddenly expanded. Despite circumstances between himself and Nell, John remained faithful to Hilly, teaching him to button his clothes and to shave. From Diana Hapgood, Hilly learned to print his name and count to twenty. Every task was weeks, even months, in the learning. As the doctor from the Army hospital had explained, Hilly had become a fear-ridden five-year-old.

As his skills grew, so did the thin trickle of confidence. Hilly wept when he forgot how to button his fly. But when he remembered, four days running, he chortled—a raucous sound, like an angry parrot.

And late in July, Hilly left the apartment for the first time since returning home. Knowing that old Gus Rabel was filling in for his son at the meat market, Nell coaxed Hilly down the outside stairs on a little errand.

Gus ushered them in. "Missus and Hilly, come in. You are looking well, Mr. Hilly." Reaching for a tiny paper bag, Gus plunged a huge fist into a glass barrel and filled the bag with oyster crackers. Handing it to Hilly, he inquired, "You still like oyster crackers?"

Hilly squawked his strange laugh and accepted the gift, bobbing his head again and again. Nell ordered a pound of hamburger and a ham bone and left with a lighter step.

That summer unraveled in heat and wind. John arranged no whist evenings. The Lundeens, sensing a conflict between their two friends, arranged none either. Increasingly, Nell fell back upon books, and especially Wodehouse. How appropriate, she thought, that her latest acquisition was *A Damsel in Distress*.

In the mugginess of August, heat rash plagued Hilly. He grew irritable and couldn't settle down. For the boy's sake, one Sunday a remote and tight-lipped John drove Nell and Hilly out to the lake.

Underway in the touring car, with the cover rolled back, Hilly stood on his knees in the backseat. The wind poured over him, drying perspiration and soothing the crawly feeling the sweat gave him as it slid down his back and from under his armpits, salting still-tender wounds.

At the lake, John told Hilly, "Take everything off." The

boy looked unsure. "It's all right, Professor. No one's going to see you."

From the screened porch, they watched as Hilly sat on the dock's edge, dangling his feet in the lake, then easing his whole body into the water. "Nice," he called, and though it came out "nithe," they laughed with surprise. And so he said it again. "Nithe."

From up and down the convolute shoreline came the subdued croaking of thousands of frogs. Hilly waded out to where the water reached his chafed armpits. "Nithe," he bellowed and stood unmoving for ten minutes before returning to lie down on the dock. All was still.

When John was sitting beside Nell, his silence was more painful than it had been at a distance. Nell was unable to launch words, while he ventured none. "This is what Hilly needs," she said at length. "This quiet."

A wordless five minutes elapsed, then: "One last time, Nell. If you decide you're ready for Washington, for me . . ."

She heard the finality.

A week passed, two weeks. Silence and absence.

Trying to say yes was like pushing against a door too heavy to budge. Then, one day in August, without warning and without reason, the door gave, and Nell plunged into the Void of Yes, as one falling down an elevator shaft. She felt the rabbity, breathless horror of tumbling through space. How had this happened?

John was less ambivalent. Laughing and kissing her hands, he said, "That wasn't so hard now, was it?"

August became September, and she was—for God's

sake—expected to make plans. In her trepidation, she was certain of only one thing—Mr. Wodehouse would be there for her. Whatever happened. Wherever it happened. He was portable. A blessed miracle.

During the past year or so, Hilly had conquered all but shoe tying, as regarded his personal toilette. He could bathe himself and wash his hair. He was, as well, intensely neat about his person and belongings.

"I told the sales girl all this, and I said it loud so anybody could hear." Dropping in on Nell on an autumn afternoon, Eudora plucked off her gloves and declined the offer of tea. "People ought to know the progress our foremost hero is making."

Disregarding Eudora's words, Nell clutched her friend's hands as if she, Nell, were drowning. And indeed she felt as if she were.

Eudora looked startled.

"I think I'm marrying John."

Elvira wrote:

Dear Nell,

We have been busy here. Dr. Kerchel passed away of a stroke in November. He was like a granddad to my Mary Cora, so we are all in mourning.

I had a strange experience three nights ago, Nell. Maybe it was because of the doctor dying. I had gone to bed and fallen asleep. Then I woke up because I heard Mrs. Kerchel's daughter Camille go downstairs for warm milk.

After Camille came back up to bed, I was lying

awake and thinking about Christmas presents for Mary Cora. We will still have Christmas, even if it's not so jolly this year.

Anyway, I was lying there and then my bedroom door opened, slow the way you'd open a door if you were afraid of startling someone. The light was dim, but I could see it was a man. He was wearing one of those creamy-colored suits with a vest and a watch chain across the vest and a little gold ship hanging from the chain. And he was holding a Panama hat.

He stood for the longest time inside the door. His face was sad. And now I knew who he was. Someone who'd never hurt a soul. So I waited. Finally, I said, "Be happy, dear."

He nodded and said, "I'm sorry."

I said, "You mustn't be."

Write and tell me you don't think I'm crazy, Nell.

Please give Hilly my love and let me know how things are with you.

Your loving Elvira

Nell had long ago guessed the identity of Elvira's lover, and the photo of Mary Cora had confirmed her surmisal. Now, she wept at the sadness of it all.

Dear Elvira,

I was sorry to learn of Dr. Kerchel's death. One can never really repair the hole left by the death of someone dear. Each blessed soul is unique, so how could we possibly replace it?

We are told that death is a punishment for original sin. What a monstrous trick for God to play on his children. I would never place a temptation in the path of my child, then punish him for being weak. All that I write on this topic is heresy, but it is true heresy, from my heart.

I don't suppose, at this distance, that there's anything I can do to lighten anyone's grief, but should something occur to you, please let me know. I will order you a copy of My Man Jeeves, and hope that it brings you a little cheer. Mr. Wodehouse has been my salvation. In the meantime, I'll drop a note to Mrs. Kerchel, sending condolences and thanking her for all she and her husband have done for you and your darling girl.

You spoke of being visited by a sad ghost. I would never think you were crazy because of that. Throughout her life, my dear Mam has been visited by the ghost of her childhood sweetheart, who was drowned in a fishing accident. Mam said that his visits consoled her. And I hope you will be consoled by your visit. This man must care deeply to make the trip from The Elysian Fields. Isn't that a lovely sounding place?

Am I a mystic? Mam always said that sort of thing was in the Irish blood. It's probably in everyone's, if they gave it a chance. I'm afraid religion has tried to put the kibosh on it.

As I look over this letter, Elvira, I discover what a heretic I am! And yet I go to Mass. Why is that? Because I am a teacher and might otherwise lose my position? If that isn't hypocrisy, I don't know what is.

Well, enough of heresy and hypocrisy.

Hilly makes slow but sure progress. He is able to stay at home by himself while I am at school. He remains unable to tie his shoes, which vexes him greatly. But, thanks to Eudora and Juliet, he is reading. Mostly The Rover Boys *and such. Each bit of progress is an enormous victory.*

My dear, would you do me a favor? Now and then, send a picture postcard to Hilly. He goes out rarely, and he loves correspondence.

A year from now, you may have to send the cards to Washington. It looks as if there might be a summer wedding. Just family and a few close friends—could you and Mary Cora make it back? No date is set. More later.

We still miss you here.

> *With much love,*
> *Nell*

chapter forty-four ☙

IN THE SPRING OF 1921, John's daughter-in-law, Mathilda, was hospitalized with diphtheria. For a month she lay close to death. During chunks of the spring and the convalescent summer, John was in St. Paul, helping in whatever way he could.

The wedding was postponed. The fabric Nell had purchased she stored in her bureau along with the dress pattern. Nell told Juliet and Eudora, "Maybe a delay is for the best." Her friends shook their heads. But Nell had seen how upset Hilly was over a change as minor as a new stove.

Old Gus Rabel bought Nell an electric stove for the kitchen and had the Acme carted away. The removal of the old behemoth required three strong men and some dismantling. As the men hefted the torso across the living room, grunting and huffing, Hilly followed, weeping and rubbing bits of the nickel trim with the sash of his robe. When the stove was gone, he stood in the kitchen caressing the sooty wall.

Nell understood. Anything so elephantine and dependable, so much a part of their lives for so long, was not easily dismissed. Yet she, the Luddite, rejoiced in the convenience of the electric stove and in the new little woodstove in the living room, meant to supplement the grudging heat from the hot-air register.

In August, John returned from his son's home in St. Paul, exhausted and ready to spend long days at the cabin. On the screened porch, Nell set aside the colander of string beans and listened as he read to Hilly from *Eight Cousins*.

Since the day, roughly a year ago, when she'd fallen into the Void of Yes, an unlooked-for contentment had stolen into her—stolen so imperceptibly and over so many months that one day she was startled by its presence and had to examine it from many angles until she could credit that, yes, she was indeed contented—even happy—with the idea of marrying John.

And she would win additional family for Hilly. Her own faraway Wisconsin family had had little presence in his life. John's son and his wife would furnish Hilly with cousins or . . . or whatever the relationships would be.

She took up the colander and resumed snapping the ends and pulling the strings from the beans. What could be more conventional or agreeable than these thoughts, and this household moment?

John had grown jowled, and his color spoke of high blood pressure, to which he paid no mind. Well, he was sixty-one and he'd driven himself hard since that first run for the state legislature. When they were married, Nell would tackle the blood pressure. He needed months—no, years—of afternoons like this one.

At the end of the day, really, John needed a wife, as he'd said—one who'd sit with him, de-stringing beans perhaps. She glanced up. What an amazing couple they were going to make. What amazing lovers.

Late September, still warm. They were seated at the picnic table. Luggage packed, John was boarding the eastbound train the next day.

Nell rose and began gathering up their lunch plates. "Would either of you like another slice of cake?"

Hilly shook his head.

John said, "Sit for a minute, darlin'."

Oh, dear, Nell thought, what's this? Was he was having second thoughts?

Looking first at her, then Hilly, John told them, "This is my last term in Congress. It's been grand, but I'm tired. Mark your calendar for Saturday, June 24, 1922. That's the day you'll be my blushing bride. Whad'ya say?"

"If I'm not blushing, will you still have me?"

Returning home the next afternoon, Nell changed out of her school clothes and into a cotton housedress laundered until its wild roses had lost their blush. From the top drawer of her bureau, she withdrew a fresh handkerchief, stuffing it into her pocket. Beneath this hanky lay the one Elvira had left behind in her hurried leave-taking. And, here, rolled away to the corner of the drawer, was the apricot pit. She held it to her face. Did she only imagine that it retained a little of its original scent?

What tales that train and the apricot had held: dark

ones—ghosts and violence and unsolved mysteries—but sunshine stories as well. Now she was living a sunshine story, the one about the happy bride that the sun shines on. She closed the drawer and two-stepped from the room.

chapter forty-five

NELL GENUFLECTED AND SQUEEZED into a back pew. St. Boniface was overflowing, a crowd beginning to gather in the vestibule and on the steps outside.

Nell wore her gray bombazine and an old black hat to which she'd attached a piece of veiling.

John was dead. He had collapsed in his Washington office, preparing for his return home.

The night before, he had called Nell at Juliet's, and they'd discussed the wedding. The Lundeens were holding the reception in their backyard. Nell's dress hung in the closet, ready. "Hilly has rehearsed giving me away a hundred times," she'd laughed. "We go over to the church every afternoon and march up and down."

John's hurriedly embalmed body was sent by train for the Friday wake and today's High Mass. In the front pew, his son, Paul, and Paul's wife and children were gathered; behind them sat dignitaries from the state capital and Washington.

The previous evening, Nell had accompanied Juliet and Laurence to the wake at John's house. Moving up the front walk, Nell had balked. *I won't go in.*

Laurence held the door.

Here was the front porch where they'd sat murmuring in the dark, watching Harvester turn out its lights and put itself to bed. And there, through the door and to the left, was the dining-room table where they'd outbid each other, slapped cards down on the oak, laughing carelessly, as if the games would never end. From the walls came John's voice: "My God, good woman, I think I'll bid seven diamonds!"

John's intensity, his brio, were worn into the carpets and wallpaper, the stair treads and furnishings. Some houses were meant to be destroyed when their owners died.

At the entrance to the parlor, Nell hesitated once more. Laurence grasped her elbow. Across the room was the open casket.

"Would you rather not?" Juliet asked in a low voice.

Nell negotiated the crowd. She could believe the stories of women throwing themselves on their husband's coffins or into their graves. She lifted John's hand and kissed the knuckles, then turned and allowed Juliet to lead her away.

She must pay respects to John's family.

In the dining room, his daughter-in-law, Mathilda, lay a hand on Nell's arm, saying, "Farmers started showing up with food around 6:00—hams and fried chickens, roast beef, legs of lamb and side dishes, dozens of them." How else to say goodbye to their fellow farmer, friend, Congressional representative, and, often as not, their lawyer? Townswomen had been up early baking pies and cakes—three times as much food as could be consumed.

"If there's a memento you'd like, Nell, please feel free,"

Mathilda told her. "John once spoke of your fondness for the epergne on the sideboard." Mathilda mispronounced the word, and Nell loved her for it.

"No. The epergne should be yours." This was a wildly improbable nightmare, and she was carrying on a wildly improbable conversation inside it. "It's too lovely for my little place. But the playing cards . . . if you wouldn't mind."

In the kitchen, eyeing their own mortality askance, men leaned against the counters, drinking, smoking, recalling John with raised voices and laughter—"You wouldn't believe it, but . . . Hell of a guy . . . Remember the time . . ."

Now, in St. Boniface, Nell was overpowered by the stench of incense. Her head throbbed and buzzed, shutting out the words of an out-of-town bishop. Nor did she hear Father Gerrold's eulogy—nor receive Communion—nor even realize the service had concluded until people began shuffling into the aisle. As she descended the outside steps, clinging to the concrete balustrade, Juliet caught her arm. "Come with us in the car."

She followed dumbly, managing to stay on her feet as the pallbearers lowered John into the ground beside his long-dead wife. She consented then to be drawn away and driven home. Larry, who had looked after Hilly for the day, left Nell's apartment with his grandparents, headed to John's house for the post-burial reception.

When at last Hilly and Nell had each gone to bed, Nell heard her son rocking and moaning in his sleep. Later, he screamed, "John, it's a bomb!"

Nell herself was too exhausted to sleep. Her eyes burned, her head and throat ached. Her body was cramped and arthritic the way a body grows when, for long hours, it hardens against reality.

Blindly she reached for the book: "There was Jeeves, standing behind me, full of zeal. In this matter of shimmering into rooms, the chappie is rummy to a degree. You're sitting in the old armchair, thinking of this and that, and then suddenly you look up, and there he is. He moves from point to point with as little uproar as a jelly-fish . . ."

How could she laugh—but she did. Long ago, Mr. Wodehouse had promised.

Monday morning, with a robe tied tight around her waist and her hair hanging loose, Nell opened the door to knocking, expecting Aunt Martha. Instead, John's partner Apollo Shane, wearing a black armband and removing his bowler, asked, "May I step in, Mrs. Stillman?"

"Of course." Perplexed, Nell stepped aside. "A cup of tea? I was about to pour myself one."

"That would be kind," he said, laying his hat on the side table.

"Milk and sugar?"

"If it's no trouble."

Spare and scholarly, Shane was a welcome figure. Devoted to John, he'd attended the wake, been a pallbearer for the funeral and burial, and probably turned up at the post-burial gathering as well. In the little that Nell had observed at the wake, he had reassured with a word here, and sympathized with a hand clasp there. Though roughly Nell's age—or even a bit younger—he possessed a grandfatherly quality of which he seemed unaware.

Setting a tray beside the bowler, Nell said, "Forgive my appearance. I took a sleeping powder last night, and I'm only just out of bed."

"I can come back later," Shane suggested.

"Please stay. Is it something to do with John?" She removed a handkerchief from the pocket of her robe and dabbed her eyes.

Shane stirred his tea. At length, he nodded. "You are free to discuss any or all of this with whom you will, but in the event you choose not to, my silence goes without saying."

Setting his cup aside, he delved into an inner pocket. Pulling out a folded manila envelope, thin string wrapped around the small button of closure, he continued, "This is not John's will. That's a separate matter. The bulk of his estate will go to his son, Paul, as you might imagine."

"Yes."

"This gift, because it is not part of the will and has already been in my keeping the past five years, will not be mentioned to the newspapers." He handed the packet to Nell. "If there's anything unclear, please call on me. That was part of my pledge to John."

"Did he expect his death?"

"He was prepared for it. His father died young of heart failure. John lived longer than he expected."

Nell wept. "I wish I had known."

"It was John's wish that you didn't. I'll see myself out." Finishing his tea, he said, "John was a grand fellow. None better. If there's anything I can do, please come to me."

Each act required more conscious thought and more mettle than Nell felt possessed of. So when she had closed

the door, she ignored the tea tray and the envelope, returning to the green chair. The atmosphere of death and loss
was too dense for even small gestures. Breathing was a
strain. She would rest until she had the strength to open
the envelope.

After half an hour, she lifted herself by the chair arms
and stood immobile for long moments before pushing
forward. What would Mam say? "Put one foot ahead of
the other, darlin'."

chapter forty-six ✒

When Nell had rinsed the teacups and saucers, she sat staring at the packet. Though she knew she had nothing to fear from it, she was loath to unwind the little string and lift out whatever lay folded inside.

Rising again, she washed her face, twisted her hair up, and pulled on a dress. She poured now-cold tea into a cup and sat once more. Hilly'd had a night of tears and violent dreams, but now he was stirring in his room. Better to read whatever was in the envelope immediately, lest he find her sobbing. She noted her name on the front in John's generous scrawl. Turning the packet over, she unwound the string, lifted the flap, and withdrew a letter of several pages.

Darling Nell,

If you are reading this, well, you know . . . But one thing you cannot *know is how much I hate leaving you. I have wanted to be here for you, always. Though I know that is wishful thinking, given my damned heart thing. I didn't share this with you because it might have caused you to make decisions in a way contrary to your own judgment.*

After the death of Gratia, Paul's mother, I was not especially eager to find another wife. Gratia and I had been happy; she had been a fine wife and an excellent mother. But I had not counted on the wonderment that lay ahead.

I think I knew from that evening in Juliet and Laurence's gazebo that I was in love. Was I terribly show-offy? I wanted so to impress you. But I was also stupidly nonchalant in those days, afraid of frightening you off. I regret the hours wasted that could have been spent . . . well, in bed. To put it frankly.

You were my heaven, so I won't complain unduly if I'm sent where doubtless many another cursing Irishman has been sent.

The Professor has been a second son and a great source of satisfaction. His safety was daily remembered in my prayers, darling girl.

And now—I must get down to business. If ever you need legal help or advice, you have only to ask Apollo Shane. He is at your service, gratis. Do not hesitate!

When you are ready, I want you to make an appointment to see Laurence in his capacity as bank president. I've put a little money in an account for you, all of which he alone has handled, for discretion's sake. So far as anyone else knows, this money will be a legacy from a distant relative.

In a safe-deposit box with your name on it are a few odds and ends of stock certificates. I'm afraid you won't be so wealthy that you can elope with the first penniless Lothario to kiss your scented hand, but I hope that these small provisions will create a pillow, a soft place to lay your head.

*With part of the money, you might think about buy-
ing a little house, a snug and comfortable place from
which you could thumb your nose at Gus Rabel, the
younger. Old Gus won't be around forever.*

*I send you a thousand embraces and a million kisses,
my own dear woman. Wherever I am, I love you.*

Your John

A separate note on different stationery said, *I'm enclosing the business card of Henry Skellings, a book dealer in
St. Paul. He will keep you informed of the latest master-
pieces from our Mr. Wodehouse. Order them!*

And now the tears flowed, but only briefly, for Hilly was
emerging from the bathroom. Nell returned the letter and
note to the envelope, shoving it between two Wodehouse
volumes in the living room.

She glanced up, then looked again.

Hilly was washed, shaved, and dressed. Though his shoe-
laces were not tied, he crossed the room with sudden dignity and laid a hand on Nell's shoulder.

"I'll get breakfast on," Nell told him, beginning to rise.

He motioned her to sit.

"Mah," he said. "Mother" was still too difficult.

"Mah." His brow creased with effort. "I look . . . after
you now."

The *Standard Ledger* dedicated a full interior page to
remembering John, with affectionate quotes scattered
throughout. Among them was one from Apollo Shane:

"John hadn't a petty thread in his fabric. He said to me,

'Shane, even the devil must have a genial streak—or else how'd he invent all these forbidden pleasures?' I spent an hour or two unraveling that, but I think he meant, 'By God, I love 'em all.' Chicken thief or saint—he'd put his shoulder to the wheel for you."

When Nell made her trip to the bank, Laurence met her, leading her to his office and closing the door. "Have a seat. Feels strange, doesn't it? I always feel like I'm acting in a play when I do business with a friend."

Nell nodded.

"Well, what this is about is the account John set up in your name. He deposited fifteen thousand dollars in it, five years ago. Of course, it's accrued a bit of interest since then." He handed her a passbook with her name on it.

She swallowed. "Fifteen thousand dollars?"

"He wanted you to have a cushion. Given the differences in your ages, it was prudent." He played with an inkwell.

"There's also a safe-deposit box," he continued, passing a key across his desk. "Mrs. Jeffers can get it out for you."

"Not today, please."

"Of course." He pushed the inkwell away. "Juliet and I understand what a nightmare this has been for you. And for Hilly. Remember, we're here."

It would be months before Nell unearthed the passbook from beneath a stack of towels in the linen cupboard. Each act of moving forward seemed a disloyalty. In not advancing, she kept John alive, as if he were in Washington.

But late at night, when Hilly was asleep, the sharp-edged fact of John's death cut through. In those hours, she huddled, legs drawn up, clutching herself, as if to present Fact with a smaller target. Then, finally, she would reach for Wodehouse.

Nell and Hilly spent that summer at John's cabin. "I don't know what we're going to do with it," Paul had told her. "You take it for now."

Not owning an automobile, Nell walked to town once a week to pick up groceries and the mail. A farmer down the road provided milk and eggs. Every Saturday, Juliet drove out, always bringing treats, starting with a quart of bootleg whiskey: "For medicinal purposes."

Nell felt close to John there, and Hilly was at ease. He swam, fished from the dock, and read, though he still preferred having Nell read *to* him. Did the printed words disorganize themselves in his head, she wondered, the way that spoken words did?

He stumbled over simple constructions. "Pass the milk, please" could emerge as "Milk . . . um . . . milk . . . please . . . um . . . pass." His difficulty angered him, and he took his feelings out on Nell. "Don't . . . tell . . . me! I . . . know!"

Late one afternoon, Nell rose from the glider and asked, "What would you like for supper? There's cold roast beef for sandwiches, or we could have sausages and beans."

"Sand . . . sand . . . rrr . . ."

"Roast beef?"

"No!" Hilly leapt up, fists clenched, and lunged toward Nell, turning at the last moment to fling a deck chair across the porch. A small table and pitcher of iced tea went flying.

Nell cowered. "Hillyard!"

Hilly ran outside, slamming the screen door and screaming unintelligibly. Hurling himself down at the picnic table,
he pounded the surface till ancient dust rose from the
pores.

"For God's sake, Hillyard, what are you doing?" Nell cried,
following him. But he moaned like a bludgeoned beast.

That night, still shaken, Nell sat staring at the moon on
the lake. *Dear heaven, John* . . . Well, it was no good crying
to John. Catching tears with the balled-up handkerchief
from her apron pocket, she shook her head with helpless
resignation and a sense of abandonment.

"Mah?" Hilly stood in the doorway.

"What is it, Hillyard?" She'd thought he was in bed.

"Sorry."

"Sit down."

He slumped onto a chair.

"We have to talk."

"Yeth."

"I was frightened this afternoon. Afraid of you. Afraid
of violence."

He puled low in his throat.

"It's a terrible thing to be afraid of your child. Something
inside feels like it's dying."

"Mah . . ."

"Let me talk, Hillyard."

"Yeth."

"Life is hard for you. You've been good, and you've
been patient, for four years. But today was bad. You cannot throw things. You could hurt someone. As it is, you
broke a pitcher."

"But, Mah . . ."

"I'm not finished, Hillyard. I know you don't want to hurt anyone. Or break things. When you feel very angry, what could you do instead?"

Hilly was silent, squirming. Was she causing him even greater frustration? But she waited. He had to understand that this was *his* problem to solve.

He rubbed his forehead and looked around as if an answer might be posted on the doorframe. Five minutes passed. Nell started to offer a suggestion, then bit the words back.

At length Hilly straightened, turning to her. "Har . . . har . . . mon . . . harmonica."

That was surely not what Nell had expected. But she closed her eyes with relief.

It was a warm day in September. Returning from school, Nell noticed one of Kolchak's trucks backed into the alley behind the meat market. Investigating, she found three men loading the old outhouse onto the truck bed. She groped to steady herself against the building.

When the outhouse was loaded, they began filling the hole from a great mound of dirt. She crossed herself and stared, unmoving, as each shovelful fell into the abyss. Finally, one of the men looked up. "Can we help you . . . ?"

Nell started. "I . . . no, no. There's no help." Puzzled, the men shrugged and continued shoveling.

chapter forty-seven ⌇

THAT AUTUMN OF 1922, another Democrat ran for John's congressional seat, a Dwight Bledsoe from St. Bridget. It angered Nell unreasonably; only John could do justice to that seat. She would feel guilty voting for this parvenu, Dwight Bledsoe, but reasoned that she could hardly neglect her newly acquired right to go to the polls.

By January of the next year, Nell had decided what to do with some of the legacy from John. First, she sent her mother a thousand dollars, with the caution not to let Paddy drink it up. "Mam," Nell wrote, "you'll know what's needed there." Her mother was not many years older than John would have been and described herself as "still on my feet, and dancing when I get the chance." She would parcel the money out with scrupulous economy.

Didn't Nell remember how her mother had educated her in all she thought crucial: house care, gardening (though that had came to naught), home remedies, manners and proper ways of doing things. When Nell's sister, Nora, had married, her mother had told Nell, "Now, Nell, girl, pay attention because you're goin' to need all this. When y've finished your high school, y've got to leave us. We can't afford you more." Weeping and slapping away the tears, her mother had embraced Nell. "We love you, but these acres won't support another grown body. As it is, I'm here on sufferance." Despite that the land had been Da's. And so Nell had left, and worked her way through teacher certification.

The second expenditure from John's money was pure luxury: a telephone. Refusing previously to be connected to the world by wire, she had caused her friends no end of inconvenience. If only I'd had a telephone when John was in Washington, she thought. If only.

When the phone was hung on the kitchen wall, Hilly gave it a wide berth, glancing the other way when he passed. Nell could have saved money by using a party line. But the extravagance of a private line so tickled her, it did seem worth the extra money.

The third outlay purchased an electric refrigerator. Old Gus Rabel was flustered. "Missus, I would have got you one," he said.

But he had already installed plumbing. The kitchen boasted running water; the bathroom owned a sink instead of a basin, a genuine enameled bathtub instead of a galvanized one, and a toilet with a water box above.

Sometimes, during an idle hour, Nell simply sat in the green chair and could not believe her comfort. *Thank you, John.* And then she fell into a black space.

It was indeed thanks to John that Nell and Hilly could afford to spend the next few summers in Mankato, where Nell worked toward her bachelor's degree at the State Teachers College, insurance against a loss of employment in Harvester. With Hilly to think of, she must be prudent.

Mankato was built on hills rising one above the other. Set in a valley of the Minnesota River, the lower part of town was breathless in hot weather, but the rooms they rented, in a house behind the campus, caught a bit of breeze from the west.

Here, where no one knew him, Hilly relaxed. But one evening Nell found him weeping. "You're sad?"

He nodded.

"Do you miss Harvester?"

"Professor," he said. "Call me Professor."

"John?"

He nodded. "Bomb." He threw his arms up in an explosive gesture.

"No." Nell put a hand over her breast. "A heart attack."

"Another thing people are hashing over," Aunt Martha said one day, as she retailed town gossip, "is how you can afford to trot off to Mankato for the summer and keep up your rent here? Flynn money, they figure." Eyeing Nell over the rim of her glasses, she added, "They're wondering how you earned *that.*"

But the bloated old woman was the color of dust, and Nell couldn't be bothered with anger.

Then, on a Saturday morning in November 1924, seventy-four-year-old Laurence Lundeen clutched his chest and dropped dead on the sidewalk outside Lundeen's Dry Goods. "He'd just told Howard Schroeder and me a joke," Anna Braun said later. "It's a good thing to die laughing."

"I was expecting this," Juliet told Nell that afternoon, sitting in the little library off her sitting room. "We're in trouble at the bank. Big losses." Juliet knew the Lundeen businesses nearly as well as Laurence had.

"The farmers?" Nell had read about the ones who'd invested heavily in equipment and land during the war. But postwar Europe wasn't buying their goods. Prices had fallen, and banks were folding.

Nell remained with Juliet the whole day, leaving only to prepare supper for Hilly. Eudora and Ed arrived at five, bearing Juliet's dinner. Eudora was wan with shock, Ed's color unnaturally high. Fine red veins laced his nose and cheeks, and he stumbled carrying dinner into the kitchen.

At Laurence's funeral, the minister read from the *Book of Common Prayer*: "In the midst of life we are in death." Oh, God, yes, Nell thought. And the longer we live, the more is it so.

Larry Lundeen, enrolled at St. Olaf College in Northfield but home for the funeral, wanted to leave school to help his grandmother.

"You're all I have," he told her. "Let me look after you."

"I won't hear of it," Juliet said. "If I don't have the businesses to worry me, I'll grieve myself to death." She patted his hand. "Besides, I'm tough as nails."

Nell's circle was reducing itself to widows and orphans. Before the month was out, Ed Barnstable, too, was gone.

"I'm feeling very old today," Eudora said one day as she, Nell, and Juliet slid into a booth at the Loon Cafe and ordered coffee and doughnuts. "I don't want to hear anything about liver pills, Mentholatum, or cascara—at least nothing more than is absolutely necessary."

"Well," Juliet said, "I have news."

"It had better be pleasant," Eudora told her.

Juliet stirred cream into her coffee. "I'm going to sell the house on Catalpa and build a new little place for myself."

"What on earth . . ." Eudora turned to face her friend.

"The house is too big and too full of memories. Right now, I can't indulge myself with memories. I have a bank to tend to."

"I think it's a wonderful idea," Nell said. "What you need now is something . . . *fun*, and what could be more fun than planning a new nest?"

"New" was a concept Eudora was not altogether comfortable with, but Nell's point was well taken and Eudora raised her cup in salute.

As they sat ordering coffee refills and a second round of doughnuts, they were perfectly aware that Harvester might look askance at recent widows being out in public enjoying themselves, but each woman had an increasing sense of Time with a capital T.

When Nell had seen Hilly to bed that evening, she sat reading *Jill the Reckless* by the light of the new floor lamp from Best Ever Furniture. Mr. Wodehouse's children were forever young, their days forever haloed in sunlight, their time forever Now. She prayed for more Now with her own friends.

chapter forty-eight 🖎

"Lucky Lindy" crossed the Atlantic in an aeroplane in May 1927. In August, Nell received a baccalaureate degree from Mankato State Teachers College. Though the two events were hardly equivalent, Nell allowed herself jubilation at her accomplishment but felt only apprehensive admiration for the flight. I'm one of the folks who happily continued making buggy whips after Ford came out with the Model T, she thought.

Before leaving Mankato, she browsed for an hour in a department store, selecting three new and daringly short dresses. From there she continued along Front Street to Lady Barbara's Beauty Salon. In the chair, she pulled the pins from her hair and said, "Give me a bob."

The hairdresser regarded her with doubt. "Are you sure?" She lifted Nell's thick, waist-length hair in her hands and peered in the mirror. "Last week, a woman was in here telling me that she dreams her hair is long again, and when she wakes up, she cries, wishing it back."

Nell shook her head. "Give me a bob."

As anticipated, the first note after her return to Harvester told her: "*you look like a whore.*" The writer had finally added the w, Nell noted, and tried to dismiss the message.

But the words robbed her of the buoyancy she'd felt hanging the three new dresses in the closet. *Damn you! Leave me my small pleasures.*

But the least change was usually cause for notice and speculation in a village. Had she met a man at college? Each day, Nell expected to hear Aunt Martha on the stairs, come to ferret out some truth. Instead, one afternoon, she opened the door to Agatha, Aunt Martha's dogsbody.

"Mrs. Stillman," the woman said, "I'm Agatha, your aunt's companion."

"Yes, come in."

Agatha was a woman with little to distinguish her, apart from a dime-sized brown mole on her chin. As she sat on the daybed, the springs squawked beneath her.

"It's old and cranky. Like Aunt Martha," Nell said. The other woman covered her smile with a cotton-gloved hand.

"What can I do for you?" Nell asked.

"Mrs. Stillman is down in bed, and I thought you oughta know."

"Has she seen Dr. Gray?"

"He says it's the dropsy. She has fluid around the heart." Agatha hesitated. "The two of you haven't always seen eye to eye, I think." She gave Nell a look of modest inquiry.

"Understatement," Nell said. "But of course I'll start coming by if you think she'd want it."

"She hasn't got a lot of friends. The sodality ladies come for half an hour, once a week. And Father Gerrold stops by. Not what you'd call entertainment." Again, the gloved hand to the mouth, as if she'd been naughty.

"Do you think she'd like me to read to her?"

Agatha considered. "If it was something light. She might enjoy that."

Over the fall and into winter, Nell called on Martha twice a week, initially bringing *The Inimitable Jeeves*. Happily, Martha found Wodehouse amusing, frequently laughing aloud. This could occasion a coughing spell but did not prevent her from waving a handkerchief and ordering Nell to continue. The wealth and aristocratic titles sprinkled throughout many of the books tickled Martha; in truth, she was not interested in the books chronicling the impecunious.

At the end of a visit in early December, Agatha told Nell, "Dr. Gray was here yesterday."

"What does he say?"

"Told me he doesn't expect her to last the winter. Her lungs are filling."

Nell pulled on her gloves. "I suspected."

"She hasn't had a happy life."

Nell paused.

"One night she was having a spell. Thought she was dying." Something in Agatha longed to be the keeper of Martha's story, the doler-out of it. Payment for thankless labor.

"She started talking. What you might call reminiscing. Said she hadn't been happy since she was a girl. Married the wrong man. She was sweet on his brother but was afraid he wasn't going to ask her, so she went ahead and accepted . . ."

Agatha glanced over her shoulder as if Martha might wander down the stairs. ". . . Bernard. Then, after she'd married him, she found out t'other one'd bought her a ring.

"Nearly did away with herself, she said. Would've if she hadn't been Catholic."

"I never knew Bernard had a brother," Nell said.

"Over t' Wisconsin."

On New Year's Eve, Nell was attending a card party at the Grays but dropped in at Martha's first. The old woman drifted in and out of awareness but seemed to be getting the gist as Nell read from *My Man Jeeves*.

"'Jeeves,' I said. It was next day, and I was back in the old flat, lying in the old armchair, with my feet upon the good old table. I had just come from seeing dear old Rocky off to his country cottage, and an hour before he had seen his aunt off to whatever hamlet it was that she was the curse of. . . .'"

"Nell," Martha interrupted, "where do we go when we die?"

Nell had not expected this question, not from her aunt. "I think we go where we long to be."

A watery cough racked the aunt. "And can we be young?"

"We can be what we want to be."

The old woman died the next day. The following week Apollo Shane phoned. "There's a small bequest for you in Mrs. Bernard Stillman's will, Nell."

"Martha barely tolerated me."

"Well," he laughed, "it's only five hundred dollars."

The bulk of Martha's estate went to St. Boniface Catholic Church for a new organ, a new kitchen, a new roof for the parsonage, and new concrete steps and balustrade.

Martha might not know where she was headed, but she wasn't taking any chances.

Martha's house, however, went to Agatha, along with two thousand dollars and the Ford. As John would say, "I'll be damned."

chapter forty-nine

AGATHA M. NIGHTINGALE—her full name—took possession of Aunt Martha's house in a passionate swoop, renting out rooms to two schoolteachers and commandeering Martha's bedroom with no qualms about sleeping in a deathbed.

After years of taking orders, Agatha finally knew ownership and independence. But since two thousand dollars would not last a lifetime, Agatha had plans.

"Mrs. Stillman," she said to Nell one day, "I've taken it into my head to write something about your . . . about Martha."

"Surely not a tribute."

"More like a short story. About her life and, you know, the one that got away. Of course I'd give her a fictitious name, but I'd tell the story pretty much as she told it to me. Kind of a deathbed revelation."

"And you would write this for . . . ?" Nell studied her surprising guest.

"Well, maybe for a ladies' magazine? Except, my English could use some help. I'd need someone to, you know, correct it."

"Editing." Yet Nell had noted an improvement in Agatha's

English just since Martha's death. With her new life, Agatha was sloughing traits acquired for her former role, including that simpery habit of covering her smiles.

"And if I sold the story, why, I'd pay the person who edited it some kind of percentage. What do you think . . . ten percent?"

"Well, it would depend on how much work the piece needed. If it were a great deal, I think fifteen percent would be fairer."

"Hmmm. Yes, I can see that." Agatha nodded, absorbing this. "But I wouldn't want anyone to know I needed help. I'd like to be the celebrity, you understand?"

"Entirely."

The long and short of it, as Bertie Wooster would say, was that Nell, no writer herself, agreed to edit the piece—if it ever saw the light of day, which seemed doubtful. But a week later, Agatha turned up with a dozen pages.

"I drove over to St. Bridget and bought a typewriter," she explained. "I don't guess magazines will want handwritten stories." She hesitated. "Should I come back tomorrow night, when you've had a chance to read it?"

Nell sat down with an inner groan to read "A Deathbed Tale," by Agatha M. Nightingale. Hardly deathless prose, raw and unschooled—but Agatha's story carried one along. And no one would identify Aunt Martha as a Chicago dowager of storied wealth living in a mansion on Lake Michigan. Nor Agatha, refashioned as the raven-haired, undervalued beauty, Bella Browning.

Editing Agatha's work turned out to be great fun. The story was shamelessly florid, with a good deal of velvet and satin, strings of diamonds and yards of pearls, but somehow that was its charm.

The next evening, Agatha announced, "I'm sending it to *The Woman's Home Journal*; what do you think?"

"Why not?"

Several weeks later, flushed and out of breath, Agatha appeared at Nell's door, arm braced against the jamb.

"*Woman's Home Journal* bought the story!" she wheezed, clutching her side. "Four hundred dollars! And they want to know if I have more." And after years of yes-ma'aming doctors' wives and bankers' wives and the Aunt Marthas of this world, indeed Agatha had *plenty* more.

Her *Woman's Home Journal* debut was front-page news in the *Standard Ledger*, complete with a photo from Eversol's Photographic Studio (retouched to eliminate the brown chin mole)—all under the headline "In Our Midst, a Celebrity."

For the next year, nearly every issue of the *Journal* boasted "A New Story from Agatha M. Nightingale." Agatha signed a two-year contract with an option to renew— nobody was going to steal Miss Nightingale away!

Nell could hear John laughing. *You women are the cat's pajamas.*

Agatha's stories survived even the stock-market crash of 1929. In fact, their absurd escapism made them more popular than ever. So, while Harvester teachers took a ten percent pay cut during hard times, Nell's fifteen per- cent editor's fee cushioned the blow.

Meanwhile, Agatha blossomed in the role of Prominent Authoress. By 1930 she was sporting a Tyrolean hat and had taken to tweeds and a walking stick. When people tittered as she sailed out of Lundeens', she took it as a tribute. To leave a wake was her fondest desire.

"Her stuff's pure drivel," Eudora said on the telephone, "but I admire her spirit. Look at the way she took hold of her life! It's an example to all women. If only I were that resourceful."

This was Eudora's first reference to an insolvency Nell had begun to suspect. Meanwhile, young Ed Barnstable was attending the University of Minnesota, and, to his mother's horror, taking a degree in veterinary science. Still, Nell thought, he and his mother might be comfortable yet—he could make a decent living in this farm community, provided President Hoover lifted the nation out of its economic morass.

Nell also worried about Juliet, who was guiding the Lundeen enterprises. At seventy-three, she was showing the strain of foreclosures.

When Nell stopped at the bank after school one Wednesday, Juliet emerged from her office, hailing, "The very person! You've saved me a call." She removed her glasses and rubbed her eyelids. "I'm taking you and Eudora to lunch at the St. Bridget Hotel Saturday. And I won't take no for an answer."

Noting the bruise-color half-circles under Juliet's eyes, Nell agreed.

Seated in the hotel dining room, the three women spread linen napkins across their laps and sipped ice water from stemmed glasses. The genius of the dining room was that

it changed so little from decade to decade: the oil portraits, candle sconces, and the liveried waiters were just as
they had been when John treated Hilly and young Larry to
dinner.

"Juliet, you look dreadful," Eudora said.

"You've lost weight yourself," Juliet countered, smiling. She set her handbag on the floor. "I'm tired of being a
banker. I have a heavy stone in my stomach, and it's called
'Foreclosure.'

"But it's nothing compared with what those people are
going through," she added. "Can you imagine watching
everything you've worked for being auctioned off at ten
cents on the dollar? The pain, the mortification?"

In 1933 Larry Lundeen packed up the life he'd built in
New York and the watercolors with which he'd eked out
survival. It was time to join his grandmother, who would
never grow old, but *had* grown exhausted. Three months
later, Juliet was dead.

After the funeral, Dr. Gray confessed to Eudora, "The
stroke was a blessing. She was full of intestinal cancer."

"And its name was Foreclosure," Eudora said.

Following the service, Nell walked home from the Methodist
Church, turning down an invitation to stop at Eudora's for
a glass of sherry. Eudora nodded. They'd talk another day.
Now they each needed to think about this particular loss.

Female confidantes like Juliet—women whose moral
judgments went beyond the conventional—were not thick
on the ground. Juliet had never judged Nell for loving John
outside marriage and had never scorned Elvira for her

pregnancy. It was Juliet and Laurence who had come to Nell after Herbert's death, almost literally saving her life.

Nell wondered now, as she had for some time: should she have told Juliet that there was a grandchild in California? But it hadn't been her story to tell, and Elvira had withheld it.

At the apartment, Hilly waited for her. He was reading *The Railway Children*, a book Juliet had given him. The spine was broken, the pages smeared with heaven knew what, some of them dimpled where tears had wet them.

Removing her hat and gloves, Nell told him, "I think I'll lie down a while before supper." She was physically exhausted by Juliet's death. As she lay staring at the wall-papered ceiling, she found in its random white-on-white pattern portals through which she could escape and often did. *On this afternoon, one of the portals—there, to the left—led her down a busy city street and into a park where she sat enjoying a Wodehouse novel. With the distant tolling of Big Ben, she recognized the city for London.*

A man inquired, "May I?" before joining her on the bench. "I find the park pleasantest at this twilight hour. What is it the French call it? L'heure bleu." His manner was such that Nell decided he was not a masher—merely friendly.

She closed the book. "Yes. I like the way the trees turn black as the sun silhouettes them."

"You're reading Very Good, Jeeves. *Are you enjoying it?"*

"You might as well ask a child if she enjoys ice cream. I'm madly in love with Jeeves. If I ever met him, I'd chase him till he said yes."

The gentleman chuckled. "I'm happy to hear it."

"I think I own every book Mr. Wodehouse has written."

"I say."

"I give his books to friends who're sick, or sick at heart. They're medicine."

"I can't let you go on. I'm embarrassed. I should have introduced myself. My name is Wodehouse. . . ."

Juliet had willed everything to Larry except the house on Second Avenue. That she gave to the village for a library, along with an endowment for a decade's upkeep and salary for a librarian—Eudora Barnstable. As usual, Juliet had acted while Providence dithered.

chapter fifty ℘

AT FIFTY-SEVEN, Nell felt orphaned. It was the price one paid for having older friends. They went their way; you remained in place.

Nell, Eudora, and the Grays were the tattered remnants of a hundred card parties, New Year's Eves, and long afternoons at the lake. Dr. Gray was taking partial retirement, inviting in a new man, Dr. White. Gray to White, Nell mused. The old order passeth.

One afternoon Nell set aside her reading glasses and Agatha's latest novella, *One Night's Indiscretion*—soon to be serialized. She glanced at Hilly as he lay curled on the daybed listening to the farm report.

How curious Hilly had been when Nell had first purchased the radio. But when phantom voices issued from the big box, he scuttled away. Later, he inched back, sitting across the room from the great mystery but staring at his shoes. If you looked away, it probably wouldn't explode.

One evening he heard an announcer he was convinced was John. "Jawn," he shouted, leaping from the daybed.

Another voice was Cora. Ghost voices came to soothe

and entertain him. Radio was now his boon companion while Nell was at school.

On a brisk morning in early March of 1934, Hilly finally mastered the art of shoe tying. For fifteen years he had persevered; now he'd show the town he wasn't an idiot.

Nell, who'd been at school, heard about the ensuing scene later. She knew from witnesses that he'd stripped to his underwear, gathered up his clothes, and rushed downstairs, to show the customers in the meat market how adept he was at dressing himself.

Once inside the front door, he threw down his clothing and began, piece by piece, to put it on, carefully buttoning his shirt and explaining, in his indecipherable excitement, what he was doing. Two women shrieked and ran into the street.

"Idiot! Get out of here!" young Gus Rabel screamed at Hilly and came around the counter, wielding a meat cleaver. Hilly cowered, frightened, recalling some past trouble with this person. But he'd waited all these years and he was going to do what he'd come to do. A nice lady, sitting on a bench waiting for her salami, smiled at him and told Gus: "He gave his mind for his country. What about you?"

"I'll use a gun next time he comes down here," young Gus vowed.

Mrs. Reverend Norton, clinging to the meat case, had also stayed, and walked Hilly upstairs. "I made him a cup of tea," she told Nell that afternoon. "I hope that was all right. He only drank a few sips, then he went straight to bed."

When Nell learned from Mrs. Norton what had

happened, she wept, knowing what a setback this would prove. Like Hilly, she retreated to the bedroom. Indeed, it would be two years before Hilly next left the apartment.

Lying prone upon the gently sagging old bed, she located once more the portal leading her to a recurring dream, this one of taking tea with Mr. Wodehouse and his wife, Ethel, the three of them seated in lawn chairs in what the Wodehouses called "the garden," as in "come into the garden."

From year to year, the dream varied only slightly. For instance, in 1934 she was wearing her summer challis, strewn with watercolor flowers.

Nell had just read Brinkley Manor *when, in the day dream, she wrote Wodehouse, asking if she might stop in at Low Wood in Le Touquet, France, to pay her regards. Wodehouse and his wife, Ethel, replied with a kind invitation.*

Of shipboard life, Nell spent little time imagining. She had seen two or three movies filmed on liners, so she proceeded directly to the moment in Le Touquet when her hero, savior, and literary companion—Plum, as he was familiarly known—swung open the door to Low Wood, welcoming her.

He was as always, perhaps more so each time. Neither strikingly handsome, nor plain featured. He was as he was meant to be: awfully pleasant to look at, with eyes full of wisdom and humor, though perhaps not of practicality. A man, she thought, who required a woman, like Ethel, with his best interests at heart.

They reposed in the Wodehouses' French garden, the afternoon warm without being oppressive. A slight breeze carried the scent of roses and something else—perhaps cinnamon. The three of them giggled over an anecdote Mr. Wodehouse had related concerning a Broadway crony.

Ah, my, yes . . . she was conversing with Mr. Wodehouse, and she was not at all self-conscious. A thrill of disbelief at her good fortune raised gooseflesh on Nell's arms. Trembling, she gathered her cotton shawl around her.

"Let me fetch a jumper," Ethel said.

"No, no. Please, I'm fine." With her tea napkin, Nell dabbed lemon curd from the corner of her mouth.

"Bring us up to date," Wodehouse said, shaking crumbs from his napkin. "How are things in Harvester?"

"Bad. Dry and hot. Crops stunted, prices low. But, worst, my dear Juliet, a pillar of our little world, Hilly's and mine, has died." She told them of the stone that had been cancer.

"Hilly," she continued, "well, he progresses, but not without difficulties." Now she relayed the humiliating scene in Rabel's.

For long moments Wodehouse considered, then said, "Well, now, let's look at it this way . . . I picture your boy holding up each article of clothing as if to say, 'And for my next trick—ta-da!—I will don these socks, one at a time! Note closely how deftly I screw them 'round, just so, toes first—these lovely socks knitted for me especial by my close personal friend the Countess of Brackingham."

This was how his magic worked. As she listened, the unyielding shard in Nell's breast, left there by Juliet's death, began breaking into smaller, more manageable pieces.

Later that March, Eudora Barnstable recruited volunteers to carry boxes of books from the Water and Power

Company to the new Juliet Lundeen Memorial Library on Second Avenue, catty-corner from the school. Awaiting these were one hundred boxes of new books, ordered by Larry Lundeen.

In June, Larry threw wide the library doors for a grand opening. A buffet of sandwiches and sweets, coffee and beer, lay ready. Everything his grandmother would have ordered, Prohibition having ended at last.

Larry and young Ed Barnstable each contributed a few words. "This is the work my mother was born to," Barnstable said of Eudora. "But, remember, Mama, you can't *order* people to read 'good' books." The knowing crowd laughed and filled their plates.

The *Standard Ledger* noted the presence of Ed Barnstable's bride of eighteen months. Blonde Brenda, who was beginning to show her pregnancy, was the off-spring of a lesser Minneapolis milling family. "Certainly not a Pillsbury," Eudora told Nell.

Eudora had hoped for a daughter-in-law as deep and true as Cora Lundeen. No such luck. Brenda was, alas, *arriviste*. Brenda and Ed had moved in with Eudora, which was fine, since Ed was establishing his veterinary practice. He had converted the old barn—once home to a horse and carriage—into his offices.

But Eudora's house was too old fashioned for Brenda, who preferred Deco. "So uncluttered." She was forever picking up Eudora's books and periodicals and stacking them into piles, so that Eudora found herself searching several tables in the parlor and hall to find that *thing* she had been reading about the Spanish-American War.

"She ordered Deco for their bedroom," Eudora explained, playing bridge with Barbara Gray, Nell, and Ivy, little Mrs. Apollo Shane. "And I suppose that's all right. It is *their* bedroom after all, and her family paid for the furniture. We stored my parents' mahogany in the attic."

"Does she pitch in around the house?" Barbara Gray asked.

"She manicures her hands and pedicures her feet and plucks her eyebrows and reads *Vogue*—I promise you she has six shades of nail enamel. If she's in a particularly generous mood, she dries the dishes, though she hates to wash them on account of the nails. I bought her a pair of rubber gloves, but they don't seem to agree with her skin."

"Well, la-di-da," Barbara chirped, to the appreciation of the others. In a small town, a certain piquancy does not go amiss at the card table.

chapter fifty-one

"It's time we found some younger company," Nell said as Eudora date-stamped Willa Cather's *Shadows on the Rock* and handed it across the library desk.

"Ivy Shane is young. Youngish."

"She's forty. We're getting old and set in our ways."

"If you're thinking of my daughter-in-law, Brenda, don't. She wouldn't be caught dead with us old hens."

"All I'm saying is, working here in the library, you meet younger women. Keep your eye out."

"Younger women want to socialize with other younger women. It's only natural."

"I suppose you're right."

"Of course I'm right."

But Nell worried. If anything happened to Eudora, she would be an old woman alone—the last leaf. Well, not really *alone*; she had Hilly, thank God. But, apart from Eudora, the Grays were the last of the crowd.

No, she would keep her eye out.

The Sunday after she'd been to the library, Nell sat by herself scanning the congregation at St. Boniface. Hilly hadn't gone to Mass since he'd come home from the war. The new priest, Father Delias, stopped at the apartment occasionally to say hello and give Hilly Communion. In the pew ahead, Nell noticed a young woman with an impatient child three or four years old. Nell smiled at the girl, who was now trying to climb over the back of the pew to join her. The mother set the child down on her lap and shook her head. The father scowled.

After the service, congregants gathered on the church lawn to discuss spring planting, the weather, and the local baseball team. Nell spied the woman standing with her child. The husband had left, but the woman was searching as if hoping to see someone she knew.

"Hello," Nell said, approaching. "We haven't met. I'm Nell Stillman. I teach third grade up at the school."

"Nice to meet you. I'm Arlene Erhardt. We just moved here last month. My husband works at the depot. He has to be there when the freight comes in."

"Of course." Nell doubted there was a freight train at this hour on a Sunday, but never mind. "Welcome to Harvester. What a lovely child."

The girl buried her face in her mother's skirt.

"Where do you live?" Nell asked.

"There was this really big room in the depot that nobody was using," Arlene replied. "Gandy dancers and trainmen used to overnight there sometimes. I'm dividing it into three rooms for us. Rent free, so we can save up for a house."

"Well, you are clever!"

"This is my little girl, Lark. Lark, can you say hello?"

The girl shook her head.

"Well, Arlene, it's nice to see a fresh face. Let me give you my telephone number." Nell dug in her bag and found a pencil and a tiny notebook. "My son and I live above Rabel's Meat Market. As a newcomer, if you have any questions, just ring me."

At home, Nell carried her purse and hat to the bedroom, calling over her shoulder, "She had the sweetest little girl, Hilly. And guess what the child's name is? Lark. Isn't that pretty? And this woman—Arlene—said she knows another new couple in the parish with a little girl, too. The Wheelers."

Setting her rosary and prayer book on the bedside table, she sat on the bed, staring out at the honey-golden May light. If not for the war Hilly might be married and have a little girl of his own.

"Things are looking up, Hilly," she said, returning to the living room. "Pancakes for lunch?"

On the following Thursday evening, the telephone rang. At the sound, Nell said, "That's Arlene Erhardt, I know it."

"Mrs. Stillman? Arlene Erhardt. Do you know a girl who babysits? I've made another new friend, and she's asked me to sub at her bridge club Friday night. But Willie has to work."

"I'd be happy to babysit, but you're probably looking for someone who'd be regular." Nell looked up a number and passed it along. "But while I have you on the line: Can you come for a cup of tea and cookies Saturday afternoon? And bring Lark? About three o'clock?" No sense in wasting time.

"My son suffers from shell shock," Nell explained, pouring tea into three cups and handing one to Arlene. The second cup she placed beside Hilly, who sat in the green chair. The rocker was too tippy when he dealt with tea.

As the women chatted, the little girl opened a picture book she'd brought with her, set it on the table beside Hilly, then climbed with some difficulty onto his lap. Perplexed, Hilly glanced at his mother, but she was engaged. Unthreatened by so small a person, he decided to accept the situation.

Lark reached for the picture book, opened it, and began pointing to animals and children, naming them and peering at Hilly for assurance.

"Cow."

"C . . . ow."

"Cat."

"Cat."

When she had flipped to the last page, Lark returned to the beginning. Again, Hilly glanced at his mother.

"Cow."

"C . . . ow."

"Cat."

"Cat." Perhaps because she herself was still wrestling with construction, the child grasped Hilly's fractured words. When he named a cow, she nodded and helped him turn the page. In this way, they passed the half hour of their mothers' visit. Like playmates, Nell thought.

When they had read the picture book three times, Lark set it aside. Straightening her skirt and patting her Mama-made curls, she said, "Now I will tell you a story."

Hilly nodded. He liked stories. Maybe one day he'd tell this small person the story of Little Lord Fauntleroy.

"Well," Lark began slowly, her face pinched in concentration, "once upon a time there was a girl named Lark and she lived by the railroad tracks and she liked trains. She liked trains a *lot*. And one day she got on a train and . . ."—she struggled for a conclusion—". . . and she didn't come back." She threw up her hands with a flourish, shaking her head and repeating, "She didn't come back."

Hilly's face fell. "Naw," he pleaded, "come back. Come back, girl."

Lark twisted around to look into his face. "Oh, all right. I guess she came back."

chapter fifty-two ☙

EUDORA LEANED ACROSS THE LIBRARY DESK, pointing toward a woman asleep on the old leather sofa.

"She checked out *A Farewell to Arms* and began reading while her little girl was in the children's room. I noticed she was crying. In total silence. I didn't want to ask why."

"What about the girl?"

"Still in the children's room."

Nell turned, heading into the room behind her, where all manner of reading was crammed onto low shelves. Squat tables and small chairs were scattered around. But on the floor, under a window where morning sunlight poured in, a child with tiny black pigtails lay sleeping, her cheeks flushed from the heat.

"Hello there," Nell said, kneeling beside the child. "Did you find a book?"

The girl woke slowly, rubbing her eyes with small fists, then wiping the drool at the corner of her mouth with the hem of her dress. She shook her head at Nell's question.

"What's your name?"

"Sally."

"That's one of my favorite names. Shall we look for a book, Sally?"

The girl followed Nell to shelves crammed with picture books.

"Here's one about a family of bunnies."

Together, they chose three books, and Nell carried them to the desk. There the child turned, inquiring, "Mama?" Spying her mother, she ran to the sofa. "Mama!" She shook the woman's arm. "Mama!"

The woman roused with effort, finally peering at her watch. "Oh."

"Are you all right?" Nell asked.

"Oh, yes. I don't know why I fell asleep like that. I seem to do it a lot lately." The woman felt her face, but the tears had dried. Pulling out a handkerchief, she blew her nose. Then, noticing the child for the first time, she said, "Sally, are you all right?"

The child nodded.

"Do you live nearby?" Nell asked.

"Yes. Close."

"I was just leaving," Nell said. "We'll check out your books and then I'll walk you home. We can get acquainted." As the group left, Eudora gave Nell a knowing nod.

Stella Wheeler was the woman's name. "Isn't that a coincidence!" Nell exclaimed. "Mrs. Erhardt mentioned that you were new in town, and had a little girl nearly the same age as hers."

Lost deep in her own mind, the woman said nothing in return. Her attention seemed to flicker on and off, like a faulty bulb. She was beautiful, if disheveled and underweight—all neck and elbows. The glance of her huge hooded eyes retreated when she was questioned directly, as if she lacked answers. Repeatedly her hand went to her thick black hair, pulled back raggedly in a wrinkled bit of ribbon.

At the Wheelers' front stoop, Nell wrote her name and telephone number on a slip of paper, as she had for Arlene Erhardt. "Just in case. Maybe I can be helpful. I've taught school here forever."

Without glancing at it, Stella shoved the paper into the pocket of her dress.

"Do you ever shop at Rabel's Meat Market?" Nell asked. "My son and I live upstairs. Drop in sometime. Bring Sally."

As she turned away, she saw the child reach into her mother's pocket and remove the slip of paper, tucking it into her own dress. What was that about? Was she afraid her mother would forget about it?

The following Saturday, Nell found both Arlene Erhardt and Stella Wheeler at her door, along with the two little girls. Stella hung back, looking coerced. Nell thought Arlene was probably a force to be reckoned with. That might be just what Stella needed.

"Oh, come in. I'm so glad you took me up on my invitation. Have a seat. I'll pour iced tea."

"I brought cookies," Arlene said, handing a pasteboard saltine box to Nell.

"My, how lovely. Home-baked. And so many. I'll get a plate."

Returning with a tray, Nell said, "I bake so rarely, it's always a treat to have something homemade." She handed around cookies and tea. "I've never been much of a baker, I'm afraid. Mam had a way with all that . . . sometimes that can inhibit a girl, you know, being afraid of not coming up to standards."

"Oh, yes," Stella agreed with vehemence.

"And Mama doesn't have time," Sally added, glancing around to be certain they understood how busy her mother was.

"Now, then," Nell said, "I'm going to get the girls paper and crayons and, if they like, they can draw at the kitchen table or on the floor."

Lark ran to help, Sally following her.

When she had fetched the supplies, Nell called, "Hilly, dear, come meet some friends, and have tea and cookies." Turning to Stella, she explained again, "My son was injured in the war. Shell shock."

Stella said, "I'm so sorry." Mrs. Wheeler was distressed, not repelled. Here, Nell thought, was someone with no emotional carapace. What courage it must take to go out in public. She hoped the woman would feel safe here.

Hilly sat at the kitchen table with his own paper and crayons. From there, he could see the little girls on the living-room floor, and they could likewise see him. Now and then, Lark rose, climbing on a kitchen chair to see what Hilly had drawn.

"That?" she asked, pointing to a figure.

"Swan," he said, though the word was difficult. "Bird."

"Oh," she said, nodding and climbing down again.

"Wite," he called after her. White.

Sally was intent on her drawing, lips pulled tight against her teeth in concentration.

Hilly walked over and ventured to look. "That?"

"Mama."

"Doing?"

"Sleeping. Mama needs to sleep." As if he might not understand, she added, "Sleep is good."

"Yeth."

In the living room, Nell asked, "So, have you ladies joined sodality?"

"Not yet," Arlene said, glancing at Stella.

"Well, it isn't compulsory," Nell told her. "I myself rarely go, though it's fun when they put on the fall bazaar. I enjoy waiting tables and visiting with the farm families—I grew up on a small farm."

"We're both converts," Arlene explained. "We're afraid they'll expect us to be A-plus, if you understand—to prove we're worthy."

Nell laughed. "Oh, yes, I understand. And you're probably right. But I don't think I'm an A-plus Catholic either."

With Nell's laugh, the atmosphere lightened and the conversation turned to books. Both younger women proclaimed themselves avid readers, though Stella admitted, "I *was* a big reader. Lately, it's harder . . . to find the time."

Nell told them of her love affair with Mr. Wodehouse, how he bucked her up when she felt low. "What would I have done when Hilly came home from the war if I hadn't had Mr. Wodehouse?" She made a mental note to order *Lord Emsworth and Others* for Stella.

Arlene leaned toward Fitzgerald, herself. "Of course, I've only read a couple of things: *The Beautiful and the Damned* and *Tender Is the Night.*" She glanced quickly at Stella, but the quiet woman was immersed in her own thoughts. "Anyway, he seems kindly toward women. Sympathetic."

"I confess I haven't read him, but I will now." Nell rose to replenish the cookie plate. "Has either of you met Agatha Nightingale? She's a writer here in town. She writes . . . *romantic* stories, for *Woman's Home Journal.* I'll introduce you." It was gratifying to be able to trot out a celebrity to impress new friends.

Meanwhile, the little girls had picked up their paper and crayons and carried them to the kitchen table, displaying the pages for Hilly and explaining what they'd drawn.

"That?" Hilly asked, pointing to Lark's picture.

"Train. Depot. I live there."

"Train you live in?"

"No. Depot."

"Train I like." He didn't connect this conversation with Lark's earlier story of boarding one and not returning.

"Did you ever ride on a train?" Sally asked him.

He nodded. "Moon on water."

"Moon on water." Grown-up talk, they thought.

chapter fifty-three ☙

WHEN HER GUESTS HAD LEFT, Nell sat mulling over the visit, concerned about Stella and Sally. Stella was clearly unhappy, but it was more than simple unhappiness, and Nell felt she must tread lightly, for fear. Fear of what? Well, *there* was the problem; she wasn't certain. Kindness appeared the only safe approach.

And Sally. What of her? What was it like for her at home? Such a little bit of a thing, and yet taking on responsibility for her mother. The father, Nell understood, was on the road five days a week, selling office supplies and furniture. And, with millions out of work, probably happy to have a job.

That year of 1937 Hilly finally ventured into the world again, sometimes crossing Main Street to the post office. Now and then he found a postcard from Elvira, like the one she sent him of waves breaking on a Ventura beach. "Wish you were here to play in the surf," she'd written.

At first he'd been timid about leaving the apartment. The outside world frightened him—but Arlene Erhardt did not. She had stopped by late one afternoon in her husband Willie's pickup.

"Come for a drive with Lark and me," she told him.

And he had gone. He and Lark sat in the back, hanging onto the truck's sides and letting the breeze blow in their faces. He laughed the open-mouth chortle that caused him to drool, but no one cared—not Lark and not the open sky.

Later in the summer, he sometimes walked along Main Street, even entering a store if something in the window piqued his interest. This came to an end when customers complained that he frightened them: his sometimes wild and impatient speech; his gimpy, drunken walk. He was a man without self-control, they said. He might be a danger to women. Businesspeople couldn't afford to lose customers in hard times, so they shooed him out, not always kindly.

For a while he remained close to home, sitting in his room, watching people come and go, especially those entering and leaving the post office. Sometimes they carried letters or packages, even large cartons.

In September, he began to wait on the bench outside the post office, offering to carry packages. Some people shoved him aside; most passed him as if they neither saw nor heard. But a few, like Stella and Arlene, let him tote their mail to their homes. Occasionally they invited him in for cookies and milk—oatmeal cookies at Arlene's, Fig Newtons at Stella's. Once, Stella forgot he was there and disappeared, probably to sleep. And people—again, like Stella and Arlene—gave him a penny or two. These he handed over to Nell. He was, after all, the man of the house.

Agatha Nightingale, once a professional companion, now had a companion of her own—"a girl" who on occasion served dinner on the screened back porch. Agatha was regularly wined and dined by her magazine in New York, so Nell wasn't surprised to find that her friend had acquired a taste for scotch whiskey. Agatha wasn't shy about offering Nell a highball, either—and Nell did not refuse.

Agatha had known difficulty. She was a sympathetic soul and, despite the stories she wrote, could keep a secret. Nell felt comfortable confiding in her about Stella Wheeler.

"Oh, dear," Agatha said when Nell had finished. "I knew a Mrs. Sonnenberg, over in Fairmont." With her handkerchief Agatha wiped sweat from her glass. "I wish I could think of something helpful, Nell, something you could do, but Mrs. Sonnenberg ended up in the state hospital. Nobody understands these things."

"I can't let that happen to Stella. There's a little girl." Nell let the subject drop. She didn't want to hear more about the hopeless case of Mrs. Sonnenberg. Pulling up her socks, metaphorically speaking, she ventured, "I sense we're celebrating. Am I right?"

And, indeed, Agatha burst out—for Agatha owned only so much savoir faire—"I have a publisher!"

"You mean *Woman's Home Journal*?"

"No, no. A book publisher!"

"A book publisher!" Nell raised her glass. "To you and your book—*what* book?"

"Well, mainly it's the stories they've already printed in *Woman's Home Journal*. Guess the title!"

"I have no idea."

"*Maidens' Prayers*. Remember, that was the title of one of the early stories?"

"I remember."

"I'll still pay you for your work, like always. Do you still promise not to give me away?"

"Of course."

"Can I tempt you with another highball?"

"Please do."

Before Nell left, Agatha said, "I know you're worried about this Mrs. Wheeler. If I think of anything, I'll call you. Anyway, she may be an entirely different case from Mrs. Sonnenberg. Don't borrow trouble."

Was that what she was doing—borrowing trouble?

In Harvester, the excitement surrounding the publication of *Maidens' Prayers* was unrivaled by anything since the Armistice. Except for the usual malcontents, like Elsie Schroeder, the town could not have been happier. Wasn't Agatha a reflection of Harvester's sophistication?

Max Hardesty, the new publisher of the *Standard Ledger*, ran a long, lavishly illustrated interview with Agatha. In each of the photos, the authoress wore her tweeds and Tyrolean hat. The walking stick, with its silver sphinx head, merited its own short paragraph.

Naturally, the St. Bridget *Examiner* also gave her space, as did the Red Berry *Weekly News* and the Ula *Flyer*. But her real coup was a page-one story in the *Minneapolis Tribune*. The paper lauded her success as another example of Minnesota's literary repute, like that of F. Scott Fitzgerald and Sinclair Lewis.

In early December, the library hosted a gala party. Larry Lundeen and Eudora laid out a buffet of cold beef and chicken, Jell-O salads, and desserts. Half the town turned out. ("The half that can read," Eudora sniffed.)

Toasts were raised with coffee and teacups, and Agatha was called upon to speak. She forsook the tweeds on this occasion, appearing instead in a "handsome Burgundy wool two-piece with peplum," as the *Standard Ledger* would later recount.

Wearing pearls and small gold earrings, she was just as her audience wished—nicely turned out without being too flossy. She had come prepared with a short written response, which she and Nell had pulled together, thanking Larry for the lovely buffet and the townsfolk for being so supportive of her writing efforts.

"I am honored by your great kindness," she said, her eyes misting. "I was raised in poverty and never expected to be more than what I was, a hired girl at least, a paid companion at most.

"I would never have had the means to be anything else had it not been for the generosity of Mrs. Bernard Stillman. Since beginning my writing career, I have wondered often about the many young women who have dreams but no means. For this reason, the bulk of the proceeds from *Maidens' Prayers* will establish a yearly scholarship for a worthy young female graduate of Harvester High School."

In a village, nothing takes one further than sincere humility—or money. Applause and huzzahs greeted Agatha's remarks. This was celebrity.

Sales of *Maidens' Prayers* exceeded expectations and, true to her promise, Agatha paid Nell her fifteen percent.

Nell had proposed donating her fee to the fund as well, but Agatha put her foot down, pointing out Nell's obligations to Hilly.

"You're not getting any younger," she said with customary candor.

The secrecy surrounding Agatha's success lent a touch of romance to Nell's life. Without fancying herself a puppet master, she was tickled to play the role of indispensable private secretary. Her life seemed almost as intricately woven as one of Mr. Wodehouse's novels but, she admitted, without his delicious to-ing and fro-ing, mistaken identities, and cordons of nemeses lined up three deep to bar the road to perfect bliss.

chapter fifty-four ⌒

"Nell," Agatha began, her tone sober. She set her teacup aside. "I've run out of stories. This second book was my swan song."

"Maybe the well is temporarily dry," Nell suggested.

"No. I'm depleted. Really depleted. It's been nine years!"

"Not possible."

"Well, it's 1938—and we began in 1929. Nine years." Agatha's eyes wandered Nell's living room, gathering memories. "It was all a miracle. Especially working with you." She hesitated. "I'm leaving Harvester."

"Oh, dear. What's happened?"

Ignoring the question, Agatha said, "I feel bad deserting you. Will you be all right financially?"

"Goodness, yes. You're kind to worry."

"Maybe you should try your hand at stories."

"But I've led such a quiet life."

"Well, in any case . . . I told the magazine I'd run out of stories. And they said they actually need an editor to beat the bushes for other writers like me. Isn't that funny? I'll be Nell Stillman for someone *else.*"

At the door, she held Nell's hands. "And about that Mrs. Wheeler: I've been thinking, and I think she's more like Mrs. DeVane, over in Windom, who had a 'spell' for several years. She snapped right out of it one day and was her old self again. Nobody understands these things."

Kindly liar.

And then Agatha was off to New York. "I'll write," she promised, and she did, regularly, retailing the glamour of New York and publishing, as well as the plain hard work of it. "To tell the truth, Nell, it's harder than writing. Or almost. What I need is an editor to edit the editor!"

Agatha's departure wasn't quite like a death, but perhaps a little.

On a tolerably warm late-July morning, Nell and Hilly walked out to the Catholic cemetery. Beyond the gates, old Adolph Arndt was carrying a bucket of water to some plantings on a recent grave. Adolph was bent and nearly blind now, but since he'd retired from the Water and Power Company a decade or more ago, he'd taken up caring for the cemetery a few hours each day, and St. Boniface paid him a trifling for his labor.

"Adolph," Nell called as they approached. "It's Nell Stillman. How are you? I've come to visit graves."

Adolph nodded. "Yes, ma'am." He doffed an old cotton cap. "And your boy with you." Though Hilly was nearing forty, he was yet a boy to Adolph.

"I was hoping to catch you," Nell continued. "I hear you raise perennials beside the caretaker's shed. Do you sell them?"

"I do."

"What do you have?"

Adolph led the way toward the shed, calling behind him, "There's some compact spirea and peonies and mock orange. You take a look and see what you like. I'll wait till late afternoon to plant 'em. Easier on 'em that way."

"That will be fine."

When Nell had chosen and was walking away, Adolph hailed her. "Ma'am."

She turned.

"About that business with the school board. Back around o-five or six. I was wrong. I hope you don't hold it too much against me."

"You did what you thought was right."

"Maybe, but I never felt good about it."

"I'm glad you told me."

Well, the poison notes hadn't come from him.

Hilly waited beside his father's grave. "Flowers?"

"A mock-orange bush. It will smell like . . . the Elysian Fields. Adolph will plant it for us."

He nodded.

"Would you like to sit a while? When you were little, you thought it might be wrong to sit on a grave. I told you your father would be glad of the company." They lowered themselves and for several minutes were silent. Around them, the air buzzed and chirped and yet seemed still. Their everyday lives distant and a little unreal.

"Bird remember?"

"Bird?"

"Big."

"Oh. The *swan*. Of course."

"White."

"Yes." Nell paused. "Is there anything you'd like to tell your father?" she asked.

Hilly considered. "Again I'll come. The harmonica?"

"Good idea." She brushed grass from her skirt. "And will you play for John and Juliet and the others?"

"Yes. And Silly my friend."

"Silly your friend?"

"My friend ambulance."

"Your friend in the war."

Hilly spread his arms, taking in the cemetery. "Wish here."

"So you could play for him? Did you play for him in the war?"

At that, Hilly began weeping and threw his body face-down on Herbert's grave. Nell patted his back and, when he had calmed, offered him a handkerchief.

Hilly rose with difficulty and shuffled toward the north fence. Leaning against a splintering post, he studied the wheat fields lying between the cemetery and the tree-hidden lake, as though he might spy in the expanse something wish-fully sought.

At the end of May, Nell retired from thirty-seven years as Harvester's third-grade teacher. There was no fuss: a small party in the home-economics room; cake and coffee; the gift of a fountain pen.

Nell wasn't affronted or disappointed. These little things were the tradition, though they did lack something. Any-way, thirty-seven years of children, most of them endear-ing; of exams and lesson plans; of pride and despair; of memories—Imogene Weatherford standing tall and sing-ing "Take Me Out to the Ball Game" during a lightning storm in December; Henry Everson weeping when his family's farm was lost—these were the real gifts she took away.

Returning from the party, she stood before her bed-room mirror, changing her clothes. She was sixty-one; her hair, now ten years in a bob, was graying in streaks. At sixty-one she had things to plan.

Were it not for Hilly and his care, she wouldn't mind growing old. Between her small pension, the funds John had left, and Agatha's fifteen percent, she would manage. But would a nursing home accept Hilly when she was gone? Was there an old soldier's home in the county? Instead of simplifying, life grew more complicated as one approached the end.

On the bedside table lay *Heavy Weather*, an appropri-ate title for her mood, though of course Wodehouse never brought her low. Gathering up the book, she carried it to the green chair in the living room.

"When, some months before, the news had got about that the Hon. Galahad Threepwood, brother of the Earl of Emsworth and as sprightly an old gentleman as was ever thrown out of a Victorian music-hall, was engaged in writing the recollections of his colourful career as a man about town in the nineties, the shock to the many now highly respectable members of the governing classes who in their hot youth had shared it was severe."

With retirement would come more leisure for this blessed passion. Nell hoped she had left her charges with a love of reading, one of the few things they could count on in life. The years could rob them of friends and farms, of youth and health, but books would endure.

She eased deeper into the chair and turned the page.

chapter fifty-five

HILLY CARRIED HIS HARMONICA to the cemetery twice a week while the weather held. Sometimes Nell accompanied him; more often he went alone, the walk perhaps reminding him of those long-ago morning runs. Invariably he returned with a fresh serenity.

Adolph Arndt reported to Nell that Hilly first played the harmonica for friends in the Catholic cemetery—Herbert, John, and Grandpa Hapgood—then walked next door to play for Protestants—Juliet, Laurence, and the others. From the radio, Hilly had acquired new tunes, among them "Nice Work If You Can Get It" and "Lulu's Back in Town." But it was "Sweet Leilani" that especially tickled Adolph.

In mid-October Eudora suffered a mild stroke, leaving her right side and speech slightly impaired. She had to relinquish her library job and thus the pride of having her own pocket money. Worse, she and her daughter-in-law now lived cheek by jowl.

Nell came to visit almost daily, bringing gossip and fresh reading material. By the following spring, her friend was walking outdoors with a cane.

But Eudora's resentment of her situation did not abate.

Her body had betrayed her. And her son was a veterinarian, instead of a doctor or lawyer. But far worse, he was married to that shallow, pretentious "debutante." "If it weren't for my darling grandson, I'd put strychnine in her coffee."

Larry Lundeen filled in at the library until the Board could locate a replacement. As fortune would have it, Desiree Navarin, whose husband owned the filling station next to the depot, had a library degree and was glad to step in.

In the spring of 1939, the Saturday before Easter, Stella Wheeler ran over young Gus Rabel's dog, killing it. Not that she had meant to.

"The poor thing," Eudora said—speaking of Stella— "she showed up at our door with the dog in her arms. It must have weighed at least half what she does, and she'd carried it for blocks."

Nell adjusted the telephone receiver.

"Unfortunately," Eudora continued, "Brenda answered the door. She took one look at the dog and said, 'Dead as a beached mackerel.' I went to the back door and called Ed, but the damage was done. Mrs. Wheeler just went to pieces, said she'd never drive again."

"She's fragile."

"Everyone knows that dreadful dog chased cars," Eudora fumed. "He should have been hit years ago."

A few days later, Nell called on Stella Wheeler around eleven, when Sally would be at school. A copy of *Anne of Green Gables* she'd found at Bender's Second Hand was her excuse.

After knocking at both the front and back doors, she tried the knobs and found the back door unlocked. The kitchen was untidy though not unduly so, as if a child kept house there. Wandering into the dining room, Nell called, "Stella?" She repeated her cry several times at the foot of the stairs.

Above, someone stirred. "Yes?" Stella's voice was thick and fuzzy, just awakened from sleep. Minutes later, she appeared at the top of the stairs, tying the sash of her robe. "Mrs. Stillman," she said, suddenly alarmed. "Is it about the dog?"

"No."

"Please . . . sit down." Stella descended, combing a hand through hair oily and unwashed.

Nell sat in a wing chair. "I brought a copy of *Anne of Green Gables*," she said, setting the book on a side table. "I thought Sally might enjoy it."

Still standing and fussing with her sash, Stella nodded. Finally, she said, "I don't have coffee or . . . or . . ." She waved a hand toward the kitchen.

"I didn't come for coffee, dear, only to drop the book off. I'm sorry I woke you."

"I was very sleepy this morning. I need a lot of sleep."

"Maybe you need vitamins or cod-liver oil. Have you seen a doctor?"

Stella started as though she'd been struck. "No, no." She grew tearful.

Nell rose, crossing to embrace her, but Stella stepped back. "I'm all right. I just need sleep."

"Of course. I'll be going." Nell was afraid she might say

or do something to upset the poor creature further. "I'll be going," she said again, turning toward the front door.

The following afternoon, Nell had just started brewing tea when she heard cries on the outside stairs. Throwing the door open, she discovered Hilly, spittle flying from his open mouth, his shirt torn, his jacket and belt missing.

"What's happened? What is it?" He couldn't speak.

"Are you hurt?" She followed as he fled to his bedroom and huddled on the bed. "Tell me!"

Mewling, he shook his head and rocked like a child.

"Did someone beat you?"

He shook his head again.

Unconvinced, Nell dropped down beside him. "Let's put the quilt over you."

Rising, she murmured, "Hot tea. Plenty of sugar."

He'd surely been attacked, though there was no blood. Her first thought was young Gus Rabel. But only minutes earlier she'd heard Gus downstairs, laughing with a customer.

When she returned to Hilly's room, he was asleep with the sheet pulled over his head.

Was Hilly's attacker the person who wrote the notes?

Though it went against her soul, Nell wanted to take down the gun and shoot the devil in the foot. Let *him* hobble for the rest of his life.

There was little point in talking to Constable Wall. Hilly wouldn't discuss what had happened.

His cemetery trips ended.

chapter fifty-six

ONCE A MONTH, until it closed for the summer, the Majestic movie theater held a drawing called Bank Night. Following the evening's movie, ticket stubs were drawn and prizes awarded—a set of dishes, a three-piece suit, cash. The June drawing featured a grand prize of two hundred and fifty dollars and filled the house with folks still Depression-squeezed.

In June 1940, Arlene Erhardt won the 250-dollar grand prize, bought a secondhand Ford coupe, and began a typing service, tearing around the county helping businesses that couldn't afford an office girl. For two years, Lark had been telling the Stillmans how her mother was teaching herself to type on an old machine that the railway had thrown out. Well, here was good news!

Nell marveled. This was the sort of canny ambition she had admired in Agatha Nightingale. She thrilled to think of women getting out in the world, finding a way to *do* something. However, from Lark, Nell also learned that Willie Erhardt was not happy about the new arrangment.

Since Hilly no longer walked out to the cemetery, Arlene Erhardt took Lark and Hilly for a ride every week in the back of the old pickup, stopping later for cake or ice cream.

Lark always lugged one of her books along to read to Hilly. Though only seven, she read as well as most third graders. "Mama made flash cards for some of the words in the books," she explained one day, licking ice cream from the back of a spoon.

Hilly relaxed with Arlene and Lark, and Nell felt that he was more intelligible than any time since he'd come home from the war. Perhaps the return to normalcy was at last beginning. Even Arlene had noticed. "He's calmer," she said, "easier to understand."

But during the fall of that year, war dispatches from Europe grew increasingly dark—German planes were bombing London day and night. Nell tried to spare Hilly, turning off newscasts and hiding the newspaper, but he possessed an antenna tuned to the war. Gradually, he grew more remote, until he no longer joined the little girls when they visited.

Through the remainder of 1940 and most of 1941, his only entertainments were *Your Hit Parade* and his radio "stories"—*Just Plain Bill*, *Our Gal Sunday*, and others. He still heard the voices of dead friends coming to him from someplace beyond the grave. He refused even the rides in the pickup.

After Labor Day 1941, Lark and Sally Wheeler entered third grade. Once the school day had ended, they climbed the stairs to report to Nell. "I wish you were our teacher," Sally complained, tossing her books beside the door. "You taught third grade, didn't you?"

"I'm sure your teacher is every bit as good as I was. Probably better."

"But she doesn't know us like you do," Sally said.

She doesn't know that people call your mother a lunatic, Nell thought, and that children are teasing you.

Arlene had kept Nell abreast of Stella's condition, which was deteriorating. "One set or the other of the grandparents are there a good deal, helping out, particularly the Wheelers—they live just over in Worthington."

Today, a freckled ragamuffin accompanied Sally and Lark to tea, Beverly Ridza, who peppered her conversation with "Godsakes" and worse, while the other two girls rolled their eyes. In addition to colorful language, Beverly came with a hearty appetite, starting with the cookie plate. "Mmmm. These're good," she said of the store-bought arrowroots.

"Well, help yourself," Nell told her.

"Only don't take too many," Lark said. "We mustn't eat Mrs. Stillman out of house and home." The very voice of Arlene Erhardt.

Nell poured more hot water into the teapot, and they all had a second cup. Later, as the girls were gathering their belongings, Beverly asked, "C'n I come again?"

"Always," Nell told her, handing Lark her language workbook. Out on the stairs, Beverly shouted, "And she *meant* it!"

A day or two after, President Roosevelt rushed warships to Britain. That evening, Arlene showed up unannounced and without Lark.

"Does it mean war?" she asked. At the word "war," Hilly flung out of the room.

"My God, I'm sorry," Arlene apologized. "I wasn't thinking."

"Well, the news does sound bad," Nell said, shaking her head.

"Poor Stella called this afternoon. She's terrified that Donald might be called up. She's . . . I don't want to say it."

As in years past, Nell bought a small Christmas tree in late November, setting it up on a table in the living room. Normally, Hilly decorated the tree with pictures cut from magazines. This year, he hung back; *Life* and *Look* were full of war images. At Nell's insistence, he eventually cut out photos from an old calendar, including one of the President and Mrs. Roosevelt. He had always been much attached to the Roosevelts and to their small dog, whom he called Falala.

On a Saturday evening in early December, Nell asked, "Would you like me to read to you?"

Hilly shook his head.

"Shall we turn on the radio? It's almost time for *Your Hit Parade*." But no; he kissed her cheek and went to bed. Nell turned on the radio anyway, hoping the music reached him.

Following barmaid's Mass the next day, Nell reheated meat loaf and sliced it for sandwiches. She and Hilly were just sitting down at the table when the town whistle blew, blaring uninterrupted. What now?

At length she rose, wiped her hands on her apron, and crossed to the telephone. "Operator?"

"Turn on the radio, Mrs. Stillman."

". . . about seven this morning, Honolulu time," an alarmingly calm voice was saying. "I repeat, planes of the Japanese air force have bombed Pearl Harbor in the Hawaiian Islands early this morning. . . . The United States

has suffered heavy losses of men, ships, and airplanes. . . ."
Escaping, Hilly knocked over a chair.

He refused to leave his room, and lay cocooned in his quilt. In the late afternoon, Nell carried a tray of tea and toast to him, but he only turned to the wall. Setting the tray on the bureau, she sat beside his hunched body. The framed photo of Silly Benjamin lay beside the pillow.

"Sylvester's on your mind," Nell said.

Hilly nodded.

"I can only imagine what it's like—being in the war together. Not like any other friendship. But remember, Sylvester won't have to be in any more wars. And neither will you."

She placed a hand on his back, hoping to connect. He lay curled in a little boat that was pulling away from her shore.

In the early evening, he cried out from sleep, "Silly! Wait!"

Once more, she rubbed his back and felt his old shrapnel wound through the flannel. "They won't make you go to war, darling boy."

Sitting in Hilly's rocker, she stayed past midnight, then drew aside the curtains, noting huge, slowly descending snowflakes. Before heading to her room, she laid a hand on his cheek. "I'll keep you safe, and we'll be happy."

He grasped her hand. "Good night, Mama."

The gunshot woke her. At first, it was part of a dream, then it was real. She threw back the quilt. Hilly's room was empty.

He lay on the outside landing, blood splattered across the freshly fallen snow, the German revolver beside him.

chapter fifty-seven ♆

Her darling boy was gone, the boy she'd sworn to protect, the boy she loved more than all the world. Crooning and moaning, she held his body until someone came—she didn't know who—leading her inside and using the telephone, she thought, because others came and carried her boy away. Someone made tea. Sometime in the still-dark hours, sitting in the green chair, she fell into a deep sleep.

The next day, Father Delias answered the rectory door, ushering Nell into his office. Though Father Delias had in the past struck Nell as a warm, even a laughing man—unlike his predecessor, Father Gerrold—the rectory had a chill, impersonal feel. The walls were white, the woodwork dark and severe, with no Doric columns or deep cornices at the ceiling. Just a simple picture molding from which hung portraits of the Pope, an Archbishop, and the bishop of the local see, each vying to look more pious than the others.

Nell had heard from someone, maybe Anna Braun, that Father Delias had told his superiors that he'd just as soon spend his life at St. Boniface, if it was all the same to them. At the time, that had endeared him to Nell. Now, sitting across a wide mahogany desk from the priest, her hands knotted around the gloves in her lap, she felt herself a petitioner in the anteroom of a peculiarly cold hell.

"Even though Hilly was a decorated war hero," she said, "no high Mass. Just something simple."

"Nell, this is hard. I'm very sorry about Hilly. But he can't be buried from the Church," Father Delias said. "I hope you understand." He leaned toward her across his desk, hand extended.

She recoiled. "I *don't* understand. Hilly was a good boy."

"No question. But he was a suicide. It's tragic," he said with feeling, "but you'll have to make other arrangements."

Nell stood abruptly.

"If it were *my* decision . . . but I have my orders." The priest's smile was sympathetic but dismissive.

Nell left the rectory without another word, her remaining belief in "Mother Church" gone. No Mother would refuse to bury her son.

Early that morning, old Gus Rabel had cleared the deep, blood-soaked snow from the landing where Hilly had lain and from which two volunteer firemen had carried him away. Now, a thin film of snow floating in the air, left over from the previous night's fall, dusted the doorstep, where Nell found a familiar-looking envelope. How *could* they?

The flap was not sealed. "*I'm sorry*," the note read.

When Arlene Erhardt heard of the priest's refusal, she hurled a drinking glass across her kitchen. Then she drove from church to church, pounding on doors, inquiring whether the minister would bury Hilly. This Nell knew from Eudora. Neither of the two Lutherans would. Nor the Baptists. Nor the Presbyterian, whose flock met in a

Grange Hall in the country. "It wouldn't be proper." "It's not our place."

Finally, the ancient Reverend Norton of the Methodists, on the eve of his retirement, agreed to say a funeral service and bury Hilly in the Protestant cemetery. The ceremony was simple, attendance sparse, many unsure whether it was sinful to be present, though they were exquisitely curious. Nell's little crowd was faithful, however. Even the three little girls came, with all their parents—except for Willie Erhardt who, Lark revealed later, had insisted that showing up was a mortal sin.

To add mystery, in a back pew, wearing the uniform of the last war, was an officer, ruddy faced and with graying hair. No one knew him, and he slipped away after the burial without introducing himself.

At the end of the day, Nell sat in the chair Hilly had bought her, caressing its arms, and thinking again about death, his death, any death. Death was the great mystery. A current was turned off. Where did that vanished power go? Was it there, vibrating in the air around her like a musical instrument whose note is no longer audible but whose strings still hum soundlessly? Finally, she turned in, wondering what that godlike figure Jeeves would have to say about all of this.

In the days following the funeral, there was a to-do about what was proper, canonically speaking, regarding burial of a suicide, this especially among those clergymen who'd refused Arlene. But Eudora Barnstable wrote an impassioned letter to the *Standard Ledger* to scotch such nonsense, followed by others from Larry Lundeen,

Apollo Shane, and John Flynn's son, Paul. As time passed, a trickle of shame oozed into the heart of the community. "But only into the left ventricle," snapped Eudora.

On the Sunday morning following Hilly's burial, a hesitant knock called Nell to her door. To her surprise, Stella Wheeler stood there, rumpled and shivering, looking unsure, her face beseeching, as if she might be turned away.

She handed Nell a package of Fig Newtons.

Stella had been at Hilly's funeral, weeping with painful intensity, confirming Nell's belief that the damaged woman had felt a special kinship with Hilly. Leading her in, Nell pulled the rocker near the little stove. Tossing Stella's coat on the daybed, she told Stella, "Sit there and warm yourself. I'll make tea."

But no sooner were they settled with tea and Fig Newtons, Stella intensely ill at ease, than someone was pounding at the door: Lark Erhardt, out of breath, eyes frantic. What on earth? "If Papa comes, don't tell him I'm here."

"I won't." Nell took the child's coat and cap. "Give me your boots. I'll carry them to the kitchen."

Noticing Stella in the rocker, Lark drew back.

"You'll have tea and the lovely Fig Newtons Mrs. Wheeler brought," Nell said. "Would you like to sit in Hilly's room? You can watch the street from there. And if you'd like to lie down when you've had your tea, go right ahead."

Seated again in the living room, Nell noticed that Stella's cardigan was buttoned wrong and that she wore no stockings, despite the cold. Stella had begun weeping silently. "The world is wicked," she said, her voice phlegmy with tears. She was depleted, operating on nerve alone. In a voice breathless, hollow sounding, like someone whispering down an empty pipe, she said, "I need to tell you something."

"Take your time."

Stella laced and unlaced her fingers. "It's about Hilly. I should have told you when it happened . . . before Memorial Day. Last year." She wiped at her nose with a balled-up handkerchief. "I'd been at the cemetery, looking after graves. Donald's cousins.

"I was leaving . . . closing the gate. A car came down the road with men in it. . . ."

She pounded her knees with her fists.

"They were chasing Hilly. All . . . he had on . . . was his shirt."

Stella began to weep again.

"Go on, dear," Nell said, patting Stella's shoulder.

"Then they saw me and . . . and they speeded up. But I saw one man in the backseat. Axel Nelson from the hotel. I looked for Hilly. But he was gone. If I'd had a gun, I'd have killed those men."

"You mustn't think of killing. It was killing that broke Hilly's mind." Nell squared her shoulders. "Now, sip your tea."

A visible quiet crept over Stella once she'd been relieved of the story. Her hands were at rest, and she laid her head against the back of the rocker.

"All of Hilly's troubles are over now," Nell went on. "You rest for a while." She fetched a blanket, then carried Stella's cup to the kitchen. Poor, broken girl.

Later, Stella's husband—a gentle, beleaguered man—came for his wife. Still later, Arlene Erhardt arrived with pajamas for Lark, still asleep on Hilly's bed.

"Sit a minute," Nell said. "What happened today?"

"Lark refused to go to Mass because the priest wouldn't bury Hilly. Willie hit the roof and dragged her to church. She ran out. Of course Willie went looking for her. I don't know what he'd have done if he'd caught her."

Nell nodded. She'd long suspected that Willie Erhardt had a temper.

"And when she comes home tomorrow?"

"Let's hope he's cooled down by then."

"Bring her back here if there's a problem."

On Monday afternoon, Nell donned a hat, pulled on her coat and best gloves, and went out.

The Harvester Arms was a rambling old clapboard with a broad porch where rockers lined up in summer, like spinster ladies gathered for gossip. The empty lobby, past its prime, was still impressive. Worn Turkey carpets looking dusty and neglected covered an expanse of oak flooring; electrified chandeliers caught the winter light and lent rainbows to walls papered with flowers no longer in the first flush of their bloom.

Nell removed the gloves, snapping them against the palm of her left hand. From an office behind the desk, Axel Nelson strode forth. "Yes?"

He was maybe fifty, slightly stooped, with a rancorous twist to his mouth. He looked at her from under thick, graying brows.

"I'm Nell Stillman—Hilly Stillman's mother."

No reaction.

"Last spring, when Hilly was attacked near the cemetery, I told myself I would shoot the man, or men, who did it."

"What's that got to do with me?"

"Yesterday, a witness came to me. This person didn't know the two young men in the front seat of the car—but she recognized you."

Nelson put up a hand. "You don't want to go around telling lies about people, Mrs.... Stillman. They might take you to court."

"They might be sorry if they did."

"What do you want?"

"I thought what I wanted was to shoot you in the foot, so you'd hobble like my son," Nell said, looking him over slowly. "But I see that you're already a cripple."

With that, she turned, and with a modest flourish pulled on her best gloves.

chapter fifty-eight ↪

AFTER HILLY'S DEATH, Nell stopped playing cards. Games felt trivial; many things felt trivial. But not reading. Reading was a bridge carrying her across a chasm of pain to places where she could view the loss of Hilly from a distance.

Eventually, Eudora said, "Let us in," adding, "it's too much trouble digging up bridge-playing women to substitute." Nell laughed.

And Eudora was right. In their own way, the women were a tonic. They shared her loss and made her laugh. Their gossip did not go amiss.

Today, the foursome of Nell, Barbara Gray, Eudora, and Ivy Shane met in the Shane living room, discussing Harvester's latest scandal: Arlene Erhardt had left her husband and headed to California with her daughter and sister.

Barbara shook her head. "Oh, dear. This kind of thing just doesn't happen in Harvester." Absently scooping up her cards and arranging them, she went on, "And with a child. I call that wrong. A child needs two parents."

"My Hilly didn't have two parents," Nell pointed out.

"That's different. You were a widow."

"I don't know this Arlene Erhardt," Ivy said. "What's she like?"

"She was so good to Hilly and me."

"That's all we need to know," Eudora said. "One diamond."

Nell hadn't wanted to get into the Arlene thing at bridge club, but one afternoon on their way home from school, Lark and Beverly had stopped in, Lark to inform Nell that she, her mother, and her aunt were moving to California. Lark had been tearful and angry, hoping her mother might still change her mind. But, all the same, the girl was fairly certain she wouldn't. "What am I going to *do*," she wept. "I like it here and I know everybody. I will probably die of lonesomeness. I think I've heard of that. I think there was an article in *The Saturday Evening Post*."

Though Nell tried to comfort and reassure the child, Lark was beyond being comforted and reassured. Reassurances simply made light of her sorrow.

"But you'll write to us?" Nell asked. "We'll miss you."

Lark nodded. "And someday I'm going to run away from California and come back. You'll see."

Re-sorting her cards now, Ivy Shane asked, "Was the husband a brute?"

"Gambled, drank," Eudora said. "Two diamonds. And I think he hit her." Nell's hands palsied at the thought, her own memories forever fresh:

The night had been raw with a dry polar wind sweeping southeast out of Alberta. The sort of cold people described as too cold for snow. Yet there was snow underfoot as she descended. The wooden steps creaked with the cold, as though they might shatter into kindling.

Light shone in a small window at the back of the meat market. Gus was working late, maybe grinding meat for

the next morning's trade. Bent double, Nell shuffled ten-
tatively, holding tight to her belly as if she could shore up
something broken or prevent a wall from collapsing. Bert
had never used his fists before.

She thrust the memories aside. Here, in Ivy's home was
not the time or place to revisit all that.

"Neddy says the little girl is broken up," Eudora told
them. She looked askance at Nell as if she'd seen something
in her friend's face that caught her attention.

"Who's Neddy?" Barbara asked. "And could we review
the bidding, please?"

"My grandson. You've heard me talk about Neddy."

Nell recalled leading Arlene Erhardt in out of a brisk
day last January and thanking her for the tin of oatmeal
cookies. "How do you have time to bake?" Nell had asked.
She set the tin aside. "Give me your coat."

"I can't stay," Arlene had said, remaining on the mat by
the door. Beneath the coat the woman was still wearing an
apron, flour dusting the skirt.

"Lark tells me you're leaving for California."

"They say there're jobs out west. Even for women." She
looked feverish. "We'll need to find something right away,
my sister and I."

"You're a brave girl."

"Not so brave," she said with a weak smile. "Foolhardy,
maybe. But I had to get away." She looked at Nell. "You
understand, don't you?" Indeed.

The parting was tearful, Arlene clinging for a moment,
then hurrying down to the street.

"Write when you're settled," Nell called after her.

At the bridge table, Nell reviewed the bidding for Barbara. "Eudora bid one diamond; Ivy, one heart; I bid two diamonds. It's up to you." Barbara had grown vague in recent months, forgetting simple things.

At our age, Nell thought, we have to be twice as alert. Is there a stain on this dress? Are these books due at the library? Did I write Mam and Nora this week?

"Two no-trump," Barbara said. "No, wait a minute. . . ."

From the West, Lark wrote:

Dear Mrs. Stillman,

I am lonesome and I might die of it and I hate California. And my school. And most of the kids. They are not nice like my friends in Harvester. We live in Pacific Beach, in something called a housing project. It's pitiful looking.

I miss you and Hilly even though I know that Hilly isn't there. Thank you for sending the picture of Hilly in his uniform. He was very handsome. I liked coming to your house and having tea and cookies. Do you see Sally and Beverly?

When we get our school pictures taken, I will send you one. I hope that you are well.

Love,
Lark

A week after Lark's letter arrived, Sally Wheeler knocked on Nell's door. Her mother, she said, was in Mankato, where she'd had an operation; Sally couldn't remember what it was called. A grandmother was looking after the nine-year-old while her parents were away.

"I think they're going to put her in the nuthouse," the girl said, compressing her slender body into the smallest possible shape in an effort to disappear entirely.

"Why do you think that?"

"Because she's crazy. She cries all the time. She stays in the bedroom and doesn't come out. She doesn't take a bath unless I make her do it, and she hardly eats anything. Doesn't that sound crazy to you?"

"Well, I don't know."

"You're just being nice." Sally chewed a hangnail. "I think they took something out of her. I hope it was the crazy part."

Nell hugged her. "Your mother loves you. You know that, don't you?"

Sally shrugged. "Maybe. But what good does that do?"

Soon after Valentine's Day 1942, Eudora called. "They've committed Stella Wheeler to the state hospital."

It was less than two and a half months after Pearl Harbor, but already windows in town had begun boasting little white flags with stars in the center, signifying a son or husband fighting the war. If the star was gold, the man had been killed. For Nell, each gold star was Hilly's.

In Hilly's room the world map was still tacked to the wall. At first, Nell tried to keep up with the battles, but now she followed them at an emotional distance. Sparing oneself life's sharp corners was a prescriptive for sanity.

But she was worried about Mr. Wodehouse and hoped that he was not somewhere being bombed.

Then one day Eudora said, "Your Mr. Wodehouse is in

trouble with the British." In France, where the Wodehouses were living, they'd been taken prisoner by the Germans, who were treating them with kid gloves, keeping the couple in comfortable captivity. In high dudgeon, Eudora exclaimed, "Do you *believe* it?"

Apparently unaware of what was happening in the outside world—the internment of European Jews in concentration camps, for instance—Mr. Wodehouse had been prevailed upon to broadcast little messages home, about his treatment at the hands of a humane Germany. The English, nightly bombarded by the Nazis, took offense, as well they might.

"And he an Englishman!" Eudora fulminated, put out with Nell for not taking up the cudgel.

Nell thought long about the news. There must be an explanation. The gentle man who had created Uncle Fred and Jeeves was not one to collaborate with murderers. After all, she'd always assumed that Mr. Wodehouse was an innocent, sequestered in the sunlit world of the Drones Club and Blandings Castle. His work—some thirty-three volumes in her own little collection guaranteed her a witty companion for the remainder of her days. When she glanced at their spines, she was shamelessly proud and refused to feel otherwise. No, she would not abandon Mr. Wodehouse.

She only prayed that the Germans wouldn't take it into their heads to do away with him before he could be exonerated.

Mr. Wodehouse, she knew, had been born in 1881, five years after her. What a comfort it was that they were growing old together. She hoped she died before he did, so she'd never have to face a future without a new Wodehouse book.

Eudora shook her head whenever she eyed Nell's book-case; when Nell actually *wrote* to him, she threw a grand fit and didn't speak to her friend for a week.

P. O. Box 63
Harvester, Minnesota
U.S.A.

November 10, 1942

Dear Mr. Wodehouse,

I'm sending this in care of your publisher, hoping that by some miracle it finds you. I feel as if I were posting a letter to the moon.

My friend Eudora, who is a great Anglophile, tells me that you are in trouble in England because of your broadcasts from Germany. I write to assure you that I do not believe you are a collaborator. My companions— the Earl of Emsworth, Aunt Dahlia, and Jeeves (that wis-est of the wise)—assure me that Eudora is quite wrong. I am far more inclined to believe them than those who are carried away in a moment of hysteria.

Thanks to another old friend, I have, to date, thirty-three of your volumes, beginning with Love Among the Chickens. *Over the years my little world has shrunk, as little worlds are inclined to do. Among those lost was the friend who, year after year, delighted me with your books.*

However, that friend kindly provided funds and connected me with a bookseller so that I might be kept current. I remind that dealer to notify me the moment you publish each of your lifesaving works.

You may regard "lifesaving" as extravagant. I do not. When my son Hillyard was in France during the Great War, your books helped to sustain me. And when he came home from that war shattered, I could not have endured the nights of worry without your help.

In more recent days, Hillyard took his own life. Though my friends have been kind, escape from grief was rare. How would I have survived without your people carrying me away to Shropshire and holding my hand in the sunlight of that place? And Lord Emsworth's Empress—that delightful pig—well, she even moved me to laugh out loud.

So, you see, dear Mr. Wodehouse, no one will ever convince me that you have sided with the Nazi savages. As we say around here, you have been "buffaloed."

It is crucial that you go on saving lives and sanity, as you have mine. Hoping this will one day reach you, I remain a faithful and grateful friend.

Nell Stillman

"GODSAKES," BEVERLY RIDZA SAID, tossing her books down on the daybed, "that Mrs. Draper knows how to give homework." The newest addition to the grade-school faculty, Mrs. Draper was the widow of a sailor lost at Pearl Harbor. "Look at all this multiplication! And language. I hate language!"

"I don't," said Sally.

Fifth graders now, Beverly and Sally were learning the meaning of real schoolwork, of theme papers and serious long division. Nell looked forward to their visits. They filled the apartment with summer all year long. But she also wondered what attraction there could be in visiting an old widow woman.

For Beverly, it was probably the store-bought cookies and weak tea. Her mother's job cooking at the Loon Cafe didn't pay for many treats. Sally's motives, however, were less clear. Though she was virtually motherless, her father had given up his job on the road and was home full-time now, a baseball coach and history teacher at the high school. Doting grandparents on both sides were frequent visitors. So it wasn't for lack of love or food that she came around.

"What news do we hear from Lark in California?" Nell asked.

"Her mother bought a bunch of secondhand stuff from some guy in San Diego. He said if you put your hand on a piece of old furniture, it'll tell you stories. Lark's gonna try it." Beverly reached for another arrowroot.

"Wouldn't it be fun if she sent us the stories?" Nell said, turning to the other child. "Sally, give your mother my best when you write. A day doesn't pass when I don't think of her kindness to Hilly."

Sally finished off her tea. "I write," she said, "but she doesn't write back. Daddy says we mustn't expect it yet. I try not to . . . but isn't it a mother's job to write back?"

Harvester saw quite an exodus during the war years: young men, who were drafted as they came of age; and older men, 4-Fs, and some women, who left for jobs in defense plants. It was the dawning of something Nell found alarming, a pulling up of roots, an exchanging of one identity for another. Once close-knit, countless families were now scattered like chaff, never to reassemble. More and more, Nell treasured those friends still gathered around her.

They had met in the bank, and Eudora suggested coffee at the Loon Cafe. The Loon Cafe had not altered appreciably in its many years on Main Street. Four booths, a counter, and eight stools squeezed into inadequate space. In its decor was no hint of a loon or any other water fowl. It could as easily be the Raccoon Cafe or the House Cat Cafe. But it was the place one ducked into for a cup of coffee. Nell and Eudora slid into a booth, each recalling their meeting here with Juliet.

"It does make you wonder about God, doesn't it?" Eudora said. "All I could think was what if it were my son or my grandson Neddy?" Word had come that the new librarian's son had been killed in the South Pacific.

Nell stirred sugar into her cup and nodded. "As I grow old, I think about God a good deal, Eudora. And not with great favor."

"It's my opinion that we give God too much credit," said Eudora. "How old was this boy? Eighteen? Nineteen? What kind of godly thing is it to kill a nineteen-year-old boy?"

"Won't you take half my doughnut?"

"No, thank you. It'd rile my stomach."

"Will they want you back at the library while the mother's in mourning?"

"I doubt it. I'm too old." Eudora pushed a ketchup bottle back and forth. "I feel guilty about her."

"Why on earth?"

"I've held it against her for taking my job."

"You didn't show it."

"Inside, I was *loathing* her. Now you know how petty I am."

Nell laughed and placed half her doughnut on Eudora's saucer. "Confession is good for the stomach."

"Now Mr. Roosevelt's never gonna see the end of the war," Beverly grieved, once inside the apartment. "That's so unfair. Who's gonna look after us?" Weeping, Beverly and Sally had climbed Nell's stairs, seeking comfort.

Franklin Roosevelt was the only president they'd ever known, a second father. On the radio, the day after Pearl Harbor, it was Roosevelt who'd assured them that we would win the war, that they must have faith. And they did.

"Mr. Truman's the new president," Nell told the girls.

"I know, but what's gonna *happen*? Are the Japs gonna win now?" Beverly pressed.

"Heavens, no."

"This Truman guy looks kinda puny, don't you think?" Beverly observed.

On May 7, following Beverly's concerns, Germany surrendered. Folks danced in the streets of Harvester and lifted their glasses in Reagan's. And on August 15, President Truman announced the end of the war. In Harvester, the news arrived at 6:00 p.m.

Nell called Eudora. "When you've finished supper, come for a drink." When her friend appeared, a golden sunset was throwing a benediction over the town. The brick wall of Kolchak's Chevrolet and Oldsmobile glowed as if from within. "All I have is a bottle of scotch that Agatha Nightingale left here," Nell told her friend.

"I'm a sherry drinker myself," Eudora said, entering and producing a bottle from a knitting bag. "I was glad when you called," she continued, pouring sherry into a glass and sitting back in the rocker. "Neddy's at a friend's, and Ed and Brenda went over to the Legion Hall. Well, you know what a bacchanal that'll be. Too noisy for me."

"Maybe it's my age, but I didn't want to be in a crowd tonight," Nell said. "Life is hurtling by the way the last grains of sand in the hourglass seem to run out more quickly than the first."

"I know. It's too much, too fast. I keep thinking of the librarian—they say she's rocky, and Brenda says she's drinking. But that's my daughter-in-law for you." Eudora pursed her lips. "Ever the Pollyanna." She sipped sherry.

"And now we have to think about those poor people in Hiroshima and Nagasaki. So many innocents." Nell poured two fingers of scotch into a glass.

"Be careful who you say that to," Eudora warned. "I said something like that in Lundeen's, and another customer nearly took my head off. 'Those damned Japs?' she said, 'How can you feel sorry for them? Think of Pearl Harbor and all our boys that're dead.'"

"How would she feel if the bomb had dropped on us? And maybe some day it will." Nell studied her scotch against the light. "The atom thing isn't going away."

"Don't you wonder how the folks who invented it feel? All those souls simply *liquefied*, for God's sake. Mothers with babies in their arms, little boys on their way to school. One minute they're joking and the next minute, their atoms are floating off in that, whad'ya call it, that firestorm."

Nell shivered. "I'm glad Hilly's gone."

"Still, no more boys will die in this war," Eudora said, raising her glass.

"I'll drink to that."

The following day, one last grubby note waited for Nell at the post office. "*Good-bye.*" One learned that some mysteries are never resolved. Still, she'd been haunted by this unseen enemy for many years; in some ways she'd changed because of him or her. The poison pen had made her examine herself closely. She would not of course have hesitated in her affair with John—nor even in the bobbing of her hair—but in other ways she doubted the pen had intended, she'd found herself wanting and tried to improve. She'd learned to forgive "enemies," for example, imagining that they too suffered hidden torments. In coming to the end of the notes, she felt a peculiar sense of loss.

But the most surprising piece of mail addressed to Nell Stillman in 1945 was this:

Dear Nell,

Forgive my presumption in addressing you in this personal manner, however I feel that we are old friends.

Your letter's delay in reaching me, for reasons too complicated to retail—except to say that they involved a ship propelled by Pigmy oarsmen, a poste restante *operated by escapees from a home for the violently illiterate, a tropical storm, and a three-legged dog with a taste for proper English—was a great misfortune for myself. I have needed just such kind assurances.*

But, early or late, your letter is cherished.

My life's companion, Ethel, seated in the armchair nearest, wept when she read your words. My own vision dimmed, nor do I credit that it was due to the spotty electricity of our present accommodations.

Nell, I enclose a copy of Money in the Bank, *a paltry thanks. You write that my words on occasion have provided allayment from grief, but I truly hope that henceforth you will read them free of that need.*

Your servant,
P. G. Wodehouse

A first edition!—and it was signed, "To Nell, jewel among women, in whose debt shall always be found yours truly, P. G. (Plum to you) Wodehouse."

With the letter tucked inside, *Money in the Bank* was placed on a pretty doily atop the corner table, beside photos of Hilly, John, and Silly. The book felt like a trophy, though she had done little to earn one. Still, her breast heaved with expansive contentment whenever her eye fell upon it.

My darling Mr. Wodehouse, where should I be without you?

Eudora ignored the book entirely.

chapter sixty ⨏

NELL LOOKED DOWN AT STELLA WHEELER, dead of a ruptured appendix. Made up and hairstyled, Stella no longer resembled the distracted, disheveled, and undeniably beautiful woman Nell had known—the woman who, even in the depths of her unhappiness, had come to Nell to confess her grief over the attack on Hilly.

Nell spoke her condolences to Sally and to her father. Hearing the inadequacy of her own words, she winced, and went on to say, "Stella was good to my son. Many people weren't. But she understood him better than most. I wish I could thank her again for her kindness." Sally sat beside her father, staring at some distant place where all of this would be a memory. At thirteen, she had inherited her mother's beauty and maybe whatever went with it.

The room was crowded and overheated, and Nell left after speaking with Sally's grandparents. Stella's mother was talking nonsense, insisting that Stella had been nearly ready to resume a normal life. But how do you fault a woman who has lost her only child? Would it be presumptuous, Nell wondered, to send her a Wodehouse?

Much of the next two years passed with barely a murmur. Life was quiet and days evaporated. What would Nell remember of this time? She thought of Thomas Mann's *The Magic Mountain*, set in a tuberculosis sanatorium. Mann made the point that it is the year empty of event that in memory seems to have passed quickly, since it contains no mileposts of occurrence to give it substance. On the other hand, a year full of event seems longer in memory because of its many mileposts.

However, one thing Nell *would* remember from the spring of 1946, after Stella's death, was Sally blowing into the apartment, slamming the door behind her, and throwing herself on the daybed in a pose to do Sarah Bernhardt proud. At thirteen, she was coming into womanhood, growing into the person she would be: beautiful, theatrical, insecure, and vulnerable.

"Now what?" Nell asked as Sally tossed her arms about in a fit of frustration.

"Beverly's mother's getting married! Some yokel farmer named Elwood Hanson!"

"Well, good for her, if he's a decent man. Why should you care?"

"Because Beverly'll be stuck in the country."

"Is that so bad?"

"It's tragic. My God, she'll be out on that farm, a million miles from anywhere."

"I don't know what to tell you. I doubt that it's a million miles from Harvester but, in any case, let's wait and see."

Sally sprang up and paced the room, turning dramatically. "I say she's betrayed me." And that was that.

Sally did not soon forgive Beverly her mother's marriage. Life was full of betrayals: first, Stella; then, her best friend. And since angry girls do foolish things, Nell was not surprised when Beverly revealed that now-fourteen-year-old Sally had dated and then dismissed young Gus Rabel's son, Billy.

That particular threat blew over, however, according to Beverly. "When Sally saw how ignorant he was, she gave him his walking papers."

No longer quite the ragamuffin, Beverly had paused and sipped her tea. "Being a football hero wasn't enough when she found out he didn't even know who John Steinbeck was."

Nell suppressed a smile.

Beverly set her cup down. "'Course he was mad. Girls don't break up with him! He went around school telling everybody that Sally was *easy*, if you know what I mean."

Nell nodded

"Which she's not. At least, not yet."

"What does *that* mean? My word, she's just a child."

"Since her mother died, Sally's gotten, I don't know— reckless? She doesn't know where she's going, and she doesn't care. Something bad could happen to her, just because she's not paying attention. I'm afraid."

Nell would later remember Beverly's fear.

From a chair drawn up to her bedroom window, Nell watched the 1949 Harvester Days throng wander up and down Main Street, where the carnival was spread out. The sound of the calliope evoked memories of John, who had always been in town for the Harvester Days, shaking hands, asking questions, laughing and escorting Nell on the merry-go-round.

In front of Lundeen's Dry Goods stood Larry Lundeen in his vanilla-colored suit and Panama hat, elegant and cool despite the heat. How like his father he looked. Nell watched him nod and tip his hat to the librarian.

And there, waving and shouting to Nell, were her girls, steady Beverly and mercurial Sally, friends once more, summer tanned and lovely. Nell blew them kisses and they blew them back. Then they meandered toward the Ferris wheel, careening through the crowd, throwing off sparks.

Nell remained at the window, trying to keep Sally in her sight, feeling unreasoned anxiety. For several minutes she lost the girl in the crush, then spied her on the Ferris wheel with a boy, no one Nell recognized.

The sun was lowering behind the buildings on the west side of the street, and stars were breaking through the thin cloth of early evening. At length Nell drew her chair away, but left the curtain pulled aside so that any breeze stirring the thick August air would find its way into her bedroom.

In the twilit living room, she poured a finger of scotch over ice cubes and sat down among the shadows. How many years since John had died? Twenty-seven? She sat in the accumulating darkness, waiting for him. He came often. Perhaps tonight he'd assure her that she was unduly anxious about Sally.

A week or so later, the front page of the *Standard Ledger* featured an article about a new high-school faculty member: Drew Davis, a Minnesota native who had taught for five years in California, served a stint in sales, and was returning to the teaching profession and to his home state to enjoy "real winters" once more. Mr. Davis would be responsible for senior English, speech, and the class plays.

His photo was sophisticated, a studio portrait. With a strong chin, deep-set eyes, and a shock of what would turn out to be auburn hair, he appeared forty-five at the outside. Nell hoped he wouldn't be too disappointed by the town's lack of worldliness.

On the way to her after-school job at the soda fountain in Egger's Drug Store, Beverly pulled to the curb in the car she now drove to and from town.

Climbing out, she hailed Nell, who was leaving the grocery store. "Mrs. Stillman!" As Nell drew near, "You've got to meet the new English teacher, Mr. Davis. He's a book person, like you."

Nell followed Beverly into the drugstore, setting her bag of groceries on the marble counter of the soda fountain and climbing onto a swiveling stool. No mean feat at seventy-four. When Beverly had donned an apron, Nell ordered a Coke. "You're enjoying English?"

"He's the best teacher I've ever had. He gives the greatest assignments. For instance, we write funny skits in English class and then we act 'em out in speech class. Sally's really good at that stuff. But . . . well, never mind." Leaving something unsaid, Beverly hurried away to take orders.

Days later, Eudora phoned. "You're friends with that little Wheeler girl." At seventy-nine, Eudora regarded any woman under the age of fifty as "little" . . . whoever.

"Yes."

"Well, I for one am worried about her."

"How do you even know her?"

"My grandnephew Cole, from over in St. Bridget, has been taking her out."

"Is that bad?"

"For her. He's trouble, real trouble. I hate to say it about family, but Hal Barnstable and his wife, Denise, are monied trash. They've neglected Cole until he's ruined. He's a senior now, but in tenth grade, he got a girl pregnant. Tenth grade! Hal paid her family off. Tell Sally Wheeler that he's a bad lot."

But one who knows who John Steinbeck is.

Days later, confirmation of Eudora's worries came from Beverly at the drugstore. "This Cole guy is bad news."

"How so?"

"Well, Mr. Davis gave Sally the lead in the senior class play. And Cole told her to quit."

"Why would he do that?"

"Some sort of test. If she loves him, she'll quit. If she doesn't quit, well . . ."

"She's not going to quit, is she?"

"No. But that's the scary part. She's crazy about this bum, and now he's broken up with her. Remember how I said something bad could happen? I think he's it."

"Is it so awful, this boy breaking it off?"

"She thinks so. Plus . . ." Beverly lowered her voice. "I think he's nuts. I mean *really* nuts. I'm afraid he'll do something. . . ."

"Why would she go out with someone like that?"

"He's one of those crippled dogs you take home and try to fix. Then they end up giving you hydrophobia."

chapter sixty-one 🙢

NELL HAD NO IDEA HOW TO INTERVENE in Sally's problem. She couldn't say, "I've been hearing stories." Sally would
hike a shoulder and flounce away.

Meanwhile, Nell was curious about Drew Davis, the
teacher directing the girl in *Our Town*. So curious, she
decided to sneak into a rehearsal. Luckily, she still had a
key to the side door of the school.

The door opened into a dark passage leading to the
auditorium balcony. But where was the light switch? As
she inched along, at the far end of the hall, the balcony
door clicked open and a dim, hurrying figure brushed by,
nearly colliding with her full on.

After the outside door slammed, Nell stood still, her
heartbeat surprising her with its ferocity. When it calmed,
she crept into the balcony, sat down, and slipped out of
her coat. No one noticed her, as they doubtless had not
noticed the previous trespasser.

The rehearsal paused, while the director sprang to the
stage and spoke words Nell couldn't hear. He was motioning, giving a direction to Sally, who nodded.

As the action proceeded, he called to Sally, "Yes. That's it."

Drew Davis was dramatically attractive. Not handsome,

but compelling, his features intense. His voice was cultured, and Nell wondered whether his California years in "sales" had been spent trying for a movie career.

She remained for half an hour, admiring the sure, patient way he handled the cast. Sally shone as Emily, each line ringing true. And Eudora's grandson, Neddy, was as convincing as a teenager could be in the mature role of Stage Manager.

Returning home, Nell banked the fire in her little stove and prepared a cup of hot chocolate. Setting it on the bedside table, she began undressing, all the while pondering her fellow interloper.

Of course it *could* have been a curious parent—but surely a parent would have spoken when they'd actually touched her in passing.

On the first Sunday afternoon in April, with a temporary softening in the weather, Nell walked across town to return copies of the *Saturday Review of Literature* to Larry Lundeen. She hadn't called ahead; if he wasn't home, she'd leave them inside the storm door. But his Chrysler was in the drive, and when she rang the bell, he answered. "Nell. Come in, come in."

"I won't stay. I just wanted to return these," she said, handing him the magazines.

"Of course you'll stay." Tossing the magazines down on a bench, he helped Nell out of her coat.

"Oh, dear, you have company." Drew Davis was sitting by the fire, a glass in his hand. Setting it down, he rose.

"Please seat yourself, Mr. Davis. I'm Nell Stillman, and I feel as if we've already met."

Larry pointed her toward an Edwardian chair.

"I remember first admiring this chair nearly forty years ago, in your mother's living room on Catalpa," Nell said.

"This woman's got a mind like a steel trap," Larry told his friend. "Now, dear Nell, what can I get you? Scotch?"

"That would be lovely." Glancing around, she observed, not for the first time, "This room is perfect."

At a console table, Larry was pouring her drink. "Nearly everything in it—except for some of the paintings—belonged to Grandmother or Mother."

"I like that—the continuity."

Addressing Drew, Larry said, "My grandmother built this house after my grandfather died. Smaller than the one they shared." He handed Nell her drink and sat on the sofa opposite her and the teacher. "Cheers."

Nell raised her glass. "Do you still paint?" she asked.

"For my sins."

"I'm glad to hear it. Someday I'll buy one of your pieces."

"Someday I'll give you one. Someday soon."

"Mr. Davis," Nell said, turning to the teacher, "I have a confession to make. The other night I sneaked in to watch a rehearsal of *Our Town*."

"No need to confess," he said. "It's not against the law."

"Well, I had a reason." She sipped scotch. "I've been worried about Sally Wheeler." She glanced first at Drew, then at Larry. "This is strictly *entre nous*, you understand."

They nodded.

"Eudora Barnstable's grandnephew Cole has been seeing Sally since last summer. Eudora says he's poison and that I ought to warn the girl." Nell twisted the glass in her hands. "I wouldn't, of course. She'd hate an interfering 'auntie.'"

Drew leaned forward. "You remember, Larry, that I said I was concerned?"

"You said she sometimes looked like death warmed over."

"She's a beautiful girl, but she's been coming to class and rehearsal looking as if she hasn't slept for a month. She's lost weight. I suspected there was a boy, but I've never seen the guy around. I don't think it's anybody in her class."

"The boy's from St. Bridget," Nell offered.

"Aha."

"She pays attention at rehearsals?" Nell asked.

"Oh, yes. Best seventeen-year-old actress I've ever seen."

"I think acting is important to her."

"It's what she wants to do after graduation." Drew finished his drink, and Larry took the glass to refill. "Normally, I wouldn't encourage it; it's a tough world. But she might as well give it a try. A year at drama school. See how it goes."

"Her maternal grandparents would probably pay for that. The grandfather is a doctor in Mankato." Nell considered. "You know about Sally's mother? Stella?"

"Larry told me. Must've been hard on the kid."

"Harder than we can understand, I think. She's very vulnerable."

They chatted for another half hour. Nell was taken with this Drew Davis, but at length, she rose. "I have to be going. Larry, thanks for the use of your scotch. Mr. Davis . . ."

"Drew," he said, rising.

"Drew, I'm happy to meet you. I feel better after our talk. I know you'll keep an eye on Sally."

Larry fetched Nell's coat. "It was time the two of you met."

The bleary winter sun was setting when Nell opened the door to her apartment. The lamp in the corner of the living room had been turned on. Sally lay asleep on the sagging daybed, one thin forearm thrown across her eyes. This was the second time in a week that she'd come by, the second time she'd fallen asleep.

On the previous visit, as she rose from sleep, knuckling her eyes like a small child, Sally had leaned toward Nell and said with urgency, "You know how sometimes you love someone—" Nell thought, Here it comes, but Sally had continued, "Not lovey-dovey love, but the kind when a person makes you feel *important*? Mr. Davis makes me feel that way, and I love him, really love him. You understand, don't you?"

Now, as Nell stirred the embers in the stove and tossed in another chunk of wood, she thought, Let me protect this child. Fetching a quilt, she laid it over the girl, then sat nearby considering her inadequacy in saving children.

Picking up *The Code of the Woosters*, she settled into her armchair. Opening to a bookmarked page, she smiled. Bertie and Jeeves were cowering atop a chest of drawers and a cupboard, respectively: "The dog Bartholomew continued to gaze at me unwinkingly . . . I found myself noticing—and resenting—the superior, sanctimonious expression on his face . . . It seemed to me that the least you can expect on such an occasion is that the animal will meet you halfway and not drop salt into the wound by looking at you as if he were asking if you were saved."

"Mrs. Stillman!" Sally sat up, panicked. "What time is it?"

"5:30." Nell laid the book aside. "Should I call your father and let him know you're on the way?"

"Would you, please?" the girl asked, pulling on her coat. "I didn't mean to fall asleep. I didn't mean . . . Oh, God. What's wrong with me?"

chapter sixty-two ↣

LEAVING LARRY'S PRE-THEATER BUFFET, the chattering group stepped into an April evening as soft as cottonwood down. In the auditorium/gymnasium, Nell and Eudora chose seats together, near the front. Eudora kept blotting her upper lip: Neddy had so many lines to remember.

They hadn't long to wait before the lights dimmed, and the footlights shone on the curtain. Drew slipped out from behind it to welcome the crowd and explain that the play was written to be performed on a nearly bare stage. "I don't think you'll mind. In fact, I doubt you'll even notice after the first few minutes."

He went on to say what a pleasure it had been working with the cast and crews. "This community has welcomed me into its midst and rewarded me with the finest young people it's been my pleasure to work with."

Applause. Drew bowed, disappearing once more. Presently, the curtain slid apart and the play began.

After the final scene had played and the cast had taken its bows, Nell and Eudora discreetly dabbed their eyes. Clearing her throat, Eudora said, "Weren't they wonderful?"

The crowd had begun slipping into wraps when the

school intercom clicked on. A young male voice issued from the speakers on either side of the proscenium. "Attention. Attention."

What was this?—announcement of the forthcoming track meet? "Attention, ladies and gentlemen." Pause. "Before you leave, you should know that the director of tonight's performance, Mr. Drew Davis, is a fairy." Pause. "A homosexual, if you prefer. Mr. Davis was dismissed in 1944 by the school board of Clarkston, California, for his perversion. Thank you for your attention and good night." Click.

"Let's get out of here," Eudora said, snatching at Nell's sleeve and pressing through the crowd. In their breakneck exodus, they parted knots of men and women, heads bent together. Once outside, Eudora plunged across the lawn, weeping. "Nell, Nell, do you know who that speaker was?" Her face was tortured. "He was my grandnephew."

"Shouldn't you go to Neddy?"

"His father will. I can't bear to go back in there. I'm so ashamed." She sobbed as she ran. "Can we go to your place?"

In Nell's apartment, Eudora accepted a medicinal from Nell, whispering, "That poor man. What's to become of him?" She dropped into the rocker.

"And of Sally? She'll blame herself," Nell said. "The boy didn't want her to be in the play."

"Does Mr. Davis have any friends here?"

"Only Larry. And they may be more than friends," Nell said. "Oh, dear."

Eudora began rocking hard. "We'll have to circle the wagons," she said, setting her jaw. "Unfortunately, that won't help Mr. Davis. The school board is probably meeting right now. He'll be gone tomorrow." She broke down again, placing her glass on the side table and taking the fresh handkerchief Nell offered. "I'm so ashamed."

"It wasn't your fault."

"It was *my* grandnephew," the old woman said.

Still heaving sighs, the handkerchief lying in her lap, Eudora resumed sipping scotch. After a moment, she cleared her throat. "I've never told you this, but when I was a girl, back in Illinois, I had a dear cousin. Leonard. We grew up together, our houses across the street from one another.

"When Leonard went back east to college, we wrote each week. He told me about his close friend Carl. They'd been friends from the first day." She teared up again but soldiered on. "Then, when they were juniors . . . well, *something* happened. The college contacted my aunt and uncle about whatever it was. And, the next thing we knew . . . the next thing we knew, the boys had drowned. Both of them."

"I'm so sorry."

"Later—well, you know how towns talk—I guessed that the boys were 'that way.' But our families never spoke Leonard's name again. Can you imagine?" She breathed raggedly and dabbed her eyes. "One day a boy is kind and intelligent, a person any parent should be proud to call 'son.'" Shaking her head, she lifted a hand in a gesture of helplessness. "The next, his high-school graduation picture's gone from the top of the piano."

Nell poured another drop of scotch into Eudora's glass.

After a moment, she asked, "What can we do, *now*? About Mr. Davis?"

Lifting the glass, Eudora considered. At length she said, "We can ask him and Larry to lunch tomorrow, before Mr. Davis leaves town." Finishing off the scotch in a gulp, she wiped her glasses on the hem of her skirt. "I know it's feeble, Nell, but what can we do?"

"I'll have them here," Nell said, squirming with dissatisfaction. Lunch was scarcely better than nothing! Still, it was decided. Given short notice, perhaps it was all that two old women could do.

Later, Nell walked her friend home. At the gate, Eudora said, "I dread to go in. Brenda will be riding a high horse, and Neddy'll be heartbroken."

Nell took the woman's hand. "This was not your fault." But Eudora did not take matters lightly, and her conscience was implacable.

chapter sixty-three ❧

"YOU *MUST* EAT," Eudora said as the two men pulled out chairs at Nell's table. "If only to keep Nell and me from nagging." She passed a platter of fried chicken and a bowl of green beans.

After Drew had delivered his resignation that morning, Larry loaded his friend's belongings into a Lundeen's truck. Now the two sat bent under the weight of events. Larry's hand shook as he forked a piece of chicken from the platter.

"You will write us, I hope," Nell told Drew. "Your work here will have an afterlife. We'll want to tell you about it."

Eudora took up the baton. "Despite everything, the play was beautiful. You're very talented, but we're very inbred and self-satisfied . . . and fearful. And somehow *proud* of all that." She shuddered.

Once they'd had coffee, the men donned coats. "I'm taking Drew to St. Paul," Larry told the women. "Back tomorrow."

Drew shook hands. "This was kind of you. Don't worry. Life goes on."

Each woman put a hand to her mouth, unable to speak, as they watched the men descend to the street. Eating on the road might have been more convenient for the men, even less stressful, but a statement of sorts had to be made to the community. What that statement was, Nell and Eudora didn't know. But it was critical, just as, long ago, Leonard's photo should have remained on the piano.

The following Friday, old Anna Braun, who still managed the local telephone company, rang Nell's number. "I have sad news. That Mr. Davis."

"No."

"It'll be in tomorrow's Minneapolis paper. Drove a car into the Mississippi. Been drinking in Mendota, so it's anybody's guess what happened."

Nell took a breath. "Should I call Mrs. Barnstable?"

"Please."

A circle tightened around Larry Lundeen. Young Dr. and Mrs. White, the librarian, Apollo and Ivy Shane, Ed Barnstable, and Nell every week made up two tables of bridge with Larry. Most of the town, however, stepped around Larry, as if he were something unpleasant on the sidewalk.

On the street, his posture was dauntless, and he appeared to go about life much as he had. But those who knew him noted his head tilted oddly, as if he listened for a sound offstage.

The one most obviously affected by Drew's death, however, was Eudora, who stubbornly maintained responsibility. She was beginning to fail. She hadn't lost her fire; she was losing the strength to put it to use.

Nell called on her daily. They sat on Eudora's screened

back porch, these porches so much a tradition in Harvester, drinking iced tea, lemonade, or occasionally something stronger.

Eudora never failed to murmur, "I'm so ashamed." Nell never failed to assure her that none of it was her fault.

"But that murderous boy is kin," Eudora said one day. "And I haven't exposed him. And Mr. Davis is dead. It's cousin Leonard all over again."

"What good would it do to expose the boy?"

"Ed didn't recognize his voice, I'm sure, but Neddy did. He's in the same fix I'm in. Wants to do something, but doesn't know what." Eudora squeezed her lids tight and shook her head.

Another afternoon Nell asked, "Would you like to play double solitaire?"

"I haven't the patience for it, if you'll pardon the pun. I'd stamp my feet if they weren't so crippled."

Nearly three months had passed since *Our Town*. The July afternoon was sticky and hot, over ninety degrees, when Nell let herself into the Barnstable house and found her way to the back porch.

"What's this?" she asked, alarmed to find Eudora in a wheelchair.

"I fell. Nothing serious, but Ed's the original mother hen. Let's not talk about it. There's lemonade in the icebox."

Returning to the porch, Nell saw her friend wholly: Eudora's body was caving in upon itself. A frame that had never owned an ounce of extra flesh had now shriveled to twigs. The proud head and long neck that Nell had often envied and sometimes likened to a lily on a slim stalk were bent over till chin nearly touched breastbone, so Eudora was forced to look up from beneath fierce brows. All this in under three months?

"Does the heat bother you?" Nell asked.

"Not so much. I'm cooling down like an old star." Eudora considered. "I wonder what happens to old stars. Do they disappear in a whiff of smoke? Sounds good to me."

"Don't talk silly," Nell said, setting Eudora's glass on a low wicker table. Choosing the porch swing for herself, she shared village gossip. "Looks as if Diana Hapgood and old Dr. Gray may be an item. I say, 'Old Dr. Gray', but is he really so much older than me? Funny how we think everyone's grown old but ourselves."

"But isn't Barbara still alive?"

"She's in the nursing home in St. Bridget. It's a sticky wicket for Charlie and Diana, as my dear Mr. Wodehouse might say."

"Well, I say 'Gather ye rosebuds.'"

They both laughed.

As she was leaving, Nell ran into Neddy, climbing the front steps.

"Mrs. Stillman. Got a minute?"

"Of course."

"Have you seen Sally lately?"

"Not since graduation. She didn't look well."

"She's a wreck."

"Mr. Davis?"

The boy nodded. "She's taken the blame."

My frail girl, Nell thought.

"She weighs about ninety pounds. Looks like a wild woman. She's cleaned her house, cellar to attic, probably a dozen times, and now she's started on the yard. She's killing herself."

"What can we do?"

"I've been trying to rope her into a show for Harvester Days. Something to honor Mr. Davis. Beverly's doing costumes. Mr. Lundeen says he'll underwrite it." Well, Eudora said that Neddy had wanted to do something, and now he was.

"And Sally?"

The boy walked Nell to the gate. "Not so far."

On her way home, Nell made a point to pass the Wheeler's. Sally was on her knees digging out weeds from a long-neglected flower border on the south side of the house. Perspiration soaked her shirt.

"You're ambitious," Nell called and crossed the lawn to stand nearby. "But it's awfully warm to be working so hard."

"Mrs. Stillman." She did not look up.

Nell was shocked by Sally's appearance. Neddy was right. The girl was skeletal, and her naturally curly black hair was unwashed and uncut, standing out from her head like an untrimmed bush.

"You've done a great deal of work," Nell said, looking toward the backyard where zinnias and marigolds, new this summer, lined up along the side of the garage.

"The yard was a mess." Sally dug up a clump of crabgrass. "You know—since my mother gave it up."

Nell felt she owed it to Stella to do something, but she

could no longer speak as candidly as she had when the girl was nine or ten. A seventeen-year-old was not so open to an old woman's suggestions or admonitions.

"Neddy tells me he's putting together a tribute to Mr. Davis. I expect you'll be involved."

Sally shook her head. "No," she said with finality.

But Nell persisted. "I'm sorry to hear it. You're a fine little actress." She tried to sound offhand. "Your mother would be proud. Mr. Davis, too." She paused. She couldn't stand here all day yammering at a girl who didn't want to hear any of this. "Well, I'd better head home. Time for supper."

She'd found nothing useful to say to a child she loved, had loved from that day in the library when she'd found Sally asleep. Here was the little girl who'd reached up to retrieve from her mother's pocket the paper on which Nell's number was written, lest it be lost.

chapter sixty-four &

WHILE SALLY WAS BURNING UP, Eudora's flame guttered. "What if we came for you with the car? Are you sure you couldn't play bridge?" Nell asked her friend.

"I'm sure."

"What if we played here?"

Eudora shook her head. "I can't sit up for long stretches."

Nell told her about *Harvey*, the movie at the Majestic, starring Jimmy Stewart. "Neddy could chauffeur you."

"Wouldn't it be wonderful if we could thank everyone who'd ever made us happy?" Eudora said, evading the matter. "Jimmy Stewart made me happy in *Born to Dance*."

"He's even better looking now. Will you please think about it?"

"I'll think about it."

Nell knew she was being humored.

What moved Sally Wheeler to throw herself into the Drew Davis tribute, Nell didn't know. Doubtless her love of him. *I really love him. You understand, don't you?* He'd not been a replacement for Stella, but a recompense. In any case, the girl did write a script for Neddy, a playlet titled

The Kingdom of Making Sense. Surely, thought Nell, there
was a great deal to make sense of in Sally's life.

A day or two before the tribute, Nell heard someone
on the outside stairs and went to the screen door.

"Is it . . . ? Oh, my," she said. "I can't believe my eyes.
Lark Erhardt."

Lark and Sally stood on the landing, Beverly trailing
them. Nell opened the door. "Oh, my," she said again, ushering them in.

And now they were sitting in her living room, drinking
iced tea and eating the familiar vanilla wafers.

"Oh, my." She couldn't quite believe that all three were
there. "My three girls together again"—her children who
hadn't gone off to war, to return in bits and pieces. "Did
you come for *The Kingdom of Making Sense*?"

"Didn't know about it till I got here," Lark said.

"Well, how do you find Harvester after ten years?" Nell
asked.

"A little bigger, I guess, but pretty much the same—
wonderful."

Sally rolled her eyes.

Nell laughed. "You're still at your grandmother's?"

"Still there."

"I think of your mother so often. I hope she's well."

Lark shrugged. "She's in Los Angeles. She works for my
Aunt Betty." This, she seemed to suggest, was no concern
of hers.

Nell stared, then changed the subject. College? Yes,
Lark was enrolling at the University of Minnesota in the

fall, likewise Beverly—Lark to study English, Beverly art. Lark had a notion to write children's books.

"And maybe Beverly'll illustrate 'em," she said, recovering her élan. "You should see the stuff she's designed for Sally's show. Amazing."

"Godsakes," Beverly swore.

"And you, Sally?"

Sally just wanted to get away. New York, probably. Maybe try acting. She tossed her head. "I'm not good for much." She sprang up and circled the room, pausing at the bookcase. "You've got a ton of books by . . ." She bent to study a spine. "Wodehouse," she said, mispronouncing the name. "How come?"

"He's one of my best friends."

"Really?" Sally said. "You *know* him?"

"Only through the pleasure he gives me." Nell flushed, as if she'd spoken of a lover.

"Sounds romantic," Sally said, straightening and looking hard at Nell. "I might try him."

Performed on the band-shell stage in the park, *The Kingdom of Making Sense* showcased Drew Davis's impact. A dozen of his students were involved in the music, set design, costumes, and lighting. The acting, Sally's in particular, neared professional quality.

Using birthday money from her Mankato grandmother, Sally had paid for printed programs listing cast and crews and stating in bold letters, "*The Kingdom of Making Sense* is dedicated to the memory of DREW DAVIS."

Nell hoped this project was a kind of expiation for Sally. Actually, when she'd visited Nell with Lark and Beverly, Sally did seem less febrile.

Ed Barnstable wheeled his mother to the park for the hour-long program, which included not only Sally's short play, but also a performance by the dancers of Martha Beverton's Tap and Toe, plus the high-school band torturing "Bali Ha'i."

An hour was as much as Eudora could manage but, until Neddy left for Yale, she would hang on, never allowing his mother to ruin him, as Denise had ruined Cole. She still groaned at the thought of Cole.

Nell spread a blanket on the ground beside Eudora's wheelchair. Getting up again wouldn't be a cinch, but she still managed. The early August evening was bathwater warm and poignant with the scent of mown grass. From the distance came the jingle-jangle sounds of Harvester Days on Main Street.

Nell recalled those bygone occasions when she'd come to the park on summer evenings to watch the penny movies projected on a fluttery sheet in front of the band shell. Was it here that she, Eudora, and Juliet had enjoyed Jimmy Stewart in *Born to Dance*? As an old woman, she luxuriated in remembered pleasures. They were that comforting, towel-wrapped brick on a cold night: baby Hilly asleep, cheeks flushed, his innocence almost painful in its perfection; and Elvira, eager, artless, standing at the door gripping an ancient carpetbag.

One of her fondest memories was of John laughing under an apricot moon in Juliet and Laurence's gazebo;

another was of Eudora sitting beside Hilly, a thick book of words and pictures held between them. And of course there had been the countless afternoons of tea and arrowroot cookies with her girls, these three young women now gathered together once more. Such was Nell's wealth. She recalled a line from Emily Dickinson: "My friends are my 'estate.'"

Toward the end of *The Kingdom of Making Sense*, Nell heard Eudora suck in her breath. "He's here," she rasped. "The devil."

"Who? What are you saying?" Nell wasn't certain she'd heard correctly.

"Cole. That's him, over there." Eudora pointed toward a young man leaning against a tree, far from the band shell but intent upon the stage. Even from this distance Nell could see that the boy was good looking—too good looking. As Sally's playlet ended, he turned, sprinting toward the street where his car was doubtless parked.

Moments later, above the sounds of Tap and Toe, Nell heard an engine gunning and tires squealing away from the curb. So that was Cole Barnstable, she thought. Dark and beautiful as a Caravaggio boy. His turning up had done Eudora no good, though the woman said nothing about it further, but merely shook her head.

As the evening's program drew to a close, Nell said good night to Eudora and Ed and headed back down Main Street, pausing to greet Agatha Nightingale's former "girl," Callie Hennessey. A decent-enough woman, she was nothing so colorful as her employer. Years later, Nell still missed the clandestine romance of editing Agatha's stories.

Climbing the stairs to the apartment, she wandered through semidarkness to Hilly's bedroom and pulled the rocker to the window. Outside, the lights of the street carnival flamed into quivering brilliance as the last shreds of milky illumination faded from the sky. On evenings like this, John sat close, and he and Nell talked for hours.

Tonight, she described Sally's playlet. "I think she's healing, but she'll never get entirely past Drew Davis's death.

"And would you believe, Cole Barnstable showed up. Eudora was upset, of course." Nell searched for a description of the boy. "In movie ads, they call his type 'smoldering.'" She sighed. "Maybe this was the last of him."

Later, she confessed her longing. She was tired, and tired of losing others. "When Eudora's gone, I'm ready."

"You sure?"

"I've done all the mischief I can do," she told him, smiling.

"Don't bet on it."

chapter sixty-five ☙

IN SEPTEMBER OF 1951, Sally left for New York and its Barbizon Hotel for young women. Her Grandma Elway, who was paying, insisted; the Barbizon was said to be safe, and a friend of Mrs. Elway's had told her she'd seen ads for the hotel in *The New Yorker*. Well, that seemed like a good sign.

Beverly and Lark headed for Minneapolis and a dorm at the University. From Lark, a postcard promised, "I'll be back."

While the girls were taking flight, Eudora was on a downward Journey.

The St. Bridget hospital was a revelation to Nell. She'd never been inside one, except for the Dr. Kildare movies. She'd birthed Hilly at home with help from the same midwife who'd delivered young Gus Rabel.

The lobby of the hospital was whispery, and the woman at the desk, with her thin, mistrustful smile, as whispery as the lobby itself. Butter wouldn't melt in her mouth. With a long, jointy finger and seeming reluctance, she indicated a hallway. "Room 23."

Nell felt she ought to genuflect before a corridor so wonderfully scrubbed and antiseptic smelling. You could see your reflection in the asphalt tile. The whole place was a little holier-than-thou.

She peeked into Eudora's room to find her friend sleeping beneath a kind of tent. Nell could sit and wait in the plastic chair by the window, or out here in the hall on a wooden bench—but she was curious. Down there, another hallway ran perpendicular to this. Neither Eudora nor the woman at the desk would be wiser if Nell snooped a little.

The new area was not holier-than-thou, but rang with strong voices, one demanding and imploring, "Do something! It's coming!" A woman in labor.

Nell backed away, feeling for the bench behind her.

"It's coming!" the woman screamed again.

"Doctor's on his way. Hold your horses." A nurse's impatient voice.

"Aauugh!" A wrenching cry. "Damn you, it's coming!"

On the bench, Nell sat, eyes closed, clutching her purse, rocking and remembering how she'd descended snowy stairs, halting twice, bent over with contractions, finally seeing the outhouse ahead of her.

The baby girl was a bloody mass no bigger than Nell's two fists. She had no way of burying it, even if she'd had the strength. She sobbed and moaned and let it slip into that awful pit.

After three days in the hospital, Eudora died of pneumonia. Nell had taken the train to visit each day, though "visit" was euphemistic since Eudora lay shrouded in the tent, either sleeping or comatose. Still, Nell read to her from Wodehouse, recalled Eudora's work during the

Great War, and described the plantings in the two ceme-
teries. "You've been loved and admired."

But she didn't again venture beyond Eudora's room.

Of course Nell carried a crock of baked beans to the
Barnstable house after Eudora's death, and of course she
attended the wake and funeral. And of course she wept,
again and again. And yet, none of it was real. Eudora wasn't
dead, not really—not in any satisfactory way. Imperious,
she still blew through Nell's apartment, exhorting, laud-
ing, bemoaning, arranging. That she hadn't arranged her
own wake was a great pity. The one organized by her
daughter-in-law resembled a cocktail party and ignored
the departed entirely.

Eudora's body was not on display. In 1951, Harvester
people still expected the deceased to be present in the
home, in an open casket—provided the body was view-
able. Doubtless one could trace this convention to a past
when prairie transport had been slow and arduous, and
folks might not have seen one another for months or even
years. One last look—and not at the funeral home, but in
a place where there was food and maybe drink. Those who
could not remember such days might find the tradition
barbaric, indelicate, but for Eudora's friends, that past was
not distant. And they were affronted that she was not present for them to exclaim over. Adding to the affront, Brenda
had already rearranged Eudora's furniture, hauling some
of it away and replacing it with Danish Modern, whatever
that was. She had surely begun the process while Eudora
lay dying.

The night of the wake, folks clustered in two camps:

Brenda's Circle, and Everyone Else. The St. Bridget Barnstables, minus Cole, and Brenda's Twin Cities relatives formed Brenda's Circle; Eudora's friends made up Everyone Else. Most of the second group felt shabby and out of place, a circumstance that would have scandalized Eudora.

A bereaved Neddy, home from Yale, looked lost as he moved among the guests, carrying platters of hors d'oeuvres. Nowhere in evidence were the hot dishes, cakes, and pies contributed by the locals.

"I'm so sorry," Nell told the young man. "I know how much you loved your grandmother. And how much she loved you. But she's left you wonderful memories."

"A lot of them." He set aside the tray he'd been holding and joined Nell on the sofa. Ever since the call had come, he'd been remembering. "I don't know if she ever told you, but when I was little—about two years old, I guess—Grandma started 'lessons.' She made it a game, so I thought we were just playing. But by the time I went to kindergarten, I could read. She was pretty amazing."

"She was kind and she had character. The best friend anyone ever had. And those are traits she's passed along to you."

Neddy shook his head.

"But it's true. I know what it meant to Sally to have your friendship this past summer."

"You think so?"

"I hate to imagine what could have happened to our girl if you hadn't been there. I think that program in the park was the saving of her."

A few minutes later, Nell expressed her condolences to Ed and Brenda, then left. Outside, the night crackled with cold, every star standing out hard and clear.

"I'll give you a lift," Larry Lundeen said, stepping out and closing the door behind him. He pulled his gloves from his pocket. "You didn't wear galoshes. You'll freeze your feet walking all that way."

"A lift would be grand."

"We'll stop at my place. I have a new painting to show you."

At the house, Larry made hot toddys, handing one to Nell. Then he left to fetch a gilt-framed and generously scaled oil painting of young athletes—several running a race in the distance, with others in the foreground standing beneath a Russian olive tree, awaiting their heat. Nell recognized the old track at the foot of Bacall's Hill, where Hilly had first run.

Larry propped the painting against the legs of the console table. "It's yours."

"Oh, heavens," Nell said, using her napkin to blot sudden tears. "Oh, my. I never expected anything like this."

"Hilly was a superb runner. And I do recall promising you a painting."

"How can I ever thank you?"

"No need." Larry raised his mug. "Chin-chin." Settling back in the club chair, he said, "I've owed you and Eudora ever since the day you made lunch for Drew and me. Apart from losing my parents, that was the worst day of my life. Tonight, at Eudora's, I regretted never finding the proper way to thank her."

"She didn't do it for the thanks." Nell told him about Eudora's cousin Leonard.

"I didn't know."

Later, Larry wrapped the painting in an old quilt, slipped it into the backseat of the Chrysler, and drove Nell home. When they'd leaned it against a wall, he said, "I'll come over in a couple of days and hang it."

After he'd left, Nell stood at her usual post, Hilly's rime-etched bedroom window. Outside, the night was as motionless as a painting, as silent as death.

Death was much on her mind; friends, a lover, even children had abandoned Nell while she stood at a lonely window, waving, as if they were headed to a party to which she was not invited. She resented their going and, even more, she resented her own seeming permanence. Tomorrow she would ask Apollo Shane to draw up a will.

Leaving the lawyer's the next day, Nell stopped at the post office and found a letter.

January 10, 1951

Dear Nell,

What a faithless correspondent I have been. The older I get, the lazier I become. I'm an old clock that's winding down, and there's no hope of winding me up again. I surely never thought I'd live to see sixty-eight— and have a daughter of forty-eight! And her children, Ann and Gregory, are . . . well, for heaven's sake, I've got to stop this.

GOOD NIGHT, MR. WODEHOUSE

And you'll be seventy-five! Oh, darling Nell, that's not possible. I would like to get back to see you in the fall. I think it's finally time. I have outlived my sins. It's very freeing to outlive your sins. We'll talk more about that when I see you.

> *With much love,*
> *Elvira*

But then Elvira was diagnosed with rapidly progressing uterine cancer and unable to travel the distance. Well, Nell thought, at least to one another we'll always be young.

Nell's girls kept in touch, each in her fashion. Long-distance calls every three or four months were Sally's signature, though she sent a telegram in 1954 when she landed the role of Millie in a bus-and-truck production of *Picnic*. "Actually met William Inge! (stop) He looked me up and down. (stop) Said I didn't have any wrinkles and therefore wasn't too old for the part!" (stop)

The previous year, Sally had told Nell, "I see Neddy every now and then. He comes into town if I'm in a show. Mostly, my shows are off Broadway. Way off. But he's always kind. I expect you know he's studying law."

"Eudora, think of it! Law, at last," Nell had exclaimed to her dead friend.

Beverly, of course, stopped by the apartment whenever she was home from the University. She was applying for graduate school.

"I wanta go all the way, get a PhD," she said. "I'd only

need a master's to teach in the art department, but can you imagine my mom when she tells people that her daughter's a doctor? God, she'll pee her pants."

And Lark penned letters, the last the most welcome. In the spring of 1955, she wrote, "I'm coming home! In September I start teaching seventh-grade English and renting the apartment above Egger's Drug Store. See you in August. Be on the lookout for used furniture."

And indeed Nell kept an eye peeled for bargains in Bender's Second Hand. She went so far as to buy a brown wicker rocker—everyone needed a wicker rocker. And would Lark be interested in Elvira's bed? "The springs are all right, if you don't mind the squeak."

A postcard from Lark begged, "Bookcases, please! Let me know the price, and I'll send a check." When Lark finally moved into the Eggers' apartment, the child was possessed of a single bed, two large bookcases, the rocker, and a student desk.

"All set!"

chapter sixty-six ☙

NELL GLANCED AT THE CLOCK on the bedside table—
7:30—turned over, and pulled the blanket around her
shoulders. Time to get ready for Mass. She still went, and
wondered why.

But she was tired this morning. And she had a right to
stay home. You didn't turn eighty-five every day. Perhaps
the two scotches last night were one too many . . . all your
fault, John Flynn, for introducing me to scotch.

Around 11:00, she flicked back the soft sheet, freeing
her feet. She'd come to appreciate old sheets, their caress
tender to ancient, papery skin. She eased her legs, thin
and crosshatched with fine lines, over the side of the bed
and stood, gathering herself. You did that when you were
old—gathered yourself.

Poking her feet into woolly slippers, she padded to the
kitchen and set a pot of coffee to percolating. The apartment held a faint, elusive scent of ripe apricots.

She passed up lunch. There was a bit of cold roast beef,
but she wasn't hungry. Instead, she shuffled back to bed.
How luxurious it was to lie abed when you were exhausted.
Not to go to Mass. Not to clean house or cook a meal. Only

lie abed and read Mr. Wodehouse and, off and on, drift to sleep. This was the reward for being eighty-five.

At eighty-five, she'd outlived her secrets, as Elvira had outlived her sins. Age freed one of much baggage.

Though Nell slept and woke and slept again, she was still drowsy when evening drew down, so she brushed her teeth and washed her face. Glancing in the mirror, she marveled. When she was young, she had looked into a mirror wondering what she could do to improve what she saw. Now she didn't notice her face, even when she was staring straight at it. There wasn't much you could do with an eighty-five-year-old face but own it.

Larry would be phoning soon. For the past couple of months he'd been calling each evening to check on her, though he said it was to gossip.

Later, she plumped the pillows, climbed into bed, and reached once more for *Jeeves in the Offing*. She would finish it tonight. For the umpteenth time. That was another thing about age. You could read the same book again and again with the same relish as the first time, because your slip-slidey mind so quickly forgot plots. No, that wasn't quite true. You could read with ever-*greater* relish because you knew with certainty that the pages were lined with treasure—even if you couldn't quite recall the nature of that treasure.

She withdrew her bookmark, its lettering nearly indecipherable from years of use: "Zephyr Playing Cards, Box 738, Hortense, Indiana. Wishing you luck in cards and in love." Touching it to her lips before laying it on the bedside table, she began reading: "Lady Malvern was a hearty, happy, healthy, overpowering sort of dashed female, not so very tall but making up for it by measuring about six feet from the O.P. to the Prompt Side. She fitted into my biggest armchair as if it had been built round her by some one who knew they were wearing armchairs tight about the hips that season. . . ."

Nell giggled, read, dozed, and thought about her long affair with Mr. Wodehouse. She recalled the day in the Water and Power Company when she had discovered *Love Among the Chickens*.

"Wasn't that fortuitous, Eudora?" As so often these days, she addressed her old friend. "What if I'd grabbed Mrs. Gaskell instead?"

Jeeves in the Offing lying across her breast, she fell into a deep sleep.

Around 3:00 a.m. John appeared beside the bed. Her darling man—he who had seen to it that she never ran out of Wodehouse. Now, he lay down next to her, closed the book, and slipped it onto the bed at her side. And now, he covered her body with his. And slowly, in the most irresistible way, the breath went out of her as she felt his weight, as so often before, rousing her and carrying her away.

epilogue ☙

Leaning against the counter in Larry Lundeen's kitchen, Lark said, "She never knew we'd planned a party." Topping up her glass of white wine, she followed him into the living room, carrying the bottle.

Long legs draped over the arm of a club chair, Sally lit a cigarette from the lighter on the coffee table. "Who in hell could know?"

"Well, *this* was her party, as it turned out," Beverly said. "This reception, Larry."

"Everybody was here."

"Except Neddy." Larry pulled up a side chair. "Too bad he had a case in court."

Sally scraped a bit of tobacco from her tongue. "Weird about the burial."

Beverly sat next to Lark on the sofa. "Well, she wanted to be buried near Hilly. And he was in the Protestant cemetery. Whad'ya gonna do?"

"So . . . a Catholic funeral and a Protestant burial. I sorta like it," Lark said. "Ecumenical. Isn't that what we call it?"

"I take it there was enough money to bury her." Sally glanced at the others. "Or did you take care of it?" she asked Larry.

"It wasn't a problem."

"Look, if you paid for it, we want to pitch in," Sally said, "and I know Neddy will, too." She flicked ashes into a heavy ashtray.

Setting his glass on the table and crossing his legs, Larry surveyed the three women. "I'm Nell's executor."

"And?"

"She left a tidy little estate."

"Hey, Lar, we remember those vanilla wafers. We drank that weak tea. We know better," Beverly told him.

"You couldn't dunk the vanilla wafers," Sally said. "They disintegrated, and you had a spoonful of glop in the bottom of your cup."

"Even so," Lark said.

"Yeah, even so," Beverly echoed.

"Thrift was a habit she got into because of Hilly," Larry told them. "She worried about what would happen when she was gone."

"But where the hell would she get any money?" Sally asked, sitting up. "A retired third-grade teacher who didn't even qualify for Social Security?"

Larry reached for a Sobranie from a silver box and lit it. "I'm talking out of turn here," he said.

"So talk," Lark told him. "We're all a little pie eyed and probably won't remember."

"You'll remember." He uncrossed his legs, resting elbows

on his knees. "She had an inheritance from John Flynn. Money and some stocks."

"John Flynn."

Beverly asked, "Wasn't he governor?"

"Congress. Before your time. They were lovers, Nell and John."

Breaking the stunned silence, Sally said, "I'll be damned."

"God, I'm glad to hear that," Lark said.

The women demanded details, and Larry retailed as many as he possessed.

At length he said, "Apollo Shane handled all this."

"I'll be damned," Sally repeated.

"Nell almost never touched the money," Larry went on. "And the stocks meant nothing to her."

"How unworldly can you get?" Sally snuffed out her cigarette and lit another.

"So where's this all leading?" Beverly asked.

"Her will divides the estate between the three of you."

"What the hell?" Sally coughed smoke.

"Who else would she leave it to?"

Lark was weeping. "Sweet Jesus."

Beverly threw her head against the back of the sofa. "This is a damned dime novel."

Larry laughed. "It is, isn't it?" He rose. "I think I'll have another Old Fashioned." Returning, he told them, "There's more."

"I'm not sure I can take much more." Lark topped off the wine glasses.

But Larry crossed to a bookcase, slipping four volumes

from a shelf. "These." He set three books on the coffee table, holding one back for himself. "Signed first editions."

"I knew she was a Wodehouse nut," Beverly said, "but signed first editions?"

"John Flynn tracked down three of them."

Each of the women reached for a book. "And the fourth?" Lark asked.

Larry read them Nell's letter from Wodehouse. Beverly let out a low whistle. "Think of it. I wonder what she said in her letter to him."

"This one she left to me," he told them, passing around the book Wodehouse had signed to Nell.

Sally read, "'To Nell, jewel among women, in whose debt shall always be found yours truly, P. G. (Plum to you) Wodehouse.' Plum?"

"His nickname."

Lark opened her *Psmith in the City* to the last page and read silently.

"What have you got?" Sally asked.

"Mike's mind roamed into the future. . . ." Lark read. "The Problem of Life seemed to him to be solved. He looked on down the years, and he could see no troubles there of any kind whatsoever. Reason suggested that there were probably one or two knocking about somewhere, but this was no time to think of them."

Beverly nodded. "Amen, Mike."

Setting his drink down, Larry pulled a folded piece of paper and reading glasses from his breast pocket. "And finally."

Using his tie, he wiped smudges from the glasses, then read,

> *To my girls: When Hilly left us, you three filled my life with joy and worry—oh yes, worry. I expect you had no idea how much sleep I lost over you or how grateful I was to lose it. My token is small payment. Let it buy a smile.*
>
> *And, darling girls, talk to me sometimes, from across this permeable boundary, as I have talked to Hilly and John and my friends Eudora and Juliet. I'm here. I'll listen.*
>
> > *Love,*
> > *Nell.*

afterword ❧

BEGINNING WITH *The Cape Ann*, I wrote a series of Harvester novels: *The Empress of One*, *What a Woman Must Do*, and *Gardenias*. In all but *What a Woman Must Do*, Mrs. Stillman, the protagonist of *Goodnight, Mr. Wodehouse*, played a crucial role in the lives of those around her, and yet I think she would describe herself as quite ordinary.

If there is indeed such a figure as Everyman, then Mrs. Stillman is Everywoman: Wife, Mother, Widow, Friend, Lover, Mystic, Teacher, Reader. I wish to emphasize Reader because, throughout her adult life, Nell Stillman falls back upon literature in order to survive the losses, humiliations, and mysteries to which we are all heir.

Since I have been for forty years an ardent fan of P. G. Wodehouse, and since I saw in his artful and noble nonsense an anodyne to pain, I thought it appropriate to combine the needs of Nell Stillman with the gifts of Wodehouse. In doing so, I hope to honor both.

It is rare that a writer of fiction finds the opportunity to celebrate an author much loved in her own life. It has been my privilege to do so—and at the same time to celebrate the power of literature to comfort, enlighten, entertain, transform, and, doggone it, make us a lot more fun to be around.

acknowledgments ✐

Thank you, Daniel Slager, for your brilliant editing. Because of your suggestions, the manuscript gained new depth, focus, and meaning. Thank you Joey Jacqueline McGarvey, dear heart, for finding and correcting my ten thousand errors in spelling, punctuation, and fact. Thank you, Doug Stewart, for being a hand-holder extraordinaire as well as the best agent ever. And thank you, Madeleine Clark, who always comes up to the mark.

Thank you, Women Who Wine—Sandy Benitez, Judy Guest, Kate DiCamillo, Pat Francisco, Lorna Landvik, Alison McGhee, Wang Ping, Mary Rockcastle, and Julie Schumacher. Please note: I have listed you alphabetically, not by age. I know when I'm well off.

Thank you, Loft Book Group and We Old Ladies Who've Been Together Forever Book Group. You keep me reading the sorts of things that inspire me to be a better writer.

As always, thank you, Daniel Sullivan, my dearest advisor, best friend, and life partner. Thank you as well to Maggie, Ben, and Kate, the Sullivan children, genius writers all.

FAITH SULLIVAN was born and raised in southern Minnesota. Married to drama critic Dan Sullivan, she lived twenty-some years in New York and Los Angeles, returning to Minnesota often to keep her roots planted in the prairie. She is the author of seven previous novels, including *The Cape Ann* (Crown, 1988). Her most recent publications with Milkweed are *What a Woman Must Do* (2002) and *Gardenias* (2005). A "demon gardener, flea marketer, and feeder of birds," Sullivan lives in Minneapolis with her husband. They have three grown children.

Interior design by Connie Kuhnz
Typeset in Warnock Pro
by Bookmobile Design & Digital Publisher Services